Catherine Bond

Moonlighter

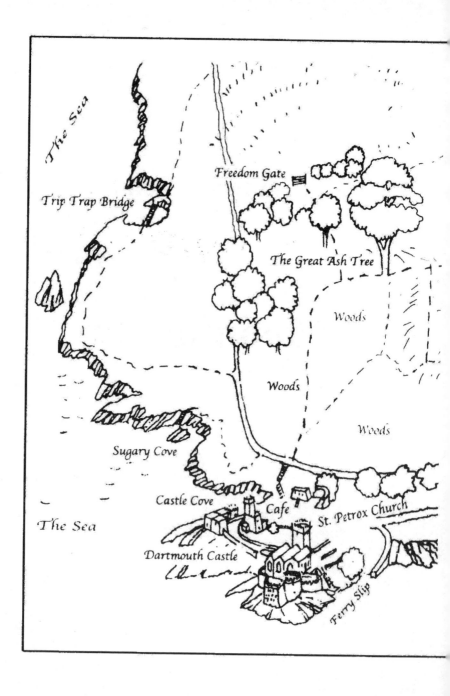

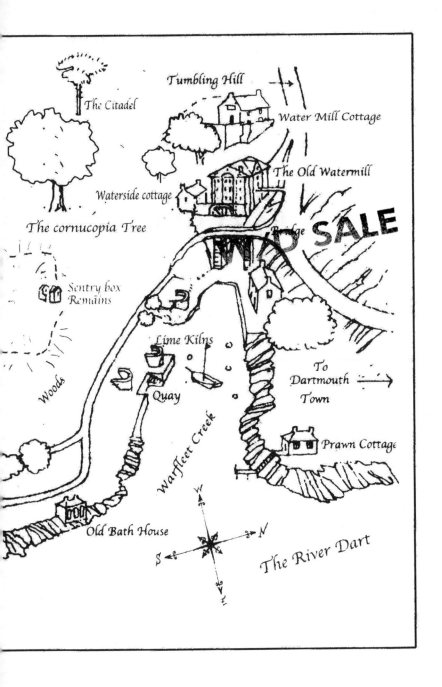

PART ONE

Chapter One
Christmas Morning

Christmas morning dawned bright and windy, ruffling the waters of Warfleet Creek, and rustling the leaves in the woods surrounding it. For the children of Watermill Cottage, a great surprise lay in store. This had been cleverly planned and secretly executed during the night by their father. When Eddie and Ellie raced downstairs after opening their Christmas stockings in their bedrooms, an illuminated saltwater tank stood in the corner of the sitting room, gently bubbling. They stopped dead in their tracks, eyes wide, and held their breath.

"Wow!" they both gasped, speechless.

"When did that get here?"

"How did it get here?" eventually came the questions.

"Dad must have done it last night!" decided Ellie quickly, and went over to peer into the bright water, gently gurgling, as seaweed waved and small fish darted between the stones.

"There's a prawn!" squealed an excited Eddie, laughing with glee. "Oh look, Ellie, there's a little crab trying to hide!"

They both marvelled at the saltwater aquarium, secretly devised without their knowledge, by Peter their father, and Sam, a neighbour and friend. They had hidden all the necessary equipment, and collected the little sea creatures and gallons of seawater to create this masterpiece. It was beautiful. The two youngsters stood mesmerised until, hearing footsteps, they looked round to see their parents peeping in through the door.

"Do you like it?" they asked anxiously.

"Like it? We love it! Thank you so much!" and they raced to hug their delighted father and mother. As daylight brightened, Peter cooked sausages and bacon, poured orange juice and piled up steaming toast; soon the family were eating breakfast together in the kitchen while Peter told them how he and Sam had set it all up in the dead of night.

"We heard nothing – nothing at all!" insisted Eddie, shaking his head vigorously.

"Not even when I kicked a bucket over and had to chase the crabs down the driveway?" laughed Peter.

A loud knock at the door disturbed them and two heads could be seen looking in – it was Patrick and Sam.

Patrick, their friend from Scotland, had shared several extraordinary adventures with Eddie and Ellie. His busy parents had bought a cottage nearby so he could return to Dartmouth each holiday from his strict boarding school and share the freedom and excitement of a waterside home, close to his best friends. His godparents ran a teashop at Dartmouth Castle. Eddie and Ellie's father, Peter, was in the Navy and often away for weeks at a time, so these kind stand-in grandparents were very comforting for them all.

Patrick and Sam were dragged off to admire the new saltwater aquarium. Sam told them seriously, "I hope you appreciate I've lost a stone in weight just carrying the water!"

Patrick asked Eddie if they could go rock-pooling but they were firmly told that Christmas Day was a bit special and no, they couldn't go. Reluctantly Sam and Patrick went home and Eddie and Ellie were soon examining interesting parcels under the Christmas tree, which they could open that afternoon.

Later, as the smell of Christmas dinner began to pervade the house, the family left together to visit friends in the neighbouring valley for lunchtime drinks.

"I can't stay too long," Mary told them anxiously.

After a short drive they reached the pretty hamlet and turned up the driveway of the Old Manor House. A toddler stood in the window, waving as soon as it saw the red car. They were welcomed inside by Speedy the Labrador, and Wolf, the small Jack Russell. Jake rushed to the door in a red jumper and red Wellington boots.

"Boots!" he pointed. Eddie, laughing, picked him up and carried the struggling child inside.

Harry and Sarah and a few neighbours were chatting, eating and drinking.

"Well, young Eddie, found a new boat yet?"

"Not yet, but we're still looking." Eddie replied.

"My brother Arthur is thinking of selling his boat *Pelican*. Why don't you have a word with him?" Harry nodded in Arthur's direction and Eddie, thanking him, moved off. Tapping his father's arm, he whispered the news to him.

"Okay, Eddie, I'll come over," promised Peter, a glass of beer in one hand and a sausage on a stick in the other. Eddie took a deep breath and launched himself at Arthur.

"Hi, I'm Eddie, is it right you've got a boat for sale?"

Arthur spun round to see who it was.

"Ah, you're Eddie, I've heard about you –spend all your time fishing and sailing and inventing things, eh? Not too keen on school, then?" and he laughed. Eddie stood there embarrassed; he didn't know what else to say. Arthur clapped him on the back.

"Not much of a one for school myself actually, made a good life farming. Now, about my boat, *Pelican*. We hardly use her now…well, things have changed." He indicated a lady sitting down with a cane walking stick beside her.

With that, Peter arrived. Soon they had arranged to see *Pelican* the next week, eaten and drunk plenty, and Mary was anxious to leave. Waving goodbye, she drove them all back to Watermill Cottage.

"Can we go out for a walk before dinner?" asked Eddie hopefully.

"Yes but be back by 2pm latest," warned Peter, laying up the fire in the sitting room.

"Don't get pestering Bridget either," added Mary. They escaped through the front door, laughing, to enjoy the freedom of Warfleet Creek, their favourite haunt. Reaching the wide spread of the glassy green water, still and smooth, they stood on the gravelly edge; Eddie picked up a few stones and expertly skimmed them across the water.

"Two, three, four, five! Here you are." And he passed some flat stones to his sister who tried valiantly to match his throw.

"One, two, oh it's no good." She sucked her teeth, annoyed, while Eddie laughed.

"Come on, let's go and see Sargasso."

They hurried down a narrow path leading to the ancient quayside, which had several lime kilns built into the back. In the end one, by a set of stone steps, the seagull lived. He had been rescued by Eddie and Ellie when they were younger and had been so badly tangled up in hooks and fishing line that his leg had to been amputated by the vet. He had remained their devoted and loyal friend ever since.

Sargasso belonged to the Seafarers and had been recently awarded a great honour because of his bravery during Eddie and Ellie's adventures. Older now, he had chosen a partner to share the rest of his life with. Her name was Seraphim; she was a pretty herring gull with a damaged wing, and the two seabirds were soon to exchange vows and become a united pair.

Eddie and Ellie came upon them in the cool brightness of Christmas morning.

"Happy Christmas, Sargasso!"

Sargasso ruffled his feathers and stretched his neck up to Eddie in delight, as the boy stroked his beloved seagull. Seraphim, not so used to humans, stayed quietly by his side, her heart beating anxiously.

"Happy Christmas from the Seafarers," proudly cawed Sargasso.

"Wow!" they both said in amazement.

"I thought you would be surprised. I have been granted the power of all-transcending language by the Spirit of the Sea for helping to find the submarines. I may talk to you now whenever I wish."

"You deserve it," said Ellie with great satisfaction, "And who is your pretty friend?" she added curiously. Sargasso gently urged her forward and told them proudly,

"This is Seraphim, she is my chosen partner and we are to be united together very soon. Warfleet Creek is to be our home." The pretty herring gull looked shyly up at him.

"She's lovely, can I stroke her?" Ellie asked him gently.

"Don't be afraid," whispered Sargasso, and Seraphim let both Ellie and Eddie stroke her.

"Here's your Christmas present." Then Eddie threw the bacon rinds to the two gulls, who gobbled them up.

"News from the Woodland, I hear," Sargasso told Eddie.

"Oh yes?" Eddie raised his eyebrows.

"That wily old owl Tolivera has been sent away in disgrace and one of the buzzard princes has gone with him to Dartmoor."

"He was horrible, I'm glad he's gone," said Ellie, tossing her head.

"We're off for a walk so we'd better go," Eddie told the gulls reluctantly and hurried up the steep hill to Sugary Cove for a glimpse of the sea. Eddie was already imagining his piled plate, full of roast turkey and the accompanying feast.

"I can hardly wait for lunch," he told Ellie. "I love Christmas dinner."

"All you think about is food," she chided him, laughing and racing ahead of him.

Eddie chased after her energetically. They reached the secluded cove with its high cliffs and wooded sides. A set of steep steps led to the beach and soon they were scuffling about in the seaweed and driftwood along the high tide mark. They threw stones, Ellie improving her skimming techniques under Eddie's patient tuition. The sea lapped and swished on the gravelly shore; it was peaceful and only the seagulls' cries and the sounds of the sea could be heard. They lounged on the flat rocks in silence for a while, soaking in the hypnotic sound.

Just as they were about to leave, a small red boat rounded the corner from Kingswear, the engine buzzing, breaking the silence. It seemed to be slowing down and edged along close to the black rocks by the old castle. Two figures could be seen dressed in yellow waterproofs. The engine cut out and their voices travelled across the water.

They're keen, fishing on Christmas Day! said Eddie.

Perhaps they're hoping to have mackerel for lunch," said Ellie, looking up at the sky. "It's going to rain, let's go!"

They headed back up the steep steps, leaving the little cove in quietness, the sea continuing its restless journey up and down the beach. Large cold drops of rain began and the two ran helter-skelter for home, arriving wet and shivering on the doorstep of Watermill Cottage, and bursting through the door.

"Phew! It's beginning to pour!" and they shook off their wet anoraks. Mary was smiling, a Christmas apron tied firmly around her, so Eddie and Ellie presumed there had been no disasters. Christmas dinner always seemed to be a worrying task for the cook, despite the fact that they had countless roast meals during the rest of the year. Eddie couldn't quite understand it.

The heavy relentless rain set in at lunchtime, and didn't stop for the rest of Christmas Day. The family were content to stay in enjoying their huge lunch, all helping to clear away afterwards and to settle by the fire with the ceremonial present opening, the Queen's Christmas message, chocolates, and unending programmes on television. There were new books to read, Christmas cake to sample, and various family members rang with seasonal good wishes. It was a happy day, just the four of them, isolated from the rest of the world in peace and harmony. It was a simple pleasure, unfortunately not enjoyed by all the inhabitants living in the small towns of Dartmouth and Kingswear that day.

Chapter Two
Floods in the woodland

As Boxing Day dawned it was still raining; swollen streams and flood water raced down Tumbling Hill to the river, leaving a spreading muddy stain in the water. The fire brigade was called out to countless emergencies, drains gurgled, and gutters, blocked with autumn leaves, couldn't cope. There were mudslides on steep hills and trees were uprooted as they lost their grip on the earth. No one ventured out, until finally at 3pm that afternoon, chinks of blue sky appeared and pink streaks flooded the sky – it was almost sunset.

"It's stopped raining," Ellie told them, peering out of the sitting room window.

"Well, you can't leave just because you're losing!" jeered Eddie.

Peter and Mary laughed at him from around the table. Ellie sulkily returned to the Monopoly board; she was about to be bankrupted as her top hat had landed on Eddie's hotel in Mayfair. She sighed and paid him the extortionate sum of paper money.

"I've only got £5 left." She took the dice and ended up in jail; but Eddie had laughed too soon and was forced to pay his father for several hotels in the Strand. Furiously he smacked the money onto the table.

"Shame," said Ellie meekly.

It did not take long for Peter to outwit them all and declare himself the winner. Accepting defeat, Eddie went to look out of the window too and asked if he could go and see Patrick.

"Yes, if you want to," his parents agreed. Ellie took up her position on the sofa with a teenage magazine called *Flirt* and buried herself in make-up, clothes and boyfriend problems.

***

For the animals in the Woodland kingdom behind the cottage, the heavy relentless rainfall had some disastrous results. The woodland path leading up to the top was now a brisk waterfall. Small families of dormice and voles sat shivering together, their tiny homes flooded.

"What can be done?" they cried out loudly to anyone who would listen.

The buzzards, high in the Citadel, in the clump of pine trees, the rulers of the Woodland kingdom, soon heard the news. Oliphant, the small white owl who lived in the second ash tree on the left, came knocking on the acorn door knocker on their closed royal door.

Oliphant had only just taken over as the deputy Ruler of the Woodland; the previous deputy, an old tawny owl, had been sacked for misconduct. Oliphant was anxious to do everything properly.

"Yes?" snapped Tween, the middle son of the buzzards, opening the hefty door himself. The white owl blinked several times and raised his head up high, staring at the impatient young prince through piercing eyes.

"We have an emergency down in the Lower Woodland. I must consult with your father. At once," he added meaningfully. The prince beckoned him in and Oliphant found himself in a panelled hall.

"Do sit down," offered the young buzzard and the owl obeyed, finding a high backed pine settle behind him. The Lord of the Woodland appeared from a doorway, clutching his russet robes around him and pulling on his matching hat.

I must be properly dressed for our first audience, he had thought to himself, grabbing his official robes from their blackberry peg.

"Ah, my dear Oliphant, a pleasure, a pleasure indeed," he welcomed the nervous newcomer.

"Trouble sir, I'm afraid," began Oliphant. "We have flood victims in the Lower Woodland; many are homeless, woken from sleep by the torrents of water. We must make a plan - emergency help, food, shelter."

The buzzard was taken aback. Help them? Rehouse them? Food? Shelter? It hadn't been thought of before: just the natural control of the population, nature's way, survival of the fittest. This was certainly a new idea and one he had not thought of. Well, what was to be done?

"Let us sit together Oliphant and consider this, come in here," and he led the curious white owl into a small study, pine panelled, the ceiling planked and arched like a small church; a low seat, padded in purple, ran all the way round. Above, it was lined with book shelves; tomes of leather-bound volumes edged in gold filled them all.

"Now, what do you think should be done?" he inquired, gazing at the small white owl, hoping he was going to come up with something. Oliphant sat nervously thinking, his eyes searching the room for inspiration. He rested his gaze on the slightly comical crooked hat of the sovereign of the Woodland, whose advancing years were beginning to reveal themselves as his eyes drooped and he almost fell asleep in the long silence. Inspiration mercifully came to the little owl: Tolivera's house was now empty. The lofty residence could be turned into a shelter to enfold the cold, wet, and homeless of the Woodland. He blinked several times, betraying nothing of the excitement that was welling up inside him at the thought of his good idea.

"Well, my lord, assuming Tolivera's house is still empty, shall we invite the unfortunate flood victims to stay at the Great Ash Tree, just until renovations can take place and the waters subside, you understand? Clearly only a temporary measure… and shall we recruit the squirrels to build a ramp so that the access to the doorway is more accessible. Most of them are ground dwellers, are they not?"

The implications of this novel idea and sensible solution to the problem were not lost on the buzzard as he absorbed the suggestion fully. He did not speak for a full minute. Oliphant's talons began to tingle with anticipation. What would he say? Would he be furious?

At last the buzzard spoke. "This is a worthy and noble proposal, my dear Oliphant. I shall set it in motion at once. I must decide on the numbers and limit them… For who would not want to come and reside in the home of the famous Tolivera, eh? Thank you for bringing this to my attention, it shall be done. Tween will show you out." And rising, he patted the little white owl on the back and ushered him out of the Round Study.

Oliphant was astonished and bewildered. So he approved of the plan? But when were they going to discuss it?

"I am glad you agree, my lord. Shall we finalise the plan? I have plenty of time now, my Lord and–"

"Later, later, dear Olly - I may call you that I hope? I shall set it all in motion. Don't worry, I shall send a long-tailed tit down with a message very soon." He patted him patronisingly.

Tween, the middle buzzard prince, appeared.

"Show Mr Oliphant out, Tween, would you?" snapped the buzzard sharply and soon the heavy royal door was closed behind him with a loud *clunk*.

"Well! Well!" Oliphant was speechless and sat in the forked branch of a beech tree to recover. He just could not make it out; he was disappointed at the curtness of the buzzard and the swiftness of his dismissal. It was a mystery. Why had he been sent away?

Chapter Three
Eddie and Patrick hear some bad news

Eddie was about to leave to chase down the Creek to Patrick's, when an idea came to him: why not try to find the shortcut along the back of the woods? Eddie first went to the shed to get a small axe. He clambered over the ancient wall to a depression overgrown and hardly recognisable. This was the path of the old leat which had fed the waterwheel. Eddie began hacking away at the strong ivy and treacherous brambles choking the whole area.

Soon he was hot and breathless. Yard by yard he moved along the path, and in the closing gloom, he finally reached the jagged remains of the lime kiln standing in a corner of Patrick's garden.

"At last!" Eddie sighed. He jumped over the wall, where the ground suddenly gave way, causing a cascade of boulders and earth to follow him. Eddie picked himself up and shook his head in disgust, he was now filthy as well as sweating and exhausted, and he wondered what Irene would say when she saw him. He made his way down to the French windows where he could see a blaze of light beaming out into the darkness. The stars began to twinkle through the sky and an owl hooted across the valley. Eddie shivered, suddenly cold, and hurried to tap on the window.

***

Beneath the cottage garden, the underground dwelling of Maudie and Maurice Mole lay covered in a fine layer of terracotta-coloured soil. Several puddles had pooled on the floor. The moles were huddled together on the bed away from the leaking roof and the cave-in of earth, wrapped in a large patchwork quilt, just their noses peeping out.

"Oh my, oh my!" squeaked Maudie. "We shall have to move again!"

"And we've only just finished making it look nice," added Maurice gloomily. "I should have taken more notice of my seaweed weather watcher; it's been looking decidedly damp and droopy recently. I don't really want to move again just yet, do you?"

Maudie looked around the tiny underground cottage. The pinecone lights flickered in their holders, and the tall clock, with its saucepan lid face and knife and fork hands, ticked gently. She sighed. No, she didn't want to pack up the handcart again and trundle off to a new place, not really.

"We can light the fire and dry it all out. Lucinda can come and help with the cleaning up, can't she?" Maurice continued, sensing his wife's reluctance to move yet again. Suddenly he was filled with enthusiasm.

"Come on, Maudie, I do believe it has stopped raining. Let's light the fire now it's getting dark, shall we?" He sprang into action, opening a wooden box lid beside the hearth, letting out a sleepy grasshopper.

"Right, Godfrey, you can start now," and straight away, the obliging grasshopper began to rub his legs together while Maudie and Maurice piled thistledown and small dry sticks into the grate. Gradually a thin plume of smoke appeared as the grasshopper set the fine down alight, and shortly afterward the sticks were crackling and the whole thing was ablaze. A small pile of logs, neatly stacked, waited beside the fireplace. Gradually warmth filled the room, as orange flickers darted their shadows over the walls. The two moles settled down in the warm glow, Godfrey went back to his box and Lucinda the spider was summoned from the large web in the corner. She ran around in circles, sweeping and cleaning the dust away, singing arias from unknown operas in a high, sweet voice. The smoke from the glowing fire travelled up the wide hollyhock chimney into the dark night air, scenting it with woody perfume.

***

Patrick and Eddie spent the evening making plans and talking about boats. Sam and Irene were watching television and the boys went upstairs to talk, pleased to be undisturbed at last.

"I can't wait for the summer now," said Eddie. Dad's going to be stationed at Plymouth, just an hour away, so we'll be doing lots of sailing."

"My dad's keen too, I just hope he gets down here. He says he will, but… I wonder?"

Patrick looked out of the window, and Eddie knew what he was thinking. Sam had let him down before. There was silence between them as Eddie walked over to join him. He could see the moon beginning to rise behind the black trees and he opened the window. Patrick knew at once what Eddie was looking for. The cold air rushed in as they gazed out, looking for a blue twinkling light from the sky, but none came.

"He will contact us one day, Eddie," said Patrick at last, freezing in the cold breeze.

"I suppose so." Eddie sighed, remembering the fun they had enjoyed with the Moonglimmer only a few weeks before.

The noise of a boat engine chugging up the river could be clearly heard, fading into a quiet drone.

"We saw some people out fishing on Christmas Day," said Eddie. "I'd love to do that."

"I don't expect many people want to go fishing on Christmas Day, except you of course," teased Patrick.

"I'll show you my presents if you like. Come on, let's close the window. Brr! It's freezing!"

"What do you think?" and Patrick indicated his presents in a corner. His parents had bought him a new set of foul weather gear and boots for sailing, two sea angling rods and reels and a large book about fishing; a new pair of expensive trainers lay in their box, and an astronomy set and telescope with a stand stood next to them.

"I think you've done very well!"

"Why don't you come back in the daylight and we'll set up the telescope in the garden," persuaded Patrick.

A voice was heard calling from downstairs. It was Irene inviting Eddie to stay to supper, which was an amazing turn of events.

"Golly, you're honoured." The stunned Patrick made a face.

"How do you like your boiled eggs? She's a hopeless cook you know." The two boys collapsed giggling on the bed. As it turned out, cold ham and pickles were not beyond the skills of Irene's cooking, with mince pies and generous dollops of cream. Eddie then told Sam all about *Pelican*, while Irene made coffee and put a tin of shortbread on the table. The phone rang shrilly, Sam quickly getting up to answer it.

"Hello, Jack. Oh no! When? Oh dear, what a shame! What bad luck!" Everyone sat still, listening to someone else's bad news.

"How's Morag? Well, of course she is. Look Jack, find the insurance policy and I'll get over to see you tomorrow. No, it's no trouble. So sorry, Jack," and he quietly put the receiver down. Irene waited while Sam shook his head, saying,

"Can't believe it. Poor Jack and Morag Fraser were burgled on Christmas Day while they were at church in the morning."

"Oh no!"

"Oh yes. And, unfortunately Morag has just inherited a great deal of valuable jewellery from a family member who died recently. They are very famous whisky distillers and rather wealthy. They brought the diamonds with them, not wanting to leave them at their castle in Inverness. The family have had a place here for years, right at the end of Kingswear– that big white house called Woodend Manor Farm. I'd better go and see what can be done to help."

"How foolish to bring them down here. They would have been much safer in a vault in the bank in Scotland," announced Irene with very little sympathy for poor Morag.

"Yes dear, you're right as always," scorned Sam, "But life isn't as easy as you think. They had been out for valuation and repair and they thought it best not to leave them in an empty house, I suppose."

"Empty castle you mean. You'd think they'd have staff there to mind them, wouldn't you?" sniffed Irene bitterly.

"It's Christmas time for everyone dear, even the staff," replied Sam curtly, clearly exasperated by his wife's indifference to Morag's plight.

Eddie, sensing an atmosphere growing, decided to cut and run. "It's getting late now, Mrs McNab, so I think I'd better be going. Thank you for a delicious supper." He smiled his most winning smile at Irene nervously. She responded weakly, her mind now elsewhere, recalling her dismay at Morag's good fortune to be married to so wealthy a man, and then to cap it all, inheriting the family jewels. Why, she and Morag had graduated together from Strathclyde University and wasn't she lucky to have met Jack Fraser in her first job as a product analyst at the distillery?

Patrick saw Eddie to the door. The two boys exchanged glances, their eyes meeting in a knowing look. "See you then, Eddie." Patrick smiled as he closed the door, not wanting to linger on the doorstep.

The sound of raised voices escaped from within.

"*Poor Patrick*," he told himself, *his mother seems so jealous of those rich people.*" And he hurried up the Creek to his own home.

Chapter Four
Oliphant takes up his position as deputy

The next day, the buzzard announced his Great Plan to rehouse the destitute victims of the flood in the Lower Woodland. A parchment notice was nailed to the trunk of the large chestnut tree by the tea shop which overlooked the sea. Word soon flew around the Woodlander Kingdom of the opportunity to have free housing in Tolivera's old residence. Applications were to be submitted to the Citadel and would be considered immediately by the two princes and the buzzard. Letters galore appeared at the door of the Citadel, neatly tied with ivy twists to prevent disclosure.

E'en and Tween went to visit the stricken homes down at the foot of Gallants Bower to check out those who had written to apply for temporary lodgings.

"Now, what shall we do about all these homeless little peasants? We can only get so many into Tolivera's house. What about the rest?" Tween wondered.

"We'll pack 'em in tightly, don't worry; if they're a bit crowded they'll want to go home even quicker won't they?" decided E'en cleverly. The homeless voles and mice had already begun their sad pilgrimage up the daunting hill, weighed down with bundles of salvaged belongings.

"Look at them all," pointed Tween. "Better get back and get ready for them."

The two princes returned to the Citadel, flying the long way round by Little Dartmouth Farm. There were several large barns where produce was stored and stacked neatly. E'en and Tween noticed them at once.

"Food for the flood victims!" they both said together, and flew in under the open end, both grabbing a small sack each and carrying their loot over the fields to the top of Gallants Bower, and dropping the sacks unceremoniously onto the grass.

"Great idea!" They sank exhausted to the springy turf to get their breath back, no notion of the theft they had just committed

At that moment, the first trickle of refugees arrived at the royal door. The buzzard and his consort welcomed them, leading them to the hastily constructed ramp that the squirrel carpenters had devised. Unsteadily, the little families edged up the sloping wood and into the most opulent dwelling they had ever seen.

"What about Oliphant, my dear?" the buzzard's wife mentioned quietly to him.

"Oh, oh yes, I'd quite forgotten him. Send a long-tailed tit down and he can come and see the results of my good idea." His wife did not dare to mention that it should have been Oliphant moving in instead of these poor unfortunate creatures, and despatched the messenger at once.

The tree was large and outspread. A door in the side was connected to the grassy hillside by a new wooden ramp which had been well constructed by the squirrels at very short notice. There was also an opening in the back, but this had a long drop to the leafy ground. The rooms were furnished with polished conker wood, fur throws everywhere and mysterious ornaments. Four chambers led off the main room, and through the narrow clefts in the trunk there were magnificent views all over the river, the sea and the deepest parts of the Woodland towards the Citadel.

The long-tailed tit tapped on Oliphant's door. Sleepily he answered it. Hearing the news, he dressed at once and was just about to follow the messenger when he saw a family of voles struggling up the hill. They were weary and weighted down with bundles.

"Stop!" he called. "Come with me, I shall carry you up the hill." And Oliphant sat on the path with wings outspread, while the voles nervously clambered onto his soft feathered back. Veronica and Vincent Vole hung on tightly and looked down through the trees to the woodland floor far below them, where their sodden home lay. Veronica gave a sad sniff and Vincent put his arm around her.

"We'll soon be back, it's stopped raining now. It'll dry up in no time once the sun comes out," he reassured his tearful wife. Oliphant set them gently down on the crest of the hill, where they gazed around in wonder.

"Welcome, welcome Woodlanders," screeched the hoarse voice of the buzzard, making them all shake in fear. Heads popped out of all the tiny narrow windows and Vincent and Veronica looked up to see some of their neighbours, Dorinda and Denis Dormouse and their countless children, all yelling and waving. Vanessa and Victor Vole, their cousins, were there too.

"Ah, Oliphant, good to see you" greeted the buzzard, nodding, his talons folded together in the folds of his russet robes.

"You see? It is all done. Just as we decided."

"Yes, lord," Oliphant said quietly, watching the vole family skipping up the ramp to join their friends in curious anticipation.

"May we have a word in private?" the small white owl enquired calmly, perching his spectacles on his nose.

"Why, yes, indeed," stammered the Lord of the Woodland. "E'en, Tween, keep an eye on ... all this." He waved his wing as the small voles and mice children all came out to play, noisily chattering and laughing. The stolen turnips, swedes and potatoes were now piled up at the base of the tree and the boisterous children began climbing and playing, hiding and sliding all over them.

The buzzard sensed all was not well, looking at the serious face of his deputy. They strolled together along the path to the royal residence and made their way up to the Round Study.

"Yes, Oliphant - are you not pleased with our evacuation plans? Has it not been a great success?" demanded the buzzard.

"I think it has, my lord, judging by the numbers of Woodland folk rehoused," Oliphant replied politely, sitting calmly on the purple window seat that encircled the room.

"Then what is it?" questioned the buzzard impatiently, tapping his long talons on the table top.

"My Lord we have both forgotten one very important thing and I have come to discuss this with you and to find a speedy solution."

"Well, what is it?" the exasperated buzzard hissed. Oliphant waited for a moment, meeting the angry eyes of the old and now almost incompetent Ruler of the Woodland.

"The Mists of Time, my lord." Oliphant said simply. The buzzard's heart almost stopped. The Mists of Time! He had forgotten all about it since Tolivera left. The underground Root Room and all its workings – all the pipes and taps and barrels, all the dates and happenings that had been recorded. The year had now nearly come to an end and there was plenty to see and plenty he did not want to see again. How could he have forgotten? What was he going to do? What if… it didn't bear thinking about. He began to get into a terrible fluster: his feathers ruffled and his eyes bulged, his talons tapped and his legs shook. He felt quite faint and lightheaded.

Oliphant watched him, icily calm, saying nothing, letting him shake and shiver because Oliphant was very angry. Very angry indeed. Instead of being a shy, retiring Dark Dweller, anxious and willing to please, he had been forced to become strong and unafraid, ready to champion what was right. He had been thrust into a position of responsibility and decision making and had discovered that he had the inner strength and courage to do it.

The buzzard, his lord and master, ruler of all the woodland, had taken his idea and passed it off as his own. He was basking in the glory of being the one who had rescued the flood victims; he had sent Oliphant away and organised the evacuation behind his back. Oliphant would never be quite so gullible again. He also knew that the buzzard was too old now and couldn't operate without him. He had once been a worthy ruler, but, no longer. He should simply retire, handing over the responsibility to his sons, provided they were capable. From what Oliphant had seen of them, he wasn't so sure.

The buzzard struggled to regain his composure, his mind racing wildly, unable to think straight. What was in the Mists of Time? Could the little folk from the Lower Woodland get into the Root Room? All those vats filled to the brim, waiting to be drunk at special occasions. Where was the key? His mind went round and round in circles. He clutched the table as the room seemed to be spinning.

"Feeling alright, my Lord?" at last enquired Oliphant, cruelly.

"What can we do?" croaked the buzzard hoarsely, his head hurting, still unable to think of a single idea or where the key was.

"I don't know, my Lord." The small white owl, determined not to help, sat gazing out of the window, his wings neatly folded.

"You must help me! You must, I command you!" shouted the desperate Ruler of the Woodland hysterically, grabbing Oliphant by the lapels of his striped waistcoat.

"Alright, alright!" eventually agreed his deputy, fending off the crazed buzzard.

"I think I know what to do." He straightened up his clothes and picked up his bow tie off the floor. The buzzard sank down on the plush purple seat, exhausted, pleading.

"You are the only one. My sons cannot make decisions yet, it is clear to me now. They have stolen food from the farm to feed the refugees. This is not the way." And he clutched his head, shaking it, sighing deeply.

"I need you, Oliphant, more than ever. Go now and do what you can."

"Yes lord," were the only words the owl could bring himself to say and he left at once, retreating backwards out of the Round Room. The solution? It was so simple.

He flew along the hilltop and entered Tolivera's house by the back door, high up in the trunk, and wound his way down the spiral staircase. Tolivera's key was still hidden in a ledge above the door, so he took it, laughing to himself.

"Dear, oh dear!" He entered the arched door at the bottom, and once inside, shot the bolts across. No one could get in now, not even with a key.

Quickly he opened the big tap while the dates flicked by in the narrow slit, as the striped liquid pooled in the silver dish beneath it. This was the stored history, which revealed itself in silent pictures, and then ran away into the drain and to a large vat to be matured into an amber pungent drink. For a very short time the process could be reversed, but then it was lost, lost in the Mists of Time – all the secret, silent observations made by the tips of the branches of the Great Ash Tree, spying on the world of the Woodland. The recent events were now erased.

Several times the little owl had sneaked down here with his friend Freddie and he knew how to get out through the venting pipe. He squeezed himself into it, took a deep breath, and shot up out onto the Woodland floor, coughing and gasping for air. Whooosh! He carefully covered the vent hole with a large stone and some dry leaves and pushed a forked stick into the ground beside it to mark the spot. It was all done, safe and secure from any prying eyes. Simple!

Oliphant had some serious thinking to do now. Should the buzzard hand the reins of power over to his sons, things could take a very different turn, and he did not like the look of it. He flew home to his home in the second ash tree on the left to contemplate his next action.

Chapter Five
Sargasso and Seraphim are united

As a new grey dawn crept over the quiet serenity of the Creek waters, a pair of seagulls made their simple vows to each other: promises for a lifetime, solemn and sincere, as they bobbed on the glinting green waters. No one else was present or required. Sargasso and Seraphim were united for ever, whispering the age-old Seafarers' words imprinted in their minds, inherited by generations before them.

The Spirit of the Sea heard their whispers over the miles of undulating ocean and nodded his satisfaction. It would be a great union, for he had a plan in place for them, the inevitable blessing of their coupling, a special gift, to acknowledge Sargasso's immense contribution. It would be a unique event in the timeless history of the sea, one only spoken of, or written about, in myths and legends.

After the quiet ceremony, friends of this unusual couple gathered for a celebration and each brought a gift of food; something from their own place in the food chain, and the breakfast feast sealed the happy union in the Seafarers' tradition.

By the time a pink dawn broke across the sky through shredded clouds, each had returned to his own resting place and the celebration was over, leaving Sargasso and Seraphim alone to begin their new life together. Happily, they left the Creek and flew towards the sea, stretching their wings in search of the remotest place to be alone together.

***

Sam McNab, unable to sleep, got up early as the first sunlight of the day spread over the slipway. He made a mug of tea and walked down to the water's edge, wrapped in a thick Shetland sweater. Once more, he marvelled that this beautiful secluded Creek was now his very own place. He sat on the large drain cover, staring out across the water to Kingswear. The birds were already feeding and two seagulls took off, skimming over the gliding water heading down river. Small birds sang the morning chorus in the surrounding trees and a blue and orange flash caught his eye further round the rocks – the darting colours of a kingfisher, so elusive, held only for a second in his sight.

He was glad he had bought the cottage, hopeful that his only son would be content to divide his young life between school and this pleasant place. Sam was growing to like it more and more and his immensely busy and responsible job seemed a million miles away here on the wooded shores of Dartmouth; the world of stocks and shares, business takeovers and company acquisitions, with its ruthless efficiency and cold decisions, seemed distant and irrelevant. He sipped his tea slowly, thinking about his friends Jack and Morag Fraser, mourning the loss of hundreds of thousands of pounds worth of irreplaceable jewellery.

The sun shone on the water, dancing its brilliant rays, and the sparkles of the ripples were bright and dazzling, flashing and blinding. The warmth reached his face and he closed his eyes and breathed deeply; shards of bright colours still affecting his vision from the sun shining in the water. He almost fell asleep in the warm morning sunlight, eventually forcing his eyes open. Where was he? He jolted awake, shielding his eyes from the diamond dancing lights reflected from the water. He felt it then; his stomach shivered with a strange and powerful sensation; he didn't want to believe it but what he was looking at had more value than anything he could ever possess. He looked again at the elusive jewels of coloured light before his eyes, and then a cloud passed in front of the sun and it was gone. Sam picked up his mug, got to his feet stiffly and walked back to his front door feeling just a little peculiar. What had happened to him? He went inside to wash and dress and get ready to visit the Fraser's, still unable to come to terms with his early morning spiritual revelation. Money had been his life.

At Watermill Cottage, Eddie was waiting for the tide to go out so that he could search the craggy rock pools for more specimens for the aquarium. He switched the light on and watched the bubbles of air bursting in the water. Some of the creatures had embedded themselves in the fine shingle on the floor of the tank. It was fascinating to see them all so close up.

Ellie came downstairs and joined him and they peered together into the glass, watching the private lives of the creatures within.

"Shall we go down to the beach today? When will the tide be out?" Ellie asked him.

"Not until about two-thirty," explained Eddie, "Nuisance, isn't it?"

First Mary and then Peter filtered down into the kitchen and breakfast was soon underway, Peter and Eddie voting for bacon sandwiches.

"What about *Pelican,* Dad?" asked Eddie. "What do you think about it? Is it going to be any good?"

Peter nudged the bacon in the frying pan, trying to wake up.

"Umm, there is one thing – it won't fit on our mooring here at the Creek. Too long I'm afraid. But," seeing his son's face, "it shouldn't be a problem, there's always someone not using theirs."

"When are we going to see it?"

"Next Wednesday, ten o'clock. Eddie, got the bread ready?"

The sandwiches completed, Eddie tipped large quantities of brown sauce over the bacon, taking such a huge bite that he could no longer speak.

"We'd better join the Royal Dart Yacht Club across the river if you want to race her this summer. I think it's Wednesday evenings."

Eddie felt a thrill of pleasure.

"Won't it be great? Can Ellie come?"

"Of course she can. I want her to. It's good to build up teamwork and stops girls fussing about their hair – too busy hauling ropes and sails. It'll make a man of her."

Eddie choked on his almost-finished sandwich.

"Don't let Ellie hear you say that, Dad."

The phone rang. Peter answered it at once.

"Morning, Patrick," and handed the phone to Eddie.

"Hello? Oh, can't you? Alright, I'll catch up with you later. Still on for the telescope? Good. 'Bye then." He turned to his father:

"Patrick's got to go to Kingswear with his dad to see some people who had a burglary." Eddie was obviously disappointed. "But Ellie will still come with me."

Good old Ellie, she rarely let him down. Perhaps he'd go and get the Moonmirror. It had been up in the woods too long and probably needed a clean and sort out anyway. He also wondered why Patrick had been hijacked by his father. As far as he knew, Patrick didn't even know them; it was strange.

"Mum and I are going to the Reynolds' today for a lunch party. Will you and Ellie be alright here for a couple of hours? You can come with us if you like, Mike and Marie won't mind."

The thought of enduring more grown-up conversation and that awful laughing they seemed to do at parties was too much for Eddie, sensing freedom for the afternoon.

"We'll be fine, Dad, honestly."

So the days' events unfolded and Eddie won Ellie round, persuading her to collect their light gadgets. They set off behind the cottage on the trail in the woods, which was thick with soft mud and covered in shingly stones washed down by the flood water.

"This is very slippery," complained Ellie, struggling until they reached the top at last.

"Phew! That was hard work," remarked Eddie, looking at his mud-spattered Wellingtons. They strode along in the fresh air, passing the Cornucopia Tree, unknown to them, where the pigeons lived. Reaching the boundary of the Woodland kingdom, they faced the tall pine trees of the Citadel, home of the Buzzards, with the five bar gate close to it. The Freedom Gate, which led to the world outside, was feared by the Woodlanders who dwelt within its boundary. Following the old pathway, Eddie and Ellie passed a large ash tree towering over the top of the hillside, once the home of the deputy ruler, the feared tawny owl, Tolivera.

The Woodland folk who had been rehoused at the Great Ash Tree were not used to humans, and hearing the footfalls of the two youngsters approaching, gathered up their children and huddled together, frightened and anxious. Instead of passing by, Ellie and Eddie stopped at the tree.

"Is it alright?" asked Ellie anxiously, looking up at the wooden hide Patrick and Eddie had constructed in the autumn.

"Someone's put a piece of wood on here. Good, I can stand on it." And he balanced on the ramp and unhooked the box from the two nails sticking out of the tree, and carefully passed the two lights down. Crack! Suddenly the wood gave way and Eddie slipped down the bank, rolling onto the grass. He laughed unhurt, lying on the ground.

"Who put that there anyway?" puzzled Ellie. "Are you alright?"

"I think so." He got to his feet.

The little creatures inside shook with fear. Humans! And so near! They closed their eyes and froze. Eventually Eddie and Ellie moved off to stand on top of the earthworks.

Where do you think Woodend Manor Farm is?" they asked each other, searching along the opposite side of the river, looking through the trees for a large white house.

"The name would make you think it's at the end of the woods, wouldn't it?"

"Oh well done, professor," scorned Ellie, "Of course it is!"

Only two houses fitted this description, one white, one grey, both hardly visible through the winter trees. Eddie gazed across the river, wondering what could possibly have tempted Patrick away from Warfleet and spoilt their plans for today? He would just have to wait to find out.

Chapter Six
Patrick meets the Frasers

Sam and Patrick were walking along the high narrow road from Kingswear Ferry towards the point, looking for the signs to Woodend Manor Farm. A steep driveway with two white pillars and high gates marked their destination. "Here it is," indicated Patrick to his father. Patrick gazed across the water, spotting the Old Watermill and the Creekside houses, the Old Bath House, the castle and church.

"Why did you make me come with you, Dad?" asked Patrick crossly, "I was going to go rock pooling with Eddie and Ellie this morning, you know."

"I wanted you to meet Jack and Morag. It might take their minds off things." He thought about the contents of the leather briefcase he was carrying, bank details and insurance information that he was going to have to discuss with Jack. He sighed.

"Let's go and get this over, I feel rather sorry for them. Anyway, there's a surprise in store for you."

Patrick frowned; he didn't like his Dad's surprises. They continued along the twisting path edged with huge rhododendron bushes, exotic trees and tropical plants which thrived here in the balmy winters. Rounding the last bend, they came upon the Georgian house sitting prettily in the gentle valley. In front of the house were several police cars, and men in plain clothes were wandering about looking thoughtful with notebooks poised.

"Oh blast, the police are here," spoke Sam bitterly.

"Oh good." Patrick cheered up immediately: something interesting at last to occupy him. One of the policemen came over to them.

"Can we help you, sir?" he asked pleasantly, looking them up and down.

"We're friends of Mr and Mrs Fraser and I've arranged to see him this morning. He *is* expecting us," he emphasised.

"Right sir, I'm Detective Sergeant Tim McDonald and I'll check if they are ready to see you. Sorry but we have a lot to do this morning, the forensic boys are inside and it's a big place."

"I quite understand," replied Sam.

Patrick spotted a man in overalls brushing the window inside. Fingerprints, he decided. They stood outside surveying the garden with its distant views of the sea; tree-covered hillsides and open fields surrounded the rear, where a few animals grazed in the distance. Some small flowering blue irises clustered beside the door. It was very quiet; the only sounds the birds singing and the murmur of voices from indoors.

"Isn't this a grand spot, Patrick?" admired Sam, "Your mother would kill for this. I must bring her over sometime."

Please don't. Patrick thought unhappily.

The front door opened sharply and Jack Fraser came hurrying out, running his fingers through his auburn hair, heavy glasses perched on top of his head.

"Sam! Patrick! So sorry you couldn't get in, the place is crawling with police. Come away in now – it's great to see you!" and he clasped Sam's hand and shook it vigorously. Then he turned to Patrick, put both hands on his shoulders and scrutinised him carefully. He saw the fair hair, blue eyes and bright face gazing back at him. He let go of him and put one arm around his shoulder, smiling.

"You've a fine wee laddie here, Sam, and no mistake. Another protégée from Burnside College, eh? Do you like the books, Patrick?"

Patrick hesitated for a second, deciding on his tactful answer while his father watched him carefully.

"Well enough, Mr Fraser, but I love it here in Dartmouth. I can come every holiday and it suits me just fine. I've a lot of friends at Burnside. Do you know the Craig brothers? They live quite near you."

"Aye, aye I do, the parents are rather good customers of mine, between you and me," and they all laughed together. This wasn't going to be too bad, Patrick admitted to himself, following Jack Fraser and his father inside the imposing front door and entering the black and white tiled hall with its large ornate mirrors on either side. A blue and white jug filled with daffodils stood on a huge table welcoming them and a tall elephant's foot held many walking sticks and umbrellas. A stag's head stared at him from a distance; several cases filled with stuffed pheasants, red squirrels and a hawk met his eyes, each standing on their own shelf, imprisoned long ago behind glass.

They entered a bright sunny drawing room painted pale yellow, where Mrs Fraser was seated pouring coffee from a tray in front of her. She had a pretty, outdoor sort of face and short curly hair and she wore jeans and a polo necked sweater. She finished filling the cups and got up at once.

"Hello, Sam, you're very welcome and this must be Patrick." She kissed them both in a friendly, exuberant sort of way.

"Come and meet Heather." And picking up a cup and saucer, she carried it over to the large bay window at the other end of the room, where comfy arm chairs were arranged around a low coffee table. Sitting in one of them with her back to them, and facing the window, was a girl. She turned to smile at them, her long blonde hair the colour of hay, her eyes light hazel brown. She was small and petite, wearing a bright pink jumper and jeans to match.

"Hello," she said politely, "I'm Heather." Patrick was surprised and embarrassed at the same time. Why had his father not mentioned Heather to him?

"I'm Patrick Mc Nab, nice to meet you," he managed.

"Shall we sit down?" urged Morag. "Come here by me, Patrick," offering him a plump, cream velvet chair.

"Now you get the scones, Sam, and Jack you bring your coffee." Soon Morag had everyone organised and they were munching on the delicious scones, enjoying the wonderful view, and it felt friendly and relaxed. Only Heather seemed shy and quiet, smiling a little, but reluctant to join in; there was just something distant about her which Patrick noticed.

Jack, Morag and Sam decided to go to the study to discuss the robbery in private and left Patrick and Heather together by the sunny window with the rest of the scones and the coffee. Patrick looked around, nervously taking in the room with its paintings and china, collection of pipes and a cabinet of silver and small trinkets. He was overcome with shyness and didn't know what to say. He finished his coffee and cleared his throat, and as he set the cups down he knew he had to say something – anything – to break this awkward silence.

"Are you here for long?"

"Another three weeks. My school doesn't start again until the 21st of January you see," she told him. "I board at St Agnes in Sussex."

"Oh aye, I board too, at Burnside, but we go back before you, you're lucky."

She just smiled back, nodding. Something came up from under Patrick's chair and pulled at his trouser leg. He jumped automatically and made a noise.

"Ouch!" Heather burst out laughing, her hand over her mouth. Patrick looked down to see a small white West Highland terrier, with a tartan bow round its neck, his trousers still between its teeth.

"Och, Robbie, leave him alone! Come on, let go!" Heather called to him and reluctantly the little dog let go of Patrick, but not without giving him a nip on the ankle first, and lay growling quietly at him. Then he launched himself into Heather's lap while she sat giggling quietly, embarrassed.

"Sorry," she finally said, looking to see if Patrick was annoyed, hugging Robbie to her.

"That's alright," he said gruffly, rubbing his ankle and inspecting it for any blood.

"He's only trying to be friendly," continued Heather anxiously.

"It's a pity he didn't hear the burglars, he'd have killed them," said Patrick, and Heather laughed loudly.

"You're right! He's a wee monster in a fluffy coat, aren't you?" and she kissed the adoring dog.

"Why didn't he hear them?" asked Patrick seriously, edging forward in his chair.

"He wasn't here. He was up at the wee Byre. It's the small cottage up the valley. Dad's fixed it up for me. I've got my music and all my stuff there and I can do what I like and not be a bother to anyone."

"Great." Patrick was beginning to relax. "Sounds really good. You can have your music as loud as you like then, no one to nag you."

"Exactly," agreed Heather, stroking the contented dog who was almost asleep.

"What sort of things do you like doing?" ventured Patrick. Heather looked out of the window for a minute before replying.

"Oh you know, the usual, music, telly, magazines." Patrick smiled at the predictable answers.

"But what I really like is archery and pistol shooting. I'm on the school team."

"Really?" Patrick raised his eyebrows. He was very surprised. This small quiet girl, pistol shooting and archery? What unusual hobbies. She looked as if she wouldn't say boo to a goose!

"I've got some targets set up at the Byre, you know, to practise with. We've plenty of bows if you'd like a go one day... would you?" she fired the direct question at him, challenging him with her eyes fixed on his. Patrick was so surprised he said yes before he knew what he was doing.

"When?" was the next dart she fired.

"Well, um... what suits you?"

"Afternoons are best really. Can you come over the day after tomorrow, say 3 o'clock?"

"Sure, why not?"

"Cool!" she replied, satisfied. It was as easy as that. They smiled at each other. Patrick was a bit shaken but remained calm. He looked across the river to the Old Bath House. It looked so different from this angle.

"Do you see that house over there, with the balcony and the doors down at the bottom?" he pointed standing up.

"Yes."

"That's where my godparents live. They run the tea shop at the castle and I helped them last Easter." Was it only that short time ago? When he had first met Eddie and Ellie and the seagull and the robin, Captain Avery, and of course the unforgettable Isabella and Ferdinand? Was it really only in the autumn that the Moonglimmer had arrived from the dark side of the moon? So much had had happened to him, he felt so different now.

"Did you like it... working there?" Heather asked.

"Oh yes, and I've made some good friends now. Dartmouth is a great place, in fact I liked it so much I ran away."

"You ran away? What, from school?"

"Not from school exactly, I didn't want to go back to Burnside so I got off the train at Newton Abbot and came back."

"Wasn't your father furious?"

"Yes, he was. But I really meant it. I was determined I wasn't going back to that boring lonely existence, not after being with Eddie and Ellie."

"Who are they?" Heather asked, puzzled, stroking the now-sleeping dog.

"They're my friends, they–" he broke off as his father, Sam and Morag re-entered the room and came towards them.

"The police want to interview Robbie now," said Morag seriously. Heather burst out laughing and Robbie opened one eye at the mention of his name.

Patrick stood up and said, "Heather's asked me to come over and have a go at archery Dad, is that alright? Maybe Thursday?"

Sam looked suitably surprised, but thankfully said nothing embarrassing.

"Sure, fine by me. Good idea!" and he smiled at the pretty blonde girl.

"Right folks, we must be off. It was great to see you, if under rather unfortunate circumstances. We'll do what we can, eh?"

Heather sat where she was and said goodbye, while Morag and Jack showed them out of the pleasant house.

"Cheerio, see you Thursday." Patrick turned and waved to the small face through the window. She held up the little white dog, pushing his paw up and down.

Sam and Patrick walked along the shrub-lined driveway in silence, both taking in the strange events of the morning. Patrick looking across the river to Warfleet Creek.

What did you think of Heather? Did you get on with her?"

Patrick was surprised at the question.

"I think so. She seemed very nice; a bit quiet and shy at first, but she's… very nice," he repeated.

"Such a shame about her accident. Jack and Morag have been wonderful. They must have been devastated." He shook his head sadly.

"Accident?" Patrick was confused.

"Aye, accident. She fell off her horse and she's lost the use of her legs. Paralysed. She's in a wheelchair." Seeing his son's face, he realised he did not know.

"Did she not tell you?"

"No, Dad, she didn't." Silence fell yet again between them, Patrick agonising about their conversation, trying to remember what he had said to her. Anything that would upset her? He hoped not. He was, however, thoroughly shaken by this revelation and he re-ran their conversation in his mind: the archery, the pistol shooting, the piano, things easy to compete in from a wheelchair. It all fell into place.

"Poor girl."

"Aye, it's a terrible shame, but she is a very plucky little lassie and fiercely independent. They've kept her on at St Agnes's because she's pretty brainy and insists on fitting in. She has loads of friends and is really popular, by all accounts. Jack and Morag are very proud of her."

"Will she never walk again?" asked Patrick sadly.

"They don't know yet but it's a year since her accident. She can still ride of course and she does, but you'd think she would never want to get on a horse again, wouldn't you?"

The two figures, walking side by side, reached the pretty little church of St Thomas of Canterbury, hiding behind its lych gate as the clock on the church tower struck one o'clock. They could see the lower ferry gliding across the river and hurried down the hill to meet it. Foot passengers were welcome on this car ferry and they squeezed along the rails and chose a spot beside the cars.

"I've forgotten to pop into the Yacht Club for a form," Sam said, annoyed with himself.

"I'll get one for you on Thursday when I come over."

"That would be very helpful, thanks son," and Sam smiled at his only child, looking at him in a thoughtful way, grateful for the first time that his legs were normal. He suddenly appreciated something he had never even thought about for the second time that day.

"Any news of the jewellery?" Patrick questioned.

"The police seemed to think someone knew they were there. No evidence of a break in, no strangers around, no tyre tracks and not much to go on. The diamonds were in a safe box in the bedroom. Unfortunately no one takes a lot of notice on Christmas morning of other people's business, too busy with their own. Very clever really."

"But how did they know Morag and Jack would be going to church?" asked Patrick.

"Well, that's a good question. It does narrow the field down. They usually do go to church when they're here, give money to the funds, etc etc."

They both said no more until the ferry reached Dartmouth and they strode up the hill out of town to Warfleet. Patrick was keen to get off rock pooling with Eddie. He noticed with satisfaction that the tide had crept out, leaving a brown shiny expanse of beach.

Irene was pleased to see them; she had spent the morning preparing a lecture and was stiff-necked and bored.

"Did you bring anything for lunch?" she asked them hopefully.

"No, should we have?" asked a surprised Sam.

"There doesn't seem to be much to eat," Irene announced apologetically.

"Well there won't be if you don't go shopping, will there?" Sam sighed, knowing that at home Irene ordered takeaway food in or they ate out. Patrick felt upset. What was wrong with his mother? He searched the kitchen and found what he was looking for.

"Leave it to me," he said, and his two surprised parents watched, as Patrick produced toasted cheese and marmite sandwiches, just a little burnt. He added half a tomato and a piece of lettuce, and served them with a flourish.

"How clever of you, dear," praised Irene, tucking into hers.

"These smell delicious!" added Sam, and the whole lot were demolished at once.

"Why don't you ring an order down to Superfoods, Mum? Just make a list out." Patrick tried to help his mother be more organised.

"We eat out most of the time at home and I don't have to bother much," Irene defended herself.

"I know, Mum, but it's different here." He couldn't believe he had to do this. His mother was cleverer than most and had travelled all over the world. Sam observed his wife and son, taking no part. This was certainly a learning curve in family life.

"You ring, Patrick." Irene told him. "Be a good boy." But Patrick was furious.

"No, Mum, it's your job. I'm not doing it, I'm going out with Eddie," and he hurried off to get ready, leaving a petulant Irene in the kitchen complaining to Sam how unfair it was.

In jeans and an old jumper, a woolly hat perched on his head, Patrick grabbed a bucket and a net and hurried out into the Creek, free at last. His mother hadn't even asked them about their morning at Woodend Farm. He wondered if she knew about Heather or cared come to that. He felt vaguely depressed and unhappy for all sorts of reasons he couldn't explain, and with hunched shoulders and a heavy heart he scanned the beach for his friend: Eddie was guaranteed to lift his spirits.

Chapter Seven
A discovery in the garden at Waterside Cottage

Far out on the browny-flecked rocks, two figures could be seen. Patrick watched for a minute and then smiled. A gust of wind blew in from the water, rippling the surface and carrying the sound of voices. Eddie and Ellie bobbed up and down over the rocks, bending to search the crevices and the sight of them filled him with joy. He stumbled across the mud and stones which were wet and slippery, noting the empty mooring lines.

That's where our boat is going to be he told himself happily. At last Eddie and Ellie noticed him and stopped, looking up, waiting for him to reach them. "Come and help us! The water's freezing!" Eddie shouted.

"What have you got?" Patrick asked, peering into the muddy water in the bucket.

"A couple of blennies and a small edible crab," he was told.

"I'll go over there." Patrick pointed to an area on the opposite side. They agreed on their hunting grounds and began trawling the weed-strewn rocky edges and investigating the pools. Ellie gently prised some pink sea anemones from their rocky home. Eddie scooped up a small flatfish and regarded it with satisfaction.

"Here's a baby plaice or sole. Look!"

"Oh good, we haven't got one of those," exclaimed an excited Ellie. "Let's see."
It was Patrick who found the prize specimen: examining a deep, clear pool he pulled up a tiny mottled lobster. "Come and look at this!"

Ellie and Edie sploshed over the mud to see what he had discovered. Eddie looked at it carefully, turning it over on his cold hands.

"I've never ever seen one of these. A baby lobster. Isn't it lovely?" he showed it to Ellie.

"Are there any more?" and obligingly Patrick plunged his hands back into the dark crevice. Something else was caught under the ledge, hard and jagged. He got his fingers round it and pulled. Out came a bunch of keys on a plastic fob.

"Not exactly what we were hoping for!"

"Somebody's obviously lost them – dropped them over the side sometime." said Ellie, surveying the uninviting treasure. Patrick put them in his pocket, and feeling rather cold in the increasing breeze, they decided to go back and put their finds in the aquarium.

"We've still got time to set the telescope up," persuaded Patrick, "haven't we?"

The three of them trudged across the muddy beach, the tide beginning to chase them and the wind hurting their hands. They found their father in the garden. He had taken the tarpaulin cover off and was inside the boat checking it over.

"Hi Dad! Patrick found a baby lobster," Ellie told him proudly.

"Good. What else?"

"Two blennies, and a baby flatfish," replied Eddie.

"Oh, and a bunch of rusty keys!" added Patrick.

"Really useful" joked Peter, looking up as Sam strolled up the driveway.

"How's she looking, Peter?" he asked.

"Not bad, not bad at all. The engine could do with a service, but apart from that and perhaps a coat of paint, she's all yours."

Eddie headed first to the toaster while Ellie foraged in the cake tins, enticed by the shortbread, mince pies and Christmas cake she knew lay waiting for her. Her mother was sitting down enjoying a film on television with her sewing in one hand.

"I'd love a cup of tea if you're making one," she called hopefully from her chair.

"Okay, Mum," yelled back Ellie. The men sat in the kitchen and the others sat in the sitting room, drinking tea and eating cake. Mary knew she would never see the end of the film and sighed.

"We're going down to Patrick's to set up his telescope," Eddie announced through a mouthful of cake.

"You boys!" Mary shook her head, smiling. "Are you going too, Ellie?"

"I don't know yet, I haven't decided," she replied, as the boys exchanged the slightest of glances, raising their eyebrows just the smallest fraction.

"You can come if you want to," offered Patrick generously, knowing that leaving her out really upset her.

Peter and Sam came into the sitting room looking pleased with themselves.

"*Sargasso*'s leaving home," Peter told them all. "Off to a new life with the McNabs."

Eventually Eddie, Patrick and Sam walked down to Waterside Cottage together, leaving Ellie, Peter and Mary sitting comfortably by the fire.

Ellie remembered the buckets outside the back door and went out just in time to rescue the contents from a pair of black jackdaws investigating the fish. One of the birds was perched on the edge of the bucket.

"Shoo! Shoo!" Ellie waved them way. Carefully she put all the tiny creatures into a smaller bowl and gently lowered each one into the bubbling water.

"That looks very nice, Ellie. You're getting quite a collection," Mary complimented her.

"Yes, of course Eddie and Patrick forgot all about them! Their nets and buckets are still out there," she complained. "They've left everything!"

"Oh well, Ellie, that's rather how boys are, off to the next thing, never clearing up." Mary told her daughter. *She'll learn!* she thought philosophically to herself.

***

40

In the garden at Waterside there was a lot of clattering and chattering, as Eddie and Patrick prepared to install the telescope. Studying the booklet of the stars and planets, they decided on the direction it ought to face.

"A bit higher I think. Up there should do." Patrick pointed to further up the steep garden towards the lime kiln. Obligingly, Eddie carried the equipment up the slope for him.

"Here? It's quite flat if we move a bit of earth."

"Yes, that should be just right."

They began to dig away at the rough ground, intending to make a platform for the spreading legs of the tripod. They were almost at the foot of the remains of the lime kiln when a strange thing happened. A hole appeared beneath the trowel that Patrick was holding and the crumbly soil fell into it; the gulf gradually widened and the soil poured into it, just disappearing.

"Look Eddie, there's a hole here!" he half shouted. "Watch out!" and Eddie moved to peer over Patrick's shoulder.

"Oh bloody hell!" he said, astonished. "What's that?" Patrick poked his trowel further into the hole, but his hand and then his arm began to vanish and he almost overbalanced.

"Steady!" Eddie gripped onto him. They stood up and backed away to have a good look at it. Eddie looked around the lime kiln and pointed.

"That's the remains of the wall around the lime kiln, and this bit is where the front edge was. Shall we have a dig around and see what we can find?"

The usual excitement began to fill him as his imagination ran away. What could it be? Memories of finding the skull of the old pirate came flooding back.

The two set to work, digging carefully this time, discovering bit by bit a large hole and wooden floor. It seemed that the lime kiln had been boarded over. Part of the wooden boards had rotted away, Eddie's fall having contributed to its final breakdown, and Patrick's probing had pushed the rotten remains down into the darkness. They pulled at the rest of the wet, earthy, crumbling wood, revealing the stone interior of the kiln, blackened with the continuous burning of lime a hundred years ago. Set into the walls were a set of iron rungs, like those used in examination shafts. The two boys looked at each other, thinking the same thing.

"Shall we?"

"No we must test them first? And only one should go, wearing a rope, really," muttered Patrick thinking aloud. "In case they're rusted out. Who knows how deep it could be?" rubbing his face as he thought quickly.

"And a torch would be good," added Eddie, realising the stupidity of entering such a place unprepared. Patrick raced back to the outside lean-to and gathered the items he wanted. He hurried back to Eddie who was waiting impatiently.

"What have you got?"

"Two ropes, a torch, and an old cupboard door."

"What's that for?"

"We'll need to cover it up after us in case someone falls into it, stupid!"

"Right," agreed Eddie, admiring his forethought. "Who's going down first?"

"Me!" grinned Patrick. "It's my garden."

Eddie nodded reluctantly while Patrick tied the rope around his waist. Eddie tied the other end of the rope to the iron fixing of the washing line. Patrick lowered himself over the edge, testing the first two rungs with his foot, then leaning heavily on them.

"They seem okay."

"Right, go on then," urged Eddie eagerly. Patrick descended several feet.

Testing the following rungs again, Patrick inched into the darkness, clinging on tightly.

"I can see the rest! There's about ten feet below me and then the bottom."

"Go on!" Eddie was very excited. Shining the torch downwards in between each rung as he moved into the lime kiln, Patrick finally disappeared and Eddie peered over the edge anxiously.

"I'm at the bottom," he soon called. "It smells awful down here. There's quite a bit of earth fallen in," as he scanned the wall with the torch.

"Something's been blocked up here, the rocks are different." He examined it carefully.

"I'm coming up," he yelled and Eddie helped him, pulling him up as he found the footholds on the wall and held onto the iron rungs.

"Phew! What an amazing find. What do you think it's for?" Patrick asked as he sat on the ground resting, breathing in the fresh air.

"Got to be something to do with the lime kiln, maybe inspecting it if it didn't burn properly," suggested Eddie. "Can I go down now?" he asked eagerly.

"Course!" grinned Patrick, untying the rope. Eddie retied it and let himself down over the edge carefully, feeling for the rungs.

"Not very easy, is it?" he said, as his head disappeared into the darkness and a chuckling Patrick held onto the rope very tightly. When he reached the bottom, Eddie felt the soft earth and stepped onto the uneven floor. At once he shone the torch around him and noticed just as Patrick had the bricked-up section apparent in the sides.

"*Umm*," he pondered, *Maybe it's just where they got the lime in and out?* He studied it until the unpleasant smell and cold dampness drove him up again.

"Coming up!" he called, and Patrick assisted him to the top.

"Phew!" Eddie rolled out of the void onto the damp grass.

"Cover it up quickly." Patrick rushed to untie the rope, hearing his mother's voice at just the same time. They put the cupboard door over the hole, then several rocks, and heaped some

earth and dead leaves on top. Gathering the telescope equipment, its initial installation having been abandoned at the chance discovery of the
gaping hole, the boys hurried down to the French windows where Irene, arms folded against the cold, was waiting.

"What have you been doing? It's almost dark." Then she hesitated. "But I suppose you need it to be dark to see the stars!" she laughed. "Come inside and get warm." And she ushered the two boys in at once, the chance for further discussions lost for the time being.

Chapter Eight
A lucky escape and a moonlight visitor

The poor stranded creatures lodged in the Great Ash Tree banged on the back door, high up in the side of the trunk.

"We can't get out!" Veronica Vole shouted out of the thin slitted windows, but her voice was lost in the whistling of the wind high on the exposed hill. Rain started to fall again and the sky grew heavy and dark, as a fierce winter storm with easterly gales approached. The inexperienced tree dwellers closed their shutters and settled down inside; no one ventured out in a storm, it was an unwritten law. As the trees waved their branches madly, the wind rose, making the noise of thundering trains approaching and soon they were driven into a terrified huddle in the opulent apartments of the tawny owl.

His curious ornaments frightened Vincent Vole – small creamy skulls resting on a shelf sent shivers through him; a dragonfly, trapped in pine resin forever, worried him; fur draped on chairs and made into cushions drove fear into him. A feeling of dread crept over him.

"I don't like this place." He shivered and shook his head.

"Come on Veronica, we're leaving," he decided firmly. "Gather up the children, I'll find a way out – wait here for five minutes, I'll be back for you." And off he went on his search. He raced around the corridors, finding the back door firmly locked; all the windows were too high, the ramp broken in pieces on the ground. He descended the spiral staircase into the dark depths and found the door to the Root Room, also depressingly locked. He looked frantically at the closed door until he noticed the large keyhole and a gap beneath the frame; was it just wide enough for a tiny vole to squeeze through? He hoped so, he'd take the chance. Filled with joy, he ran back to the room where his family were sheltering.

"Let's go! Quickly now, I've found a way out! Does anyone else want to come with us? We're not staying here! This place has a bad feeling to me." announced Vincent bravely, looking around at his surprised neighbours. Silence.

"We'll come," whispered Dorinda and Denis, hugging their three children, Dodo, Davy and Dorrie. No one else answered.

"Anyone else? See you all soon, I hope." And Vincent led the way down, down and reached the door of the underground Root Room. The grown-ups wriggled under the door and the children squashing themselves flat, managed to push each other through the key hole, sliding down the other side into the mysterious and strange smelling room. Burps and gurgles, bubbles and pops, could be heard coming from the pipes and barrels.

"Coo, what's this, Dad?" asked Davy, gawping at the complicated apparatus of pipes and dials.

"Nothing to do with us, lad. Don't touch" he insisted firmly. "Now, how do we get out?" wondered Vincent and Denis. They searched and sniffed in the dark corners of the tree roots, scrabbling and scratching until they found a gap where the earth was soft and the roots large.

"We can get through here," panted Vincent. The children followed their parents through the newly scratched tunnel out into the Woodland, emerging into the darkened air with its wintry chill. Scampering down the path, they were sheltered by the trees and heavy undergrowth, and they arrived at last back home which thankfully had almost dried out, just left damp and musty. Shouting goodbye to their friends, they curled up together for warmth, exhausted and glad to be back. Dorinda, Denis and their three children did the same in their round hollow. Asleep in the warm leaves they were unaware of the terrible fate of those they had left behind.

Cracks of thunder and jagged shards of lightning lit up the sky on the summit of Greensward Bower; a shaft of brilliance struck the tree with ferocious power. Almost immediately fire engulfed the Great Ash Tree; the topmost branches flamed and then went out, leaving much of it blackened and stark in its grisly greatness. No one was left alive.

***

On the small remote island which was linked to the mainland at low tide by a sandy causeway, Sargasso and Seraphim idled away their special time. It was a secret place where the mussels and oysters contained small seed pearls, and wild purslane and lush watercress grew in the natural stream dividing the small valley. They feasted on the rare food and drank the pure crystal water. A pair of sea otters joined them for games in the sea and obligingly threaded the pearls onto a thin band, which Sargasso hung around his wife's neck.

Together the two birds spent many carefree hours soaring high over the wild expanse of cliffs, flying low over the tufted grasses and deep rocky crevices, and watching the thunderous winter sea foaming into the inlets at high tide, spurting plumes of white spray into the air. It was exhilarating and exciting to see the power of the ocean and they were filled with pride to be part of this constantly changing, mighty Seafarers world.

Sitting on the sandy shore on the last night of their retreat together, watching the moon's waning light spread its silvery blanket over the sea, they saw a figure begin to slowly creep out of the water towards them. Round and black, silhouetted against the light, its plodding, slow legs rhythmically straining its heavy body further and further from the lapping water, pushing nearer and nearer to the fascinated pair. They felt no fear, watching until the moonlight cast the creature into better view. It was a turtle, the black eyes in his wrinkled head watching them as it purposefully made his way towards them. He had been instructed to cross the seas from warmer waters to bring news to this special pair of birds.

They were the chosen ones, selected for their characteristics of loyalty, steadfastness and courage, which would be tested by the burden they had been chosen to bear. The wisdom of the Spirit of the Sea, gathered during all his long years, had helped to make this momentous decision: they would be the ones, before it was too late and Sargasso too old.

Ptolemy the turtle, whose age would never be known, continued his journey, eventually reaching the webbed feet of the watchful pair. He too wore a shell around his withered neck and Sargasso recognised at once that he was a messenger from the great Sea Lord.

"I salute you and bring you greetings of happiness; may the brightness and calm of the moon bless your union, Sargasso and Seraphim." And the ancient turtle nodded his head as the moonlight shone on the smooth shiny shell of his back.

"Thank you, Old Man of the Sea," replied Sargasso. "We are honoured by your visit."

"We are to watch together," explained the turtle, "it is all arranged. We must wait for the planets to align themselves in the eastern sky. Be patient my friends, the time is not yet right, but the Long Night Moon will wait for us." And he turned his head to indicate the lop-sided moon rising in the darkness, just waning off its full glory.

The creatures remained silent, watching the night sky, as gradually three bright lights appeared quite close together.

"At last!" breathed Ptolemy. "Mars, Jupiter, and Saturn. Do you see them?" and the gulls nodded, wondering what was coming next. Soon, two more bright glows came up from the horizon and took their places in the sky.

"Venus and Mercury," the turtle announced proudly. "They are all here." The five planets shone together onto the deserted beach for the first time for twenty years.

"Go down to the water's edge and wait quietly," Ptolemy instructed them, and hesitantly the pair of gulls did as they were told, paddling silently across the flat sand to the first lapping wave. From the farthest end of the long shiny beach a light began to shine and rose above them, travelling across the sky. It disappeared in the distance, leaving the faint arc of a rainbow under which they stood. It was a moonbow, its coloured fantasy faintly visible, directed from the moon above them. Sargasso and Seraphim gazed up at the moonbow with its pretty soft lights and gradually it melted away before their eyes. From the darkness behind them the turtle appeared.

"You have been blessed by the power of five planets and walked under the arc of the moon, and you shall be the first ones," he told them, his head nodding.

"First ones to do what?" asked Sargasso, puzzled. "You will see. I shall return after the Moon of Winds strikes the sky with its sharpened cusp and grows to maturity. I am proud to have witnessed this night and to have been your messenger. It is now all in place; we have only to wait with patience for what will come. I wish you a happy night together." And the turtle began its ponderous journey across the wet sands, met the first wave with gladness and was soon floating away on the tide, the moon shining steadily across the water and glinting on the creature's back.

"But what does it all mean?" asked Seraphim, when she could see him no longer. "Why did he come? How did he know we were here?"

"The Spirit of the Sea sent him – he knows all things," explained Sargasso, questioning to himself the strange happenings of the night.

"They are still there! Look!" He and Seraphim gazed up into the vast expanse of sky above their heads; the five planets suddenly beamed down fiercely together upon them and the two gulls felt drawn to the sky, irresistibly urged to fly up, up, up into the brightness and they soared together over the moonlit sea. All thoughts had vanished, nothing mattered, nothing, except to strive higher and higher, until eventually they mated on the wing, held weightless in the sky by the pull of the five planets, and gradually as the light lessened they floated down to earth, wings outspread, and dreamily fell asleep in the sheltered valley, on the secret island tucked away in the quiet corner of Devon.

Many astronomers remarked that night on the exciting phenomenon of the five planets aligned together in such an unusual phase of the waning moon, and took photographs to capture it forever. The following morning, the seagulls awoke refreshed, their memory of the previous night more like a dream and happily they returned home across the waves to Warfleet Creek, where in the shelter of the lime kiln, Seraphim began to collect twigs and sticks to fashion a perfect nest.

Chapter Nine
Choosing a boat, and a new acquaintance

The whole family set off on Wednesday morning to visit the boatyard, spread out on the edges of Old Mill Creek, an inlet up the River Dart towards Totnes. Many boats of all shapes and sizes littered the quiet muddy flats. A large crane stood alone, and nearby an assortment of heavy vehicles waited. It was a hive of serious work, as the New Year would swiftly lead to spring, when there would be a high demand for boats to be returned to the water.

Peter parked the car and out they all piled. Several stone buildings with lighted windows gave a clue to where John Morrison, the boatyard owner, might be found. He was on the phone but waved them to sit down on the assorted plastic chairs around the room. The walls were adorned with navigation charts from all over the world – Brittany, the Canary Islands, Tobago and the Azores were among some of the romantic names Eddie in particular was fascinated with.

"Now," said Mr Morrison at last, "sorry to keep you. *Pelican* isn't it? Let's go and see her right away." They introduced themselves as they wandered towards the row of boats wedged upright, their masts and wire shrouds jangling in the breeze, and stopped beside a navy blue shiny hull with its red-painted keel, the letters *Pelican* neatly painted in white on the side.

"Here she is." Mr Morrison patted the paintwork affectionately. "Just been antifouled and painted. Careful of the ladders, and mind your heads!" Eventually everyone squeezed down into the compact Moody 33 and gazed around inside: a small neat galley, tiny toilet and washing facilities, two cabins and a central seating area. The deck had been newly varnished and all the ropes, cleats and sails replaced. Together, Peter and John inspected the engine and everything below decks.

"Isn't it fantastic?" Eddie finally managed breathlessly, totally smitten by the small compact craft. "I could live on here," he added confidently.

"Hello up there!" A voice called from the boatyard below where Arthur and Margie stood beside the ladder. "Everything alright?"

Eddie's head popped up, grinning.

"Brilliant!" he beamed.

After the viewing, everyone returned to the office to discuss the possible purchase in more detail. Soon Eddie and Ellie were bored and took a wander around the exciting place, noticing two old ruined castles half-hidden in the larch trees on either side of the inlet. Further on a rushing stream ran out from under a stone bridge, its origins lost in a mysterious valley, rocky and overgrown, leading upstream. An old mill house stood by the bridge, its waterwheel intact, the wooden slats encrusted with moss, now silent and still. An old man was tending a vegetable plot outside, turning the soil with a fork, the prospects of spring planting on the horizon. The two youngsters wandered down the path towards him.

"Hello" Ellie called brightly to him. He looked up and took his pipe out of his mouth, his brown wrinkled face breaking into a smile as he rested on his fork.

"Mornin' young lady. What you doin' here? Come to buy one of them fancy boats?" and he fished in his brown waistcoat pocket for his matches, struck one and sucked furiously on his smoking pipe, coughing and clearing his throat. He stared intently at the pair.

"Holiday folk are you?" and he struck another match expertly, his blue eyes fixed on them.

"No, we're not!" Eddie exploded hotly. We live at Warfleet Creek, in Watermill Cottage; do you know it?"

"As a matter of fact I do." He smiled impishly. "I was born there!" and he puffed away on his now well-lit pipe calmly, waiting for a reaction from the children.

"Were you really?" Ellie was almost unbelieving. "Really? At Warfleet?"

"I was and that's a fact, me and my five brothers and sisters. All born at Waterside Cottage down by the slipway. Used to be a farm down there where me Dad worked. 'Tis where I learnt to love the soil." He looked away, thinking back in time, pungent smoke erupting from the burning pipe.

Eddie at once thought about the shaft in the lime kiln he and Patrick had discovered. Did this old man know anything about the bricked-up door? It must have been there then because of its age.

"Which house did you say, lad?" came the question from the curious old man, eyeing them up, still grinning, his blue eyes twinkling as he wiped his mouth with the back of his hand, where it was moist from smoking the pipe. Eddie answered quickly, repeating himself.

"We live at Watermill Cottage, you know, at the top of the Creek?"

"Oh yes, I know it, wasn't even there in my day, only an old thatched cottage there with ducks and a pond down by the stream."

"Yes, we know, we've been told." Ellie nodded, memories flooding back to her of a previous adventure.

"Did you ever go into the lime kiln?" suddenly ventured Eddie, "the one in the garden at Waterside?" Ellie looked extremely puzzled, frowning, while Eddie waited nervously for the answer. The old man took out his pipe and looked hard at them before replying.

"And what do you know of that, young fellow-me-lad?" his blue eyes staring into Eddie's face, "Eh?"

"Only that it's boarded up and there's an iron ladder going down into it. The wooden top has rotted away and fallen in so you can see down there," Eddie explained, telling only half the truth.

Watchful now, the man took out his matches again and a silver object, and pushed the smouldering tobacco down into the bowl of the pipe, then applied another flaming match to it. He sucked furiously again, Eddie and Ellie watching fascinated.

"Well, I'm suppose you're goin' to find out anyway, come to think of it. Kids these days don't take no for an answer, I should know," he told them philosophically. "You be careful mind, that ladder was put there a long time ago. Now, down that kiln, right at the bottom, there's a doorway blocked up."

Ellie's eyes were wide and her mouth even wider. Eddie clenched his fingers nervously, waiting.

"That doorway leads into a tunnel, a trial seam, mined over a century ago when they was looking for tin and coal, so you be careful. 'Course you can't get into it now mind, but I expect you'll want to go and poke around in there like kids do and get dirty and suchlike. So you take care missy, don't want you falling in, do we?" and he gave her a lovely smile, his blue eyes twinkling in his brown weather-beaten face; he was a slight build with small features and a strong wiry body. Ellie was bursting with curiosity, and grabbed Eddie's arm.

"What's all this about Eddie?" she whispered furiously at him, "You've got to tell me!"

"Well now, is this your mother comin' to find you? I'd better get back to my soil, this isn't getting my broad beans in, is it? Come and see me again and tell me what that old shaft is like after all these years. All these years, well I never." He watched Mary fast approaching his gate.

"We didn't know where you'd gone," their mother called breathlessly to them, reaching the low wall surrounding the old house. "I hope you're not bothering this gentleman." And she smiled at them all, glad she had found her two wanderers.

"Good morning. Here's a lovely lady," smiled the old brown face cheekily. "I'm Ezekiel King and it seems we've got something in common."

"Oh?" Mary was very puzzled.

"You won't believe it, Mum, he used to live at Warfleet!" burst out Ellie.

"Really?"

"Long time ago now." Ezekiel shook his head.

"Well that is amazing I must admit, but, we must go now I'm afraid. Your father is ready to go. Come on then. 'Bye bye Mr King, nice to have met you," she added. Mary ushered her brood away quickly.

"'Bye!" shouted Ellie, following her mother at once.

"'Bye." Eddie stared at him for a moment longer, reluctant to leave. He was cross with his mother as they hurried back to the boatyard, where they found Peter and Mr Morrison exchanging a certificate from a marine surveyor, guaranteeing the boat's seaworthiness.

"That's it then," John told them, and Arthur and Peter shook hands in agreement.

"Have you bought it then, Dad?" asked Ellie. "Is it ours now?"

"Well almost," replied Peter "just the money to find, Ellie. Any contributions?" he joked. Eddie was very pleased, but he had been riveted by the information Mr King had luckily given him, and was dying to get back and tell Patrick at once.

Arthur and Margie seemed very relieved at the successful sale and told Peter they were going to book a cruise with the money.

"You've got the boat you want then, Eddie?" Arthur smiled at him. "I hope you have a great season this year, you're just the right age - my, you'll have some fun! She's a fine little racer; good luck with her," he added generously, looking just a little sad.

"Why don't you come out with us and show us how she sails?" replied the boy, suddenly sensing his loss.

"Good idea, Eddie" added Peter, proud of his thoughtfulness.

"Well, I, um, might well do that. Thank you," Arthur decided, rather pleased.

So it was all finalised and the excited family returned home, buying fish and chips on the way for a celebratory lunch, Eddie only half as excited as he should have been and Ellie, impatient and frustrated, waiting to find out what had been going on. She knew better than to discuss Eddie's revelations in front of her parents, and sat in quiet fury during the journey back to Warfleet.

***

Nobody noticed the small red boat hugging the shoreline, making its way down river. The only eyes that observed its passing were those of Seraphim, as she sat in the lime kiln where she had carefully created her nest; it was an unusually large nest, tightly packed together, constructed of driftwood lined with strips of seaweed and then a layer of moss and feathers. No other seagull had ever made a nest like this - they were usually a rough tangle of sticks that looked as if the wind had blown them apart, but she knew her instincts were right and carried on just the same. She sat in the empty nest looking out to sea, because, as yet, there was no egg in it. Seraphim observed the two figures passing by, then they disappeared out of her sight.

At the small cove below Woodend Manor the occupants of the small red boat cut the engine and got out their fishing rods, glancing around to make sure nobody was about. Content they were unobserved, they attached two large magnets onto the special strength lines and the heavy rods, mostly used to catch very large fish. Throwing the lines over the side each splashed into the water, sinking quickly.

"Them markers have been washed away," one said to the other. "Must have been the storm. Bloody nuisance, we'll have to guess where they are now."

The two men wound and re-wound their reels for almost an hour, cross and desperate in the end by the empty lines returning, the magnets attracting nothing but a pair of old iron pliers.

"We'll have to leave it; someone will notice I'm missin'" reluctantly spoke the bigger of the two fishermen. "Let's go."

And heaving their gear on board the small boat, they revved the engine furiously and chugged back up the river resentfully, creating an illegal wake in their anger at their unsuccessful search.

Chapter Ten
Surprises in the woodland

The whole woodland was in mourning as the Woodlanders stood around in little groups, tearful and unbelieving, staring at the charred and blackened branches at the top of the Great Ash Tree. Veronica Vole clasped her husband's arm, sniffing away large tears.

"We were so lucky," she kept repeating. "What made you want to leave?"

"I don't really know," admitted Vincent, "there was just something creepy about the place that said death to me." He shrugged his shoulders unhappily. "If only the others had come with us - I should have made them listen." And he gulped, feeling waves of guilt and remorse washing over him. In her heart Veronica was so very thankful her own children were safe.

The Woodlanders had been called to an extraordinary meeting at the Citadel at Noonday by the Dark Dwellers clock. Gradually all the creatures began assembling, first to witness the lightning-struck tree and then to talk and gossip, shaking heads and reminiscing, remembering families now gone forever.

In the Round Study at the Citadel, the buzzard, his consort and his two remaining sons were awaiting the arrival of Oliphant. The buzzard, visibly advancing in years now, was very shaken. This was a tragedy of the first degree, especially as he had ordered the evacuation of the Lower Woodland.

"This is all my fault," admitted the buzzard to his wife dejectedly.

"But it was that pestering white owl, Father, who made you do it," insisted Tween.

"Yes, of course," agreed E'en.

"This was a natural disaster my dear, the fire, like the flood, a chance happening, a freak of our world of nature," consoled the wife of the Ruler of the Woodland wisely.

"Our Lord Sunna, Spirit of the Woodland, controls everything that happens on the land, as the Spirit of the Sea controls the oceans," sighed the buzzard. "This was sent for a reason, it must have been: two disasters in one week, very unlikely. It's time to give up my throne, I'm sure of it." Now he'd said it, it didn't sound so bad; he was tired and couldn't sleep. What would be next? A plague? All the decisions and responsibilities seemed to be crushing him. Perhaps it would be good to let it all go; hand it on to the next one, whoever that might be. He peered out of the oval window to see scores of creatures arriving, creeping over the grassy hill, assembling in little clumps. He sighed.

"Pass me my robes, dear," he asked his wife reluctantly, who silently provided him with gown and hat. As he arranged his fur collar, Oliphant was shown in by a black rook.

"Take the roll call before I come down, will you?" the buzzard ordered the rook. "Are all the Council Members present?"

"I *am* checking, Lord, most are here," replied the rook grumpily.

Dear, dear, thought the buzzard, *even he's getting old now!* As he stared unseeing out of the window again he was overtaken by a vision of heathery moorland, granite boulders and clear rushing streams; of sunshine warm on outstretched wings and the sweet chorus of the wildest of birds that only inhabit the humanless landscape of high Dartmoor. He suddenly longed for the peace and stillness of that remote place of his ancestors. What a pleasure it would be to return to its simple beauty! Maybe, maybe. He remembered he had banished his middle son Tween and the rascally owl Tolivera to just such a place. Now he was dreaming of it himself.

"How strange the circle of life is!" He shook his head. He was disturbed by his wife touching his wing tip.

"My dear?" she said quietly, "Mr Oliphant is here." The buzzard turned, ready to accept whatever the white owl said. After all, it was all his idea in the first place. Oliphant bowed.

"My lord, this is all very sad, very unfortunate. I feel truly sorry for all these Woodlanders families."

Aha! thought the buzzard, *I can feel an apology coming! Quite right too! It was all his fault!* He puffed himself up haughtily, preparing for what was coming next.

Oliphant had not slept since he had heard the news, woken by a tearful Vincent and shaking Denis from his daytime slumber. Was it only three days ago? He had raged and cried, paced the floor of his treetop dwelling, begged forgiveness, searched his conscience and asked for guidance from the ethereal Spirit of the Woodland who he knew to be somewhere. Finally, a calm serenity had shrouded him, blanking out his wild rantings and eventually he found a sort of peace; this tragedy was *not* his fault. It was an accident, plain and simple. He had tried to help those poor unfortunate creatures and somehow disaster had resulted from a freak storm. It was terribly sad, but there it was. The Woodlanders had made their choice but fate had conspired against them all.

At last he had dozed by his small fire, exhausted by his grief, until the clonking of his acorn chimes woke him half an hour before his audience with the Lord of the Woodland. He felt refreshed, and drank a cup of camomile and foxglove tea to settle his mind. "Well, here goes!" he told himself firmly, brushing his tufty head with his long teasel brush, and now here he was in front of the buzzard and his family, standing firm, calmly telling them what he sincerely believed.

"My Lord, this is all very sad, very unfortunate; I feel truly sorry for these Woodlander families." And he paused. "Such tragedies befall us in life and we must accept this. A freak storm - we were not to know. We should all move on now, help the survivors and be glad that some were left alive."

"What?" the buzzard was astonished. "Come, come,

Oliphant, will you accept no responsibility for this… this… good idea of yours? Surely?"

"No, my Lord."

The buzzard was silent; his wife and sons stared hard at him, furious and frightened, willing him to banish the white owl and send him packing as he deserved. What would happen now?

"Then I shall retire." The words came out of the mouth of the buzzard without his consent, slipping out from the darkest recesses of his mind, his secret longings turned into thoughts and the thoughts into spoken words. His wife fainted and his sons gasped: Tween wanted to cry and E'en felt sick. Oliphant stood calmly by, watching. He would not falter; this weak and elderly leader must go. He suddenly despised him.

"Then Lord you must," came the cool restrained voice of Oliphant. "We shall announce it at the Council Meeting. I shall act as deputy until a new ruler is appointed." The buzzard's consort returned to consciousness, fanned by her son E'en, and stammered,

"No, my Lord, not you! He must go!" and she pointed a wizened claw at the owl. But the buzzard went to the oval window and stared once again at his subjects assembled below, representatives of all the living creatures in the Woodland, and knew Oliphant was right; he felt glad, glad to be going. His time was over; it had ever been so in the animal world, his world of the Skywingers and Woodlanders. A challenge was always made by someone younger: it was right, after all.

Seizing the moment, ignoring the stunned family, Oliphant led the buzzard by the wing out of the Round Study, past the two rooks who were on duty and who had been listening in disbelief at the door.

"All present, Sire," they mumbled to him as he passed. The buzzard seemed to be in a bit of a trance and walked unsteadily to the topmost branch of the Citadel, where his subjects were spread out before him. It was a clear bright day, with a slight breeze, and pale winter sun weakly breathed warmth over them all. Regaining his composure in the golden brightness and looking towards the sun, the Lord of the Woodland spread out his wide wings so the light shone through his pale feathers; it was a great sight and all the little creatures below were in awe of him. Old and forgetful as he was, he looked magnificent.

"Subjects all, we must never forget the great power of the world around us. Such power in the form of lightning was responsible for our sad losses this week. We cannot apportion blame to anyone. The flood victims had settled into their temporary homes, happy together, well fed and among friends, this was what we did for them. Alas it did not last – *but* – we did something! Are we not all brothers and sisters in adversity?" and a cheer broke out from all the listeners; this was the buzzard's finest speech. He hushed them.

"And now I am leaving you." Gasps from the crowd were heard. "My time is over. Mr Oliphant will act as Regent of the Realm until the Great Spirit of the Woodland decides on a new ruler."

At that moment the sun passed behind a cloud and it was quiet and still. The buzzard folded his wings and hopped away into the royal bedchamber, and lay down beneath the indigo blue covers where he fell asleep, no one daring to open the closed door. He was free at last! Unable to face the crowd, the rest of the family had watched from a narrow slitted window below, shocked and trying to come to terms with their new situation. It was unthinkable.

Oliphant then stepped forward to the stunned gathering, looking small and white and timid.

"My friends, this is a time of change for us all. Do not fear for the future, we have princes enough to find a good leader. The Great Spirit of the Woodland will guide us. All will be well and we will be united. Nothing will change, be assured of that. My door is open to you all. Now eat and drink and accept the news of today, for tomorrow awaits us!" His eyes blinked as he looked around the many faces staring at him; he was hoping for their immediate support, but it was too soon: the shock had been too great and he felt no enthusiasm from them at all.

The squirrels, who had been charged with the task of supplying refreshments at very short notice, turned out in clean aprons and served hot elderberry wine flavoured with scented geranium, and slices of seed cake sprinkled with crystallised violets. It was very well received, just right after the shock they had all suffered, and the wine mellowed the hearts of the Woodland nation. The small white owl drifted among them on a getting-to-know-you mission. He was very changed from the shy, gentle, unsure bird that had plotted with the robin so timidly in the months before. Would he be equal to the task? He was confident he was.

Chapter Eleven
Patrick has an archery lesson

It was Thursday morning before Eddie could make contact with Patrick. By then he had been through a thorough grilling from an exasperated Ellie, who demanded to know everything the boys had discovered.

"But we only came upon it by chance, Ellie, while we were putting up the telescope tripod. I did knock some of the earth down the night before, climbing over the new wall," he admitted guiltily. "I think I started some sort of landslide. The earth just gave way. We didn't know it was there, honestly." He tried to disentangle himself from her persistent questioning.

"Well, I want to be there the next time you go down there," she insisted.

"So, Mr King, who we met yesterday, knew all about the tunnel because he lived here. That seems most odd, and it was already blocked up then?" Ellie reaffirmed all Eddie had told her. "And it was in the old ruined lime kiln that the mine shaft was dug for exploration?" she repeated.

"Yes, Ellie," wearily confirmed Eddie. She really could be a pain sometimes; he longed for Patrick's quiet undemanding company.

"I'd like to get hold of Patrick and tell him about Mr King and make some plans. I think I'll go and ring him." Eddie decided to make his escape.

Ellie let him go, satisfied she knew everything, and made her way into the garden armed with breadcrumbs.

"Freddie, Freddie, something for you!" she called.

Freddie was not under the shrubs by the garden wall because he was staying with Oliphant. He'd gone for a few days until the crisis in the Woodland was over. Hearing the terrible news of the deaths of the homeless families, he knew Oliphant needed a friend to steady his nerves and keep his morale up.

Eddie returned almost immediately.

"I can't see Patrick this morning, he's gone to Kingswear again, back to see the Frasers. Funny isn't it? Why did he need to go again? Irene wouldn't tell me and Sam's in town." He kicked a small piece of gravel with the toe of his shoe in a bored way. Ellie shrugged her shoulders.

"Oh well, something more important's come up. That's all."

At Kingswear, Patrick was just getting off the ferry, feeling a little nervous and wishing he hadn't agreed to go over to see Heather. His father had reminded him to call into the Yacht Club for a membership form. Dutifully he opened the large wooden door and entered the paved hardstanding where some small dinghies were laid up for the winter. This club enjoyed exclusive river frontage and was comfortable and well patronised.

The steward and his wife were washing glasses and tidying up.

"Yes?" asked the steward pleasantly.

"I'd like a membership form, please," he replied.

"For a family would that be?"

"Yes, I think so." Soon he had the appropriate form in his hand.

You need to be proposed, I'm afraid." added Philip the steward apologetically.

"That's no problem, I think the Frasers have said they'll do it," replied Patrick.

"Oh the Frasers, that's fine, they come in here quite regular when they are here. Terrible 'bout the robbery, have they got anyone for it?" he asked, polishing a glass. "We've had the police in."

"I don't think so, not yet," Patrick told him. "I'll bring this back as soon as we've filled it in. Goodbye, and thank you." And he made his way out of the comfortable lounge bar, anxious to leave, stuffing the form into his jacket pocket.

That's that done. He sighed. Now he had to go to Woodend Farm. There was no escape. A young man raced past him on a mountain bike, long hair flying. He almost knocked him over.

"Sorry, mate!" the boy turned grinning. "Late for work!" and pedalled off around the bend.

Stupid idiot! complained Patrick to himself. *Nice bike.* He looked across the river which was a dark glassy green. The castle and the old church all looked quite different from this side of the river. A fishing boat chugged into harbour, gutting its catch on the way home, surrounded by screaming gulls.

Poor Heather, he thought suddenly, and he made up his mind to try to get to know her and her funny little dog. *I'll tell her all about Eddie and Ellie, and maybe they'll be able to come next time.*

Arriving at the gateway he saw the boy on the bike, only this time he was sweeping up the dead leaves along the edge of the driveway. He had a thin cigarette gripped between his lips. He raised his eyes and acknowledged Patrick with a jerk of his head.

"Visiting are you, mate?"

"Um, yes," replied Patrick shyly.

"Round the bend and straight on."

"Thanks," smiled Patrick, and walked on feeling the boy's eyes staring into his back. He heard him whistling as he continued sweeping. He yanked the old iron bell-pull down. A deep jangle could be heard from within. He waited for a while, then the bark of a dog greeted him as the door was flung open. Heather sat in her wheelchair.

"Hello, Patrick." She smiled cheerily. "Shh Robbie, that's enough now," as the yapping dog insisted on one more bark.

"Come away in now," beckoned the girl, wearing blue jeans and a black sweater with her hair in a pony tail. He followed her straight through the house down a long tiled hallway. At the end a door lay open, inviting them into the garden beyond.

"Come on." She turned and smiled. Obediently Patrick followed her out into a paved terrace with a gate at the end, and together they followed the smooth path with a slight gradient which had obviously been constructed with wheelchairs in mind. Ahead, Patrick could see a small cottage surrounded by a paddock where a chestnut horse looked curiously over the fence. A wooden stable stood in the corner of the field, bundles of leather tack hanging from the open doors and a New Zealand blanket draped over one corner.

Heather spun the chrome outsides of her wheels expertly, while Patrick walked beside her.

"What's his name?" He pointed to the horse who was watching them with interest.

"Her name," Heather corrected him. "Ginny Come Lately, Ginny for short. It's one of Mum's favourite songs from the sixties. Ginny's a real beauty, gentle and patient. Here." And she fished in her pocket and gave him some sugar lumps. "She loves these."

Patrick approached the horse timidly.

"Hold your hand out flat and keep it still. She doesn't bite people, she's too nice," Heather told him proudly. Delicately, Ginny picked up the sugar with her soft pink whiskery mouth, and nodded her head, ears alert, watching him intently. Patrick gently stroked her, feeling the smooth silky coat, warm and glossy.

"She's lovely," agreed Patrick, pleased the horse had been so friendly.

"The archery stuff is kept in the other side of the stable."

The door was extra wide to accommodate the wheelchair. Inside it was warm and smelt of wood. Heather gathered up a couple of bows, and the strings, gloves and armguards they would need, giving Patrick two boxes of arrows to carry. Together they went behind the stable to a flat bark-covered square where targets had been hooked onto two trees. The surrounding area had been netted off to prevent the arrows disappearing into the trees beyond.

"The targets are made of straw, Shady brings them out for me," She explained.

"Who's Shady?"

"Will Lane, he helps us out. His parents run the village shop. We call him Shady because his surname is Lane!"

Patrick realised it was the boy on the bike. *Hmm,* he thought nastily, *I wonder if the police have spoken to him?*

Heather demonstrated stringing the bow and he was given a leather armguard to wear so that the string didn't snap back onto his outstretched arm and bruise it. The arrows had notches at the end to fasten the string into and he wore leather finger-gloves to pull back the string. Heather was good teacher, and keeping his elbow in line, he pulled the string back beneath his chin and let go. It fell to the ground short of the target.

"Well done!" praised Heather.

"It's quite difficult isn't it?" said the surprised boy.

"Try again," encouraged Heather, and soon the whole box was empty. Patrick did manage to hit the target twice, but nowhere near the yellow centre. Another box later and he was improving.

"Hi there!" and Morag appeared, striding up the path.

"Hello, Patrick," she said smiling. "How are you getting on? Is he a good pupil, Heather?"

"He's not bad, getting the hang of it now I'd say," she laughed.

"At least I've hit the target," protested Patrick.

They put the arrows into a stand and hung the bows onto pegs fitted onto fencing posts. Everything had been planned to give Heather maximum independence. Walking the short distance to the cottage, the three entered by the split stable door.

Morag and Patrick sat down at the small pine table while Heather filled the kettle. No help was offered and she busied about fetching everything she needed, which was all at convenient heights for her. Soon they were sipping the steaming coffee and munching biscuits, enjoying the view of the sun on the hillside from the open doorway.

Patrick soon forgot himself, and Morag and Heather teased him, dragging his life story out bit by bit. Surprisingly, the solemn, shy Scottish boy poured out his secrets while they listened quietly.

"So that's me," he finally said, realising that he had been doing all the talking.

"Well, we're pleased to know you Patrick McNab!" and Morag hugged him quickly. "I'll leave you to it. What's next, Heather, for the poor wee man? Shooting? Riding? Cross country racing? He'll be sorry he ever set foot in Woodend!" And off she went laughing, a pretty, slim figure in her red sweater and matching corduroys. She turned and waved once.

"I like your mother," nodded Patrick.

"She's okay," was the modest reply.

They cleared up the cups together and returned to the archery ground. A further hour was spent, only this time Heather joined in. Patrick was rather humbled. She was exceptionally proficient and made him look very much the beginner.

"It's only practice," she told him apologetically. "You're getting the hang of it now. Wait till you hit your first bullseye!" as another of her arrows hit the yellow circle with a thwack!

It was thoroughly enjoyable and Patrick forgot very quickly that Heather was disabled. He just didn't seem to notice anymore. She was also very pretty, with lovely blonde hair and an agreeable, kind nature.

She looks like her mother, Patrick thought. Looking at his watch, he decided it was almost time to go. They found the arrows and put all the archery equipment away in the stable next to Ginny.

Patrick said goodbye to the horse and he and Heather made their way back along the path to the house, where they exchanged phone numbers, and waving goodbye to Morag and Heather, he left by the front door.

What an amazing girl, Patrick thought, *I really enjoyed that,* and walked steadily on until he reached the small village square. He went into the post office for a bar of chocolate.

A pleasant lady, small and bright, served him.

This must be Shady's mother, he decided. Another customer behind him confirmed his suspicions.

"Morning, Mrs Lane., said a mournful voice.

"Morning, Abel," she replied. "Busy?"

"Oh yes, always busy cleaning up and doing a few repairs, you know. Churches always need looking after. Constant work there is. Never stops, wears me out it does."

Patrick took his chocolate, and seeing the ferry arrive at the slipway, hurried off. He smiled. *Shady Lane!* What a name. He bought his ticket and watched the tugboat make its way through the dark river to the other side. He was almost sorry he was going home.

Chapter Twelve
An afternoon exploring

Ellie was welcomed at the Castle Teashop by Bridget and George with open arms. She felt very guilty as she had not given work a thought since Christmas.

"Lovely to see you, dear," Bridget smiled.

"I see that brother of yours down on the cove!" chuckled George. "What's he up to today?"

"We got the most wonderful present from Mum and Dad," enthused Ellie, "A saltwater aquarium! So we're gradually putting specimens in it," she told them proudly.

"That sounds wonderful," agreed Bridget and George. "We'd love to see it."

"Oh you shall," Ellie assured them, beginning to help them. The three worked well together, and as always in the holidays there were plenty of people interested in Bridget's delicious cakes and creamy whipped hot chocolate.

Eddie searched the crevices and pools, pulled up large boulders and waded in the slippery edges, finally producing a small eel, another species of crab and plenty of little blennies. With cold hands and rather wet clothes, he was looking forward to getting warm in the café. Turning to climb the path, he noticed a red boat across the river, moored up in a tiny cove. *That wasn't there yesterday,* he told himself.

He trudged up the many steps and joined Ellie, to Bridget's delight, trailing seawater behind him. He sat at the quiet corner table by the kitchen and was supplied with hot chocolate and chocolate brownies.

Ellie offered to stay and wash up for a while.

"You know what that means, don't you?" she hissed at Eddie.

"What?"

"You can't go down to the lime kiln until I come back! You promised!" Her eyes flashed at him.

"Okay, okay." He raised his eyebrows and nodded.

"Alright, I'll see you at home."

As Eddie was leaving he turned and asked, "Have you seen anyone in that red boat? The one moored across the river? Do you know when it was put there, George?"

"It seems to come and go. Sometimes I'm too busy to notice, of course."

"Well, keep an eye out, would you, if you see anyone using it? There was a robbery over at Kingswear on Christmas Day."

"Get away!" George shook his head.

"Yes, and some very expensive jewellery was taken. They're friends of Irene and Sam, the Frasers from Inverness. Do you know them?"

"I can't say I do but their whisky is famous alright! I'll try to keep my eye on that boat for you. Do you think it's connected to the theft, then?"

"Don't know, but Ellie and I saw it on Christmas morning, that's all,"

Eddie set off for home, walking slowly with his bucket of treasures. At the Creek, Sargasso flew along the grey rocky edges to greet him.

"Eddie!" he cawed, delighted to see him.

"Sargasso! Where is Seraphim?"

"She's nesting," the seagull told him proudly. "We are united now and hope to hatch our first chicks in the spring."

"That's great news, Ellie will be so pleased. We've bought a new boat called *Pelican* and Patrick is to have our little green one. Can you keep a look out for a small red boat that may be going up and down the river? We'd like to know who's using it."

"Of course."

Sargasso hopped up the beach on his strong yellow leg. They parted on the slipway and each returned to his own domain, a comfortable easiness still between them. Eddie was anxious to return to the lime kiln and thought carefully about what tools he would need to try to break through the bricked-up doorway. It might be better to wait until Irene and Sam had gone out. *Blast!* It was the only way to keep it a secret. Eddie gritted his teeth crossly. There was always something in the way of the things he wanted to do.

He organised the tools as best he could and as luck would have it, his parents told him they were taking Irene and Sam to Plymouth.

"I hope you and Ellie don't mind."

Eddie tried to cover his utter joy at this news.

"No, no of course we don't mind. We'll be fine here, don't worry about us."

"That's alright then," said his parents, somewhat relieved.

Great! thought Eddie triumphantly, just as Ellie returned home. Waving to their parents they chased off to the garden at Waterside Cottage.

"Couldn't have worked out better. We'll have to work like blazes to get these rocks out." Ellie was very excited and couldn't wait to see into the old lime kiln. They scraped the earth and leaves off the cupboard door. Soon the black gaping hole was uncovered and the iron rungs leading down the side could be seen. Ellie peered in, kneeling down on the edge.

"Shine the torch, Eddie," as she gazed into the dark earthy-smelling shaft.

"Stinks, doesn't it?"

Fetching the ropes for safety, in case one of the rungs gave way, they tied a bucket onto a rope and Eddie and Ellie clambered down the iron ladder slowly and carefully while Patrick shone the torch down. Reaching the bottom, there was just enough room for two.

"Here's the bricked-up doorway." Eddie showed her. "We're going to try and break through. Are you ready for this?"

"'Course I am!" she retorted angrily. "Give me the chisel, I'll go first!"

Patrick lowered the bucket of tools and Ellie began chipping away at the loose-looking mixture of rocks and stones. She was very good at it and seemed to have the right knack. Eddie passed the small rocks up in the basket to Patrick, who chucked them over the boundary wall. Ellie worked like a demon and soon there was a gap large enough to see into. Eddie could hardly contain himself.

"Let me see!" he asked excitedly.

"Wait a minute, I'll just get one more out." And she pulled another large stone from its rocky bed. "It's all quite dry behind here," she told her agitated brother who was bursting with impatience. "Now have a look." And she changed places with him in the tiny space.

He shone his torch into the jagged aperture and saw an opening leading into darkness. Casting the beam around he could just make out wooden beams surrounding the wall and ceiling at intervals. The air smelt mouldy but no gas met their nostrils.

Ellie was pretty exhausted and climbed up the iron rungs, falling onto the grass with relief.

"Phew, that's hard work!" she told Patrick, who looked at her messed-up hair, dirty face and obvious exhaustion.

"You look as if you need a break." And she didn't argue with that.

"Can I go and have a look now?" He leapt down into the black hole to join Eddie at the bottom. They had proved the doorway led somewhere and there was evidence of iron hinges where a door had hung once.

"Come on, let's get enough stones out so we can get in!" encouraged Eddie, and somehow he and Patrick managed to chip enough rocks away until the hole was large enough to squeeze through.

"Grab this bucket Ellie, it's full," called Eddie, as he and Patrick helped to push the load of rocks upwards.

"If we do go into a tunnel, because I'm sure that's what it must be, we've got to be careful. Should we all go in or leave a lookout? What if we get lost or stuck or trapped somewhere? It could be dangerous. What would we need to keep safe?" His mind was racing ahead. Ellie sat thinking too. This sounded a bit scary and not quite so much of an adventure. Going off into a dark place under the ground? Why, there might be mice or rats or both! *Ugh!* She shuddered. Where could it go? Would it be wet in there? Would the tide come in and fill it up? They could drown.

"I don't think I want to come," said Ellie, suddenly full of fear and dread of a dark unfriendly place. "You go with Patrick, I'll stay and keep watch. What will I tell Sam and Irene if they come back?"

"The truth! We can't hide a mineshaft in their garden, can we?" Eddie told her scornfully.

"Do you think that's what it is?"

"Yes, I do. There's lots of places in Cornwall that have these in their gardens."

"Why don't you take a ball of string with you and you can unravel it, and that way you will know where you've come from, or I'll be able to find you if you don't come back."

"Don't say that!" Eddie made a face and laughed, but he didn't actually think it was that funny. "But it's a good idea in case the torches run out. Go home Ellie, would you, and get me some more batteries? Please? Go through the woods, it's quicker. I've hacked a path behind the wall."

It was much easier, and she was back in no time with the batteries, two balls of red wool and a roll of garden twine.

"I thought you might need these," she panted. "That shortcut's brilliant. Saves the hill."

Eddie disappeared down the iron rungs following Patrick. He turned once.

"'Bye Ellie, see you later, don't worry about us. Tie this end up to that stone." And he passed her the red wool end.

"Don't break it, will you?" she said anxiously. She almost wished she was going with them.

"Be careful won't you?" she called, and impetuously climbed down the ladder, putting her head into the space to watch them go. Two lights danced on the earth-and-rock walls ahead. Stout wooden posts and beams neatly placed at intervals could be seen. The red wool disappeared into the darkness and so did the boys. Only their voices echoed back to her. She felt suddenly very lonely and awfully tired as she went carefully back up. It had been an exhausting afternoon. All she could do was watch and wonder. They would come back, wouldn't they?

Chapter Thirteen
A risky adventure

Down in the damp and musty tunnel, Patrick and Eddie were marvelling at the engineering skills required to have built such an excellent shaft. Playing their torches around the walls and roof, different colours of rock and stone with sparkles and shiny streaks reflected back off their torchlight. Occasional trickles of water ran down the walls and there were some puddles in places, but generally it was amazingly dry. There was a strong smell of mould and old cellars.

"Where does it go?" puzzled the boys after they had gone about 100 yards, their backs aching from stooping. It was not quite high enough to stand up.

"Umm, not sure, either out towards the castle or across the river," decided Patrick.

"Surely not!"

"Where else would it go?"

They fell silent, both rather taken aback at the idea of actually being under the river. It was a frightening prospect. Flashing their torches up at the roof, Eddie spotted something in the dark earth above him.

"What's that?"

"It's a black rubber cable of some sort." It was fastened to the wall with big metal clips. "Here's another opening." Patrick shone his torch on a much narrower side tunnel. The cable ran along the roof, down the wall and disappeared into the smaller hole. Patches of white fluffy mould and small rocky lumps appeared as the rock structures changed.

"What would that cable be for?" asked Eddie, thinking hard. "It can't be electric or gas, that's impossible."

"Then it must be a telephone cable, mustn't it?" reasoned Patrick, "I wonder how long it's been there? Was this tunnel built especially for it, do you think?"

Both boys were very puzzled. The tunnel went on and on. There was no debris at all, merely strange chambers at intervals in the wall, blackened and empty. Patrick shone his torch on the floor around one of them.

"Candle wax I reckon. Those niches are for candles to light it up."

"Yes, you're right," agreed Eddie, looking curiously at the blackened shiny hard wax.

"If it's been lighted once then this tunnel must have been used for something regularly. You wouldn't bother to make these niches if you were just laying a cable and leaving it, would you?" reasoned Patrick. "Maybe the tunnel was already here and it was very convenient for the cable."

"Possibly, and that low side tunnel was dug afterwards to continue its route wherever it went."

"This is far too well-constructed for a cable, this is a proper mine shaft shored up with pit props and strong beams," said Patrick, shining his torch forward and backwards around the roof.

"Do you think it's safe?" Eddie asked anxiously, worried in case it was foolish to continue. In his wildest dreams he had never supposed the tunnel would be so long or so well-constructed. The cold was creeping in however, and the smell was oppressive. Their necks were getting stiff from bending over.

On they continued, until the floor began to feel as if it was going uphill. Then the wool ran out and Eddie fastened the large ball of twine to its frayed end. Shining the torch in front of them, they could see that the walls were changing colour to reddish earth interspersed with rocks and occasional shells.

Ahead a door appeared, and the boys heaved great sighs of relief. Their secret worries suddenly evaporated. Patrick clutched his friend's arm.

"Look, look, we're at the end." And staring into Eddie's face he said slowly,

"Where do you think we are?"

Eddie shook his head, and not given to wild imaginings merely told him quietly,

"We'll soon find out won't we? That is, if we can open the door."

"I expect it's locked," said Patrick gloomily, "and we didn't bring any tools with us did we?"

But the door was not locked, just an old iron latch to lift and it swung creakily open, after a bit of a push on the old timbers to help it. Both boys nervously flashed the torches around, to find themselves in a small circular room made of cut stones with a set of granite steps curving upwards. An iron handrail followed them round. Two narrow windows, dirty and blackened, let in a very little light. At the top of the steps another door stood enticingly closed, made of heavy oak with great iron hinges. The floor they stood on was flat and black. Cobwebs hung from corners and the air smelt stale and musty.

"Shall we?" asked Eddie, raising his eyebrows at his friend.

"We're not stopping now!" answered Patrick, and they crept up the cold granite steps to the doorway. Standing together in the gloomy half-light, they pressed down on the same latch mechanism as before, expecting the door to remain firmly shut. A large empty keyhole sat just below the latch. With a loud click, the latch sprung up, making them both jump. They tried to pull back the door, and with a groan it freed itself from its wooden surround and gradually eased weakly open to reveal daylight. A small hallway lay before them, and opposite them was another door. Three narrow windows with wide ledges filtered light into this room. Rushing to look out of each of the different windows, neither boy could believe what they could see and shouted loudly to each other.

"I can't believe it! It's impossible!"

"I know exactly where we are! It's amazing! What a find!" Their voices rose with excitement. Then they started laughing and they stood together and laughed and laughed, full of a hysterical mixture of surprise and relief. When they stopped and wiped the tears from their dirty faces, both returned to the same window and looked out.

The view before them spread out over a small shingly beach, across the wide expanse of shining river towards their very own Warfleet Creek, the hills and the woods beyond. They were almost exactly opposite where they had come from. Eddie could see his own house quite clearly as he stood on the bottom floor of Kingswear Lighthouse. The tunnel had led them from the garden at Waterside Cottage all the way beneath the river and up inside the old lighthouse. This was perched halfway up the cliff placed there in 1864, over 100 years ago, to guide vessels into a safe harbour. The boys ran excitedly from window to window, rubbing the old glass clean with the sleeves of their jumpers.

"What's the time? How long have we been?" asked Patrick suddenly. "Ellie will be going mad, wondering what we're doing!"

Eddie looked hard across the river.

"I think I can see her in the garden. She's got a red jumper on, hasn't she?" He pointed through the glass, now somewhat clearer.

"Oh yes, I can see her. Come on, we'd better go back. Shall we pick up the string?" They had abandoned it at the foot of the steps at the first glimmer of light. It had trailed through 600 yards of tunnel.

"No, let's leave it just in case. We'll tie this end up. I'll have to replace it for Mum, she's bound to notice it's gone!"

They had spent more than enough time away. They would have to leave the pleasure of exploring the lighthouse for another day. One thing they had noticed was that the main entrance door in the hallway was very firmly locked. Nobody could get in, except through the tunnel, without the key.

We'll bring Ellie next time," Patrick assured Eddie.

"She'll be so excited. Dad may be back by now and I don't want them to find out about the tunnel yet."

Reluctantly they retraced their steps down into the cellar room darkened by brambles and ivy which had overtaken the windows. They closed the door behind them.

"It's quite secure because that main door is locked. Weren't we lucky neither of these doors were locked?"

They stooped down and chased along the tunnel much faster now, sure that they were not going to trip over things or find a rockfall in front of them.

"The cable doesn't come all the way along here, or we've missed it somewhere," noticed Eddie.

"You're right. Keep an eye out for a small side shaft. It's easy to miss in the dark."

Searching carefully along the strange walls, sure enough the cable disappeared into a dark narrow aperture on their left, neatly fastened to the wall.

"Ah, here it is. It must go down the middle of the river out towards the sea, then." Both agreed on this. Tired now and aching, eventually they arrived back at the opposite end and gingerly eased out of the old doorway into the dead end and the daylight, eyes squinting at the brightness.

Ellie screamed, seeing their legs, shoulders and heads appear out of the jagged rockwork.

"There you are! I thought you were never coming back! You've been a whole hour, a whole hour! What have you been doing? Oh do tell me, I'm dying to know," she pleaded, pleased and thrilled at their safe return.

The boys clambered up the iron rungs, by now exhausted, and set about covering up the shaft again, anxious it should not be discovered.

"Just wait a minute, Ellie," said Patrick breathlessly, "we mustn't let anyone fall down here. It's got to be safe," he insisted, checking the cupboard door by standing on it. Rocks, leaves and earth followed. No one would ever dream it was there. At last, satisfied it was hidden from view, the boys flopped down on the ground, completely exhausted. Ellie sat beside them, quite prepared to wait and savour all the news she knew they were about to tell her.

"You'll just never guess in a million years where we've been, Ellie," said Eddie mysteriously. "But we could see you when we got to the other end."

"You could see me?" She frowned, thinking. "But that means you must have been outside, in the daylight."

"Yes! Yes, go on," encouraged Patrick.

"You don't mean it comes out at Kingswear? Surely not! But that means you must have been under the river..." she puzzled thoughtfully, looking at both their faces intently.

They smiled and nodded together.

"Yep, you've got it! Honestly it's true." And Ellie just sat open-mouthed in disbelief.

"It's really true. It was quite an incredible journey. We never thought it would be so long. It's a proper mining shaft, must have been an exploration test seam for copper or tin or coal or something. Guess where it comes out?"

"Go on!" Patrick encouraged her.

"I can't, I just can't, tell me, just tell me!"

"Ok, it comes out at… Kingswear Lighthouse!" they both chimed together, and fell about laughing.

"Never! What, right inside? Oh, do let me go and see." And she narrowed her eyes to look across the river to the opposite bank, where the white tower of the lighthouse, nestling in the rocky cliffs, could be clearly seen. It seemed unbelievable.

The sound of voices disturbed her silent gaze and all their eyes met in dismay at the realisation that all their parents were home.

"Hello?" came the inevitable shout, and wearily they rose to their feet. Sam and Irene strolled through the French windows onto the small patio.

"Whatever are you doing out here?" questioned Irene. "Come inside and get warm, we've got lots to tell you," and she beckoned them impatiently. "Come on, you can make us some tea."

Her arrogant orders were the last straw. There was no hope of discussing their exciting discovery or of planning any research trips to the lighthouse. For one lingering moment they glanced across the darkening sky and the black glinting water to the lighthouse they could quite clearly see but had never really noticed.

"I can't wait to go over there," Ellie whispered. "I can feel an adventure coming on!" She giggled and the boys nodded, their shining faces agreeing with her. All three were thrilled at the prospect of finding out a lot more about the secrets of the lighthouse.

Chapter Fourteen
Unwelcome arrivals

In the Woodland, life was changing very swiftly. Oliphant had blossomed as the Regent of the Woodland. He had forced the buzzard to resign. The Great Ash Tree lay empty, unhappily associated with the tragedy of the fire. The buzzard's consort, mother of the three princes, had accepted the decision to leave and was packing up their belongings. She hoped the rest would restore her husband to better health. They were off to highest Dartmoor to visit Treen, her son, and Tolivera, the previous deputy of the Woodland. There, under the guidance of a great eagle, they were helping to rebuild a community shattered by forest fire, hopefully learning new skills and lessons in humility, kinship, and wise governing.

. She admitted now that her two other sons could do with just such lessons in life: spoilt, selfish and too immature to take over their woodland community, this break would be character-building for them both. Hopefully her princes would learn quickly. She had put aside all vengeful thoughts about Oliphant and accepted that her husband was old, and not as he was. He had been a fine ruler but his time we over. Oliphant could have his moment of power for a while because she would return with one of her sons taking his rightful place as heir to the Woodland.

Oliphant had decided that he must establish his authority quickly. He must show a clear lead in the dangerously fragmented community. He gave orders to the squirrels that the regent's house was to be thoroughly cleaned and a flock of magpies were to move his own sparse belongings up to the Great Ash Tree. It was soon done, and Freddie kindly house-sat for his friend down in the Lower Woodland. He had never had a real home before and in his declining years it was a pleasure to have a refuge indoors out of the bitter winter temperatures.

A small group of black jackdaws had spread from the eaves of the old watermill into the trees at the foot of the woodland where they watched and waited, patient but with evil intent. They had heard mutterings of discontent and listened to worries from the more openly opinionated birds. The bluetits gossiped furiously among themselves and the foolish blackbirds, empty-headed and shallow-minded, would talk to anyone prepared to listen. Eventually the jackdaws gleaned enough knowledge to understand the political situation: the buzzard, Ruler of the Woodland, had gone, and a small white owl from the Lower Woodland had been appointed regent. There had been a flood, and deaths from a lightning strike, and everyone was very scared and uncertain of the future. What unhappy events!

The jackdaws listened sympathetically. The more they listened the more they were told, and the whole promising picture unfolded. In a huddle together, they plotted and planned. Their leader was an intelligent sharp-beaked fellow known as Jack B Quick. He was amusing and gathered people around him with his wit and charm. Life had been too quiet and Jack quite fancied himself in a posh house at the top of the hill. They wouldn't know what had hit them, these dithering, clod-hopping country folk! Jack and his lads laid low and waited. There was plenty of time, they mustn't rush.

In the quiet home in the second ash tree on the left, the robin and the owl had many informal discussions. Oliphant was finding out how difficult it was to be the one at the top. Everyone flocked to him with their problems and questions and expected him to know all the answers. Endlessly he racked his brain instead of making them use theirs. It was not easy to be Lord of the Woodland.

The robin listened attentively to his friend, made camomile and valerian tea, and offered it to the small white owl, accompanied by the one thing guaranteed to cheer him up: squashed-fly biscuits.

"Why don't you take advice from the doctors at the Cornucopia Tree?" he suggested. "They might be able to help you, just at the beginning you understand, until you get the hang of things."

"Ummm," considered Oliphant, chewing deliciously on the tasty biscuits.

"You know, Freddie,that is a very good idea, very good indeed. I just might do that if I can find the time."

Freddie so wanted to help Oliphant through this time of change and see him emerge a strong leader, admired and respected. One more thing was on his mind. Out he came with it.

"What do you think you will do with the Mists of Time?" he enquired gently, refilling his acorn cup with the pink fragrant tea. Oliphant stared thoughtfully out of the small window overlooking the Lower Woodland. He watched a jackdaw and a seagull land on the roof of the old watermill.

"I can see that it's a source of valuable information if it's used correctly," he finally said slowly. "It would seem to me that spying on all our friends is unacceptable, but that to be informed of what is going on is different. Or if evidence is needed for, well, any unfortunate goings on. Do you agree?"

Freddie thought about this carefully. "I think I do."

"As I am to be living there, it will be so easy to open up the Root Room again and check everything is working. We'd better get it up to date. That is… if you'd like to help me. I don't really trust anyone else. Would you, Freddie?"

"Of course," agreed the robin at once. "You won't forget your visit to Dr Dew and Dr Yew, will you?" he added as a gentle reminder.

"I shall go today, I promise."

"Good."

A loud cawing noise was heard outside. Then several loud squawks and the hysterical outraged screams of small birds. It was coming from the garden of Watermill Cottage. Freddie peeped out of the elevated oval door and realised there was a squabble going on. It sounded serious. Even Mary heard the racket and looked out of her kitchen window.

The jackdaws had surrounded the wooden bird table and were taking it in turns to gobble everything on it, and the robins, bluetits and finches were being driven away. An outraged fight had started.

"Go away, you horrid great things! That bird table is not for you!" An angry Mary banged on the window. The jackdaws lined up cheekily on the garage roof, waiting. Most of the bird food had been eaten anyway.

"Let's go, we've had enough. They're welcome to what's left!" sniggered Jodie, Jack's younger brother.

After the watermill had been abandoned, the jackdaws had successfully nested and multiplied in the great eaves of the old building. Now they seemed to be everywhere, large and menacing.

Freddie and Oliphant looked at each other from the secluded tree top, having witnessed the fracas.

"Umm, they're beginning to take over," was Freddie's perceptive remark.

"I expect it will sort itself out. I'm off to the Cornucopia Tree, I'll see you later." And he swiftly adjusted his yellow bow tie and set off purposefully. Arriving at the tree, he pulled the familiar rope and heard the conker shells jangle far away upstairs.

Soon the door swung open and he proceeded up the spiral staircase with its glass cabinets on either side, full of amazing potions and concoctions in interesting glass-stoppered bottles. Verity, the white dove, greeted him and she bobbed a curtsey at the new Regent of the Woodland.

The two doctors, Dr Dew and Dr Yew, looked up from their large partners' desk, bespectacled and studious. They stood at once.

"Good day to you-oooooo, Mr Oliphant," they cooed together, and Verity led him to the window seat. The doctors left their desk and sat beside him, waiting patiently.

"Continue-oooo," one of the pigeons urged him. Oliphant didn't quite know what to say now he was put on the spot.

Everything seemed to jumble up in his mind: the pressures and worries, the decisions and guilt, all his misgivings. Where should he start? He opened his beak and tried to talk but the doctors shook their heads.

"It is too difficult for you-oooooo, everything is so new-oooooo." And with a flick of a wing he was ushered by Verity into a tranquil room.

"Sleep on the Cloud of Ease." She directed him to a wonderful bed where he lay down, saw a rose-coloured sky above his head, and fell asleep instantly. While he was asleep Dr Dew spoke to him in a calm, monotonous voice which he could hear quite clearly but could not respond to.

He was told that they had no elixirs to help him. Everything he needed was there already in place within him, he had only to find it. He could never be the sort of ruler the buzzard had been because he did not possess the inherent genes of a great hunter-predator. Yet he could be immensely strong and fierce in his own right. His main asset was his own simple nature: his direct grasp of what was right and his great compassion. He was a Dark Dweller, and the doctor told him that night would be his strength, and darkness his greatest helper.

The owl did not understand but the voice continued to reassure him. If he only believed in himself, soon he would see. He was left alone to sleep a deep and relaxing sleep, serene and quiet. For after all, what owl did his work and thinking in the daytime? No, blackest night was his time.

The doctor returned to his partner and together they quietly discussed their diagnosis and prognosis. All was entered in neat hand in the large ledger, but on this occasion Dr Dew asked Verity for the invisible ink. It wouldn't do to have the fears of a new ruler made public. Then both waited patiently, smiling to each other. They were expecting a visitor, their anticipation evident.

The owl slept for many hours. Freddie, waiting for his return, grew restless and impatient. He became so anxious that he left the house in the tree to seek his friend.

It was by now late morning, the sun had broken through and the breeze was very slight. The Woodland, clothed in its winter attire, was brown and colourless and yet tiny green buds were just beginning in the wild honeysuckles' tangled strands, and fine spears of snowdrops were pushing through: the first signs of spring.

Reaching the top of Gallants Bower he searched for the Cornucopia Tree but was blinded by the sun shining through the Freedom Gate and over the Citadel. Everything was suddenly quiet and still. He felt warmth on his feathers, and a great tiredness came over him.

I must have come up that hill too quickly, he told himself. *I feel a little lightheaded.* He stopped to rest on a dead mossy branch.

A brown figure was darting through the woodland. It had a child's face and was dressed in bracken and leaves, with sturdy legs and pointed shoes. The sun's beams seemed to be following it wherever it went and it was so nimble and sure-footed it seemed to be dancing. The robin pretended to be asleep with his eyes half closed. He was intrigued with the bright sunny figure exploring the woodland in such a carefree way.

He disappeared from view and Freddie decided to follow him along the path heading towards the Cornucopia Tree where the tiny figure melted in through the doorway and was gone.

Inside, the visitor was greeted by the doctors with great joy and led to the side of the sleeping owl. There the child held out his hand and touched the white feathers of his subject. A warm jet of golden light surged from his fingertips into Oliphant who stirred slightly in his dreams, drowsy and comfortable.

"Thank you, Lord Sunna, we owe everything to you-oooooo," cooed the pigeons quietly together.

The child smiled and danced around the tree house, touching each bottle and jar which twinkled as a sunbeam entered each one.

"And the buzzard is gone?" came the question.

"He is, my lord."

"Then all will be well. You'll see." And off he danced down the stairs and out to inspect the rest of his kingdom. For this was Sunna, Spirit of the Woodland, whose powers extended over most of the land. As the seasons changed, his power increased: a child in spring, growing through boyhood in summer, a man reaching maturity in autumn, and finally an old man in winter. As the cycle of the year spun round, the woodland spirit completed the circle of life. Happy and bright with youth and vigour, he was at his most joyous in spring. By winter he was strong, and determined to meet the greatest challenges his one year required of him.

The pigeons cooed excitedly together. A visit from the great Lord Sunna was a hugely meaningful event. One of the days of the week had been named after him and he was always associated with thunder. It did make the wise and learned doctors wonder… wasn't the great storm just at the fading end of the year? Just at the time when the old Sunna was preparing to die? Dr Dew had made a few notes in his Woodland diary and carefully locked it away.

The fleeting Spirit of the Woodland passed through every path and blessed every tree and plant on his way back to the foot of Gallants Bower. He stopped sharply. He could feel waves of discord pulsing towards him and the air became heavy. Lined up in the old sycamore trees fringing the boundary of the watermill were many grey-headed jackdaws, their beady eyes all fixed upon him. They were waiting.

Sunna's youth made him fearless and he continued confidently. As he skipped beneath them they let out a raucous screech to frighten him, but it was in vain, the boy was undeterred. He looked up smiling, opened his mouth and blew gently. A tremendous gust of wind surged out and toppled the birds from the trees, scattering them hither and thither with terrified shrieks. Laughing to himself the boy continued down the narrow path to the stream that poured down Tumbling Hill, drank to quench his thirst and continued up the other side of the valley. He disappeared in a glowing haze. The jackdaws picked themselves up, thoroughly shaken. It was their first encounter with the Spirit of the Woodland and his awesome power.

Oliphant woke up on the Cloud of Ease, stretched and felt wonderful. He got up, and peered out of the door to find the rooms empty. He left quietly by the spiral staircase, to see Freddie asleep on a mossy bank just outside. It was warm and sheltered in the sunshine. They had both been asleep for several hours and neither would have any recollection of what had taken place.

Chapter Fifteen
Ptolemy appears and Abel has a problem

Sargasso and Seraphim waited patiently at the nest she had built inside the lime kiln. It was not as other seabird's nests, haphazard and flimsy; this nest was securely woven and deeply lined with feathers from her own breast. But no egg came. Seraphim became anxious.

"Shouldn't the eggs have been here by now?" she asked her devoted partner.

"I'm sure they will arrive. Wait just a little longer." And he fetched her some tiny shrimps as a treat. Day after day they waited, watching out across the windy river, seeing the gusts changing the patterns on the water endlessly. One good thing that came of all their patience was that Sargasso made several sightings of the red boat moving up and down the river. He flew over at once to see who the occupants were. They always had fishing rods rather too big for the sort of fish caught in Devon's sheltered waters, and twice he caught snatches of conversation borne on the wind. Sargasso did not recognise them. They were not part of the angling fraternity constantly and keenly fishing every weekend around the estuary. These two always covered the same stretch of water, talking quietly to each other. Once, one of them became angry and raised his voice and his fist, but the other one calmed him down, looking quickly around for observers. They didn't notice the seagull. It certainly was strange behaviour.

As the days went by, the moon became larger and larger until it arrived at the eve of the Moon of Winds. The moon was full at half-past midnight, shining its blue-white light over the water.

Seraphim was awake, aware of splashing sounds coming from the steps at the end of the Old Quay where they sat stone still and frightened. They watched in fear as wet and shiny, the lumbering turtle Ptolemy clambered towards them.

"My faithful friends!" he greeted them. "You have been waiting for me for many days, I know this. Your patience has been tested, but see, your reward is here." From around his middle he unwrapped a sheeny, gauzy mesh. The seagulls watched.

"The time has come, Seraphim. Step to the water's edge with me. Hold the corner of this sea blanket and lower it into the water." She did as she was told. The shiny mesh glinted in the water and she held it very tightly. The turtle chanted slowly some words she did not understand.

"Now pull it out." And again she obeyed the turtle's command.

"Sargasso, now you. Take the sea blanket and toss it up into the air." And the bewildered seagull followed his instructions, holding the gauze with his beak and throwing it upwards. The fine filmy mesh rose high into the air, caught the light of the moon on its shiny surface and floated gently back down to the grassy quay, as the turtle again chanted his strange words.

"Now, place the blanket in your nest and we will sing together. Take your place, Seraphim, and be ready."

The turtle and the two gulls softly crooned curious music beneath the glorious light of the moon as waves lapped on the rock-lined shore. The wind rose and the trees whistled eerily in the trees behind them. They fell into a trance as the sweet sounds filled their souls, and gradually out of Seraphim's body a single large, pearly egg emerged. It was enfolded in the sheeny, shiny, gauzy blanket which had been blessed by the sea and the sky. All three felt intense excitement and were thrilled with the arrival of the long-awaited egg.

"When your egg hatches I am to be the appointed guardian of your offspring. I have dedicated the rest of my life to its nurture and safety. You will be parents to an exceptional fledgling. Together we will be responsible for its journey through this world. And now, Seraphim, you must remain sitting on your precious egg until you hatch it. It will take much longer than usual and you will need still more patience. Sargasso and I will help you and in one moon cycle the shell will break."

Sargasso and Seraphim looked at the wrinkled old turtle and were a little afraid. What was going to happen? Why was their egg different? Why was there only one? But it was too late to turn back save the unthinkable - to smash the egg. It couldn't be done. Sargasso knew Seraphim would never allow it and in his heart he knew he couldn't do it. Together they rested through the remainder of the long night and the egg stayed furled in the gauzy net made from the sea and the sky, warm and safe.

***

At St Thomas in Canterbury Church in Kingswear, Abel King was searching frantically for a set of keys he had lost. As the verger of the parish church, his duties were many and included opening and closing the church and the hall, cleaning and sweeping the floors and path and polishing the many brass ornaments and church decorations. He was quiet and small but extremely nosy and knew everybody's secrets. He knew how many bottles of communion wine were stored in the crypt, and that one had gone missing last Christmas morning; he knew that Joe Ferris, after his holiday in Portugal, had slipped a few escudos onto the collection plate. He also kept an eye on who came and went among the wealthy holiday home owners; some turned up on Sunday mornings to worship in the quaint old church which offered beauty and peace far away from the commercial world. Yes, Abel King knew a lot. He cycled each day from the Mill Cottage at the head of Old Mill Creek which he shared with his father, Ezekiel.

"Drat and blast it!" He was getting crosser and crosser, but search as he might, he could not find those keys. They belonged to a small shed at the back of the hall where old curtains, redundant robes and several broken chairs lived. It was where Abel kept his own secret, but he not visited this shed for several weeks now. There was someone else who had a key and Abel was going to be forced to confess that he had lost his. It was all very annoying.

Abel left the tidying up of the hymnbook cupboard to go outside and make sure that the clock was keeping good time. It was about to chime on the hour. Shady Lane came cycling furiously up the hill towards the lych gate, his hair flying behind him.

"Morning, Abel," he puffed. "Busy?"

"As always. You late for work?"

"Not really, no more'n usual!" He grinned at the sour, unsmiling face.

"Getting anywhere with solvin' that robbery, are they?" Abel asked, coming round the churchyard to check the hands of the clock.

"The police seem to have finished up at the house. We've all had our fingerprints taken, proper game it was! Better go, Abel. Oh, and one interesting thing is, they reckon it's a local job! Yes! Fancy that!" as he fed Abel's obvious interest.

"Really? Wonder what makes 'em think that?"

"Dunno, seems odd to me. I mean who'd want all those diamonds? Nobody would be able to sell them would they? Stands to reason. 'Bye now!" and off he went up the hill and disappeared over the top.

"Who indeed?" Abel asked himself. "Chance would be a fine thing." And he hurried to look at the tower as the clock started to chime loudly. He finished his morning's work and made his way to the Railway Tavern, a local pub overlooking the scenic railway line which once had proudly carried passengers to Paddington station.

"Half of cider and a cheddar ploughmans," he asked Sally the barmaid who took his order at once.

"I think I'll sit outside today, girl," he told her. "I'll be in the garden." And he walked through the pub out into the whitewashed yard where several wooden tables and chairs had been set out. The sun was shining which took the chill off the air and although it was winter, the yard was quite sheltered and warm. Abel didn't want to run the risk of being overheard. He was meeting somebody today.

Five minutes later Sally appeared with his cider and his lunch.

"Here we are, Abel. You're a brave one outside today!" and she left his food on the table and went back inside. Soon the latch lifted on the back yard door and it opened to reveal a middle-aged man of insignificant appearance wearing a cloth cap, a thick tweed jacket, grey trousers and laced boots. His hair was grey and he had grey stubble over his face where he hadn't shaved. He glanced around anxiously and then slid into a seat next to Abel.

"Got your note, what's up? I've brought me key." He fished in his pocket to find it.

"Give me a bit of bread Abel, that looks a fine lunch, sure it does," he wheedled, and relenting, Abel broke him off a chunk of the warm crusty bread.

"And a piece of cheese to go with it wouldn't be hurting you," continued the man.

"Oh, alright," grumbled Abel, passing him over a slice.

"Thing is, Ben, I've lost my keys. The one to the shed is on the ring," he confessed.

"Have you, now."

"I'll have to get another one cut. Give me yours, will you? I'll go up to Harcourt's now and get it done in my lunchbreak. I'll be back in half an hour and meet you by the shed. You'd best not stay here, Sally will be back for the empties in a minute."

The man who was called Ben took a pickled onion off the plate and a swig of cider from the glass, looked longingly at the rest of the crusty bread, and got up leaving the key on the table.

"See ya then."

Abel frowned at the man as he left by the same yard door, closing it behind him. Could he trust him? He wasn't sure.

Ben Murphy shuffled unnoticed through the few streets of Kingswear to a small garden retreat, reached through a thick iron gate. It was a public place but few visited it, tucked away in a sunny sheltered nook on the hillside. He'd taken a ten-pound note out of Abel's pocket as he sat close beside him, and carrying his paper bag closely he sniffed the gorgeous savoury smell of the hot pasty he had bought himself, and a bottle of beer to go with it.

"Well," he told himself, "if he'd shared his lunch as any good Christian would have done, I wouldn't have pinched his money, would I?" justifying his mean actions to himself. "Stupid eejit!"

Ben's cunning mind, developed out of poverty and self-preservation since childhood, ran over the interesting facts Abel had reluctantly offered him. So he had lost his key, but where? he wondered. This middle-aged Irishman was a wandering agricultural worker; picking daffodils in Cornwall in the spring, strawberries and soft fruits in Devon in the summer, and apples in the Vale of Evesham in the autumn. During the cold winter months when he was homeless he had to find somewhere to stay, and this year he had happened upon Abel King.

He had persuaded him after a brief acquaintance to let him sleep in the shed behind the church hall where, under a pile of worsted wool choir garments, long discarded, Ben had enterprisingly made a cosy bed from the broken chairs and snored away the winter nights. He had told Abel it was his Christian duty to help the homeless, over several pints of cider in the Railway Tavern. Abel had offered him the spare key and Ben had willingly accepted it. He often lurked in the church while Abel performed his daily duties, and sometimes Ben offered minimal help, just enough to keep his bed assured for a few more weeks until the chilly fields showed the green spikes of daffodils far away in Cornwall, and the first income of the year arrived.

Ben enjoyed his itinerant lifestyle, getting easily bored. He was not averse to a bit of stealing if the opportunity arose, which of course it surprisingly had, here in quiet Kingswear.

Why was Abel so anxious about the keys? Was there something he hadn't told him? He began to worry. The sooner they located the package the better it would be. Munching his delicious pasty and washing it down with good ale, Ben's thoughts turned to Ireland and his great-grandfather's cottage lying idle and rundown, just as he had left it all those years ago. He was going to buy it back and restore it. His dream was to end his days in County Clare, gazing out over Doonbeg. Shady Lane had presented him with the opportunity and he wasn't going to let anything spoil his dream. For now it was tantalisingly close; so close he could almost see the clouds scudding over the newly thatched roof of his ancestral home, and he couldn't let this chance slip away. He would have to be very careful and watch Abel from now on. He pursed his lips and swigged the last of the beer from the bottle, closing his eyes and falling asleep, dreaming of his beloved Ireland. One day he would be there when he opened his eyes.

Chapter Sixteen
A confession from Patrick

Some bad news broke the next day: poor Patrick had to go back to Scotland early. He only had a few days left. He was devastated as they talked on the telephone together.

"Isn't it sickening?" he grumbled to Eddie. "Mum's got things to do in Glasgow and she thought it would be nice if we travelled together! She'll probably lecture me the whole way. Can it get any worse?"

Eddie had to agree that it couldn't. Irene was the last person he would want to be cooped up with for seven hours.

"When's half term?"

"End of February."

"That's not too bad," Eddie reassured him.

"Would it be too selfish of me to ask you not to go down into the shaft without me?"

There was silence - a long silence.

"Eddie, are you still there?"

"Yes, I'm thinking. I suppose I don't really mind."

"Thanks, Eddie. I don't think I could bear it. But... I need to see you and Ellie to tell you something. Can I come up?"

"Of course."

"'Bye then."

Eddie went to tell Ellie that Patrick was expected. She was watching the creatures in the aquarium, the light was on and there was plenty to see.

"Why is Patrick coming up?"

"He's got something to tell us."

"Hmm, wonder what that is?"

"How do I know, stupid! He's here now anyway." Eddie watched Patrick's head bobbing past the window. The back door opened.

"Hi." And they both turned towards him. He stood there looking at them.

"I've got something to tell you. I should have told you sooner, I don't know why, I just didn't for some reason."

Eddie and Ellie were puzzled by his awkward manner and kept quiet. Patrick walked to the window and looked out. He seemed strange and unsettled. Then he turned to them both and said,

"The Frasers, over at Kingswear, you know? Dad and I have been over there a couple of times."

The others nodded. "Yes?"

"They've got a daughter called Heather, and I've been to visit her... Well, she invited me over first. She's really nice and I've told her all about you and I was just wondering, if you've got time... maybe you could go over and visit her? I'd like you to meet her. Do you see?"

He looked out of the window again.

Ellie didn't see. She couldn't quite understand. Why had he not told them about her? She felt angry and hurt.

Patrick spun round.

"I know you think it's strange me not telling you but Dad started it, he didn't tell me she even existed. His little game, but... she's disabled. She's in a wheelchair." He paused. "She rides and does archery and pistol shooting, and she's got this little dog, he's a real menace, and... I really admire her guts. I know you'll get on with her. I was going to bring you over with me next time. Her father has a mooring down on the river, Eddie, and I was thinking of asking him if you could put *Pelican* there in the spring." Patrick ran out of things to say and sighed, looking rather desperately at them both.

"I just wish I had a bit more time here. It's always the same, I never want to go back." He turned and looked out of the window once more, as if he couldn't bear to face them.

For once Ellie and Eddie were silent, digesting the news Patrick had just revealed.

Ellie was in fact feeling pangs of jealousy. Patrick was her friend and she had never needed to share him. She stared stonily, unsmiling as she tried to come to terms with the strange emotions she was experiencing. Eddie was more interested in the news of the mooring than in Heather. So what, she was disabled? He didn't care.

"Its fine with me," said Eddie "It's not a drama. I am interested in the mooring of course as well as Heather!" and he smiled impishly at Patrick.

"Ellie?" Patrick tried again to re-establish some sort of approval from her. "I am sorry I didn't tell you about her before, I thought—"

"Thought what?" interrupted Ellie frostily. "That I wouldn't like her, be horrible to her, make fun of her? What did you think?"

"No, Ellie, of course not! None of those things, you're not like that! Will you let me phone her? She's really looking forward to meeting you, honestly. Please? I'd so like you to."

"You haven't told her about our adventures, have you?" Ellie asked in a small voice. She didn't want to share Captain Avery, Ferdinand or Isabella with anyone.

"No, of course not!" Patrick was horrified. "I wouldn't do that."

"Okay, let's not get stupid over this," sighed Eddie, suddenly having enough. He hated conflicts. "Patrick hasn't committed a crime, Ellie, he's just made a new friend. He is allowed to, you know," he challenged her.

"I know that!" she spat at him sharply, "But he kept her a secret… deliberately." Her glare at Patrick was accusing.

"Yes, I did, but the more I got to know her the more I felt we would all get on together. She's got a beautiful horse, Ellie, you'd love it, and her own cottage in their grounds." "Oh really," was her biting sarcastic reply.

At that, the phone rang and Eddie ran to answer it. It was Arthur to see if *Pelican* needed to be delivered anywhere or left in the boatyard. Eddie promised he would give the message to his dad. When he returned to Patrick, he was alone and very quiet. Ellie had walked out in a fury.

"Ignore her, she'll get over it," advised Eddie patiently.

"Look, why don't we all go over to Kingswear together?" he suggested to a depressed and deflated Patrick. "We can get another look at the lighthouse. Maybe we should call on Heather and break the ice. Come on, no time like the present. What do you think? Ellie's just put out, that's all." Privately he thought she was probably jealous.

After some thought, Patrick spoke.

"I'd like that. I think it's a good idea. I'll go and suggest it to Ellie, shall I?" Eddie nodded and Patrick went to find her. She was in the garden on the little seat by the pond, watching the goldfish. He sat beside her. She didn't look at him, keeping the silence, but she pointed to a frog coming up for air.

"We could all go over today. We could have a look at the lighthouse and maybe say hello to Heather?" he dropped the bombshell heavily. Ellie remained silent.

"Only if you want to." He tried again.

She finally spoke. "I don't mind," she said in a non - committal way. "Might be alright, I suppose."

Patrick took this as a yes.

"I'll tell Eddie but I think you've got a surprise in store. Trust me."

"Okay." She shrugged, trying to push her hurt feeling away. She didn't want to go at all.

Chapter Seventeen
A new friend from Kingswear

One hour later they were on the ferry chugging over the river, breathing in the crisp fresh air and the smell of the sea. Seagulls called noisily overhead as the three tried to forget their quarrel. Patrick looked around appreciatively.

"I miss this so much when I get back to Scotland," he told them both. Ellie began to feel pangs of guilt. Poor Patrick. Always leaving, always longing to come back.

"Half term is not so far away, you get such a long time off. More than us!" she grinned at him.

"Have to have some perks!" he grinned back. Eddie was pleased; everything seemed to be alright again, thank goodness.

The ferry docked with a thump, the cars revved their engines and all the passengers hurried off. Ellie actually felt quite excited. The clock chimed eleven o'clock as they passed.

"Fancy a bar of chocolate?" Eddie asked, diverting round the corner to the post office. All three trouped into the crammed general store and chose their favourites.

"Should we get something for Heather?" asked Ellie, choosing a small box of Devon fudge.

"Good idea, I'll pay for it," Patrick offered, and the pleasant lady behind the counter smiled and took the money.

"On holiday, I expect?" she asked them, wrapping the fudge in a paper bag.

"No, we live in Dartmouth," answered Eddie. "Just visiting some friends."

"Not many youngsters here now, of course," said the lady shaking her head. "Mostly holiday homes and retired rich folk. 'Course my son's still here, can't seem to get rid of him!" she laughed. "Have a nice morning."

"'Bye," they said politely and left the shop, noticing a man outside with a bucket and cloth just about to clean the windows.

104

"Mornin'." He nodded to them. "Takin' a walk around the coast?" He began to splosh water in the bucket and took a soapy sweep across the window.

"Yes, it's such a lovely day," answered Ellie as they sidestepped the sudsy water.

"Aye, shows up all the dirt, this sunshine, and the grubby fingermarks." And the man turned back to his work. As they strolled along the sheltered road from the village, a bicycle bell startled them from behind. Turning abruptly, Patrick saw the long-haired boy he had met before.

"You again!" he laughed cheekily, "and you've brought your mates this time, eh?"

Patrick nodded to him.

"I'll tell Heather you're on the way. See ya later!" and he pedalled off furiously, hair flying in the wind, darting in zig zags all over the road. He turned once and waved.

"He's got a nerve," complained Patrick. "What's it got to do with him if we visit Heather?"

"Who's he?" Eddie was interested.

"That's Shady Lane, he helps out at Woodend."

"Shady Lane? What a name!" laughed Ellie, intrigued.

"I think his name is Will but he's called Shady because of his name, which is Lane. Probably deals in drugs," added Patrick nastily.

Half way along Beacon Road they could see the octagonal top of the lighthouse, with its windowed turrets. A copper ball and ornate weather vane marked the top.

"The lighthouse," pointed Eddie as they approached it round a wide bend in the wall which ran alongside the river's edge. The entrance had an elaborate gate leading to an iron studded door, sadly locked. Patrick and Eddie stood still, hands on the wall, unable to believe they had crossed the river through an underground tunnel and arrived exactly inside this beautiful old building. How could they get inside? All three looked at each other. How could they find out?

Eventually, undecided about what to do next, they moved on along the road, soon passing an unusual Devon cottage which was reached through a gate and a set of steps.

"Keepers Cottage, now what does that tell you?" Ellie pointed her finger triumphantly at the boys. The penny finally dropped.

"Ahh, I see what you mean!" laughed Eddie.

"Shall I?" Patrick opened the chipped old gate and ventured up the steps, grassy and unused. At the door, a tarnished ship's bell hung. He swung the rope and grimaced at the noise which sounded extremely loud. Nobody came. The windows were dusty with cobwebs; dirty net curtains drooped miserably.

"It looks deserted. No one lives here anymore." Patrick tried the firmly locked door.

"Never mind, let's get going. Everyone in Kingswear must have heard that racket."

Disappointed, they continued along the lane looking across the river and out to sea.

"It's quite an important place for a lighthouse," decided Eddie. "I think there was one over the turret at the tea shop as well. It's a pretty difficult entrance to find from out at sea, that's why they put the daymark up here on the top of the point," he explained.

"We're here." Patrick pointed to the entrance of Woodend Manor Farm, winding into a dark driveway, hidden by tropical plants and dense bushes. Reaching the large white house, all stood on the doorstep full of uncertainty.

"You ring," urged Ellie.

Patrick pulled the black iron bell-pull and heard it jangle inside. Ellie and Eddie looked all around, admiring the wonderful view and gardens. They could see the Old Bath House and the castle ferry slip across the river. No one answered the door. Walking around the side, Patrick could see the garage door open and the empty space. Suddenly Will's head appeared around the corner.

"Hiya! We're round here. Come on." He beckoned, his sleeves rolled up and his hands wet. They followed curiously to the central courtyard at the back where, on a table in an old tin bath, a small dog was having a soak in steaming water. Heather, wearing a red anorak, was seated in her wheelchair, holding a soapy brush.

"Keep still you, little terror!" she scolded him and looking up, saw Will returning with Patrick and two strangers.

"Hello," she said in a surprised voice, pleased to see Patrick again. "You've brought your friends! Look Robbie, you'd better get out of your bath and get dressed." She laughed. "Help me lift him out, someone!" and obligingly Ellie picked up the large brown towel and shortly the little dog was wrapped up, rubbed dry, and his tartan coat fastened up. Will lifted the tin bath down and poured the water away in the central drain.

"Mustn't get cold must you?" Ellie told the dog, who was wagging his tail.

"Come inside," Heather requested, and everyone followed her into the large kitchen which was painted lemon and pale green.

"Now, you must be Eddie and Ellie, you've got to be." She smiled at them. "Patrick's told me about you. You live over at Warfleet, don't you?"

Will had disappeared off into the yard and Eddie could just see him through the window, hanging the bath up in one of the garages.

She's pretty, thought Ellie, seeing the small blonde girl smiling at her. She had taken off her red coat and had a white jumper and denim jeans on. Her hair was untied today.

"Would you like a drink or anything, lemonade? Tea?" she asked.

"No, thank you," they replied as Robbie sniffed them each in turn and then barked at Patrick.

"He doesn't like me for some reason!" and everyone laughed.

"Do you know anything about Keepers Cottage?" suddenly asked Eddie. "It looks empty. We saw it as we came past."

"It's been like that for ages. I think the keeper of the lighthouse lived there once. I'm sure it used to be part of this farm and estate."

"Really? So maybe your dad's got the key? What about the lighthouse, then? Who owns that now?" Eddie demanded to know. Ellie and Patrick glanced nervously at each other. Had Eddie gone a bit too far? He was bordering on the nosey, but Heather didn't seem to mind. She thought for a moment.

"Well, the Harbour Authority I suppose. It's automated now so there is no lighthouse keeper. That's why the cottage has been empty for years. Are you interested in lighthouses then?"

They all waited for Eddie's answer.

"It's exactly opposite our house," he told her with a winning smile.

"I can find out from Dad and maybe you can go inside it. Would you like to come and see Ginny? She's up at the stables. Do you like horses?" she directed her question at Ellie.

"I do, but I don't know much about them, and I don't ride," she confessed.

"Doesn't matter. Come and help me feed her. Shady's going to muck her out today. I try to help as much as I can." Patrick hastily broke the silence, knowing what the others were thinking.

"Do you sail, Heather?" he asked.

"I've been on Dad's yachts and I love being out in the fresh air and the wind. What about you?" This time she directed her question back at Eddie.

"We've got a little Cornish shrimper which we keep at our creek. Dad's just bought a Moody 33 and I can't wait to go out in her. Trouble is, we've nowhere to moor it at Warfleet - but we'll find one." He reassured her with another winning smile. She smiled back, nodding.

"Will you sail too, Ellie?" Heather asked her. "I see the boats going out on a Wednesday night from the Yacht Club."

"I expect Dad and Eddie will enjoy the racing more than me. I really just like going for a sail and maybe taking a picnic," she confessed.

"Come on then, let's go to the stables," smiled Heather, and they followed her as she wheeled herself out of the kitchen, pushing the door open herself. The others were uncertain how much to help her. They didn't want to do the wrong thing and embarrass her. Walking alongside her she pointed out the stables and the cottage, the farmland and the livestock, and told them about the little cove with its steps to the river.

"It's called Silver Cove, very tiny with a minute beach. I expect you can see it from across the river."

"Does your dad have a red dingy?" Eddie asked.

"I don't think so." That eliminated the mysterious red boat then, thought both the boys together.

"Shady has a boat, it might be his?" Heather added.

I knew it! thought Patrick triumphantly. *I'm sure he's mixed up in this tangle somehow!*

They tracked up the winding path and reached the stable where the blond boy was busy removing the straw into a small trailer. Ginny poked her head over the stable door at the sound of voices. Heather soon saw that they each had a job to do.

In a while the tack was polished, stable swept, hay replaced, and Ginny was brushed and groomed and thoroughly spoilt, enjoying the attention. Shady finished his work and went off back to the garage.

Ellie and Heather seemed to like each other and the horse won everyone over.

"Let's have coffee now," suggested Heather, indicating the cottage nearby. Ellie was most impressed with this and she realised that Heather had real independence here; everything had been specially adapted for a wheelchair user. The three watched curiously as she busied about producing coffee and shortbread efficiently and quickly.

"Here you are," she said as they sat down in the tiny kitchen-diner. Voices could be heard outside.

"It's Mum and Dad back."

Walking up the path were Heather's parents, Jack and Morag Fraser.

"Entertaining, Heather?" smiled her father. "Who have we got here then? I know Patrick, of course."

"These are my friends from Warfleet Creek," Patrick said quickly, "This is Ellie and her brother, Eddie."

"Great to meet you," smiled Jack. "So nice to have some young people around. Heather misses all her school friends when we come here."

"Now tell me all about yourselves," begged Morag prettily, and gradually she got each one to talk about themselves.

"So you sail?" Jack was impressed. "Very useful having a dad in the Navy. What sort of boat have you got?"

Eddie told him all about the purchase of *Pelican* and just happened to mention their search for a new mooring as the Creek one was too small.

"Well of course, you must use my mooring down here at Silver Cove. Please use ours anytime. Get your father to give me a ring, I mean it now." And he smiled a big smile at them all.

"That sounds wonderful," Eddie replied gratefully, his careful plan falling into place exactly as he had hoped. Patrick flashed him a conspiratorial glance.

There was a cough outside and then a knock at the door.

"Excuse me, Mr Fraser, sorry to interrupt you, but we'd like to interview that young lad Will Lane again." The detective in charge of the robbery was standing there.

"Really?" everyone looked shocked; everyone that is except Patrick, who nodded smugly to himself. *I thought so.*

"Oh dear!" said Mr Fraser and Morag together, looking upset.

"He's down in the garage," said Mr Fraser, and got up at once. The two men returned to the house, leaving them all to draw their own conclusions. Eddie changed the subject, at once sensing the gloomy atmosphere that had descended over them.

"Mrs Fraser, I was wondering if you could tell me anything about Keepers Cottage, or the lighthouse for that matter. Do you know any of the history connected to it?" he asked rather desperately.

"Now, let me see," said Morag, glad of something else to think about.

"I'm sure we still own the cottage, though of course there's no one there now. It hasn't been occupied in our time and we took the farm over from Jack's parents. We must have the key somewhere, probably in the office. As for the lighthouse, I think the original old light is still there but I don't think we can get inside." She pondered. "Why are you interested, Eddie?"

There was a short silence, eyes meeting all around the room.

"We live directly opposite it, and I am rather keen on old lighthouses," he added convincingly. Ellie stifled a giggle and hastily turned it into a cough. Heather was intrigued; she sensed something was going on. Patrick refused to meet her steady gaze.

"I can have a look in the office if you like," Morag offered.

The small entourage wound down the gentle slope towards the main house. A police car drove off with two occupants in the front seats.

"Oh no, I think Will's had to go to the police station," Heather said in a voice betraying her anxiety.

"Don't worry, it's just routine, I'm sure," comforted Morag.

The back door opened and Jack let them into the warm bright kitchen.

"Come into the office," invited Morag. Inside the neat, well-organised room Morag hunted in the drawers of the desk. Eventually, to everyone's delight, an old, rather pretty key was found - the key to Keepers Cottage. In a dusty ledger brought down from a high shelf, some useful information was found.

Mrs Fraser read it out clearly. "The last tenants were a family called King. Several generations of lighthouse keepers seem to have been here. You see, the lighthouse had to be manned when the light was fuelled by oil - quite a responsible task keeping the light burning, you know. I think it was too small, so the cottage always went with the job. Very interesting isn't it?"

"That's great, thank you," enthused Eddie.

"I expect the family will be mentioned in the parish records," added Morag thoughtfully.

"Can we go and look round the cottage, Mum? Would it be alright to have the key?" asked Heather out of the blue.

"I don't see why not, but I'd better ask Jack first." And she left the room leaving the four youngsters on their own.

"That would be brilliant, Heather!"

"Sounds exciting!"

"Are there any steps?" No one had thought about the wheelchair.

"We'll get you up somehow," grinned Eddie. Mr Fraser appeared in the doorway.

"Don't know what you'll find there, not much I expect, but you're welcome to have a look around if you want to."

"Oh good, Dad, that's great." Heather seemed very pleased. "Come on, let's go now." She suggested, seizing the moment. Quickly they gathered up their things and headed down the driveway to Keepers Cottage, full of excitement at what they might discover.

Chapter Eighteen
The police get a new lead, and Keepers Cottage gives up its secrets

At the local police station things were getting difficult for Will. His parents had been forced to close the post office as their son was under eighteen and couldn't be interviewed alone. Mrs Lane was very upset and Mr Lane rather angry.

"What have you been up to then?" demanded Jim. "Eh?"

"Leave him alone, Jim," warned Iris, "How can you think that he's mixed up in all this? He's your son!" she sniffed.

"I ain't done nothing, Mum, so don't you go worrying. It's just a mistake, that's all," Will reassured her brightly as he looked around the bleak police interview room, feeling rather scared. Two policemen walked in and sat down opposite Will.

"We just want to clear up a few things, Will," said Detective Sergeant Tim Mc Donald, opening a folder with a lot of statements in it. The older man said nothing, just leaned back in his chair unsmiling, staring at the three nervous people before him.

"About this key, the one that was kept at the stable, we've got your fingerprints off it and interestingly another set which we haven't identified. Now, any ideas who the other prints might have been from? Who did you give the key to? Eh? Better tell us at once, come on."

"But I didn't! I didn't give it to anyone. No one ever comes up there. Honestly, only the family and me. I don't know mate, really," Will insisted anxiously.

"Will, do you realise how serious this is? This key, we are sure, is how the intruder got in. There was no break in, nobody forced the windows, doors, broke any windows; no other keys are missing or left Mr and Mrs Fraser's possession. This is the only way. Do you understand? You are in a very, very serious position. You might as well tell us now and spare your parents all this." He reached forward and glared at Will, who was now extremely frightened.

Mrs Lane burst into tears and sobbed into her handkerchief and Mr Lane tried to comfort her.

"Look, son, it's no good. You can't hide it now what you've done. Just tell them, okay? For your mum's sake, eh?"

Will ran both his hands through his hair and sighed deeply.

"Why won't you listen to me, Dad? I haven't done anything wrong. I did not steal that necklace or anything else," he insisted once again. Trickles of icy fear were beginning to reach his stomach and pool into a large puddle of anxiety. They surely couldn't believe it was him?

"How did you know there was a necklace, boy? Tell me that!" demanded the detective triumphantly, pointing an excited finger at him.

"Because I saw Mrs Fraser wearing it the night before Christmas Eve. They went to Col Rigby-Todd's for drinks. I was there delivering the Christmas tree just before it got dark. Fetched it in the trailer from Barton Gabriel that afternoon. I helped to get it into the house, and Heather and I put the lights on it."

"What time was that?"

"Early evening. They went out, I dunno, maybe sixish, wasn't really looking at the time, but you can ask them, can't you?" argued Will, suddenly sensing a chink of hope.

The detective wrote this in his notebook and sat back in his chair, thinking. *Blast!* He couldn't get him to confess. There was one other unidentified set of prints taken from the stable door. Will's, of course, were everywhere.

"Who else knew that key was there? Who else goes up to the stable? Have you had a friend help you, or visit the house recently? Anyone you haven't told us about? A girlfriend maybe?" he smirked nastily.

Will tried to think. He searched and searched in his head frantically.

"You haven't been messing about with some girl up there, have you?" snapped Jim Lane nodding, youthful memories flooding back to him.

"No, Dad, I haven't." Will sucked his teeth angrily. The only thing he could think of was when the Frasers were still in Scotland and Ginny had thrown a shoe, he had taken her to Cotterbury Forge for a new one. He had asked Abel to give him a hand to get her into the horse box. Together they had coaxed Ginny into the trailer and Abel had accompanied him to the forge and back, helping Ginny down the ramp and into the stable. He had gone into the house to put the keys of the Land Rover back... But he knew Abel, he worked at the church and helped various people out, including his mother, with odd jobs... It couldn't be Abel.

I'll tell them anyway. It'll get them off my back, thought Will selfishly.

"Only Abel King." announced Will quietly.

"Abel King? Don't be ridiculous, Will! He's a good Christian, works at the church. Helps us out! Don't go making out he done it - that's wicked!" shrieked Iris Lane at her son.

"Hang on a minute, who's he?" The exasperated policeman got his pen ready again.

"He helped me once take the horse to get a new shoe. He's alright, and he came with me to collect the Christmas trees from Marldon," Will suddenly remembered.

"Better check anyway," the detective announced, and took Abel's details. "Where will I find him?"

"At St Thomas's Church, he's the verger there. Very conscientious he is too," added Mr Lane.

"Right, okay, Will, you can go now for the minute." There was no evidence and no proof to hold the boy.

Pity, he'd have fitted in a treat. Typical! thought Detective Tim McDonald. They all sighed great heaves of relief as Will and his mum and dad were ushered out of the interview room and driven home to Kingswear.

***

While Will was at the police station, Eddie, Ellie, Patrick and Heather were enthusiastically searching Keepers Cottage. Arriving at the gateway, the boys lifted the wheelchair up the few steps to the path which led to the old front door with its peeling paint and dirty glass. There had been a lot of giggling and showing off as Heather was unceremoniously picked up and deposited on the path.

"Right, who's got the key?"

"Me!" Heather shouted in glee. "So, shall I be first in?" waving the key enticingly.

"Yes, you can scare the rats away then!"

"Oh, shut up!" laughed Heather. Luckily the keyhole was at waist height. She turned the old key and pushed the door. Nothing happened and they all laughed.

"Well push it, Heather," Eddie told her, "Don't be so feeble."

She pushed her wheelchair closer and gave the door a shove. This time it opened.

"I think I'll just squeeze through." And she did, manoeuvring herself forward into the dark entrance.

From the small hallway it opened out into two rooms, a kitchen and scullery and a sitting room with a large stone fireplace. At the end of the sitting room some stairs led up. Two small mullioned windows looked out across the road, the wide river and the castle entrance to the grey sea beyond.

The house was almost empty; some old advertising leaflets lay pushed behind the front door and plenty of cobwebs adorned the ceiling and corners. Ellie explored the kitchen with its old wooden cupboards, stone sink and wooden draining board. A door led down some stone steps into the scullery to another low sink, storage shelves, a tin bath and a lot of spiders. A stable door led onto the overgrown garden which could be seen through the window.

"It's quite nice," she told herself.

"Look, Heather, come in here." Heather wheeled herself to the doorway. Inside a drawer Ellie had found a key on a piece of string, an old kitchen knife, some rusty scissors, and a strange wooden and metal handle. There was also a white handkerchief with blue flowers embroidered on it, now yellowed round the edges and dusty. The letter *M* was clearly stitched in one corner.

"Strange things," mused Ellie. "I wonder what the name was. M? Sad, isn't it? All that's left from somebody's life."

"Yes," agreed Heather, "I wonder where the key's from?"

She passed it over on the string and Heather turned it over in her hand.

Ellie ran her fingers around the back of the drawer and felt a piece of paper which was caught in the back. She bent down, and with the rusty scissors prised out several sheets of yellowed thin paper folded tightly together in an envelope. Very carefully she unfolded it as the paper almost split apart at the folds. She could just make out the faded ink written in beautiful small letters. It was dated 1892.

The Lighthouse, Noank, Connecticut

My dear Mary Anne

I can hardly write this letter to you, but I know I must reply with speed. Since your dear Daniel passed away I have prayed so hard to think of the best thing to do, but I fear you shall all starve if I do not agree to your request to have one of the twins. Sister dear, Tobias and I will take little Ezra, give him a home and bring him up as our own. I can hardly bear to write these words but I must. I am so sorry to hear you have to leave the lighthouse but glad you have found lodgings at Warfleet Creek.

117

Send little Ezra on the mail ship from Liverpool under the care of Mr Samuel Codner Esq, who travels to Connecticut and was introduced to me by Rev. George Watson. He will contact you shortly. Provident indeed, you may agree. I never dreamt my childless home would be filled at last.

Write to me with all speed, God bless you and little Amos,
Your loving sister,
Martha Brady

"Oh, how sad!" Ellie looked up rather upset by what she had read.

"What's the matter?" Heather asked.

"I've found this letter down the back of the drawer. Read it." Ellie passed it over. "Careful, it's a bit fragile."

Heather read the contents of the letter, which revealed the emotional struggle of the two sisters, who were, it seemed, both married to lighthouse keepers. The shabby envelope was addressed to Mrs Mary King, Start Point Lighthouse, Start Point, S. Devon, and dated 1892.

Ellie looked out of the window for a moment. Wasn't the old man she and Eddie had met at Old Mill Creek called King? Ezekiel King, the one who had lived at Waterside Cottage? Could he be related to the Mary Ann King in this letter? It seemed a bit of a coincidence, and they all had names from the Bible.

"What a shame. This Mary Ann had to give one of her boys away to her sister in America. Isn't that awful?" Heather folded it up carefully, put it back in the envelope and handed it back to Ellie.

"I've never been to the lighthouse at Start Point but I've seen the light flashing there a hundred times," she said.

"It's a nice walk there, a tarmac path," Ellie added carefully.

"Let's see if this key fits anywhere," Heather said brightly, changing the subject so they proceeded on a tour of the house;

but the key didn't fit in any of the other doors. The boys were upstairs, their voices echoing all around. Two tiny bedrooms, with eyebrow windows were located in the thatch.

"Look, Patrick, you can see our house from here." They gazed out of the dusty window. "There's nothing really here, is there?" as the boys opened each cupboard and looked up chimneys. "Let's go back down."

So they hurtled down the wooden stairs, making a loud noise.

"Needs a few mod cons, doesn't it?" remarked Ellie. "But we can't find anything to fit this key. I'm cold now, let's go shall we?" and Heather agreed. They closed the door and the girls did the locking up.

"What shall we do now?" they asked each other. Eddie and Patrick knew where they wanted to go… down the steps to the old lighthouse.

"Hang on, what if the key fits the lighthouse door?" asked Eddie. "It's possible isn't it? Let's get it and try, shall we?" He looked to Heather for a decision.

"It's okay by me," she said slowly, realising that she would not be able to get down to the lighthouse.

Eddie and Patrick ran back for the key and Ellie and Heather wheeled the short distance to where the lighthouse stood, its pretty top visible above the road.

"We'll think of a way to get you down there don't worry. Maybe the key won't even fit," said sensible Ellie to her new friend. The boys returned waving the key.

"Got it!" They grinned like a pair of Cheshire cats. Eddie leapt down the twisting steps with its iron handrail and then stopped. He looked back.

"What about Heather? Let me see first if the key fits and then we'll have a think, okay?"

Ellie and Heather rolled their eyes at each other. Patrick stood by, saying nothing. He didn't want her to be left out.

Eddie reappeared, face alight.

"Opened first time! Come on! Ellie, you bring Heather's cushions. Patrick, you and I will give her a fireman's lift. Okay Heather?" His enthusiasm was infectious.

"Okay" was her curt reply, as she unbuckled her waist strap. With very little fuss the boys followed Ellie, carefully carrying Heather into the small circular entrance and placing her on her cushion on one of the stone ledges.

"That doorway opposite goes down to into the cellar and these stairs go up to the lighthouse itself," Eddie told her.

"How do you know?" Heather was puzzled. "If you haven't been here before?"

"Oh, but we have!" the boys told her triumphantly.

"Don't be silly!" Heather looked at Ellie for back-up, but she was nodding.

"Tell me! Tell me!" Heather pleaded. "How can you have been here before? It's not possible."

"Oh yes it is," laughed Eddie and Patrick, "we discovered a tunnel from Warfleet that goes right under the river and comes out here! It's down there." They both pointed to a large oak closed door. Heather stared hard at it. It was unbelievable that through it lay a hidden tunnel. She thought for a moment in silence.

"But why would anyone dig a tunnel through there? What could it possibly be for?"

Patrick answered first.

"They used the lime kiln to dig a trial seam for tin ore we think.We found a large black cable running off a smaller tunnel, which could be for a telephone cable. There are candle holders, so somebody long ago used to creep across the river to the lighthouse. Don't you think it's very exciting?"

"Yes, but there is definitely a mystery here. Something must connect it all together."

"Well now we've found the key we can use the tunnel.It actually comes out in Patrick's garden."

Heather shook her head in disbelief.

"Maybe it was two families that connected the two places."
She glanced at Ellie who gave her the slightest shake of her head.
Heather took the hint and looked at her watch. "I really ought to
be setting off for home."

Eddie and Patrick carried her up to the wheelchair.

Locking the door they asked, "Can we keep the key?"

"If you take good care of it. I won't tell Dad yet."

They were all thrilled with the outcome of their afternoon,
ready to piece together the mystery. Whoever had lived in the
cottage must have known about the tunnel. And what was the
story of the poor woman who had given her child away?

PART TWO

Chapter Nineteen
The birth of Cornelius

As dawn broke in the eastern sky on a dull, cold morning in January, as owls hooted and seagulls called across the blue-grey sea, Seraphim was startled from her drowsy endless sitting by a strange noise. She could hear a faint tapping from beneath her; she shifted her large body on her clumsy legs – yes, there it was again, tap, tap, tapping coming from the warm egg. The wind blew cruelly from an easterly direction and whistled as it skimmed over the Creek and up the valley beyond.

"Sargasso! Sargasso! Wake up!" the alarmed gull cawed to her sleeping mate. At once he was at her side to examine the large egg. They heard a tiny voice calling,

"Mother, Mother, let me out!" Each bird looked at the other, terrified.

"It's our child calling!" They were both very frightened, and then the voice came again.

"Mother! Mother!" accompanied by more insistent tapping. Completely unsure of what to do next, both birds kept very still. There was a splashing sound and then, clambering up the steps, glistening with water, Ptolemy appeared; the large, ungainly, turtle had returned.

"I have heard the voice of my little master calling. Open the shell, Seraphim, do not be afraid. This is a day of celebration. Your son will be with us soon. Help him."

Obediently Seraphim pecked the shell and many cracks appeared in it. Sargasso helped to remove the pieces as the egg shattered into sections. Gradually the little creature inside unfurled its limbs and began to emerge from the shell.

"This is your son, Cornelius," announced Ptolemy proudly. "The Spirit of the Sea has sent him to you as a special gift. He is to cross the boundaries of all the kingdoms and join us together. He is a new species. Welcome him and be proud."

The three watched as the small damp thing came to life. It yawned and stretched its arms. It shook its head and the wet curls glistened. It crawled out of the cradle of the remaining shell and into the soft moss and downy feathers Seraphim had gathered long ago.

Looking proudly at this new life, the turtle and the gull parents examined their offspring curiously. He was almost a miniature human child with curly hair and blue-green eyes, just the colour of the Creek water on a dull day. Folded neatly behind his feathered back were grey soft downy wings; he seemed to be wearing long shorts made of scaly fish skin, shiny and smooth; his feet were encased in leather that was seamlessly joined to his legs. As Sargasso looked closely, he could see his feet were those of a mallard duck, with webs of skin between the toes.

"He's not quite human," whispered Seraphim to Sargasso.

"No, but he's not quite a bird either," replied her husband.

"No," added Ptolemy, "he encompasses all things," as he looked at the infant's scaly lower body which resembled his own. The child's curls dried quickly in the breeze to a golden shine.

"I'm cold, Mother," he called to Seraphim in his tiny voice, "and I'm hungry too."

The small herring gull, full of motherly pride and devotion, wrapped him in the sea blanket and snuggled up to the tiny creature. Ptolemy beckoned to Sargasso.

"Come, we will fetch food for him. You and I will take turns to feed him."

So the two creatures dived under the water to gather a special ferny seaweed that grew in the deep and never reached the shore. When they returned with the unusual sea plant they carefully fed it in morsels to the hungry child. Seraphim looked constantly at his beautiful face, with its small nose and tiny lips, his pretty ears and long eyelashes. His golden curls framed the cherubic face. He yawned and soon fell asleep.

"Isn't he beautiful?" she asked the watching pair, as he slept on and on, his feathered chest rising and falling as he breathed.

"Can he swim? Does he need clothes? Can he walk? How will we look after him?" Suddenly Sargasso was filled with doubts: this was not a simple gull chick, or a fish, or a child. What were they going to do with him? They began to panic.

"Hush, hush, my friend," soothed Ptolemy, "that is why I am here to provide advice and guardianship. You, his parents, will provide love and care. Together we will succeed. Today you must prepare yourself for some visitors. The news will soon spread of his arrival."

Sargasso and Seraphim were rather taken aback at this news. Visitors? But who? The only person Sargasso wanted to show his precious child to was Eddie. *Won't he be amazed?* he thought to himself, *and won't Ellie adore him?* He was amused at the prospect.

That winter's day was cold and uninviting. The sun didn't shine or the clouds part to break the grey gloom and a damp mist held fast in the chilly still air. The bird boy slept on; the two gulls and Ptolemy became accustomed to his face and the rest of his strange little body. Dusk fell early that afternoon on the cold lonely quayside.

Just as the daylight dimmed and an early darkness began to cast its cloak over the world, a faint noise could be heard in the distance – a soft high-pitched chiming noise like a thousand tiny bells ringing far, far, away. Sargasso raised his head and listened. He knew what it was and smiled. The silver spiralled shell he wore around his neck began to make a humming noise and then a whispered voice spoke to him.

"Sargasso, Seraphim, it is I, the Spirit of the Sea. I am travelling across the oceans to see your child. Wait up for me, I shall be with you this night, wait for me." And the voice faded away.

"Will we hear the silver tinkling shoals, my dear?" asked Seraphim. "Are these the visitors that wish to see our child?"

"Yes, they and others, Seraphim. The Spirit of the Sea is journeying across the world tonight. Try not to be afraid," he calmed her. Ptolemy nodded at them both and slipped into the water with a splash. He went to fetch food for their guests. Out into the deepest waters of the bay he swam to collect the blue-grey strands of the royal ferny weed that only grew in dark sea caves. He returned with a large bunch filling his wrinkled mouth, shaking the sea water from it as he clambered up the steps.

The darkness was broken suddenly by a bright light above them: a lantern held on a long stick waved in the wind. Then an elfin child appeared sitting on the branch of tree, dressed in leaves, smiling.

"Don't be afraid, it is I, Lord Sunna, Spirit of the Woodland. I have come to light the path of the new child and to welcome him." He lowered his lantern and slid down the knotty branch of the bay tree. The lantern was made of fine twisted honeysuckle with twenty glow worms packed inside.

"This is my gift to him," he smiled. "Welcome to the Woodland kingdom. We are your closest neighbours. I invite you to visit our leafy paths and refresh yourself at our crystal streams."

He bowed and laid his lantern on the cold ground where a circle of light sprang around them all. The bird child laughed at the pretty light and the elfin spirit sat cross-legged a short distance from them.

"He is rather small to be so great," remarked Seraphim to Sargasso, who merely nodded wisely.

Soon more splashing was heard at the foot of the steps and Ptolemy lumbered over to see who it was. There in the dark water were two dolphins – Doryana and Diadem, grey and shiny, their noses peeping out over the granite steps.

"Welcome little master, and greetings Sargasso, old friend. You and your wife are well deserving of the honour of this child. We have brought presents," they clicked.

Ptolemy beckoned to the gull parents protecting their son and hesitantly they revealed him in his cosy nest.

"Let me see my new friends," said the child in his tiny voice, and he sat up and began to climb over the driftwood and crawl to the steps. Sargasso and Seraphim were so alarmed they tried to stop him but the old turtle held them back.

"Leave him, he will come to no harm." Reluctantly they let him go. The small child crawled to the very brink of the steps, where he sat with his tiny legs and webbed feet dangling over the edge.

The dolphins edged closer, each with something in their mouths and as the boy held out his hands they slithered up the steep steps and in turn laid a small item in his hands. Ptolemy then bowed and took the presents from the boy who patted each dolphin on the nose, delighted with them. They clicked furiously together and the child laughed and chuckled.

"Thank you, thank you," he said.

"He understands what they are saying!" gasped an amazed Seraphim.

Sargasso, who had been granted the power of all-transcending language by the Spirit of the Sea, also understood.

"We have travelled to the far North of the world to bring you a lodestone gem. It will guide you. Then we swam to the Southern Ocean for black pearls and coral. This is our gift to you, little master," he heard them say.

Their smooth grey coats shone in the circle of light provided by the obliging glowworms. Ptolemy placed the black and glittering gem around the child's neck, held with a tiny thread of black pearls and a coral clasp.

"Let us watch together and wait for our lord, the Spirit of the Sea." And everyone listened carefully, as in the distance again came the faintest bell-like rings on the wind. They sat quietly as the small child climbed back into his nest and promptly fell asleep.

Gradually the moon rose above them, shining down on the glinting moving water as the level of the river began to slowly rise and fill and small wavelets disturbed the surface.

"He is coming, it will be soon," nodded Ptolemy with satisfaction, and he beckoned them to the edge of the old quayside to wait, all except the sleeping child. The waves grew larger: some had white crests, gently petering out with a hiss on the remaining shingle of the tiny beach. The ringing became louder and louder until at last the silver tinkling shoals burst out of the water in front of them in a shimmering sparkling cloud of small fishes. They had reached the end of their journey and flung themselves over and over in the now turbulent sea, full of hundreds of silver-scaled glinting bodies. It was a spectacular sight, caught in the lustrous light of the moon.

Next, four white horses reared up on the crest of an incoming wave, and were immediately reined in by their master, his white curled locks dripping seawater and his beard flowing and foaming beneath the white water. He wore a circlet of three silver fish, head to tail, curved around his head. The horses ceased prancing, snorted and then fell silent as the water gradually stopped frothing and lapped darkly around the Creek, now as full as the highest of tides.

The tall figure in his white robes stepped from behind the horses onto the stone quay and held out his hands in a gesture of friendship. He patted the two dolphins, who clicked and nuzzled his hands, and he smiled and nodded to Ptolemy and the seagulls. He bowed in the direction of the Spirit of the Woodland.

"He is come at last, this child of the Sea, the Earth and the Sky. Let me see him. Bring him to me."

Obediently Seraphim took the tiny child in her beak and presented him to the smiling Lord of the Sea.

"Come Lord Sunna, Spirit of the Woodland, we will name and bless him together." The elfin creature obeyed and stood beside the tall figure. The boy awoke at once as the great man cradled him in his arms and stared into the lovely face of the child with his greeny-blue eyes and golden curls. He stroked the small downy wings tightly folded and saw the fish-skin scales of his lower body. He felt the small webbed feet, supple and soft in his fingers.

"Welcome, Cornelius" he whispered, and passed him to the Lord Sunna, who put his hand into his pocket and removed a handful of sand which he sprinkled over the boy. As it touched him the minute particles turned into tiny specks of light and illuminated his whole body. Taking him back, the Spirit of the Sea held the child in his sea blanket up above his head, offering him up to the bright pale light of the moon. The sea sparkles glowed brightly. Taking off the fish circlet from his head he placed it on the boy's curls. Immediately the fish closed together to fit the small head.

"This is my gift to you. These silver fish are a sign of friendship, one each for the Earth, the Sea and the Sky: Tellus, Caelum and Altum Mare. They will never leave you. Each one is responsible for you in this world so that you will learn to swim, walk and fly." He placed his finger on each fish and lit it up for a second.

"Thank you," whispered the boy, who was then handed back to the waiting Seraphim. She returned him to the nest and sat with him as he snuggled down into her warm feathers, yawning.

"Let us eat now," directed Ptolemy, and the strange gathering sat together and ate the royal ferny weed, which had originated on the western shores of Killarney. The elfin Lord Sunna uncorked a small wooden cask he had brought, with the dew of summer mornings and the frosty rime of winter's chill added to it. They ate and drank under the strength of the largest moon ever seen and the power of its light entered the sleeping creature and he grew even as he slept.

"I shall return next year on the Moon of Winds to visit Cornelius," said the Spirit of the Sea. He bowed to Lord Sunna and snapped his fingers. At once the horses rose up and were ready:

"Come Neptune, Triton, Aquarius and Aquamarine. Goodbye, my friends. Watch over the boy who is part of us all, for he is our future. Up! Up!" he called and the horses reared and snorted and kicked out across the water. Immediately the waves began to undulate and soon white-crested tops carried the four horses and their majestic master away over the sea, followed by the dolphins.

Lord Sunna yawned and said, "Goodnight Seafarers, goodnight little Cornelius." And he went over to touch one of the silver fish on the child's head. "Tellus will guide him through the ways of the Woodland. He shall be my messenger. Goodbye." Then he skittered off up a branch and disappeared into the dark trees.

Only Ptolemy, Sargasso, and Seraphim were left. Cornelius slept in his sea blanket which had been blessed by the sea and the sky under the moon so long ago. It had been a very exciting and eventful night and they were all tired and ready to go to sleep. The two birds huddled together in the lime kiln with their precious charge and Ptolemy slept at the foot of the steps on the mud and shingle of the outgoing tide. The moon meanwhile continued its journey across the sky, leaving a fraction of its power behind, embedded in the bones of the tiny creature who had been offered that night light, guidance and friendship.

Chapter Twenty
The death of the buzzard, and worrying developments in the woodland

Far away on the highest tor on Dartmoor, the buzzard, his wife and two remaining sons took refuge in a large, bleached tree. This tree was a landmark, with its strange twisted branches that would never see buds or leaves again. The decline of the buzzard was rather shocking: from a proud, arrogant leader with gimlet eyes and a fine polished beak he had diminished in stature to a shabby, hunched figure, tired and haggard. Without the trappings of royalty around them, the young princes, E'en and Tween, had to fend for themselves. They learnt how to hunt and chase, to stalk and kill. Their blood ran high and they tasted true freedom, the freedom of wide, open spaces, without boundaries or fences. Time ran by unchecked without restraints or curfews; they shed the shackles of parental control, now their father was too old and their mother too weak. They were forced to make choices and decisions about themselves, and to face the consequences of their own actions. There was nobody else to blame.

Soaring above the glorious landscape, the two brothers grew up as nature had intended. The past diminished and both entered a new phase of self-confidence and belief. Duty, responsibility and royal codes of behaviour seemed very distant now. Freedom was good, the taste of it intoxicating. In a few short weeks these young princes were transformed and truly travelled the road to maturity.

One evening, having hunted all day and eaten the raw flesh of their victims, they returned happy and invigorated to the stricken elm tree to the sad news of their father's death. Their mother wept tears of despair and frustration.

"What will I do now?" she sobbed. "What is to become of me?" Her sons comforted her as best they could.

"One day, Mother you will return to the Woodland with us. One day," E'en promised.

"We shall perform the final ceremony for Father," promised Tween.

At dawn the next day, each carrying one wing of their dead father, the two buzzards flew ponderously to the highest tor on the moorland and dropped his body from a great height onto the jagged granite teeth below. It shattered into tiny pieces of blood, bone and feathers.

"Let the Sun parch him, and the Rain carry him, and the Earth receive him," they chanted together proudly, and it was done. The royal Lord of the Woodland had returned to the elements of Nature.

"Now, brother, we must decide who will succeed him."

"It is the eldest son who takes the throne, is it not?"

"As you wish."

"It is decided then." And their conversation was at an end.

E'en did not want to go back and resume the reins of office, not yet. That was in the future. Both the birds were content to idle their days away in the glorious freedom of the moorland for just a little longer. Their mother, who was obliged to stay with them, cared little as she mourned the loss of her husband. She was now left to the mercy of her three sons.

***

Down in the Lower Woodland, there was a feeling of unrest. During the dark and cold days of the New Year many more jackdaws appeared, lured by the charm and fast talking of Jodie and Jack B Quick. Their offers of plentiful food, good nesting sites in the disused watermill and brash boasts of waking up the sleepy valley, proved attractive to wandering groups of birds. Soon they were everywhere with their black eyes and bold manners. They chased the voles and their children, fought the smaller birds on the bird tables, squawked at each other's jokes, and took over the nearby trees to laze around in arrogant gangs jeering and mocking anyone passing by. It was all quite terrifying for the little ground dwellers of the Woodland, who had survived the flood and the fire only to be bullied and terrified by these invading hoards.

Jack and Jodie grew bold and began to explore the upper regions. They discovered the empty palace at the Citadel and had already located the Great Ash Tree where Oliphant now dwelt alone.

"It'll be a pushover!" laughed Jodie, "There's only him, that pathetic small white owl. He's in charge now. He's a joke, eh Bro?"

"Some fight he'll put up!" laughed Jack. "We'll be up there in no time, living in the lap of luxury. Then it'll be different, you watch! They won't know what's hit them."

They plotted and planned together, Oliphant blissfully unaware of the impending danger. Jodie had discovered the buzzard's store of dewdrop wine quite by accident as he sat in the branches of the Citadel one day looking out over the blue sea. He had heard a loud popping noise below him and hopping down to investigate, opened a small doorway in the trunk. There inside were casks of wine neatly labelled and stacked. One of the bottles had burst its cork and the contents were seeping gently out.

I can't waste that! he told himself, and filled his beak to taste it.

My, that's good. And he struggled to straighten it up to stop the leak. "I can feel a party coming on," he said gleefully, and hurried back to tell his brother.

Jack was delighted. "Good idea, I'll tell the gang it's party time. Tonight? No point in wasting time, shall we say Starshine?" and off he went to start the buzz around his Woodland cronies. Some of them were rather intrigued by Jack B Quick, with his cheeky ways and persuasive charms. He and his brother had tried to win over the quieter birds and bring them into their ever-increasing circle, and so it was that late that night, under a black star-studded sky, the birds gathered at the Citadel, not very far away from the Great Ash Tree, just along the path.

The merriment began. The dewdrop wine was consumed in large quantities by everyone. Jackdaws and rooks, blackbirds and small brown sparrows, woodpeckers and a crowd of long-tailed tits turned up, many out of sheer curiosity.

Great lumps of bread and cake filched from bird tables all around the area seemed in plentiful supply. Shrieks of raucous laughter echoed around as Jack and Jodie told their favourite jokes and encouraged their friends to party.

The youngest woodpecker, Wolfgang, was told to start drumming out an insistent beat on a nearby tree and the three Nightingale sisters soon began clapping and dancing to the rhythm. Everyone joined in shaking feathers and stamping feet, heads gyrating to the irresistible beat until some sank to the ground exhausted and fell asleep while others became even wilder, encouraged by Jack and Jodie.

A few turned sheepishly away and slid off home before they could be noticed. Once the dewdrop wine was finished, Jack demanded more.

"Open another one, shall we?" he shouted to his brother.

"Why not?" and soon another cask was smashed open with a huge knotty branch.

"All this could be ours!" smiled Jack. "Somebody's got to shake this place up a bit. It's dead round here, deadly dull and boring."

He strolled over to the Nightingale sisters, Nora, Nancy and Nina, who were sitting on a convenient log. Jack's eyes lit up at the sight of the three lovely sisters, preening their feathers and fluffing themselves out daintily.

Jack was wild and handsome with a dark, cruel streak in him. He wanted to show off to the girls.

"Come on, you three beauties." He strutted up to them, eyeing Nina as the prettiest. "We're going to have some fun now, coming to join us?" he invited them with a smile. The three birds twittered to one another, giggling.

"What did you have in mind?" asked Nina coyly.

"We're going inside to finish the party," bragged Jack. "You three deserve a palace and that is what you're getting." Jack continued with his daring plan, his arrogance driving him on as he tried to impress Nina.

"Fancy a look up here?" he pointed to the doorway of the Citadel, beckoning to the remaining birds, still enjoying themselves.

"Why not, we're up for it!" shouted a pair of rough jays, cackling,

"And count us in will you?" added ten other rooks who always did everything he told them.

"Do you think we should?" questioned Wolfgang Woodpecker nervously. His parents had emigrated from the Black Forest many years ago and always behaved very correctly.

"Hell, yes!" shouted Jodie. "It's just rotting away with no one in it. If that white owl hasn't got the guts to take it over for himself, why shouldn't we?"

There were yells of agreement as many of the birds, unused to drinking such large quantities of the precious dewdrop wine, lost their minds and stopped thinking for themselves. Jack had them at his mercy now. He felt elated, and the burning desire to conquer the Citadel was fuelled.

"Let's do it!" he shrieked, and soon many helpers were smashing the lock until the door swung drunkenly open and hung on its hinges.

"Go, go, go!" urged Jodie. The angry band squeezed through and rampaged up the polished pine spiral staircase, jeering and shouting.

"This isn't a good idea," whispered Nina, Nancy, and Nora to each other. "Let's go, come on, there's going to be trouble here. Imagine what Dad will say?" They looked in horror at the wine-crazed crowd surging forward, and quietly tiptoed away.

By the time Jack noticed they had disappeared it was far too late: the takeover bid that he had orchestrated to impress the sisters was already in full swing.

Upstairs, things went from bad to worse as each stateroom was occupied and acts of wanton violence were wreaked on the undefended palace. Eventually most of the intruders fell asleep in unlikely places and Jack and Jodie, finding the buzzards' state bedroom, tucked themselves up for the night beneath the royal monogrammed quilt.

"We've done it, bro," whispered Jack to his younger brother but he received no answer; only the rhythmical snoring of his exhausted bedfellow replied. Smiling, Jack closed his eyes in the palace he had coveted for many months.

"So easy," he breathed to himself, as he fell asleep, contented.

Chapter Twenty-one
Oliphant takes control

The next morning the band of squirrels, who had been frightened out of their wits by the noise the previous night, ran to the Great Ash Tree and hurtled up to the large main door, knocking wildly until Oliphant sleepily opened it.

"Mr Oliphant ! Mr Oliphant! You've got to help us!" cried out the tiny squirrel voices as they tumbled over each other into the opulent hallway. Oliphant was overwhelmed by their numbers.

"What's happened?" he asked, bewildered.

"They've come! They've come! Those black-feathered villains! Those dastardly interlopers have taken over the Citadel, what shall we do?"

Oliphant was astonished at the news. Being a Dark Dweller he had been out hunting far away all night and consequently had heard nothing. He was outraged, and could feel his anger warming up his feathers at the thought of it. He seethed in fury and his eyes became narrow and piercing. He blinked several times.

"This cannot be allowed to happen. The Citadel is for our ruler, the Lord of the Woodland. We must drive them out..." he told the anxious squirrels, "...but we must not be hasty, we need to think and devise a good plan, one that will work. Give me a little time to think this over. Don't worry, they shall not get the better of us. Come back to me tomorrow at twilight and I will have news for you. Go now. They shall have their day. Tomorrow will be ours, my friends."

He spoke with sincerity and conviction and the little creatures trusted him. Suddenly he seemed to be the voice they were looking for to calm their fears.

"Until tomorrow then," whispered the leader of the squirrels, reassured at last.

"Yes, yes, go now. Try to avoid the Citadel, keep to the Lower Woodland," advised Oliphant, smiling at them as he quietly closed the door.

At once the smile left his face and the instincts of a hunter took over.

"You have made a great mistake, Jack B Quick. For now I shall have no mercy. I would like nothing better than to tear you to shreds! You and your stupid brother and the rest of your followers. Enjoy your one day of false pride for it shall be your last," he vowed cruelly, as his gentle heart turned to stone to protect the Woodland and its quiet creatures.

He gathered his key and went down the spiral staircase; down, down, even deeper, to the entrance of the underground Root Room housed beneath the Great Ash Tree. It was here that events of the Woodland were recorded, gathered in from the tips of every branch, from where the sap ran down into great barrels to be stored.

Oliphant moved the heavy table with the wide silver dish on it to just below a large barrel. He positioned the tap above the dish and slowly turned it on. The date flicked by above him in a narrow viewing slot. It was yesterday's date.

Slowly the striped syrup of many colours flowed onto the silver surface and spread out. Pictures began to appear as he viewed the extraordinary happenings of the previous day. Fortunately Jack and Jodie knew nothing of its existence and had only discovered the dewdrop wine by accident. Was it only a matter of time before they attacked the Great Ash Tree and he himself would be ousted? Oliphant felt sure it was. Then the Root Room would be invaded and the private life of the Woodland laid open for all to see. No, this could not be allowed to happen.

The small white owl watched the swaggering antics of the two bullies and their followers with a heavy heart. However, his sadness was gradually replaced with courage, and a fierce intention overwhelmed him, until he believed himself to be invincible. He would gather a strong band of Woodland folk around himself and inspire them to follow him. They would defeat the raggle-taggle invading jackdaws who dared to usurp this woodland throne.

His second thought was to go to the Cornucopia Tree for help and guidance from the pigeons he had drawn such strength from. Then he remembered their wise words just before he had taken office, that night would be his strength and darkness his greatest helper. He did not know he had been blessed by the hand of Lord Sunna, Spirit of the Earth that night, as he lay sleeping at the Cornucopia Tree, and as he sat quietly in the gurgling noise of the underground distillery, a plan began to unravel itself from the tangle of thoughts in his head. Every nut and bolt had to be in place before he began. In the meantime he had to defend the Great Ash Tree.

He made a list of his soldiers in this gallant fight. Some he would have to wake from their winter slumbers; some might refuse him altogether; many would be afraid for themselves and their children. The plan had to be perfect, watertight from every angle, or none would join him. It would take time. He must have peace and rest to complete his daring strategy. He would sleep now.

He lay down in the large circular bed with its ornate carvings and its heavy embroidered coverlets. His head touched the plump feather pillows and he slept for many hours. Dancing dreams filled his thoughts, turbulent and vivid. He saw dark creeping figures and ghostly white faces; he heard screams and squawks, shouts and pleas for help; there was blood running down the trees and feathers floating in the wind. He tossed and turned, not wishing to see any more, but suddenly he glimpsed the sun breaking through, heard the morning song of the birds and far away he could make out a figure standing on the top of the Citadel surrounded in bright light and smiling; everything was peaceful and the chaos seemed to be at an end.

He drifted on into a deep and untroubled sleep. Thoughts and ideas slotted into an ordered plan, and he woke several hours later to the hum of an early bumble bee and a ladybird softly making its way across the window pane. He opened his eyes and knew what he had to do. The way forward was clear.

Leonora the ladybird spoke to him. "Good morning, Oliphant, we have travelled from Tresco to join you as the weather is unusually inclement. We felt great longing for the wooded shelter of Gallants Bower. I hope we are not too early," she apologised, "it is not yet quite spring."

"Too early? No indeed, it is extremely fortunate you are here. I might just have a little favour to ask of you and your scarlet brigade."

Boris, buzzing outside the window, saw Leonora and he too entered the bedroom to greet both his old friends.

"Ah, Boris, just the person I need," smiled Oliphant with satisfaction. "I think you had better wake up your musical band. I might have an early performance for you. Go and tune them up as soon as you can."

Boris and his brothers liked nothing better than buzzing harmoniously all day. They were hoping to find a new and glamorous queen to impress and now Oliphant had an early engagement for them! He buzzed off busily to alert his brothers.

The small white owl, filled with purposefulness, knew he needed the help of Faithful Freddie, his friend and mentor. Together they would lead their followers to victory. He sent a long-tailed tit down to fetch him. These were always hanging around the latest incident, gossiping, and they were full of the occupation of the Citadel by Jack, Jodie and their cronies. Freddie came at once and by the time he arrived he had been told the news and was of course rather horrified.

"What a thing to happen!" he greeted his friend, fussing and fluffing out his feathers.

Oliphant dismissed the excited long-tailed tit who was hoping for snippets of news, but the door was firmly closed.

"I've thought of a plan, Freddie, and need your help." This was not a request, this was an order.

"Of course, Oliphant. I will support you in any way I can," agreed Freddie at once.

"Good. We need the whole Woodland to rally round this time in order to get rid of these fiends, these usurpers, once and for all," insisted the owl in a deadly cold voice, and Freddie shivered. He wouldn't want to be on the wrong side of Oliphant now. What a change there had been in this timid white owl since he had taken up the challenge of ruling the Woodland as its deputy!

"Come and look at the Mists of Time and see for yourself." Together, down in the Root Room the robin and the owl re-ran the incredible events that had led to the occupation of the Citadel.

"The cheek of it!" was all Freddie could say, the evidence enough to make clear to him the gravity of the situation.

"So what is your plan?" the robin inquired.

"First of all we must block off all their escape routes, and that is the most difficult part, because they can simply fly away! So I have enlisted the help of Boris and Leonora. Luckily the weather on Tresco is very cold so they have all returned several weeks early. This could prove to be very advantageous," Oliphant smiled.

Freddie nodded as his friend continued gravely.

"The squirrels are most abundant in numbers and probably the bravest. They shall be armed with prickly conkers and catapults. When they run out we shall re-arm them with burdock burrs, and that's where you come in. I want you to enlist the help of the voles and the dormice to collect some."

"What?" came the horrified voice of Freddie.

"Yes, I'm afraid we are going to have to wake them up. Everyone must help to defeat these foes so soundly that they will never come back."

"Yes, Oliphant," agreed Freddie. "I see."

"Next, Maurice and Maudie. We need them to dig plenty of molehills around the Citadel and the Great Ash Tree to give cover to the ground dwellers. Can you arrange that?"

141

"I'll try."

"The most delicate negotiations are yet to come and for this, Freddie, I need your advice."

Freddie nodded nervously, feathers twitching.

"I want to use Nina Nightingale as a decoy. Jack is crazy about her but we need to try and persuade Norman to let Nina help us. He is very strict with his three lovely daughters and I'm not sure if he even knows they came to the party at the Citadel. How do you think we should tackle this tricky problem?"

Freddie sat silent for a while. It was going to be difficult. In fact he was rather shocked by the suggestion.

"You see we must get all of them out of the Citadel somehow. I thought Nina might be the answer but... maybe I'm wrong," said Oliphant. He stared out of the window waiting for his friend to reply.

Freddie took a long time to deliberate and at last he was ready to speak.

"I feel sure that Norman will not give his permission if he feels Nina will be in any sort of danger. Perhaps this is the best way to tackle it: enlist the help of the whole family. Arrange a picnic to be held at the foot of the Great Ash Tree. Offer a cask of the Mists of Time to which we have added an elixir from our doctors. Those fiends will go anywhere for a good time. We've just seen that very clearly. What do you think?"

Oliphant mulled this over, trying to visualise this plan. It was a good one, one he would never have thought of.

"Well done, Freddie, I think it will work. Norman can keep an eye on all his girls but we must offer them shelter here to avoid any..., well, unpleasant things that the girls might see. Excellent, it is a good and sensible idea." Freddie was thrilled.

"Now can you set the other tasks in motion and I will go and see the Nightingales and the Underconstumbles? We also need a supply of nectar for Boris and his friends."

The two birds parted company, each with a lot to accomplish and much persuading to do to enlist the support of the

Woodlanders. Would these measures prove to be too unpopular with the small woodland folk? Was waking some of them from hibernation just a step too far? Was it madness to try to defeat the jackdaws? Only time would tell.

Chapter Twenty-two
Abel is interviewed by the police

The police car drew up outside the white cottage just over the bridge at Old Mill Creek. It was late afternoon, and Detective Sergeant Tim McDonald had already checked that Abel was not at St Thomas's Church at Kingswear. The cottage was very old indeed, tidy and well maintained. The large vegetable patch stretching beyond was a gardening masterpiece – neat, freshly dug and organised with rows of indeterminable green things. A great deal of time and care was lavished on this soil.

He approached the low black door and knocked. He waited, hearing activity from within, and soon a wrinkled face set with two brilliant blue eyes appeared around the slowly opening door.

"Yes? What would you be wanting?" the voice enquired as gradually the door opened. A small wiry man belonging to the startling blue eyes was revealed.

"Good evening sir, does Abel King live here? I'd like a quick word with him if that's alright?" asked the policeman politely.

"Oh would you, well you'd better come in then, he's having a bath."

Tim McDonald stepped inside the low doorway, careful not to bang his head, and followed the man into a small sitting room. He was shown to a seat.

"I'll tell him you're here then. I'm Ezekiel King, his father. In trouble is he?" questioned the grinning brown face and twinkling eyes.

"No sir, just following a line of inquiry." He was left alone to survey the room. The walls were stained with pipe smoke which clung in the air and several old oil paintings also had a nicotine coating. A woodburning stove glowed brightly and a neat pile of logs lay in the stone hearth. Slightly worn cottage furniture was clean and well used and a jam jar with snowdrops sat on top of a small gateleg table, a surprising touch in the absence of any wife appearing. A colourful rag rug lay on the floor, reminding Tim McDonald of his grandmother's scullery many years ago. All seemed tidy and orderly.

He heard voices upstairs and several doors banging. Then the old man appeared again.

"He's not pleased but he'll be down directly," nodded the brown face, which reminded Tim of an otter without the whiskers.

"Tea?"

Hardly daring to refuse, the policeman nodded. He sat back into the comfortable chair and for the first time that day relaxed, as the large clock standing in the corner ticked the minutes of life sombrely away. Abel, upstairs, dressing in his clean clothes, was thinking fast, his mind racing. He'd have to watch what he said. Taking a deep breath in front of the mirror, he brushed his thinning hair and laid his mother's silver-backed brush back where it belonged. He was ready.

The tea and Abel arrived at the same time just as Ezekiel had planned. He didn't know what was going on but he'd try and give his son a fighting chance.

"Well sir, just a few questions if you don't mind," began Sgt McDonald, sipping the strong brown tea in the willow-pattern cup.

"We're investigating a diamond robbery over at Kingswear at Woodend Manor Farm, and I'm led to believe that you are acquainted with one William Lane. Do you know this lad, sir?" He looked directly at Abel, waiting.

"Oh yes, I do, his parents run the post office next to the church."

"And what is your connection with Will Lane, sir?" pushed Tim, his pen and notebook now brought into action.

"Umm, very little really. I know he works at the farm for the Frasers."

Steady lad, don't give too much away! thought Ezekiel, his teeth gritted as Tim McDonald pounced on the information.

"You know his employers then?"

"Only by sight, they attend St Thomas of Canterbury Church in Kingswear when they're here."

"So as the verger you're at the church on a Sunday?"

"Yes, I'm always on duty when there's a service. Open up, put on the heating, I gives out the hymnbooks at the door so I sees everyone who comes in," he said proudly. *And a toffee-nosed bunch they are too,*" he thought to himself.

"So you saw Mr and Mrs Fraser on Christmas morning, then?"

"Yes, sir. I opened the two doors up for that poor little maid to get her wheelchair through. Still, they've got everything money can buy to make life easy for her," he added with a hint of bitterness.

Be careful Abel, why don't you shut up a bit! worried his father. "A top up of tea, Sergeant?" interrupted Ezekiel desperately, lifting the old brown teapot towards the policeman. There was a pause as the cups were refilled. The eyes of the father and son met and Ezekiel gave a wary frown.

"Have you ever been to Woodend Farm?" A direct dart was now fired. Abel paused to think, playing for time to compose his answer, knowing he had already given himself a watertight alibi for Christmas morning. Ezekiel held his breath and curled his toes in his leather slippers.

"Yes, sir."

"How many times?"

"Just the once."

"And when was this?"

"Oh, back along a bit now. Just after Will passed his driving test. He had to take the horse to Cotterbury Forge to get a shoe and needed a bit of help with the trailer."

"Do you drive?"

"No, I went to help him load up Ginny and hitch up the horsebox onto the Land Rover. It were a bit tricky for 'im."

"Did you go into the house at any time?"

"No, sir." Abel looked up into the policeman's face. This was the truth.

"How long were you at the farm?"

"Oh, 'bout an hour I suppose."

"And did you go with Will to the blacksmith's?"

"Yes sir, I did. The lad couldn't manage by himself, that Ginny can be a handful I can tell you."

"What happened when you came back?"

"We unhitched the horsebox and took her up to the stable, then I left him when it were all sorted."

"Did you get paid for this work, helping Will? Surely you wouldn't do it for nothing? Or maybe you would, a churchgoer like you?" Tim McDonald threw the challenge down.

"I didn't get no money sir, it don't bother me, just gave the lad a hand and had a trip out into the country, see? But he's a good lad and he gets me some baccy now an' again, for me dad."

"Did he give you some this time?"

"Yes sir, I think he did." Abel nodded.

"Have you ever helped Will to do any other tasks around the place?" Tim McDonald leaned forward and got closer to Abel. Something about his manner alerted Ezekiel and he automatically reached for his pipe and leather pouch at the mention of baccy and began to fill his pipe, waiting for his son to answer.

Abel stared out of the window, the sun's rays casting a beam through it into the room, catching dust in its light, suddenly making the rest of the cottage seem dark.

"I went with the lad to fetch the Christmas trees from over Marldon way. They were a bit heavy for him. We got one for the church and two for the farm."

"Did you go inside the house when you helped Will? Did you, say, help him carry anything inside?"

Abel had to answer truthfully because three other people had been there when he and Will lifted the 16ft tree into the hallway.

"Hardly inside, sir, just into the hallway, 'twas a big un, 16 feet if I remembers right."

147

"Which day was that, Abel? Can you remember the time?" Abel could because it was long past his supper time when he got home and he was not pleased. That young maid had asked Will to help her decorate the tree, put all the high baubles and trinkets on it, and he had to walk back home tired and hungry.

"'Twas the night before Christmas Eve, I can't remember the exact time, 'bout early evening. It were cold and dark and raining."

Tim McDonald wrote all this down, leaned back in his chair and drank the remainder of his tea. It seemed to signal that the interview was over. Abel plucked at a ragged nail on his thumb edge. His father picked up the signal: Abel was nervous. He always picked at his nails and bit them when he was anxious. Sure enough, the thumb went up to his mouth.

He's mixed up in this, sure as eggs are eggs, Ezekiel thought with a sinking feeling.

"Well, I think that's all." The policeman shut his notebook and fastened the elastic band round it.

"Any more tea?" Ezekiel obliged, and on a polite refusal he escorted Sergeant Tim McDonald to his smart police car and it disappeared down the lane. Abel looked out of the window to watch him go.

Ezekiel frowned and pursed his lips. *Now for that boy!* He'd get the truth out of him.

Abel waiting nervously for his father, quite sure he couldn't lie his way out of this one – his father knew him too well. He picked automatically at his fingers, dreading each footstep of the approaching man. As he entered the room their eyes met: two filled with guilt and two with fury.

"What the devil have you been up to, lad? What have you got yourself mixed up in? This whole thing is a nest of evil and lies, isn't it?" He put his face up close to Abel's, spitting the words out. "Isn't it?" he repeated. Ezekiel wanted to shake his son until his teeth rattled. "How could you be so stupid? Those rich folk, they'll always get the better of the likes of us. They've got influence and connections. Now, you'd better tell me all you've done and I'll see if I can think of a way out of this mess. You stupid, stupid young fool!"

Abel didn't even try to argue. It was all a mess. The diamonds were lost, even his keys were lost. He didn't trust Ben Murphy, and poor Will Lane had been taken off and interviewed twice now by the police. He didn't really want the boy to take the blame... No, it had all gone wrong. He looked out of the window, reluctantly admitting to himself he had been a fool, lured by the idea of getting rich quickly and easily. He turned to his angry father and decided to tell his story. He sighed heavily and said, "Sit down, Dad. I'll tell you how it all happened."

"You'd better not tell me any fairy stories, son, I know when you're lying."

So Abel told the tale, right from the beginning, of how he had overheard chance conversations about the inheritance of the diamond collection by Morag. Of their impending visit to Kingswear for Christmas, and presumed usual attendance at their local church on Christmas morning. The lucky break when Will asked him to help with Ginny. He had seen with his crafty eyes the keys to the back door left on a nail in the stable wall. Will had had no idea Abel had watched from the passenger seat of the Land Rover.

That was when Abel had pieced together his plan. When Ben Murphy and he had met in the Railway Tavern they had both heard the talk in the bar of "those whisky people who lived on the point". Ben, who didn't even pretend to be honest, talked Abel into letting him stay in the storage shed for the winter. He had told him it was his Christian duty to help the homeless. Against his better nature Abel had let him, even giving him a key, and gradually as the plan had matured, he realised that Ben was the perfect accomplice. Abel also had the use of a small boat belonging to some generous people who attended the church. They only visited Kingswear three times a year at the most. As the plot was perfected, Abel thought it was just getting better and better.

He arranged the key and prepared the boat, the rope, and the marker buoy, and while he was at church that Christmas morning, Ben stole the diamonds. Then he met him after the service and together in the boat, they motored to the quiet cove, dropping the metal box with its attached rope and marker buoy over the side. Later, armed with heavy fishing rods and mammoth magnets they would easily recover the box, divide the spoils and each make a new life, free and rich. Easy!

But sometimes life conspires against us and Abel had firstly dropped his keys overboard – keys to the shed, the church and his home. Then the Boxing Day storm had broken the rope and buoy away from the box, and it had presumably drifted with the strong tide, because they had not been able to recover it – not yet. Lastly, and the most upsetting for Abel, was the unfortunate involvement of Will Lane. He liked the boy, and felt guilty.

Ezekiel listened gravely to his son's foolishness. How had he expected to get away with it? Had he intended to abandon his father when he received his share of the diamonds, he wondered, thinking back on his son's behaviour. Not that he cared, he was past all that. Many cruel blows in his life had hardened his heart.

"So that's it really, not quite how we'd planned it, I'm afraid."

Abel finished talking and leaned back in his chair, suddenly tired of it all and wishing it would all just go away.

"That young copper, he's on your case, I can tell you that, boy. Oh yes, he's a smart one. You wait, he'll be back." Ezekiel puffed away on his pipe thoughtfully. "A right mess this is."

Abel nodded miserably. "I know, I know," he repeated, and then fell silent. The clock ticked and the room seemed to stop in time. Abel felt drowsy and exhausted. He closed his eyes as his father sought for an answer, deep in thought.

Ezekiel knew one thing –if the diamonds were recovered the search for the thieves would not be so urgent. He knew he could bully Abel into retuning them, but what about Ben? Would he be so willing to give it all up? He was also a great danger to Abel: he knew everything and could thrust the blame onto Abel and disappear. Pay him off! It was the only way Ezekiel could see, but how much would it take to keep him quiet? And would it ever be enough? He could keep coming back for years to pester them. No, that wasn't the way.

If only he had known that at that very moment Ben Murphy was unlocking the old church shed. He'd had his own plans all along. He packed his belongings into a canvas fishing bag and moving a heavy chair aside, lifted up a short floorboard. He took out an old Dubbin tin and looked inside with satisfaction, just to make sure it was still there. Wrapped in white tissue sat a large diamond necklace sparkling its icy brilliance. He smiled at it.

"Come on my beauty, you and me, we're going home. Not long now." And he stroked the cold, glinting stones and replaced it in the tin. The tin went far down into the deep pocket of his dirty old poacher's jacket, where he patted it. He had always known the diamonds were there, just a little insurance policy in case things went wrong.

Whistling, he walked up to the large car park on the quayside and hitched a lift with one of the refrigerated fish lorries out onto the main road. He heard the steam train hoot and sat back in his seat with satisfaction, looking at Kingswear and the River Dart for the last time.

He'd got what he wanted; enough to buy back his grandfathers' cottage in County Clare. Let Abel keep all the rest... if he ever found them. He grinned to himself.

Chapter Twenty-three
Heather does a little detective work

The following morning, Heather wheeled herself along the road which led to the small hamlet of Kingswear. She was determined to find out from the parish records who had lived in Keepers Cottage all those years ago. She entered the church grounds under the lych gate and opened the black door to the church, and soon she was inside waiting for Mr Dodds to appear.

He came bustling in, his thin hair over his large glasses. He swept it away impatiently.

"Hello, young Heather, now I've brought my keys, what's all this about, eh?" he questioned her as he selected the key to the parish office, opened the door and beckoned her inside.

"I'm doing some research on the lighthouse and the cottage that belonged to it. I'm trying to find out who last lived there," she explained, trying not to tell him too much.

"I see." Mr Dodds looked a little strangely at her. "I see." He unlocked a large black cupboard and showed her a pile of books, all large and dusty.

"So about what year would that be, dear?" he asked her patiently. "All the books are dated, you see."

"From about 1892," Heather answered brightly.

"Long ago as that, umm, let me see." And poor Mr Dodds began heaving the large ledgers about.

"Not that one, that one, not that one either," he muttered to himself, hair and glasses falling over his nose. He swept them back again impatiently. "Now we are getting nearer. Ah good, here we are… Got it!" he announced triumphantly.

"Fantastic!" Heather breathed a sigh of relief as the big black ledger was carefully placed on the table in front of her.

"We own Keepers Cottage you see, and the lighthouse keeper always used to live there. It's just a bit of fun finding out something about them really," she explained with a charming smile.

"Well, well, well, a historian in the making, eh?" chuckled Mr Dodds, won over. "I must be off now, just leave the book where it is when you've finished and I'll put it away later. Now, where is Abel King this morning? He should be on duty, I'm sure." And off he went muttering to himself. Heather couldn't wait for him to go and as the door clunked shut, she settled down with her notebook and pen at last.

In her pocket she had the fragile, yellowed letter that she and Ellie had discovered in the back of the kitchen drawer in Keepers Cottage. Very carefully she unfolded it and spread it gently on the table to check the date. The letter was dated 1892 and in its faded ink the address from The Lighthouse, Noank, Connecticut, could be made out. The battered envelope was addressed to Mrs Mary Ann King, Start Point Lighthouse, South Devon.

"King," said Heather to herself, "but Mr Dodds has just said Abel King is supposed to be here this morning. Is he connected to them in some way? A relation perhaps?" She opened the book with its yellowed pages, but there was nobody called King in the parish. The Lighthouse Keeper in 1892 was a Mr Arthur McQuinn, Beacon Road, Kingswear. She suddenly realised she was looking in the wrong parish because Mary Ann King had lived at Start Point and her twins would be registered in the local village church. *Blast!* If one of the King boys had followed in their father's footsteps, they would not have been old enough to be in charge of the lighthouse until about 1916. How stupid of her. She wheeled herself to the open cupboard and tried to look down the dates on the spines of the black bindings. She wrestled with the book marked 1914-1918.

Of course, the Great War. All the men were volunteers. Her heart sank. *Maybe they were excused duties if they were needed badly at home? Everybody couldn't just leave for the war effort,* she thought hopefully. Turning the yellowed pages carefully and hardly daring to hope, she reached 1914 and ran her finger down the column. A man called Hinton lived at Keepers Cottage. On she went to 1915; Mr Hinton was registered again at that address.

She moved to 1916 and her finger suddenly stopped. Her eyes grew wide and she gave a short gasp. There it was! Amos King, Keepers Cottage, Beacon Road. Then, in the marriages: Amos King, 25, married Jenny Newman, 22, from Newmans Farm, Weeke Hill, in the parish of Dartmouth. Then, later, in the births, twin boys, Ezekiel and Luke.

More twins! thought Heather. *All names from the Bible. What were the names of the twin boys belonging to Mary Ann King?* she referred back to the letter again.

"I fear you shall all starve if I do not agree to your request to have one of the twins, sister dear. Tobias and I will take little Ezra for you."

Scanning over the words further on, she stopped again.

> *...send little Ezra on the mail ship from Liverpool under the care of Mr Samuel Codner Esq who travels to Connecticut and then on to Newfoundland. He will contact you shortly...*

Poor woman, Heather thought. She heard a door open and close and footsteps slowly approaching. She waited as the door squeaked open: Abel King stood there, broom in hand, a short man, his thinning hair carefully parted and smeared over his shiny head.

"Sorry to disturb you, Miss. Just cleaning up," he said gloomily, eyeing the large black ledgers.

What does she want? he thought to himself nastily. *Nosy madam.*

"Anything I can help you with?" he offered politely.

Heather stared at him. "Maybe you can!" she told him brightly. "Are you Abel King the verger?"

"What if I am?" he questioned rather cautiously.

"Do you know anything about Amos and Ezra King?"

"Well of course I do! Amos was me grandad and Ezra was me great-uncle. He went to America, long time back."

"Was he the lighthouse keeper here in Kingswear?"

"Aye he was, and his father before him. It was a family tradition for the Kings," he said proudly. "'Course, they don't need anyone now, all electric it is. All gone now," he said rather sadly.

"Do you know anything about Mary Ann King?" probed Heather.

"I do, she was me great-gran and when her husband Daniel died she had to leave the lighthouse. It was down Start Point and 'cos she got no money, her sent one of they boys to her sister. She had to move to Waterside Cottage down Warfleet."

Wasn't that where Patrick lived now? She couldn't quite piece it all together.

"Her son Amos, he was my grandad, and Ezekiel, my dad, was one of his twin sons. My dad still lived in Waterside Cottage when he was a boy. We still kept in that cottage with Dorcas my mother until we moved up Mill Creek. Then she died." He sniffed and nodded, "See, that Keepers Cottage only went with the job. When you retired you'd got no home. So we always kept on Waterside from Mary Ann's day. That charity man, Mr Codner, he bought it for her. He was the one that took Ezra, so the story does go in the family."

Heather was so delighted with all this information that she shut the book quietly. She had learnt a lot, but from Abel, not from the Parish Records.

Abel looked sort of faraway with his eyes fixed on the window as he remembered things from long ago. He carried on, seemingly not noticing whether Heather was listening or not.

"'Course, my Uncle Luke, Dad's brother, he was killed in the war 'bout 1940. Dad was right cut up 'bout that, came back from the war to find me born and his brother gone. He's never got over it really. That's what they say about twins, isn't it? Must have been terrible for they boys Ezra and Amos torn apart through poverty. But you know, he took a place up just like his brother, both lighthouse keepers; he found a place reminded him of Devon in Noank in Connecticut; lovely place right on the water's edge."

"You haven't got any letters or anything from him, have you?" asked Heather suddenly.

"Dunno. I could ask me dad. He sent us a card at Christmas times but he didn't come to Mother's funeral. Didn't find out 'till it was all over. Too far away. 'Tis all sad really, poverty, death, loneliness. Sad old times, eh?"

Heather sat silent.

Abel came back from his daydream and remembered Ben Murphy. He jolted into action. "Hmm, got to get on, Miss. Can't stop here talking," and he hurried out of the office. Good Lord, he'd forgotten about Ben. What was he going to say? His dad had made him go to work today while he thought about how Abel was going to try to redeem himself. It was certainly a tangle.

"Leave me," he had ordered his timid son. "Leave me to think this out. Get off to work early, go on you lazy skitter!" and he'd willingly obliged, anything to get out of the way.

While Heather made some notes of everything that he had so agreeably told her, Abel was about to get a nasty surprise. He opened the old church store room with his newly cut key, only to find there was not a single trace of Ben Murphy left. His makeshift bed was dismantled, blankets neatly folded, clothes, bag and belongings had vanished. Even his old poacher's jacket and winter boots had gone. Abel was dumbfounded. Where had he gone? Had he found proper lodgings somewhere? A new job? He looked around the tidy room frantically but Ben had evaporated into thin air. He'd definitely gone. A cold feeling of dread crept over Abel. He'd gone for good, leaving Abel to take the blame, leaving him alone to face the inevitable consequences. Abel panicked and ran out of the door down to the post office on the square. He burst in.

"Why Abel, what's wrong?" asked Mrs Lane, surprised to see such speed from the usually slow, surly man.

"Have you seen Ben Murphy today, Iris?" he panted. "Has he been in here?"

"Why let me think. Yes, yes, no, it was yesterday afternoon. He came for some baccy and I gave him some change for the phone. That's right, and two of my pasties. He likes those!" she added proudly.

Abel's heart sank to his boots. He knew then that Ben had run out on him. He only ever used the phone to ring his brother Pat in Limerick.

"Do you know where he went?" Abel asked hopefully, clutching at the faintest chance.

"No, I don't I'm afraid. I'll ask Jim. Jim? Are you there?" she called through the door leading to their upstairs flat. Jim appeared reluctantly, smoking his pipe.

"Abel, what is it?"

"Did you see Ben by any chance yesterday, Mr Lane?"

"Aye, aye I did. He was walking up the quayside with a bag over his shoulder and that dreadful old coat of his on. That smelly one, it's awful." He made a face. "Something wrong? Pinched your wallet, had he?" Jim laughed.

"Jim! Don't say such a thing!" and Iris folded her green cardigan around herself and rolled her eyes at her husband's tactlessness.

"No, no, I reckon he's moved on. Didn't say goodbye, that's all," sniffed Abel, dropping into a deep despair now.

"You'll get no thanks from the likes of him," said Jim rather sharply, puffing on his pipe. "Taken your help and kindness and gone. That's rather typical, he's that sort. Up to no good, probably."

"Eh Jim, you don't reckon he's mixed up in that robbery up at the farm? Those whisky people, you know, the diamonds!" Iris's eyes grew wider.

"Could be Iris, could be," nodded Jim in agreement.

"Thanks." Abel could bear it no longer and slipped away almost unnoticed as Mr and Mrs Lane discussed Ben and his wicked ways at great lengths.

He's left me! Left me with all this on my plate! Oh God help me! Abel was distraught. He went back to the shed and sat with his head in his hands, not knowing what he should do.

I'll have to go home and see Dad. I'm really scared now. It's all gone wrong. I'll have to go home! Panic struck him and he couldn't think any more. He locked the door and got his bike out of the church porch and set off grimly for his home. *Dad will know what to do. Dad will know what to do*, he repeated in rhythm to the pedals turning, his only thoughts to get back to his father.

Heather closed the books with satisfaction and piled them up on the table for Mr Dodds to put away. Shutting the door, she wheeled herself out into the main church, left by the front door and began to push herself home, checking first that the precious letter was in her pocket. She patted it in a satisfied way. The mystery of the sad separation of Amos and Ezra, the lighthouse keeper's sons, was about to be unravelled.

Chapter Twenty-four
The clues add up and the police edge closer

In his office, Detective Sergeant Tim McDonald tapped his pen on the table as he read through the notes and statements he had taken over the last few weeks. Something was definitely unfolding but he couldn't quite put his finger on it. He had a slight feeling of excitement, as if he was on the brink of seeing it all clearly. He looked out of the window at the grey clouds collecting overhead. *The church is perhaps the key,* he said to himself, nodding. *The Frasers had to be at church for the thief to get in, but— what if they hadn't gone to church that morning?* He sighed and scratched his head. The person who stole the diamonds knew the Frasers had gone to church. How did they know? They lived so far along that lonely road and hadn't any servants. What if one of them had stayed behind? How would the thief have known? He must have been stationed in Kingswear village or in the church to ensure they were all inside. Did the Frasers take their car? *I don't think I've asked them. Blast! How stupid of me!* And he banged his fist on the table. If they had walked, that gave even more time for the crime to be committed. He flicked back to Mr Fraser's statement:

"Morag, Heather and I left the house at 10.30am to be sure of getting Heather in and seated by 11.00am when the service began; she hates a fuss."

Half an hour was surely too much time if you go by car – five minutes' drive, five minutes to park, five to get Heather into her wheelchair, and so on. No, they must have walked. *What was the weather like on Christmas morning?* He tried hard to remember. He had been staying at his girlfriend Nadia's house. She was off duty on Christmas Day from the local hospital where she was a nurse. They had walked to her parents' for lunch, it had been cloudy and then just after they had sat down to eat, the rain had started and hadn't stopped. So at 10.30 am on Christmas morning it would have been cloudy, mild and dry. *I bet the*

Frasers walked to church, he decided triumphantly. *Now, the question is, who saw them?* As soon as the thief or thieves verified the Frasers' intention of going to church, the plan could go ahead, knowing they had one and a half hours maximum to complete the job. Tim McDonald's mind went back to the church. He needed a connection between the church and the village, and the Frasers. He thought again about Will Lane and Abel King; either could have seen the Frasers, but Abel had stayed at the Christmas service. Back to Will again. He fitted the bill but somehow Tim doubted him. Abel could have had an accomplice, but who? Was Will seen around at 10.30 am? He'd have to check his alibi again.

He sifted through the papers. Will's statement said he was in bed at 10.30 on Christmas morning. His mother and father had told the same story, but it was possible to have slipped out down onto the jumble of terraced roofs without anyone knowing. Tim thought hard and then decided that he would go and see Abel again, but this time at the church, away from that wily father of his. He had seemed a bit nervous and reluctant to talk. Maybe he was hiding something and afraid of his father? *I think I'll bring him here to the police station, that'll frighten him! Yes.*" He closed his notebook and got up, taking his jacket off the peg. *I know I'm nearly there. I just can't quite fit the pieces together, but I will!*

***

Mr Dodds returned to St Thomas's church, humming to himself. He was a retired bank manager and took a keen interest in the church. He went into the parish office and noticed Heather had lifted down another book. "She's been busy!" he said admiringly. "Plucky little maid. The Great War, eh? Not many men left in Kingswear during those years." And he put the ledgers away and locked the cupboard. He went back into the glowing warm church he loved and noticed the Children's

Society collecting box was missing from the entrance table. *That's funny, I was going to empty all the charity boxes this week and take the money to the bank. Very odd.* He searched the church. The box for the Children of Ethiopia was gone from the Missionary alcove in the Lady Chapel. Who could have done such a thing? And why wasn't Abel here? He might have seen a stranger lurking around. It was all very annoying.

Just at that moment Tim Mc Donald arrived.

"Good afternoon, sir. I'm Detective Sergeant Tim Mc Donald. I was hoping for a word with Abel King. Is he around today?" he asked pleasantly.

"Ah Sergeant, I'm Philip Dodds, the treasurer here, and well, I'd like to help you out but Abel doesn't seem to be here at the moment and I'm afraid I've just discovered some of our charity boxes are missing. I'm hoping they've just been misplaced over Christmas, but…" He shook his head and sucked his teeth. "I'm not suggesting there's any connection with Abel, don't get me wrong. Abel does outstanding work for St Thomas's, outstanding. He's loyal and reliable, quiet, and—"

"Not here, unfortunately," interrupted Tim McDonald. "Any idea where he might be? At home, do you think?"

"Well of course it's possible, but he doesn't usually go home until 4.30pm and he's pretty good. Probably about church duties somewhere."

"Okay sir, let me know if the boxes don't turn up won't you? It's a pretty sad thing to take money from a church."

"Oh yes, I agree Sergeant, I agree wholeheartedly," said Mr Dodds, looking through his hair with his glasses balanced on the end of his nose.

Tim Mc Donald left the church and went towards the post office to buy a bar of chocolate, his afternoon treat. *Wouldn't do any harm to have another chat with Iris and Jim Lane anyway.*

They were both behind the counter with a mug of tea.

"Good afternoon, Sergeant," greeted Jim warmly.

"Hello, just a Jupiter Bar please," asked Jim, fishing for the change. The transaction complete, he bit into the chocolate appreciatively. "Have either of you seen Abel King today?" he added casually, chewing away.

Jim and Iris looked at each other and Iris wrapped her cardigan around herself, folding her arms purposefully. "Now that's a coincidence, he was in here only half an hour ago. Seemed a bit upset. Looking for a friend of his, that Ben Murphy." Iris rolled her eyes.

"'Course, I saw him yesterday heading up the quayside, and good riddance I say," added Jim.

Tim McDonald stopped eating his creamy hazelnut bar.

"Ben Murphy? Now who's he? Just remind me."

"He's that dirty old fella that wandered into town before Christmas. Shifty Irish bloke, one of those immigrant agricultural workers, you know, picks fruit and veg. I expect he's gone back to Cornwall to pick daffodils again."

"Was he a friend of Abel's?" asked Tim, delving in his pocket for his notebook and pen. Iris and Jim looked at each other and their eyes met. Should they tell Abel's secret? They didn't want to get him into trouble. As far as they were concerned, Abel was a good Christian who had helped steady their Will down a bit and given him a helping hand at the Frasers'. Those rich folk were always wanting Will to do something. Mind you, they had paid for his driving lessons and let him have the Land Rover, but that meant he could do even more work for them, didn't it? Just a little twinkle of an idea sparked in Iris's mind as she remembered that awful night they had gone to the police station with Will, and he had mentioned Abel then. What was it about? She tried to remember. Yes, it came back to her: he had helped Will once with the horse and to collect the Christmas trees from Marldon Farm. She also remembered how cross she had been at Will, trying to implicate Abel.

"But you went to see Abel, didn't you, after Will told you about the horse and the Christmas trees? You've already cleared him, haven't you?" questioned Iris closely.

"We haven't cleared anybody, Mrs Lane, not yet, not until we catch the person or persons who perpetrated this crime," said Tim McDonald with a deadly serious face.

"Oh... oh I see," replied Iris quietly. She searched for her handkerchief up her sleeve. So her Will wasn't out of trouble yet. She blew her nose and sniffed. Jim decided to take over, he could see what Iris was thinking and it wasn't good. He cleared his throat and began.

"Thing is, Sergeant McDonald, that Ben Murphy had nowhere to stay during the cold spell we had afore Christmas. There's an old shed just behind the church where they keeps extra chairs and old books, things like that. Well, Abel let Ben sleep in there... I know that for a fact, and Abel being a good Christian and all that, he thought he was doing a kindness to him like."

He looked at his wife. He'd done it now, told Abel's secret.

"How long has he been here then do you think? Sleeping in the store room?" asked Tim quietly, writing in his notebook.

"About six weeks I'd say, what do you think, Iris? Six weeks?"

"Yes Jim, definitely," agreed Iris. "Because he's always been in and out of here for packets of tea and bread, and he's very fond of my homemade pasties as well," she added proudly. "In fact he bought two yesterday."

Jim realised that fact was quite important.

"He was leaving! That's why he bought two, Iris, because I saw him off up the quay and he had that old bag of his over his shoulder, He's left and that's why Abel was so upset. He told us he didn't say goodbye."

Tim's mind was racing ahead of them both. Ben King was the missing link. This could be the vital clue.

"Look, Sergeant McDonald, this puts us in an awkward spot. We don't want to get Abel into trouble. Nobody knew that fella was sleeping there. He would slip in and out like a shadow. The vicar, Rupert Watkins, he's in charge of three other churches and he bobs about from one to the other. He lives at Galmpton. Abel and Mr Dodds seem to do most of the day to day work. The vicar wouldn't know Ben was even there."

"No," agreed Iris, "he was practically invisible. Mind you, he gave us one or two fish he'd caught, which was quite nice of him."

"Yes, but you've given him the out of date bread and cakes, Iris."

"Ssh Jim! Don't get me into trouble!" hushed his wife, terrified of the policeman.

"Alright, alright, I didn't hear that." Tim Mc Donald calmed them down.

"Now, I'll just verify a few more things with you and then I'll leave you in peace." However, just as he spoke, Mr Dodds came in.

"Hello Jim, Hello Iris, packet of Rich Tea biscuits, please. Hello again, Sergeant McDonald. Still looking for Abel?"

"Just came in for a bar of chocolate, sir, actually," smiled the police officer coolly.

"I have found the missing boxes, Sergeant."

"Good, that's good." Tim was pleased.

"Trouble is," added Mr Dodds, "they were both empty – cut open and the money gone. The boxes had been dumped in our compost heap and rather badly hidden in the dead flowers. Terrible isn't it? Terrible."

Iris and Jim kept extremely quiet, frozen to the spot, frightened of saying anything in case it got somebody into trouble.

"Ah," said Tim. "That's made it into a theft now. We'll have to fill out a crime report. Shall we go back and do it now?" and he led Mr Dodds out of the post office towards the police station. It was all falling into place. It was obvious now that Ben King had taken the money then left town in a hurry. The fingerprints could be checked on the boxes. Had he got the diamonds with him? Even if he had, he'd still need cash to travel until he could sell them, which explained the empty charity boxes. Getting rid of the diamonds would be difficult. The police had published pictures of the jewellery everywhere, including in newspapers and magazines to alert the diamond trade. No one in their right mind would touch them – would they?

***

At that very moment, Ben Murphy was in a remote shepherd's shelter, half way to Wales, having hitched several rides, first in the fish lorry, then with a supermarket trucker. He was boiling up a billy can on a primus stove, dropping in the crab claws which the kind Spanish driver had given him. He warmed his hands in satisfaction. This was the life he'd missed. Travelling from place to place, foraging and fending for himself. Soon he'd be buying his ticket at Fishguard, off across the sea to Ireland. He couldn't wait.

When he'd eaten his crab he carefully washed the claws, dropped the diamond necklace into the biggest one and replaced the empty clean claws into the plastic bag. Nobody would look in there, especially when they started to smell, as they always did.

He packed up and set off whistling towards the setting sun, oblivious of the trail of facts that were beginning to lead to him.

***

Abel, however, was not feeling so carefree. Despair and panic were clouding his thoughts. He arrived home sweating and panting and threw his bike against the fence. He burst in through the low wooden door.

"He's gone, Dad, he's gone! Disappeared! He's taken everything! The shed's empty. He's left me to take the blame, the dirty pig! After all I've done for him. Him and his sneaky ways.

Why has he done it, Dad? It's just not fair!" A torrent of words poured out as Abel searched the home frantically for his father. His dad appeared from the garden shed, grinning, dresses in lovat green combat clothes and with a black knitted hat on.

"Dad, what are you doing?" Abel was stunned.

"We're going fishing, lad, get your things and I'll explain later. We don't need any bait!" as he held up a small metal detector from behind his back. Abel nearly fell over with surprise. He didn't need Ben Murphy now. *Good old Dad!* A wide grin spread over his face.

***

By the time Tim McDonald arrived at the old cottage by the bridge up Mill Creek, it was dark and empty. No one had answered the door.

"Blast!" swore the furious policeman. "Now where have they gone?" Just when he thought he was getting somewhere. He got back into his car. It was dark now, he'd have to leave Abel for another day. As he drove away he was determined to set up a missing person's inquiry and bring Ben Murphy back for questioning. Could he be the missing piece in the puzzle? Only the fingerprints would tell.

Chapter Twenty-five
Preparations for conflict

In the Woodland, news had been posted of the birthday picnic for Nina, one of the Nightingale sisters. After a great deal of persuasion, Norman and Noreen agreed to let the picnic be the starting point of the Woodland's reply to the takeover. Every dweller was outraged at the bullying tactics of Jack B Quick and his gang, everyone would do their bit to drive him out. Shelter was offered to those who did not want to partake in the fighting at the Great Ash Tree should things get seriously nasty.

The plan was this: new earthy defence hillocks were to be provided by the tireless digging of Maurice and Maudie Mole. Oliphant had offered them a permanent home under the fortress wall of Gallants Bower as a reward. It was too good an offer to turn down and the tiny moles had blinked, swallowed, and bravely agreed to Oliphant's request for help. The owl heaved a sigh of relief, having already planned the deployment of their ground soldiers, the voles and mice.

Artillery fire would be provided from the trees by the many fearless squirrels. Catapults and conker shells would be the primary weapons and beechnut husks and burdock burrs would be secondary ammunition. Oliphant and Freddie hoped the bombardment from the sky would be the final disabling factor. Providing Boris and his buzzing band of followers with sticky nectar had proved to be difficult in winter, but luckily some honeysuckle still covered hedges by the coastguard's cottage and Oliphant had ordered it to be requisitioned, as the nectar was vital to the success of the whole operation. His trump card had been the discovery of an attractive, slumbering queen bee lodged in the bark of his very own home. Just what Boris was looking for to start a new colony.

Leonora and her followers were to entice the jackdaws away from the picnic towards the Citadel and lead them into the firing line of the main battle location. The ladies polished their wings to an alluring brightness and repainted each other's spots to a brilliant shine. They buffed their black-spurred boots and pulled on long fishnet gloves. A touch of scarlet lipstick, a twirl of black mascara, and they were ready.

The squirrels deposited stores of prickly conker shells in the nooks and crannies of the trees. The mice and voles nibbled off dry, hollow stems to make pea shooters. Denis dormouse and Victor vole were to take charge of the ground troops behind the hillocks. The hollow stems, when blown, emitted an eerie, ghostly sound and when they were filled with hard berries they turned into efficient weapons, stinging and painful.

Oliphant and Freddie called a secret meeting of the group leaders and Norman and Noreen to check the final details. Everything had to be planned meticulously to avoid confusion in the thick of the impending battle. During late afternoon the picnic would take place and as it was to celebrate Nina's birthday, friends and family would gather by the Great Ash Tree where feasting, merriment, and party games would follow. Oliphant would offer a cask of the Mists of Time and each glass that the jackdaws drank was to be spiked with a few drops of an elixir. It was up to the Underconstumbles to decide the nature of the elixir. The little white owl trusted the doctors' judgement implicitly. He knew one thing – he never wanted Jack B Quick or Jodie or Jed ever to return to their Woodland Bower.

He questioned his troops to hear their completed plans. Denis and Vincent were sure their men had been drilled, practised the accuracy of their shooting, and placed their ammunition close by. A bonfire would be lit as the sign of the attack to begin. Everyone agreed it was a brilliant plan. They were ready!

Norman Nightingale was to have one very important job. He was in charge of the elixir from the doctors and was to guard it at all times to ensure it did not get put into the wrong glasses. Noreen, Norman and Freddie were to bundle the three Nightingale sisters into the Great Ash Tree through the back door to safety. Any other Woodlanders who sought refuge were also welcome to shelter there.

"Is that everything?" asked Oliphant, looking round his faithful troops, united in this one purpose. He felt proud and suddenly afraid. What had he involved all these good people in? What if some of them were injured? Or worse? Had he led them into strife, violence, and perhaps bloodshed? Nobody wanted the jackdaws to rule the Woodland so this unfortunate action was necessary to regain peace and justice for all. Oliphant quickly reassured himself that he was doing the right thing; the plan *would* work – it had to.

***

As the sun rose weakly over the grey granite tors of high Dartmoor, the branches of a large dead elm tree took on a rose-coloured glow from the dawn's reflection. A small sunlit figure appeared bobbing and weaving through the tough bushes of holly, blackthorn and gorse scattered over the landscape. It was time. Sunna, Spirit of the Woodland, had come to reclaim the rightful Ruler of the Kingdom of Gallant's Bower. He had watched the prince's progress from spoilt, petulant teenager to a mature adult, ready to assume the responsibility of ruling and decision-making which were the lifelong duties of High Office. E'en was expected to find his own consort, and a new young couple would rule together. There were other princes to take care of their aged mother.

Lord Sunna approached the tree where the buzzards roosted and laid his hand on the lichen-covered bark. A shiver of light transmitted at once to the top of the tree and woke the three birds. Sunna then jumped to the topmost branch and stood in front of the startled buzzards.

"Awake! It is I, Sunna, Spirit of the Woodland, I have come to claim you, E'en. You are summoned to Gallants Bower, for today you must take back your throne and assume your rightful place. After the conflict they will be ready to accept you. Today, in the name of peace, blood will fall for you onto our sacred ground. You must be worthy of the sacrifice. Be ready, the spirit of your ancestors will guide you and the seeds of wisdom which I shall plant will grow inside you."

The buzzards all listened in silence, stunned by the appearance of Lord Sunna. The old consort, widow of the Lord of the Woodland, bowed her head. It was time.

Sunna held out three small brown seeds in his hand, harvested from the Tree of Life, and E'en moved forward to eat them.

"The first is for Justice." The buzzard pecked it and swallowed.

"The second is for Wisdom." He pecked that one too.

"And the third is for Mercy." And the buzzard pecked it and swallowed twice to be sure.

"Ultimate power is a heavy burden to carry and easy to let fall. It draws undesirables to itself and many crave to unwrap its coverings for the prize inside. Beware of false friends, E'en, and seek to know yourself. Respect the smallest in your kingdom for they are many but together they have great power – power even to challenge yours. You have one year to prove yourself. As I grow old, at the end of my reign, I shall seek you. Your deeds will be recorded and judged and the future of your crown will rest on them. Go now, take up your throne, for tonight your people will welcome you. The Spirit of the Woodland salutes you!" and Lord Sunna touched E'en's fine feathers. The young buzzard felt a warm sensation of indescribable joy flow through him. He turned to his mother and brother, nodded to each, and flew off. He did not look back.

Chapter Twenty-six
The day of reckoning

On that fateful day, Jack and Jodie grew bored in the royal residence high up at the Citadel. Restless and brooding, they stared out across the fields and trees to the grey sea and the misty rain-laden horizon beyond. Winter had not yet yielded its chilly grip. The take- over of the old residence had been a challenge, a bit of fun, something to motivate them. They had flouted an age-old authority and won. What now?

"It's not *so* great up here, bro, is it?" questioned Jodie, pecking up crumbs of clover cake off a monogrammed plate.

"Those Nightingale sisters don't seem to fancy us anymore either," sighed Jack, sipping drearily from a crystal goblet full of wild strawberry lemonade.

"But I'll tell you this, bro, this'll cheer you up, there's a picnic planned today for Nina's birthday."

"No! Stop it Jodie, you're just trying to make me feel better. Good try!"

"Cross my heart and hope to die, I'm not! There really is a party up here today. I heard those noisy squirrels chattering about it."

"Well, well, well." Jack's eyes glittered, appreciating the delights that might be in store for him. "Thanks Jodie, you've made my day!" and he went off whistling to the bedroom to polish his feathers and sharpen his claws. Jodie called after him.

"Shall I round the boys up?"

"Oh yes!" came the reply. Off Jodie went to spread the word among the Gallants Gang. This was going to be a good day, he could feel it, and he shivered with a little tingle of excitement. Life was never boring, not around Jack B Quick.

I've always rather liked Nora, the quiet one, he admitted to himself. *I think I'll go and look in my treasure box and see if there's anything in there she might like.*

So it seemed that Jack and his gang were almost on the hook; they had taken the bait as Oliphant and Freddie had predicted.

At home, in the graceful branches of a larch tree, Norman and Noreen Nightingale went over the plan again and again, trying to convince themselves that nothing could go wrong and that none of their daughters would be in danger at any time.

"Mr Oliphant has assured us it will be alright," said Noreen quite confidently.

"Yes, I know," replied Norman. "It's alright for him. He doesn't realise what three teenage daughters are like. They're all fascinated by those dark, handsome scoundrels, that's the trouble. They think we're a lot of old fuddy duddies spoiling their fun. Remember when we were young, Noreen? Trying to dodge your dad and mum when we wanted to be alone?"

"Norman! Hush!" flustered Noreen and then laughed girlishly. "I remember!"

"Well then, you can see the problem."

"I'm sure it will be fine. We've both seen all the careful planning by Mr Oliphant, and once the girls are safe inside the Great Ash Tree those wretched jackdaws will get their comeuppance. I can't wait!"

Norman said no more, not convinced but unwilling to cast doubts that might worry his wife. He turned his thoughts to his most important task of the day – the collection of the precious elixir from the Underconstumbles.

"Just going to the Cornucopia Tree, my dear. I won't be long," he called to her. Reaching the ivy-covered dwelling, he rang the bell and heard the dried conker shells jangling above his head.

The door opened quietly by itself and he went in and up the spiral staircase, past the dazzling array of bottles, jar and potions. Verity, the white dove, met him at the top, wearing a white starched apron. She cooed gently.

"Welcome to you-ooooo, Nightingale true-ooooo, they are waiting for you-ooooo," and she beckoned him forward into the large and spacious surgery, The two doctors, Dr Dew and Dr Yew, were seated one each side of their huge partners desk.

"Good morning," greeted Norman.

Verity approached him, offered him a seat and fetched a tray of instruments.

"Just one small thing to do-ooooo," she cooed reassuringly. She held out a long wooden instrument in her claw and tapped his beak with it. At once Norman put out his tongue. With the instrument she took some scrapings, then nodded to him, and Norman obediently shut his beak. She took the long instrument carefully on the tray to the doctors and all three disappeared at once into a side room, leaving Norman very puzzled.

Verity soon returned with a pale magenta liquid in a glass for him to drink.

"Rose-coloured Dreams," she told him. "Just a precaution."

In the small treatment room Dr Dew and Dr Yew Underconstumble were mixing the golden particles from the nightingale's tongue with the Elixir of Musical Appreciation.

"A very satisfactory solution, my dear."

"I'm glad you think so, dearest," said the other, adding a few drops of kingfisher blue. Then, swirling the liquid with a silver spoon, it was ready.

"There!" With great satisfaction, they poured the elixir into a blue-ribbed bottle and corked it.

"What a peaceful way to end a conflict," they decided together. "Jackdaws have always been rather raucous individuals, don't you think?" Wrapping the bottle carefully in a large leaf and tying it with several strands of old man's beard, the doctors summoned Verity, who took it to Norman, waiting nervously in the large room.

"For you-ooooo," Verity smiled, handing over the precious package. The two doctors sat down at their desk again to fill in the large open ledger.

"Two drops will do-oooo," they spoke together. "Choose only a few-ooooo for they will turn blue-ooooo for a day or two-oooo!" and they both laughed together at their brilliant plan. Norman was bemused and a little scared at this mysterious responsibility. Verity sensed his deep apprehension and nodded to the doctors. At once they stood up and each put a wing around the small brown nightingale.

"This is a tangle we must undo-oooo. Understand this: no harm will come to you-oooo. All will be well in our takeover coup-oooo," and then Verity escorted Norman and his precious package out of the Cornucopia Tree, down to the woodland floor.

Every possible thing was now in place. There was no going back, and when Norman reached Oliphant and Freddie at the Great Ash Tree later on, it was clear that nothing would stop them. Not now.

***

The Battle for the Citadel began at midday. Maurice and Maudie Mole took over their new residence beneath the roots of the crumbling fortress wall, built in the Civil War. Maurice wanted to be ready to repair the many hillocks which were under his control. Vincent and Victor Vole and Denis Dormouse quietly led their followers to the camouflaged bunkers, where, armed and primed, they slid unnoticed into position. The squirrels scrambled up the trees in the sycamore grove between the Citadel and the Great Ash Tree and, waiting obediently in the crooks of the trees for the signal, promptly fell asleep. Boris and his band began the delicious task of gorging themselves on wild honeysuckle nectar until they were so heavy they could hardly fly. Leonora and her ladybirds gathered together in a myrtle bush to check on their seductive make-up one last time.

At two o'clock precisely the Nightingale sisters and their family arrived at the Great Ash Tree. They were welcomed by Oliphant, calm and confident. His forward planning had resolved everything – or so he thought.

As the squirrels were all busily occupied they could not do the catering, so a small party of hedgehogs had been woken from their winter hibernation and begged to help in the woodland struggle. The good-natured creatures had agreed, and now, dressed in aprons and bow ties, were helping to staff the birthday picnic. Strings of berried lights had been strung from branch to branch. Long streamers of silver birch bark fluttered on the branches. A large birthday cake packed with nuts and berries and decorated with glazed flies stood mouth-wateringly in pride of place.

The guests began to arrive and Nina, looking shy and very pretty, greeted them and took the small gifts offered to her graciously. The crickets set up their instruments and tuned up for the dancing. Glasses of hot, spicy elderberry cordial were circulated.

Soon the hubbub of talking and laughing spread like an echo through the Upper Woodland. Oliphant and Freddie crept to the topmost branches of the ash tree to survey the troops, hidden so cleverly not very far away.

The music and laughter reached the ears of Jack and Jodie, now gleaming at their dazzling best. Eyes bright with anticipation, they nodded to each other, winked, and left the Citadel to gate crash the party. They crossed the chosen battle zone unaware of many fierce, cold eyes watching them, hidden in the hillocks, dark hollows and overhead branches. Leonora stared icily from the myrtle bush and Boris dozed sleepily above her. They could wait a little longer, it would be worth it.

Jack and Jodie strolled in arrogantly, each with a small gift under his wing. Approaching Nina, they bowed in a sweeping gesture, wished her a very Happy Birthday, and pecked her on each cheek.

"Thank you! Thank you very much!" Nina said sweetly, unwrapping the two gold, gauzy boxes at once. Inside were a pair of earrings and a gold necklace, both stolen by the jackdaws from unsuspecting holidaymakers on the beach. Norman, seizing the moment, prepared their fateful drinks, adding two drops to each, unseen by anyone.

"Here you are, boys! Welcome to the party, it's going to be quite a day!"

The crickets struck up again and music blasted out, with persistent drumming compelling everyone to dance to the rhythmical beat. All the rest of the black jackdaws soon came creeping in and mingling with the dancers. Norman carefully ensured they all had two drops of elixir added to their drinks, which he served himself.

Oliphant appeared, cheerfully dressed in a red spotted bowtie and offered Norman a cask of the Mists of Time which was carefully placed on the table and then uncorked. Jack caught sight of it and nudged Jodie. This was going to get better and better. Each brother seized a Nightingale sister as they joined the crowd already swaying to the music. The smoky liquor was offered round and enjoyed by everyone. Norman suggested games and Noreen organised musical chairs, apple bobbing, and blind man's buff. Food was served and the cake cut. Nina blinked shyly as everyone huddled round to sing Happy Birthday. She was flushed and excited and looked so pretty that Jack was overcome with a desire to kiss her.

"One last game!" announced Noreen. Oliphant and Freddie looked at each other.

"Why hasn't the elixir worked?" whispered Norman. "They both seem just the same."

"Don't worry, it will," replied Oliphant confidently. "Ready for the signal?"

Noreen and Norman had agreed to each take one of their daughters and Freddie to take a third into the safety of the Great Ash Tree.

"Light the bonfire." The hedgehogs obediently struck flints and the dry twigs began to blaze as a faint darkness crept over the sky.

"Now!" Oliphant nodded.

"Come on, let's hide," whispered Jack to Nina, pressing her wing closely, and Nina giggled, snuggling up to him.

"Come on! This way!" he urged.

Suddenly, Leonora and her troupe of lovely girls appeared enticingly and the other jackdaws stopped in their tracks.

"Corr, I love ladybirds, don't you?" said one to another, "Don't mind hiding with one of them, eh?"

Each jackdaw forgot what he was doing and followed an eyelash-fluttering, long-legged ladybird. They left the party group as the red-and-black sirens beckoned and enticed them along the path towards the Citadel. Even Jodie forgot to follow Nora to a hiding place, but Jack held Nina's wingtip tightly and pulled her along the darkening path. She was in the shadow of the bonfire and where her father couldn't see her. Norman was looking everywhere for her, sudden panic seizing him.

All at once, Boris and his buzzing band zoomed in from overhead, and screaming loud zzzing noises drenched the jackdaws, including Jack, Jodie and Nina, in a spray of sticky nectar. The ladybirds all flew off out of the way of the honey shower, their job done. Brave Boris had ensured the birds would not be able to fly away. Then the wailing noise from the leafy hillocks started – a frightening, ghostly noise, the signal from Victor, Vincent and Denis.

Nina was terrified and tried to run but it was getting hard to see as she wrenched herself away from Jack, falling over in the honeyed mess; leaves began to stick to her and she rolled down a slope, coming to rest in a hidden hollow. She lay still, panting. Jack called her name but no words came out, just a sweet whistling. His feathers felt prickly and sticky and as he looked down he was horrified. He was blue all over. Bright kingfisher blue. What had happened? He looked around and saw that his friends dotted along the path had all turned blue too. The wailing from the reeded pipes confused them all. Jack tried to catch up with his friends but things started hitting him. Large, hard berries rained down on the blue jackdaws.

"Ouch!" he said, but only a faint birdsong was heard. The jackdaws were terrified now, running in all directions, hampered by the sticky honeysuckle nectar, unable to fly away. No voices could be heard, only sweet birdsongs rather similar to an evening nightingale's call.

Jack and Jodie tried to make their way along through the sycamore grove out into open land, and as they limped along drenched in nectar unable to communicate they made bright blue targets obvious to all, even in the closing daylight.

The squirrels began to fire serious ammunition from their treetop positions and sharp thorny missiles assaulted the stricken enemy. Two young birds, Joe and Jan, were badly hit: one broke a wing and the other was punctured in the breast. As they lay gasping on the path, Leonora and her band shot out of the trees and kicked them with their spurred boots. Soon the birds lay still, blood spilling onto the earthy pathway. Leonora shrieked with laughter.

"That will teach you a lesson," she yelled. The ladybirds turned out to be the most vicious of all, and continued to attack the grounded birds, whose blue feathers floated in the melee.

Back at the Great Ash Tree, Norman, Noreen and the timid birds and animals who had been sheltering were all now frantically searching for Nina, calling her name out loudly.

"Nina? Nina?"

They began to spread out into the Woodland. Maurice and Maudie immediately snuffled and snooped around the picnic area and found Nina down in a small hollow, covered in sticky leaves and very frightened.

"We've found her!" shouted Maurice and Maudie together in their tiny voices and the frantic parents arrived at once on the scene.

"Come on Noo Noo, we've got you now," as her father carried her back to the berry-lit picnic area. Many hands helped to wash the poor nightingale's feathers with rainwater and soon she was dry and enjoying the fuss and another piece of birthday cake. Maurice, Denis and Victor climbed up onto the ash tree to tell all the others it was safe to come out. The cricket band began to play again, trying to create a distraction from the faint noises coming from the far end of the Woodland by the Citadel.

Oliphant and Freddie flew along to see the results of the battle, not prepared for what they would see. Several bodies littered the ground, with many feathers and patches of blood; injured frightened birds cowered in corners at the foot of tree trunks. Only sweet birdsong was heard when the jackdaws tried to open their beaks. Jack and Jodie, still alive, huddled together unable to comprehend what had happened.

Darkness fell and as Oliphant began to summon help for the injured, a bright light burst out from the top of the Citadel, surprising everyone. Looking up, dazzled, Oliphant could see a large majestic buzzard with his wings outspread. Below him with his finger tips alight, spreading brightness all around him, was Lord Sunna, Spirit of the Woodland.

"Oliphant, explain what has happened here. Robin, gather all the Woodland people here. I have good news for you all." And the robin nodded and flew back to the Great Ash Tree to tell all the others.

Oliphant, trembling and fearful, knowing he had planned this battle and its sorry result, flew to the lower branch of the pine tree and waited. E'en sat on the topmost branch, silent and powerful, looking down on them all. Oliphant shook in fear. Two dead, many injured, it was all down to him.

Lord Sunna came to sit next to him. He spoke gently. "This was a drastic action to take. It has ended in tragedy for some, injury for others, but let there be no mistake, these birds had sought power and possessions which were not theirs, you had courage, Oliphant, to make a decision. It is a consequence of war that some die. You have done well. Leonora, come forward!"

He suddenly turned his lighted fingers up to the top of the sycamore grove some way off where Leonora was hiding, and drew the ladybirds to him in a beam of light.

"You have displeased me. Revenge was not yours to take. You and your followers will care for the wounded and you will stay in the Bower for one year. All travel is forbidden. Go and do my bidding," he pronounced. "Summon the Underconstumbles to me, Oliphant."

Freddie appeared with a trail of followers: dormice, voles, moles, hedgehogs, squirrels, the nightingale family and the musicians. Everyone gathered at the foot of the Citadel talking excitedly to each other, looking up at the buzzard perched on the very top.

"Is it him? Is he back? Can he be better? Who is it? Which one can it be?" The inquisitive voices went around. The buzzard sat in a golden pool of light, still and silent, waiting for Lord Sunna to give him the signal.

The two pigeons arrived flustered and worried, with Verity the white dove close behind them.

"Come, sit beside me," invited Lord Sunna, as nervously the birds obeyed him. Verity remained on the ground.

"Explain the elixir you chose, please," asked Lord Sunna.

"Yes, lord, we shall do-oooo," answered Dr Dew and Dr Yew together. "Those who drank it turned blue-oooo to single them out from the innocent and true-oooo and the guilty lost their raucous voices and were only able to sing to you-oooo."

"Is this reversible?" asked Lord Sunna.

"Oh yes my lord, in a day or two-oooo their voices and feathers will return, they shall be good as new-oooo. We assure you-oooo." cooed the Drs Underconstumble.

"A wise choice then, you have not betrayed my trust. A gift to you." And he offered them a crystal phial which glittered and sparkled in the light. "A secret from me to you."

"Thank you, my lord." They both bowed, and flew to join Verity below.

"Jack B Quick, you and your remaining followers shall be escorted to the Freedom Gate and cast out. The injured will remain as a testimony to this sad night. You are lucky to have escaped death." Turning to the other birds he said. "Take them now, faithful friends. All those who were persecuted by these birds will now rid us of their tyranny. Go now!" ordered the Spirit of the Woodland.

"Forever banished! Do not return!" His fingers pointed to the petrified jackdaws, their untidy feathers a sticky mess. Blue and voiceless, they had two days to survive until their natural plumage returned.

They were hustled and jeered to the five bar gate and then cast in silence into the darkness; to the savage wild winds, left to the mercy of the weather and hunting birds of prey. Some shivered as they watched the birds disappear into the blackness. Small faint birdsongs were heard, then silence.

Returning to the Citadel, Lord Sunna called to them all, tired and sad.

"And now I will introduce you to your new Lord of the Woodland, to E'en the rightful ruler, grown in wisdom to meet the challenges of today. Greet him in our custom and welcome him!"

Then the Spirit of the Woodland shone his fingers onto the bark of the tree and the light was almost too bright to bear. Some of the small Dark Dwellers and a few of the Earth Dwellers were afraid, but Oliphant and Freddie led them in a special woodland call of two notes, one high and one low, repeated three times. They waited, looking upwards to E'en, once a prince, now a king: the new Ruler of the Woodland. What was he going to say? What was he going to do? What did the future hold now?

Chapter Twenty-seven
An underground journey, and danger at the lighthouse

Heather arrived home breathless and excited, the precious notebook tucked into the back of her wheelchair. She pushed open the kitchen door and manoeuvred her wheelchair inside.

"Hello," greeted her mother, "I wondered where you were. What have you been doing?"

Heather's face was full of joy and her cheeks were pink. She rushed all her words out at once. "I've made some fantastic discoveries today Mum, you wouldn't believe it, all about the people who used to live in Keepers Cottage and worked in the lighthouse. It's so amazing and so sad as well. I must phone Patrick and Ellie to tell them all about it. You don't mind do you?" She turned and headed for the door.

"No of course not, I'll make some tea if you like and then you can tell me all about it." Morag was thrilled to see her daughter so keen and interested and making new friends.

Heather wheeled herself off into the hall to use the telephone. Both Ellie and Patrick were surprised to receive her call. "Can you come over very soon? I've got some really exciting news!"

"Brilliant, we're all dying to hear about it. Soon as we can," came the urgent promises.

Heather put the phone down. Not soon enough was the problem. That river in between them was such a nuisance, sighed Heather.

Patrick ran up to Watermill Cottage after the phone call and minutes later the three were already plotting to go to Kingswear.

"Why don't we go across through the tunnel?" asked Patrick daringly. "I mean, now we know it's there it seems such a waste not to use it. It's much quicker!"

Eddie laughed at this crazy suggestion, but thinking about it, knew it was the answer.

"You're right you know, and why don't we take the Moonmirror with us? Wouldn't it be fun to make it work in the old lighthouse? The lighthouse hasn't been used for years. We could show our invention to Heather. What do you think?"

The others were all in agreement.

"Good idea. Why not?"

"How will we get out at the other end?" worried Ellie. "The door onto Beacon Road is kept locked."

"Well Heather will open it won't she, dummy!" Eddie shook his head at her. "She's got a key, hasn't she?"

"Just want to be sure, that's all." She made a face at him defensively.

"When shall we go?" asked Patrick, hating it when they bickered. "We've got to phone Heather back and tell her what's going on."

"Let's go tonight!" suggested Eddie. Ellie wasn't so sure, she looked doubtful but didn't want to disappoint Eddie. Everyone was quiet for a moment, thinking.

"What shall we tell our parents?" Ellie voiced her fears.

"What about saying that we are going over to see Heather – staying for the evening – then we'll come back on the ferry? Dad can pick us up at the other end. At least we can go one way in the tunnel, can't we?"

There was a pause. It seemed on the face of it a reasonable idea: telling all their parents just enough to satisfy them but still leaving them the secret excitement of going under the river in the newly discovered tunnel. Ellie gave a shiver. A tiny bubble of fear kept bobbing up and down inside her; the fear of darkness and rats wasn't very far away. Was the tunnel smelly? Was it wet? She didn't dare ask.

"Ellie, you ring Heather, tell her what she's got to do and we'll go and check the Moonmirror's charged."

The two boys disappeared pretty quickly. Ellie went to look out of the window. She could see the lighthouse up on the hillside. The bubble bobbed up again. Could the tunnel collapse?

Could it flood? What if they got stuck and couldn't get out? She began to feel prickles of sweat under her tee shirt, and felt sick.

I could leave a note for Mum telling her where we are. I've got to. Eddie will be furious but I don't care. I don't think I'm brave enough to do this, Ellie fretted; she would write the note.

Eddie came rushing back. "It's at least half charged. Aren't we lucky?" He was very excited and went to get ready.

"Good," smiled Ellie. Alone, she went to the desk in the dining room and composed the note:

> Dear Mum and Dad,
> You know we have gone to see Heather for the evening, but what you don't know is that we have discovered a tunnel from Waterside Cottage down through the old lime kiln in the garden. It comes out at Lighthouse Beach across the river. I know Eddie will be cross with me for telling but I had to.
> Love Ellie xx
> P.S. Please don't worry. Eddie and Patrick have been over and back through it once already.

She sealed the envelope quickly and put the note on her mother's pillow.

The plan went well. Three sets of puzzled parents asked a few questions, were satisfied with the answers and shrugged their shoulders – kids! Well, they were nearly fourteen now.

Eddie packed the Moonmirror into a holdall and at four o'clock they were saying their goodbyes and leaving to collect Patrick.

"I'll pick you up at 8.30pm from the lower ferry," nodded their dad from the doorway. "Okay?"

"Okay, Dad," they both replied, and sped off down the Creek dressed in very warm clothes. Each had a torch and spare batteries. Patrick was waiting, wearing a red knitted hat and grinning from ear to ear. Luckily his parents were out so there was no problem going up into the garden and disappearing.

Ellie, who actually thought she might be sick, took some buttermints out of her pocket and handed them round.

"Sweet, anyone?"

Up in the cold damp garden they impatiently swept rocks, leaves and earth away. The sour, mouldy smell crept out at once from the dark hole. Ellie shivered, and they all switched on their torches.

"You go first Eddie, then Ellie, and I'll follow," suggested Patrick, knowing Ellie would be happier in the middle. She glanced gratefully at him.

***

On the Kingswear side of the river, Heather was busy getting herself ready and collected the key from her father's office. She was to make her way to the lighthouse and open the main door, then wait for the three underground travellers to arrive. She was excited and nervous for them all.

"I'll come along with you to meet your friends," smiled her father. Heather couldn't think of a way to say no to him, so she agreed.

"Okay," she shrugged, her heart sinking in despair.

***

Eddie, Ellie and Patrick went down the runged ladder and eased themselves into the jagged aperture. It was quite a squeeze and there was a lot of giggling and unhelpful pushing. Ellie swallowed her fear of the dark and shone her torch all around once she got inside the tunnel.

"Is the red wool still there?" she asked, looking everywhere.

"Should be, we didn't break it or untie it did we, Patrick?"

"No, it's here, look." Patrick found the wool on the floor, a bit damp and dirty now.

"Good," said Ellie, quite relieved.

"Come on, follow me and do try to keep up, Ellie," Eddie called back.

"I'll push her, don't worry!" shouted Patrick.

The three stumbled along the incredible route, with its wet walls, glinting rock particles, mould and damp. Ellie held the wool loosely between her fingers and it seemed to give her confidence. It was the proof that the tunnel would lead her out at the other end.

Eddie pointed out the black cable disappearing down the side tunnel, and Patrick shone his torch to show her the niches cut into the wall. It seemed like an uncomfortable dream as they could hardly stand up straight and their backs and necks ached after a while.

Eventually the ground sloped upwards and Eddie shouted back, "We're nearly there. Look, here's where the red wool ran out and I tied the garden twine on."

The walls changed to a reddish earth with shells dotted in it.

"Thank goodness." Ellie found the damp, earthy smell rather horrible and she couldn't wait to see daylight again.

Patrick caught up with her and felt for her hand to help her up the last bit. Ellie blushed in the darkness but she appreciated the warm human contact, and the last of her fears vanished. *Patrick is so kind,* she thought gratefully.

"Here's the door, look!" called Eddie, and grabbed the iron latch. Ellie was shivering now as the door swung creakily open and she couldn't wait to see what was on the other side. A small circular room with a set of granite steps reaching upwards appeared, with its tiny dirty windows letting in daylight.

"Is this the bottom of the lighthouse?" She voiced her hopes aloud. "Let's hope Heather is waiting on the other side of the next room."

Eddie rubbed his neck which had become stiff and sore. "What did you think of it, Ells?" he proudly asked his sister.

"I still can't believe it." She flashed her torch around in amazement. "What's that?" pointing at a small square black place in the wall.

"Where?" questioned Eddie impatiently.

Patrick went to examine it. He felt all around its edges. "It's a small door. Look, at the bottom those are flood boards, to stop this room from flooding." He bent down to look more closely, and tried to slide the blackened board out of the way but it broke in half. "Rotten," he muttered. The rest pulled out easily.

"Look up there!" Ellie pointed. "A handle hanging on that nail."

Eddie came over, and he and Patrick slotted the handle into the square hole, turned it, and the small door ratcheted back on an old iron track in the floor. It opened unsteadily onto the cold windy beach. A blast of chilly wind entered. The door was three inches thick of tarred heavy timber.

"Lucky the tide is going out. Close it quickly," shivered Ellie. So they closed it with the handle, which was hung back on the wall.

"How did we miss that?" Eddie wondered. "Anyway, let's get on and find Heather. Just one more door."

So up the cold, granite steps they went, to the heavy iron-clad door with its great hinges. Patrick and Eddie freed the cumbersome latch and pushed it open. They were now in the tiny hallway entrance which was surrounded by stone ledges. Opposite them was another door, level with the road, and hopefully Heather was on the other side.

Ellie ran to one of the narrow windows and looked out. She could see across the shingly beach and the lazy water to Warfleet Creek, marvelling that she, Eddie and Patrick had in effect walked under the river.

Hearing voices, Heather, who was waiting anxiously on the other side, banged on the door. "Hello? Are you there?" and putting the large key in the lock, turned it with a satisfying click and opened the door. Three faces were looking at her. "Oh my goodness! I can't believe you actually came under the river! Wasn't it scary?" Heather was bursting with excitement.

"Yes it was," admitted Ellie, "but it was fantastic!"

"What's in the bag?" Heather wanted to know.

"Aha! This is what we wanted to show you," said Eddie and Patrick together proudly. "This is the Moonmirror, one of our inventions."

"Oh? What does it do?"

"Wait and see, my girl." Eddie wagged his finger at her. "Professor McNab and I will demonstrate later. First, let me get you up onto the next level."

The only way to get Heather up the narrow stone steps was to carry her. She pushed her arms and Ellie lifted her legs, like going up the stairs backwards.

"You won't need your wheelchair, there isn't enough room up here!" So they left it in the entrance and seated Heather in a wooden captain's chair conveniently placed by the window. A circular stone bench ran around the turret, and above their heads the old oil lamp with its many lenses and glass prisms twinkled proudly. The light was beginning to fade, darkness approached, but the view was still excellent.

"Tell us your news then," said Patrick as they all sat down at last.

"I had real trouble with my dad, he decided to walk along with me. It was terrible!" laughed Heather.

"Where is he now?" asked Patrick, thinking hard.

"He's gone into our neighbour's, Mr Dodds, the church treasurer. He's the one who helped me with all the ledgers in the church, and… I've got some interesting news."

"Come on, tell us!"

"Ellie and I discovered a letter at Keepers Cottage that day, tucked way back in a kitchen drawer. This is it." She produced it out of her pocket. Eddie and Patrick reached for it but Heather held it out of their grasp.

"No, no, too fragile, let me read it to you!" She carefully unfolded the thin yellowing pages and read clearly.

> *The Lighthouse, Noank, Connecticut*
> *My dear Mary Ann,*
> *I can hardly write this letter to you, but I know I must reply with speed. Since your dear Daniel passed away, I have prayed so hard to think of the best thing to do, but I fear you will all starve if I do not agree to your request to have one of the twins. Sister dear, Tobias and I will take little Ezra, give him a home and bring him up as our own. I can hardly bear to write these words but I must.*
> *It grieves me to hear you have to leave the lighthouse but we are glad you have found lodgings at Warfleet Creek. Send little Ezra on the mail ship from Liverpool under the care of Mr Samuel Codner Esq. who travels to Connecticut and then onward to Newfoundland. He was introduced to me by the Rev. George Watson. He will contact you shortly. Provident indeed, you may agree. Mr Codner is held in high regard in America.*
> *Write at once with all speed, God bless you and little Amos. I never dreamt my childless home would be filled in such a way.*
> *Your loving sister,*
> *Martha Brady*

"And the address on the envelope is: *Mrs Mary Ann King, Start Point Lighthouse, Start Bay, S Devon,* dated 1894. Now, what do you think of that?" asked Heather triumphantly.

Eddie spoke first.

"So – is there a connection?"

"'Course there is." Patrick thought and spoke at the same time. "Plenty of connections, and I'm just beginning to see them."

"Come on then, brainbox," encouraged Elle.

Patrick began. "Mary Ann King took lodgings at Warfleet and the entrance to the tunnel is at the same house, my house, Waterside Cottage. She had to leave Start Point when her husband the lighthouse keeper died, but she must have had a connection with this lighthouse. Maybe her son was once the lighthouse keeper here and lived over a Waterside. Pretty convenient way to go to work, eh?"

"Yes, but nobody is going to build a tunnel for a lighthouse keeper, it must have been constructed by a mine exploration company first," argued Eddie.

"But just listen to what else I have found out. Ready? The King family seem to be a long line of lighthouse keepers. We now know that the twins, Amos and Ezra, were separated as children and their mother and aunt were both married to lighthouse keepers. One emigrated to Connecticut to a lighthouse at Noank and the other, Daniel King, died at his post at Start Bay. Now, I have discovered by chance that one - Abel King, note the biblical names this family favours," Heather raised her finger, "is the verger at St Thomas's Church here in Kingswear. He told me only yesterday that Amos was his grandad and definitely the lighthouse keeper here. His family kept on the cottage at Waterside because Mr Codner had bought the cottage for Mary Ann from an American charity."

"I suppose when he gave up the job, Keepers Cottage went too," mused Eddie.

"Exactly," Ellie and Heather said together.

"But don't you remember, Ellie, going to the boatyard and meeting that old boy in the garden. What was his name?"

"Ezekiel King?" offered Ellie.

"Yes, he told us he had lived at Waterside when he was a boy."

"Well then, he must be Abel's father and a direct descendant of Amos, whose—"

"—brother was sent to America!" finished Patrick, and they all fell about laughing.

"I've had enough of all this," admitted Eddie, who was getting bored. "But good for you, Heather. Now you have tracked down the King family. Well done."

"Thanks." Heather looked down at her notes.

"Well, now for the Moonmirror," announced Eddie, standing up. The girls rolled their eyes at each other. *Typical!* Rather self-focused, as always.

The two boys began assembling their new invention in the world of physics.

"Professor Mc Nab, continue." Eddie urged.

Patrick bowed to the amused girls. He cleared his throat and began. "Good afternoon students, today's lecture is about renewable energy. Solar power, I am sure, is familiar to you, but lunar power is not. Here before you is our new invention, the Moonmirror light, based on the light of the moon. This is reflected by mirrors and strong magnified glass to strengthen it. From the glass panel, the energy is created in the silicon strips and is stored in a small battery, which in turn, illuminates the bulb."

He and Eddie then put the components together.

"Aren't you going to switch it on, after all that?" complained Heather.

"It's not quite dark enough. Just wait a bit longer and we will."

"Interesting news about the King family, isn't it?" Ellie remarked. "Of those twins, Amos and Ezra, that were separated, Amos was Ezekiel King's father, and Ezekiel also had a twin brother, Luke, who was killed in the war."

Patrick's interest was sparked again. He looked up and said, "So the last lighthouse keeper here was definitely Amos. Was he the one who left the letter in the drawer at Keepers Cottage?"

"He must have been, and the letter was a sad memento. Maybe he kept up his duties until he died. He could have used the tunnel to go to light the lighthouse lamp and come back each night to the cottage at Warfleet. Very convenient, eh?" Patrick was amused by this idea.

***

They couldn't have dreamt that at that very moment Ezekiel and Abel were making their way down the dark river, dressed in commando gear from the Second World War. They even had camouflage grease smeared over their faces.

Ezekiel's plan was a good one. Under the cover of the fading light, they had set off. First they had crossed the bridge at the Old Mill and silently crept through the woods, skirting around the Naval Colleg Quay to where the boats were kept. Here, bold as brass, they stole a small clinker dinghy and rowed it across the river. Then, after tying it up, they walked along the railway line to the marina at Kingswear where the red boat was kept. A kind couple from the church had befriended Abel and given him a key to their boat, to use any time for fishing. This was where they were headed. The underwater magnetometer, a relic of the war, would come in very useful. That tin box had to be found and the jewels returned, or they would have no peace for the rest of their lives.

Abel was failing, his energy level dropping. It was his turn to carry the metal detector and it seemed to weigh a ton.

"Look sharp lad, not far now," encouraged Ezekiel, slapping him on the back. Abel stumbled and nearly fell over as his father chuckled to himself. *What a weakling!* Not like his brother, Luke – they'd had a few scary times together in France, doing raids on the docks at St Nazaire. They'd done some paddling together, blackened faces, scared witless, risking all for their regiment.

"Give it to me!" and he snatched the cumbersome instrument off his tiring son, exasperated by his weakness.

"Cor, it's heavy, Dad," complained Abel rubbing his shoulder.

"You're lucky the Germans aren't after you, you'd soon pick it up then."

At last they reached the marina and found the red boat, and they settled themselves down, breathless and sweating.

"Fuel okay?" asked Ezekiel.

"I think so," puffed Abel. *Think so! Bloody hope so*, and Abel crossed his fingers silently. He was exhausted.

Gently Ezekiel coaxed the engine into life and keeping low revs eased her out of the congested marina. Hugging the river's edge they passed the Yacht Club pontoon and slipped away from the small town, chugging up the river in silence as the tide ripped past them on its way out to sea. It was quite dark now.

"Where should we start?" asked Ezekiel. "We've got to allow for plenty of drift. Did you find the marker buoy, son?"

"No, Dad, me and Ben spent hours looking up and down this river. Not even a sign of it."

"I expect one of the fishermen has picked it up, but you do know exactly where you dropped the box don't you?" Ezekiel asked harshly.

"Yes, Dad, right opposite the cove, at the bottom of the garden."

"Good," sighed his father, "got something to go on then. Could have drifted either way, then got stuck on the bottom. You've got the key, haven't you?"

Silence.

"Haven't you, Abel?"

"Um, we did have it, Dad, but we had a set each, and you see…"

"See? See what?"

"I think I dropped mine over the side, and Ben, he had the other one. Ben – well, he's gone, hasn't he ? I only got the one, and then…"

"Ah, shut up your whining, you're useless! Useless, do you hear? We'll have to smash the box open, that's all. Probably rusted anyway." And the man ground his teeth in annoyance and sighed again. "Just let's get this over with now. We've got to find that box."

Abel cowered in the boat. His dad just made him go to pieces. Always did. Treated him like a Royal Marine. It wasn't fair; if that Ben Murphy hadn't run out on him...

"We'll find it, Dad, don't worry, got your magic wand with us, haven't we? Just think what Uncle Luke would say if he could see us now. We'll be there in a minute." Abel softened his father's mood by the very mention of his uncle and they sat in silence, edging up the river in the darkness.

Ezekiel almost believed he was with his brother again, out on a daring raid in enemy territory, blackened and invisible against the searchlights and sentries of the U-boat docks. He looked around constantly and bit his lip. In five minutes they would be at the target; his heart pounded and his mouth was dry. He and Luke would not fail; they never did, they were twin brothers, thinking and feeling the same, the perfect team.

Chapter Twenty-eight
Things go badly wrong

At the foot of the tree-lined cliff, below Woodend Manor Farm, there was an inlet cut into the rock. A steep path led from the garden to the water, where iron rings had been drilled into the rock to tie boats up long ago. It was exactly here that Ben and Abel had cast the red metal box into the sea, secured on a chain to a mooring buoy. Hours later the storm had risen up for several days and ripped their plans apart.

"Just here, Dad," pointed Abel, rocking the boat as he stood up quickly.

"Right." Ezekiel cut the engine to let the boat drift. He switched on the underwater metal detector and lowered it into the black darkness.

"Every tin can and teaspoon will be registering, you wait," as he watched the needle flickering. Once or twice they hauled up some discarded metal objects: a pair of pliers and part of an exhaust pipe. A fishing boat chugged by, causing a strong wake, and the boat rocked violently as the surge hit them broadside on.

"Steady!" called Ezekiel to his companion. "Nothing here, let's try a bit further out."

So they moved a little down river. The tide was helping, pushing them in the direction of the sea. The magnetometer scanned the seabed. Suddenly the needle flickered and the red light glowed brightly. Ezekiel let the strong line out with the huge magnet, and bingo! It locked onto something.

"Pull her up, lad!" hissed the excited man and he and Abel dragged the rope up as an old chain noisily chafed on the side of the boat.

Abel made a silent prayer to his own Lord and slowly and surely a muddy, chipped red box appeared out of the water. Abel leaned out dangerously, tipping the boat in his excitement, and grabbed at the small object that had caused so much trouble and strife.

"Careful boy, you'll capsize us!" shouted Ezekiel in panic but Abel held fast and dragged the box and himself into the bottom of the boat, sprawling backwards in a tangled heap. *At last!* He hugged the muddy box to his chest.

"Well done, good effort!" chuckled his father, watching Abel floundering in the boat like a freshly landed plaice. "Work's not done yet, got to open that damned lock now. Pass the tools over, will you?"

He put the metal detector down carefully in the boat. "Might have another go, see if there's any more treasure down there on the way back," he grinned.

***

In the lighthouse turret, darkness had well and truly fallen, and Eddie and Patrick were itching to turn the Moonmirror on.

"Ready?" As the current flowed out of the batteries and into the bulb, the old lighthouse came to life again. Not only the Moonmirror shone out, but some of the lenses and prisms above them were caught by the light and reflected far out across the water.

"Hoorah," clapped the girls, shading their eyes from the brightness of the glare.

"Isn't that wonderful," breathed Heather, "how clever."

Down on the river, Ezekiel, Abel and the small red boat were caught in the bright glare. Shocked and terrified, unable to understand what had happened, they were both transfixed like frightened rabbits. Ezekiel had prised the lock on the box open, breaking it roughly with large bolt shears. He was standing up in the boat hugging the box to his chest when the white light had illuminated him and he stumbled against the side of the boat. The box swung open and Ezekiel shouted out,

"No! No!"

Before he could close it, a long diamond necklace snaked out from the hinged opening and slithered over the side, disappearing into the water with hardly a sound. Ezekiel tried to jam the box closed but a long diamond brooch was caught in the hinge.

"Damn it, you bloody thing!" Ezekiel roared, took a step, lost his balance, dropped the box and fell over the side with a splash.

"Dad! Dad!" screamed Abel, too frightened to move as everything happened in front of him and glittering diamonds bounced and spread across the bottom of the boat.

Hearing the shouting, the four young people stared out into the light they had created on the black river.

"Look! Look! There's a boat" cried Ellie, shading her eyes.

"And somebody's fallen in," pointed out Patrick.

"What can we do?" agonised Heather. "How can we help him?"

"Where's your Dad?" asked Eddie. "He can phone the coastguard. There's a lifebelt ring down on the beach below here. I'll go."

"Dad's at Gunners Quay, just along from here at Mr Dodd's house, but he might have gone now."

"Doesn't matter, they'll have a phone." And Eddie and Patrick hurried down the steps to the main door. "I'll go down to the beach and try and get the lifebelt to him," Patrick shouted. "That black door will open, it goes to the beach doesn't it?"

"Alright, see you later," yelled Eddie, and disappeared along the road.

"Try to keep the light on them, Ellie," Patrick called up to her as an afterthought.

"We'll try," she replied bravely, hoping there was enough charge left to keep it alight.

Heather and Ellie watching from the window saw splashing and then no more, as the man disappeared from the circle of light.

"Oh God, he's drowned!" Heather gasped. "He's just gone! Where is he?" and she strained her eyes, desperately trying to see him. Ellie moved the light beam around and caught the splashing arms again as the water was reflected in the white glow.

"He's still there! Look!" she pointed. "He's swimming to the bank!"

Ezekiel was very lucky. The tide was slack, just on the turn, the water slowing down and ceasing its powerful drag. He was dazed and confused, the cold water numbing him.

"Bloody Germans and their search lights," he muttered. "Luke's a gonner, poor old Luke," as his mind wandered in confusion and returned to the Second World War. His brother had been shot as they canoed together on a covert mission and Ezekiel had been left to fend for himself to try to re-join his comrades.

He dragged himself to the shore and managed to get a footing on the steep rocks. The receding tide was another stroke of luck for him. Tiny shingle edges were revealed, just enough to step along the bank. He felt on his belt for a hand grenade. *I'll put their lights out for them*, he promised himself grimly.

Abel, unable to comprehend the fact that his father had suddenly disappeared, was left alone and very frightened in the boat. He gripped the sides as he slowly floated out to sea, staring at the diamonds scattered on the wooden planking.

Ben's gone, Dad's gone, what shall I do? Those wretched diamonds have caused me nothing but trouble. I've a good mind to throw them all over the side! He started to sob bitterly as his cold hands fumbled to collect up the priceless collection of Scottish ancestral jewels. Several large brooches, a small diamond tiara, two bracelets and matching necklaces, rings, earrings and two diamond combs were roughly pushed back into the dirty, wet box.

Eddie had run along the road to Gunners Quay, down the steps past the two proud canons and banged on the front door. A light could be seen above the door in the fanlight so he knew somebody was in. Mr Dodds opened the door and was surprised to see a boy standing there.

"Yes?"

"I'm sorry to bother you, sir, but there's been an accident on the river and we need to call the coastguards. Is Mr Fraser still here?"

"Why yes, we've just been discussing that queer light from the lighthouse."

Eddie was anxious to make the phone call. He stepped inside and asked,

"Where's the telephone?"

"I'll see to that, what's happened exactly?" He was leading the way downstairs. "Jack, a boy's here, it's…?"

"Eddie."

"Eddie says there's been an accident and we need to call the coastguards at once!"

Jack rose to his feet immediately.

"Not Heather! Please not Heather!"

"No, no, she's fine, she's operating our Moonmirror light with Ellie. That's what you could see. No, sir, a boat's been spotted with two men in it and one of them has fallen overboard. The other one is drifting out to sea. We need to ring at once!" he told them desperately.

"Right." Mr Dodds went at once to the telephone and called 999, asking for the coastguards and giving the location.

Eddie and Jack opened the French windows and stepped out onto the terrace. They scanned the river, and saw that as Heather moved the light she caught the red boat in its glare, now passing the castle's entrance.

"There it is!" Eddie pointed and Jack saw it at once. Mr Dodds came to join them.

"They're on their way, sending the lifeboat rib out at once. Yes, I can see it now. Well the tide's turning, he shouldn't go too far. No sign of the other one, then?" He looked doubtful.

"Had they got lifejackets on?"

"Don't know, but the one in the boat hasn't," Eddie replied, shaking his head.

"Foolish, foolish of course." Mr Dodds sucked his teeth three times. Eddie remembered his father's words last summer: "you're just a little brown blob in the water and you can't be seen." How wise he had been.

Patrick meanwhile had twisted down the steep granite steps, through the small hall and down into the darkness. He switched on his torch and found the black door. Putting the handle into the square hole, he ratcheted the door open on its small metal track. It ground open and a rush of wind chased in, making Patrick shiver.

A siren sounded far away in the distance. He stepped out onto the beach, his eyes accustoming themselves to the darkness, and glanced behind him to the lighthouse turret. Two small figures could be seen, and the bright light spreading out from the glass window. He felt very proud.

Turning to locate the lifebelt ring, which was hung on a post at the back of the shingly beach, he was immediately grappled to the ground by somebody. A stinging blow hit him across the face, then a hard clunk whacked him on the head, and he passed out cold.

"Got you!" Ezekiel was pleased with himself. He had crept along the shoreline to the beach, just below the illuminated lighthouse. He bent to examine his prisoner. He rolled him over... but it was just a boy! A boy! He wasn't wearing a uniform either. He thought frantically for a moment, and suddenly it all became clear and he realised where he was. He was in Devon on the beach, just where he had played as a boy when his dad had worked at the lighthouse. What was he doing here? Why was the light on again after all these years? Then he heard the sirens getting nearer and nearer and a boat chugging on the river, and remembered. *Abel!* Where was Abel? Drifting out to sea no doubt, in the red boat. Somebody had called the coastguard. He'd be rescued soon, so no time to lose. He felt sorry he'd knocked the boy out, but he'd got to get away. He dragged Patrick to the shelter of the cliff away from the river's edge and ran through the small black door, bending low. He knew exactly where he was going.

Down he went to the large heavy oak door that led to the tunnel, and disappeared. He caught his foot in something and almost fell. It was the green garden twine. Swearing, he untangled the string from his shoelaces and then he realised the significance of that damp thread. He had lost his torch in the fall and had no light of any kind but he wasn't frightened. He'd been through that tunnel many times with his father and now with the string to guide him he felt sure it would lead him to safety.

Chapter Twenty-nine
A most exciting evening

At Watermill Cottage, Mary went upstairs to put the laundry away in her bedroom. An envelope on the pillow caught her eye. She opened it at once, and put her hand to her mouth as she read it. She sat down heavily on the bed, the facts sinking into her brain. She looked up through the French windows across the river. It was beginning to get dark and the water rippled lazily, dark and shiny.

It couldn't be true! Her children couldn't have gone under the river, through some tunnel, it just couldn't be true! She sat there for a minute, her heart pounding, everything swimming in her head. *Peter!* Where was Peter? He wasn't home from work yet, and she looked at her watch. Five-thirty, he'd be here soon. Mary was frantic; she didn't know what to do. She looked out of the window again at Kingswear and noticed a strange thing. The old lighthouse had a pale light shining out from its glassy turret. It looked like... well, it looked like Eddie's Moonmirror light, but it couldn't be. Could it? Mary smiled grimly to herself, shaking her head. Yes, it could be. Eddie, Ellie and Patrick had gone to the lighthouse to show Heather the Moonmirror, through this tunnel they had discovered.

The back door banged and Peter called out, "Hello?"

Mary ran to find him. "Oh Peter, I'm so glad you're home! The children have done something terrible! I'm so frightened, what can we do?" And she burst into tears.

"Tell me, Mary, what is it? Come on now, stop crying. I need you to tell me or I can't help them," and he knelt down by her chair. "Come on, what's happened?" He was very worried indeed. His wife wasn't prone to tears.

Through her jerky sobs, Mary told him about the letter she had found.

"Little wretches! Fancy doing that, I've never heard of any tunnels. God, it can't be safe."

Mary began to cry again.

"Look, I'm going to find them. Get the number of the Frasers at Woodend Farm and as soon as I find out anything I'll let you know. It's the only thing I can do."

"Peter, I've just thought of something. The light's on at Kingswear lighthouse, look. That is Eddie's Moonmirror I'm sure. That means they're alright."

"I'll give them alright, little fools!" Peter was angry now. He put his boots on and a waterproof coat, grabbed a torch and a hard hat from the garage and left saying, "Don't worry, Mary. Ring the Frasers for me. Okay?"

She nodded, waving from the window, drying her eyes with a tissue. Peter raced down the Creek and reached Waterside garden. He saw at once the hole with its iron ladder leading down.

He swung himself down the ladder; being used to ships he was quite at ease. He recognised at once that it was a proper doorway that had been bricked up. That was a good sign because it meant all this had been constructed properly. He took a deep breath and forced himself into the dark tunnel. Quickly he made his way along, shining the torch before him.

Thank God it's not leaking, he sighed gratefully. A heavy black cable clipped neatly to the wall disappeared down a small side tunnel. *Telephone cable,* he told himself. He was beginning to get backache from the low ceiling but ignored it. Reckoning the journey across the river was six to seven hundred yards, and hoping he would soon be halfway, he suddenly heard a noise. He shone his torch in front of him and was horrified to see a pair of eyes in a dirty face. A man dressed in what looked like combat clothes with a blackened greasy face loomed up at him.

"Who are you?" Peter challenged him. "Have you seen my children?"

Ezekiel was furious to find somebody coming in the opposite direction; he had so nearly got away. He stood back with his legs apart, firmly planted on the rocky floor, and slowly unhooked the hand grenade from his belt. He held it out in front of Peter's face. "Look, see this? I can blow this tunnel to kingdom come. Now, you let me pass and I'll be on my way. I got no quarrel with you. You'll find one of your boys on the beach. I'm sorry but I had to hit him to get away. Now, make up your mind."

Peter stood aside at once. He wasn't going to tackle a man with a hand grenade even though he wasn't frightened of him. "Fine by me." And Ezekiel pushed past him and disappeared into the darkness.

Phew! Peter breathed heavily and then worried about the boy on the beach. Patrick or Eddie was lying injured out in the cold. What was the tide doing? He hadn't noticed in his haste. He began to run, and finally reached the end of the tunnel, up the sloping hill, into the entrance, where water was beginning to lap in through a small open door.

The tide's coming in! Peter realised at once. He crept out of the low opening to find himself on Lighthouse Beach with the tide advancing. A crumpled figure lay under the cliff, not a flicker of movement showing. He raced to the body to find Patrick with a bruise on his face and blood coming from his hair. Peter knelt down, calling Patrick's name quietly. He knew better than to try to move him.

"Come on old man, I'll get help for you." He checked at once that he was still breathing and mercifully he was. As Peter turned his head towards a noise in the distance, a boat chugged towards him, lights piercing the darkness. A lifeboat rib was towing a red boat in. Immediately, Peter flashed his torch at them. Slowing their speed, they came gingerly to investigate, assuming it was the missing man.

Peter shouted to them that Patrick had a head injury and the coxswain radioed for a doctor to be standing by at once. "We can't move him until the doctor sees him." Peter offered to stay with him until they returned.

The rib headed off quickly to deliver Abel to the police waiting at Kingswear, keen to investigate the strange happenings on the river. The local doctor hurtled out of his cottage and stood on the jetty at the Yacht Club. As the lifeboat pulled in, the crew bundled him on board and returned at full speed to Patrick, who had now regained consciousness but was feeling sick and groggy.

Peter managed to refrain from questioning him, but only just. He was very anxious that Eddie and Ellie did not try to return to the tunnel, especially with that madman around. Doctor McAfee declared Patrick fit to be moved and the injured boy was stretchered onto the lifeboat and delivered to Dartmouth hospital for observation overnight.

Peter entered the lighthouse and climbing the steep stairs two at a time reached the turret room where Jack, Mr Dodds, Heather, Eddie and Ellie were all squashed in together, wondering what on earth was going on.

"Dad! How did you get here?" Eddie was totally bewildered to see his father, who by the look on his face, wasn't too pleased with them.

"Patrick's gone to hospital by boat. Some scoundrel attacked him on the beach, bashed his head and knocked him out."

"Oh no!" They were all horrified. Eddie began to stammer,

"But…. but, he went down to throw the lifebelt to the man who fell overboard. I wondered where he was. I didn't worry… Is he alright?"

"Well he's conscious, thank God, got a bit of bruising. We'll see tomorrow. I suppose Sam and Irene think he's with you, having a good time at Heather's." Peter rolled his eyes, not too happy with his offspring. He turned to his daughter. "If Mum hadn't found your note, I don't know what would have happened. Why didn't you tell us about the tunnel? It was very irresponsible of you. I came to find you, then I was stranded on the beach with Patrick on an incoming tide, waiting for the lifeboat. Not the best of evenings I've ever had."

"Oh dear, we're so sorry, Dad." And Ellie burst into tears. The whole thing had got the better of her. Heather was devastated about Patrick. Eddie went red and pursed his lips together.

"Sorry, Dad. We just wanted to come under the tunnel to show Heather the Moonmirror. I wanted to make the lighthouse work again, that's all. I didn't realise there would be all this fuss," he said defiantly.

"Well, we can discuss this 'fuss' later," Peter told him sternly, "but you can thank your sister for having the good sense to tell us where you were, otherwise Patrick might have been in real danger."

Jack realised that tempers were high, and said "Why don't you all come back to Woodend Farm with Heather and me and we'll have something hot to drink? We can phone everybody to tell them the news. Especially your mother, she must be frantic. Yes? Come on, I'm intrigued with all the things that have happened tonight, and Morag will want to hear about Patrick."

So before Peter could protest, he found himself making his way along the road, one arm around each of his children, Heather leading the way. Even Mr Dodds came, he didn't want to miss out on the excitement. The lights shone out brightly as they approached the big house and Morag, hearing voices, opened the front door.

"My, my, quite a gathering! Come along in!" Something had obviously happened but thankfully her daughter and husband were alright. Beside the fire they drank hot tea and buttered toast, and then Jack poured the men a whisky.

"Try this, Peter. Philip, hope you like it, it's a new blend we've been trying."

Morag was very sorry to hear about poor Patrick, and Heather badgered her to phone the hospital to check on him. Jack rang Sam and reassured him that his son was in good hands. Mary was relieved to hear from Peter but was rather shocked to hear about Patrick.

Everyone could sort of see that the Moonmirror had been a great idea and that the old lighthouse had looked magnificent rekindled once again, but Eddie's success was spoilt now, knowing that Patrick had been injured. If only he had gone to find him.

There was a loud ring at the doorbell and when Jack went to see who it was, Sergeant Tim McDonald was standing there.

"Good evening, Sergeant McDonald," greeted Jack. "What can I do for you?"

"Good evening sir, may I come in? I have some interesting news for you and Mrs Fraser."

"Of course. Don't be surprised at the amount of people here because we've been having a bit of an evening."

Jack led the policeman into the warm room with its blazing fire, where he was introduced to everyone. He only knew Mr Dodds and Morag.

"Did you catch that mad army guy with the hand grenade?" asked Peter at once. "Did he do the robbery? He looked the type."

Everyone looked at Peter in amazement.

"What army guy?" Jack was puzzled.

"Shall we find somewhere quiet to discuss this, sir? I need to make a few notes." And Sergeant McDonald stood up and ushered Peter, Jack and Morag into the privacy of Jack's office. Mr Dodds was disappointed, now he wasn't going to hear what was going on.

Tim McDonald turned back. "Mr Dodds, I shall need you in a minute."

Philip Dodds smiled appreciatively, "Of course, officer."

Tim announced that the police were holding Abel King in custody and that he had been arrested on suspicion of stealing the diamonds from the Fraser's house on Christmas Day.

"But he couldn't have done it, he was in church all the time. We were there on Christmas morning. You must have made a mistake, officer," burst out Morag.

"Well you see, madam, he had an accomplice, and although he didn't actually remove the diamonds himself, we think he masterminded the robbery and the events afterwards. We've caught him red-handed with a boatful of diamonds! He's pretty distressed because the man he was with is his father, and he fell overboard."

"Was he drowned?" Jack was horrified.

"Doesn't seem so, sir. Last seen swimming for the shore." Sergeant McDonald turned to Peter: "And now perhaps, sir, you'd be good enough to tell us about this man you saw?"

"Yes, of course. I've had such a strange evening. I returned from work to find my wife very distressed. It seemed our children, Eddie and Ellie, had disappeared through a tunnel they had discovered, leading from Warfleet Creek, which apparently came out inside the old lighthouse. I went to find them and bumped into this crazy fellow, all dressed up in combats, greased face, the lot. I told him I was looking for my children and he took a hand grenade off his belt and threatened to blow up the tunnel if I didn't let him past. Of course I didn't even try to stop him, but he did say he had hit one of the boys, and for that he apologised. Then he ran off. I knew it had to be either Eddie or Patrick and was very worried. I found Patrick injured and unconscious on the beach and the lifeboat already on call."

"Thank you, sir." The policeman wrote everything down. "I suspect that was Abel's father. Both were dressed in clothes which apparently had been kept since the Second World War. I expect the hand grenade was the same vintage, and harmless, sir."

"Don't you believe it, officer, I've been trained in such items. A bit rusty maybe but I wasn't prepared to risk it," Peter assured him.

"I need to make a phone call, Mr Fraser, may I?" and Sergeant McDonald and Jack went to find a more private phone.

"Send a car out, Jenkins, at once. We are looking for a man aged seventyish, dressed in combats, greased face, may be dangerous, in possession of a hand grenade, so be careful. Warfleet area, name of Ezekiel King. Wanted in connection with the jewel robbery at Woodend Farm. Get lively!"

They returned to the office together.

"Have you recovered all the diamonds, Sergeant?" asked Jack.

"No sir, I'm afraid not. Abel has told us that several pieces fell over the side when his father was trying to open the box, but there are a lot left. You can come to the police station tomorrow to identify them."

"How did Abel get involved?" asked Morag, sadly.

"We shall know more tomorrow, ma'am. He wasn't in a very good state. We're hoping he can make a confession and statement in the morning."

Morag looked disappointed.

"I can guess if you like, Mrs Fraser, but this is strictly off the record. Do you understand?"

"Of course!" Peter, Morag and Jack shivered in excitement.

"We think Abel befriended an Irish itinerant agricultural worker called Ben Murphy who came to Kingswear homeless and looking for work. Oh, ask Mr Dodds to join us, he needs to hear this."

Jack obligingly fetched him. He sat quietly, eager to listen. Sergeant McDonald repeated what he'd said about Ben Murphy. "Abel, being a kind soul, offered Ben a place to sleep in the old church lock-up store, without permission of course. Were you aware of this, Mr Dodds?"

"Certainly not! I had no idea anyone was sleeping in there. It's full of old choir robes and spare chairs, and well, junk."

"I suspect they heard about your inheritance, Mr Fraser, and hatched a plot together. It was in the local paper I believe, an article about the whisky heiress."

"Yes it was," admitted Jack, "I thought it was good publicity!"

"I have seen Abel in the Railway Tavern with a rough-looking sort of man. Was that him?" asked Philip Dodds.

"Probably. He's disappeared, run out on Abel, but we've got a missing persons search out on him now. We'll get him, don't worry about that." Sergeant McDonald continued: "Abel knew when you were coming. Again, local gossip. Will Lane had asked Abel for help several times at the farm. He knew if you came for Christmas you would attend morning service. We think Ben did the actual robbery, somehow getting into the house, and together they dumped the jewels in the river to be collected later. Abel's father obviously decided to help him as Ben had left him holding the baby. It all went wrong somehow. We'll find out tomorrow."

"Do you think that Ben fellow took the money from our boxes?" asked Mr Dodds indignantly.

"Almost positive, sir, he needed the cash to get away. He also did very well from the post office. Jim and Iris were very kind to him. He even took two of Iris's pasties on his escape!" laughed Tim. "I expect his fingerprints are all over the place. We'll soon see."

"We've lost a very good church verger," sniffed Mr Dodds. "Abel was a dedicated Christian, devoted to the church."

"Well, instead of helping others, sir, he succumbed to temptation and helped himself!" laughed the policeman. Mr Dodds was not amused.

"All this is speculation of course, not fact, so please do not discuss this with anyone else. Will Lane will be questioned again but I feel sure we have the right man." The sergeant smiled at Morag.

"That maniac I met in the tunnel, he's this poor chap's father, is he? He escaped from the beach when the boat capsized, is that right?" asked Peter.

"Yes, sir, we think he was helping his son recover the stolen property. Shall we join the others now?" Sergeant McDonald firmly closed his notebook. They went back into the sitting room and joined the waiting group.

"We saw that boat, didn't we, Ellie?" burst out Eddie as soon as they were all together. "I remember now, on Christmas Day we went for a walk before lunch and saw them. We thought they were fishing! It was the same red boat."

"...and the storm came the very next day. I expect they marked the place with a buoy and the storm ripped it out. They lost the jewels and they have been looking for them ever since," finished off Jack Fraser.

"We've seen that boat several times since then and they've had fishing rods. We just thought they were... just fishing," laughed Eddie. "Maybe those keys we found are theirs!"

"Good, that's very go, we've got witnesses now," smiled the policeman.

There was a knock at the door and Jack opened it to find DC Jenkins standing outside.

"Car to take you all home, sir." And so the various people were despatched home for the night. Eventually the Frasers closed the door and Morag, Jack and Heather were left on their own. Heather sat with Robbie on her knee.

"Sad, isn't it?" she said wistfully, looking into the fire. "We shall never use those diamonds, probably hardly ever wear them, we didn't buy them and we didn't ask for them, and yet look at all this terrible stuff that has happened because of them! It makes me feel awful. People must hate us because we've got so much money. I never really thought about it before."

Mary and Jack exchanged glances.

"What would you do with the diamonds, Heather?" her father asked quietly.

Heather stared into the flames and thought for a while. The room was filled with silence. No one moved, and ideas flashed through Heather's head and seemed to be drawn up the chimney and into the air outside, like the flames flickering and dancing before her.

Eventually she spoke.

"I'd like to keep one piece of jewellery for me, and one piece for Mum, then the rest I think I'd sell and with the money, do something for the people of Kingswear. Not sure what, but something to improve people's prospects or children's' futures, that sort of thing."

Jack and Morag swallowed, and tears glistened in both pairs of eyes.

"Then that is what shall happen, just as you have said, Heather," her father said quietly. "We'll talk about it tomorrow."

Heather, still looking into the fire, smiled and said dreamily, "Tomorrow? Everything is going to be different tomorrow, isn't it?"

Morag wondered what exactly Heather meant. Was it the decision about the diamonds? Was it the frightening events she had witnessed this evening? Patrick's hospitalisation and Abel's imprisonment; the possible drowning of a deranged father? Or was it the glances and laughter she had noticed between her new friends, especially Eddie? Morag had her own thoughts about this.

Chapter Thirty
A satisfactory conclusion

Ezekiel was well aware of the escape and evasion tactics required to outwit the police. Nobody was going to capture him! His Commando training from so long ago had been rekindled and was now renewing his mind and spirit.

He was heading towards Beesands village, where his cousin Josiah had run the village pub for years. He kept to the fields, travelling along the hedges where there were plenty of places to hide. When he was exhausted he crept into the outhouse of a convenient farm and lay in the straw close to a very surprised pig and her piglets in the next concrete byre.

His age, 72, was against him; he was tired and needed to sleep. At first light he woke, stretched and set off again, finding some turnips to gnaw on. He made his way around the coast, stealing a bottle of milk from a cottage doorstep and downing it gratefully. He even put some money on the cold granite step to replace it. *Must be getting soft in me old age!* he chuckled to himself.

At last, weary and aching, cold and damp, he arrived at the Cricket Inn and knocked on the door. He had already washed his face in a cold stream to get rid of the camouflage grease. Josiah's daughter Enid opened the door.

"Uncle Ezekiel! What a surprise! We're just having breakfast, come on in and join us!"

"That'll do," he smiled, and sat down with the large family. "Well cousin, nice to see you, been a long time!" Josiah lit his pipe after his breakfast.

Lying skilfully, Ezekiel ate and talked.

Enid's husband Matthew announced he was going scalloping later that morning.

"I'd love to come, just fancy a blow on the sea. Got room for a spare crew?" asked Ezekiel gently.

"Why yes, Uncle, got one off sick today, now there's a bit of luck," laughed Matthew, pleased.

So half an hour later, full of breakfast and far from shore, the *Lizzie Ann* was making her way across Start Bay. Ezekiel was putting miles between him and his pursuers.

The police were getting nowhere with their search. The trail seemed to have gone strangely cold.

***

Ben Murphy stepped off the ferry at Cork harbour, much to the relief of the passengers sitting near to him. That old fellow stank! Everyone had kept their distance from him, he could see their noses wrinkling in disgust as the smell from the old crab shells got worse.

Whistling cheerfully, he headed off towards the west. A lorry driver he had spoken to in the bar, as they drank a pint of Guinness together, picked him up a few miles along the road.

"Where are you going?" he asked Ben kindly.

"Doonbeg," said Ben, hopefully.

"Hop in then, I'll get you as near as I can. Alright?"

"Now that's an offer I can't be refusin'! You're a grand man." And Ben climbed into the cab. Not long afterwards the driver regretted his kindness as slowly the smell reached his nostrils. It was enough to put him off his rashers, slice of wheaten and the mug of tea he was anticipating at his next stop! Pooh! He opened the window an inch.

Three hours later, fed by the friendly driver and deposited five miles from the village, Ben Murphy whistled and smiled at the side of the road, heaving his old bag over his shoulder. *Haven't I the luck of the Divil himself!*

He set off with renewed determination to walk to Doonbeg Bay. A low, single storey whitewashed cottage had been a constant vision in his dreams on restless nights; golden thatch, green half-door with a fuchsia hedge around the garden and red geraniums in the small glass porch.

"I'm coming home, Grandda, I'm coming home," he promised.

The reality was somewhat different. As the grey rain fell, a wet, bedraggled man approached Briar Cottage. The roof was mostly gone, the door hung on its hinges, and every window was broken. Tall weeds and rusty iron implements graced the garden. Ben shivered. In the misty distance the sea murmured, waves crashing, grey and white, but to this travel-weary soul the vision was still strong.

Won't take me long. I'll get her back into shape. At least it's empty, no tenants to burn out.

He was not discouraged. To him it was the most desirable place in all the world, and hopefully one necklace from the great Scottish Collection would do it. He must be patient. In good time he would make it happen. He was here now and he wasn't going to leave his ancestral land ever again. He breathed in the damp misty air. He was home!

***

Nobody seemed to remember or care about Abel King, sitting silently picking at his nails in the empty white cell. Without his father he was sad figure; without Ben, there was no one else to take the blame. He sniffed and wiped his nose on his sleeve. There was a knock at the door. He jumped in fright. What now? He didn't want to go to Exeter Prison – the thought terrified him.

A policeman opened the door loudly, keys jangling, and showed a familiar figure in.

"Mr Dodds!" Abel was so very pleased to see a friendly face.

"I'll leave you sir, half an hour alright? I'll keep my eye out for you." And he pointed to the cell window in the door.

"Good morning, Abel." Mr Dodds spoke in a kindly voice. "I thought you might need a little help today. If you like I could represent you. It's a little unusual, but not against the law. I was training to be a solicitor before I became a bank manager. Not good with the darker side of life, you see. Not good at all. But I'll do what I can to help you out. Whatever you've done or not done, Abel, you didn't do it to me and we have always got on, haven't we?"

Abel nodded silently, the kind words upsetting him. He didn't deserve this. He'd done wrong and he knew it.

"I did it Mr Dodds. I did do it, I'm really sorry now, I really am. Very sorry. Ben's gone and me Dad's drowned. It's all terrible." He sobbed wet tears into his hands which covered his ashamed face. He sobbed with his shoulders heaving in great gulps. All his guilt and worry, fear and dread welled up and poured out. He was inconsolable.

"Now, now." Mr Dodds patiently patted his shoulder in an embarrassed way. "This won't do, Abel, it won't help." He handed Abel a large white freshly ironed handkerchief. "You'll feel better now you've got all that out of the way. Let's begin at the beginning, shall we? It may not be as bad as you think." So, kind Mr Dodds began to listen as Abel gathered his thought and told him everything.

***

The following morning at Watermill Cottage, Eddie and Ellie were undergoing a thorough grilling from their father and mother.

"You'd have thought we committed the robbery," remarked Eddie bitterly. Ellie remained silent and upset. She hadn't done anything except try to prevent Eddie from killing them both in that awful tunnel. As was her way, she remained stubbornly loyal to her brother until it was all over.

"And now we must go and visit Patrick, and then we are going over to Woodend Manor Farm to apologise to Mr and Mrs Fraser for involving Heather in this fiasco," said Peter sternly. "I don't know what they must think, bringing Heather into all this the first time you all go out together. Really!"

Peter went on and on and Mary grew tired of it. The children were sulky and defensive; Peter was cross and continued to complain about everything.

"Oh, let's go and see Patrick then, shall we? No harm has really been done, Peter. Come on, they take after you, you know, spirit of adventure and all that Navy stuff?" She twinkled her eyes and laughed.

Peter suddenly realised that perhaps he would have done exactly the same thing, and maybe he had been a bit hard on his youngsters.

"Okay, but let's wait and see how Patrick is before you're off the hook, you two." And he wagged his finger at them both. Ellie and Eddie glanced at each other. They knew it was going to be alright, and heaved a sigh of relief.

The family were at Patrick's bedside in twenty minutes, where he was enjoying being the hero of the hour. He had a large dressing on the side of his head and a purple and red eye peeping from it. Two pretty nurses, Nadia and Kate, were busy looking after him and five other men on Britannia ward.

"Nice to have a young man for a change," winked Kate, as she had shown the excited Ellie and Eddie in.

Eddie had spent all night feeling very guilty.

"When are you coming home?" asked Ellie, shyly handing over a box of Patrick's favourite chocolate toffees.

"Tomorrow," Nadia told them. "Just waiting on the x-ray results."

"I'm very sorry I left you," blurted out Eddie. "I thought you were on the beach waiting for the lifeboat. I should have come down to make sure you were alright..." He stopped, getting upset.

"No, no, don't be ridiculous!" Patrick said at once. "Nobody could have known he'd be violent. It's not your fault. Don't say that!" and he became upset too.

"Alright, alright," soothed Mary, "It's fine now, you're all heroes. There's some exciting news from Woodend Farm to tell you all. Morag rang to tell us most of the diamonds have been recovered. Just one or two missing."

"Wow, that's fantastic news!" they all agreed, exchanging excited smiles.

Mary continued, "If you hadn't gone to the lighthouse to show Heather the Moonmirror you wouldn't have caught those two retrieving the diamonds. It was all just good timing. You all played a very important part. You see?" She looked at her husband triumphantly. Peter was thrilled at this information. The children would not be blamed now for what had happened.

"Heather and her father have been in to see me already," Patrick told them. "She says it was the most exciting evening she has ever had!" Eddie and Patrick's eyes met. They had got away with it – just.

An hour later they arrived at Woodend Farm. Peter had insisted his children apologise to the Frasers. Will Lane was sweeping the path by the front door.

"Good morning," he said pleasantly, leaning on his broom.

"Hi!" greeted Eddie and Ellie, a little awkwardly.

"Fine goings on," nodded Will, "was it you lot that lit up the lighthouse?"

"Yes," Eddie replied shyly.

"Heather told me. Lovely it was, lovely! Poor old Abel, feel sorry for him, there's no harm in him, you know." Will shook his head. "I've got to go and talk to that Sergeant McDonald later on. Right glad I am it wasn't me."

"Come on then, ring the bell," Peter said impatiently. Will returned to his sweeping.

"Like to see that light of yours sometime," he called cheekily to Eddie, who laughed and nodded, sticking his thumb up. Ellie giggled and looked at her father. He didn't think it was funny.

Morag greeted them and led them into the kitchen where Heather was baking scones.

"Mmmm, something smells good." Eddie sniffed appreciatively.

"You can have one in a minute," she told him. Dressed in red today, she looked very pretty indeed and Eddie gazed at her for just a bit longer than normal. Morag made coffee, and seated by the big bay window in the drawing room, the two families shared Heather's treacle scones, an unusual Scottish treat.

"Really nice," Eddie commented, munching, as Jack strode in to join them. He smiled.

"Seen Patrick?"

"Oh yes, just been to the hospital."

Eddie and Ellie immediately apologised for involving Heather in such a serious incident.

"Nonsense, nonsense, it was all an adventure, good character-building stuff. Sam and Irene are a bit shell-shocked but got a result, didn't they? Did you hear our news? All the diamonds recovered except three pieces. Not bad, eh?"

"That's great," agreed Peter. "Do you know which pieces are missing?"

"Yes," replied Morag. "A graduated necklace, a pair of teardrop earrings and a large pendant, a single stone. It was brought back after the Boer War by my great-grandfather, Montague Fraser. It is a rather special champagne diamond. It actually wasn't one of my favourites but it was worth a lot of money."

"You could send divers down to try to find it?" suggested Eddie helpfully.

"Don't you worry about it, laddie!" chuckled Jack. "Let the insurance company in Edinburgh do that!"

"We're going to sell the diamonds anyway," announced Heather. "Set up a scholarship or educational bursary with the money, something for local children. Aren't we, Mum?" She turned to her mother.

"Why yes, that's what Heather has decided," Morag replied quietly.

"Great idea, isn't it?" added Jack enthusiastically.

"That's brilliant," said Eddie admiringly, giving Heather a flashing smile. She blushed and returned the warm smile.

"I'm glad you all agree."

Having cemented their friendship well and truly the families parted, everyone feeling the visit had been very worthwhile.

"Come and visit us next time," offered Mary. "Heather can help fill the aquarium."

"I'd like that," was the reply.

As they sat on the ferry in the fresh air, many thoughts swept through the minds of the four people huddled together. *What a difference a day makes,* as the old song went. It was so true. Everything had changed. Heather was right: things would be different from now on.

Chapter Thirty-one
An end to the mystery

Eventually the facts trickled out, and the village gossips on both sides of the river had a field day exaggerating everything. The harsh reality was that Abel took the blame for it all in the absence of Ben Murphy, who had evaporated off the face of the earth. Nothing could be proved as Abel's fingerprints were not on the keys or in the house, and Ben could not have his prints taken to match the ones the police had found.

Ezekiel had been tracked down by detectives to the Cricket Inn. His hand grenade had been confiscated, and although he had been eliminated from the robbery inquiry he could still be accused of being an accessory to the recovery of the diamonds and assault. Tim McDonald knew he wasn't a real villain; he had willingly come to the assistance of his son in a desperate attempt to help him.

Ezekiel was soon back in Mill Cottage, shaken, tired, a little confused and very cross with Abel. If you were going to commit a robbery you could at least do a proper job and get away with it, he thought irritably.

He slept off and on in his armchair by the fire, dreaming of his brother Luke and old times with his family. Many memories had been stirred up; memories of Amos and Jenny, his parents, of the lighthouse, and the mystery and excitement of the tunnel opened up for the cable-laying for the first international telephone connection between Europe and the UK. Memories of him and Luke fishing and sailing and eventually their call-up into the army; all these thoughts swirled round and round. His sadness at the loss of his brother, his disappointment with his milky-faced, frail son and the death of his beloved Dorcas. It was then that his heart had sealed over and refused to bear any more pain. His garden and the solitude of the Creekside cottage were the only pleasures left to him now. Tired out by the last few days, Ezekiel fetched himself a tot of rum, stoked up the fire and gazed into the flames, sipping the familiar fiery syrup. Visions of Dorcas's pretty face swam in front of his eyes; she was laughing. He smiled as he drifted off to sleep. Luke, strong and brave, beckoned to him with a cheeky grin. Ezekiel smiled back at him as he eagerly left the chair to join them. He never woke up again.

***

Mr Dodds broke the news to Abel, who sat stunned and silent in the police cell. He was about to be let out on bail.

"But... but Dad was strong and fit, he was never ill," stammered the quiet man, bewildered and unbelieving.

"He'd had a hard life. The war, providing for a family, losing his wife, who knows? He died peacefully, Abel, and he's probably left everything to you – the cottage, his savings. You'll be alright, you wait and see." Kind Mr Dodds comforted Abel as best he could.

Sergeant Mc Donald appeared, and gently during the next hour he and Philip Dodds got all the rest of the information they needed from the frightened man. The last pieces of the puzzle were slotted together. It seemed that Will Lane had unwittingly been the source of much of the information Ben and Abel had relied upon.

During lunches at the Railway Tavern they had found out when the Frasers were around, where the jewels were kept, important facts about alarms, locks and keys, all supplied cheerfully by the talkative Will over a pie and a pint. Abel had discovered where the key to the house was kept the day he went to the stables to help Will with Ginny. A key hung on a nail inside the stable door opened the back door, and the alarm code was chalked above it. Abel had watched him slyly from the passenger seat of the Land Rover; it was so easy

He had said nothing and noticed everything. Ben Murphy had used this key to get into the house on Christmas morning.

When the Frasers arrived at church that morning, the whole family, Abel gave Ben the nod and the robbery had gone into motion. Hiding the jewels in the prepared red box after church, they got the boat out and sank the locked box, chain and marker buoy to be recovered later with strong sea fishing rods and heavy-duty magnets. Simple. Or so it would have been, if the storm hadn't ripped the buoy out and let the box drift away. Since then, the two men had spent many frustrating hours trying to recover it.

Will Lane had in fact been totally innocent of any involvement in the robbery, but his casual attitude to the privileged information he was entrusted with had been a huge factor in the theft. The idea had grown from a seed planted in Abel and Ben's minds. Idle tongues in small villages could be very dangerous, as Tim McDonald knew only too well. Silly, foolish Will.

All attempts to trace Ben Murphy had failed. Even Abel knew very little about him except that he had a brother Pat in Limerick. The detectives from Kingswear had handed the case over to the Guardai – the Irish police. There was not enough evidence, other than his tearful confession, to convict Abel. The fact that he was found with the diamonds didn't prove he had taken them.

Abel was released into the hands of Mr Dodds, who assured him his job at the church was still available. After all, he told Abel cheerfully, the Christian faith is based on forgiveness. Most people would forget about it, given time. He was expecting Abel to be given a suspended sentence, and encouraged him to enrol in a community service scheme at the local college, helping teenagers with learning difficulties to read and write.

Abel found he had a great deal of patience with these disadvantaged youngsters and helping them get their lives started again made him feel very good. Even Heather took an interest in it and promised to devote one evening a week to the project: she was becoming quite good friends with Abel. The strangest things bring people together, thought Mr Dodds quietly to himself one morning, as Heather turned up in the church office.

"Great news, Mr Dodds, the case against Mr Abel has been dropped. Mum and Dad don't want to press charges and there is nothing the police can do. We've recovered most of the diamonds, so – no harm done!" She twinkled a smile at him.

Philip Dodds' pale straw-coloured hair fell in his eyes as he looked at Heather. He swept it away impatiently.

"That is fantastic news, Heather."

"We're going to sell the diamonds, you know. I've got plans for the money. I've just enrolled Will in our new class in the village hall. Computers are Kids' Stuff," she laughed.

"Really? Maureen, my wife, might like that. She's terrified of our computer." Mr Dodds was very interested.

Everything was different, as Heather had predicted. Many people had been affected by the diamond robbery and its ripple effect continued throughout the village. Heather, Patrick, Eddie and Ellie became an inseparable four. They took turns riding Ginny and fought and argued over an archery tournament held outside Heather's cottage. All too soon, school loomed up on the horizon. Patrick would have to make the long train journey to Edinburgh, Heather would be driven to West Sussex, and Eddie and Ellie must return to their local schools, a boat or bus ride away. It was a miserable prospect.

"Let's have a party!" suggested Ellie. "I'll ask Mum. Let's have a good send-off and cheer ourselves up! Shall we?"

"Yes, and we'll ask everybody! What about hiring the village hall?" asked Heather, perking up.

"We can have music in there and make as much noise as we like," grinned Eddie.

"Great idea!" agreed Patrick.

So after consultation with their parents and a phone call to Mr Dodds, the party plans began to take shape. Heather printed invitations and posters on her computer, watched by a mesmerised Will.

Mr Dodds was persuaded to hire a local band, The River Raiders. Will and three of his friends had been messing around in a garage for years, driving all he neighbours mad. Two played guitars, one a keyboard, and Will was on the drums.

"I never knew that you played in a band, Will." Heather was full of admiration.

Jack and Morag volunteered to supply the drinks, Mr Dodds sorted out a licence, Irene and Sam, Peter and Mary agreed to organise the food. Abel was to sort out tables, chairs, the crockery and the cutlery from the church kitchen. Even Bridget and George were roped in, to help with the supper. Invitations went to the police station, the hospital, the lifeboat station, coastguards, village shop and the ferry crew.

Mary asked Heather and Ellie to scout around for some spring flowers to decorate the tables with. The day before the party, Heather was delivered to Watermill Cottage to wander the paths around the church and Creek in search of flowers with Ellie, while Eddie and Patrick went fishing at the castle. Ellie helped the wheelchair down along the Creekside path, where they spotted the first primroses and some hazel catkins.

"Look there, let's pick those. Where does that go?" Heather pointed, noticing a smooth path leading towards the river.

"That's the ferry slip, do you want to go down?" Ellie asked.

The wheelchair fitted easily down the path.

"You can see our house from here," said Heather. "I could swim across on a calm day," she laughed.

This path led down to the water but a set of steps barred the way. "What a nuisance. I can get out and bump down the steps on my bottom. It looks so lovely, there's a tiny rocky bay there."

"Will you be alright?"

"Yes, come on, don't fuss about me."

Ellie watched silently as Heather lowered herself out of the chair, turned round and sat on the ground. She shuffled neatly down the steps and dangled her legs over the edge of the tiny inlet.

"Heather?" began Ellie hesitantly, "How did you hurt your back?"

After a short silence the answer came. "I fell off Ginny – she lost her footing going down a hill and I went right over her head and damaged my back as I hit the ground."

"Will you always be…you know, in a wheelchair?"

Heather sighed. "I haven't severed my spinal cord. It just didn't seem to work, no messages get through at all, so I can't tell the muscles what to do. It's been a year now, so, to tell you the truth, I haven't tried to walk for a long time, because well… it's so frustrating and disappointing."

"I see." Ellie wished she hadn't asked.

They sat together in silence, enjoying the closeness of the water and the swish of the waves in the tiny inlet. Cormorants and oystercatchers skimmed across the surface of the river, calling loudly. Something caught Heather's watchful eye.

"Look at that! What is it, Ellie?" The two girls peered into the water. The shadow of something passed by beneath them, then another strange shape swam into view. Both disappeared into the waters of the dark inlet.

"That looked like a turtle, didn't it?" Heather turned to Ellie in excitement.

"It did," agreed Ellie, "but what was that other thing?"

"I don't know. Let's wait for them to come out again, they've got to come out sometime."

Both girls stared intently into the clear moving water, seaweed swayed and shadows were cast on the sandy bottom. Suddenly a dark shape appeared – a turtle, swimming practically beneath them. Alongside him was the strangest thing they had ever seen – a small neat creature that was neither fish nor bird, but its head was human and it definitely had a little face. Ellie and Heather pointed to it at once, calling out in excitement, but the two swimming shapes turned left and disappeared quickly along the dark rocky shore.

"What was that?" Ellie wondered out loud. "One was definitely a turtle and the other thing looked like a sort of fish, but I'm sure it had a funny head? What do you think?"

"Yes, yes," Heather nodded emphatically, "it was exactly as you said. Could it have been a seabird?"

"But it didn't have a beak, did it?" and they both laughed, a little puzzled.

***

Ptolemy and Cornelius had been out fishing for royal ferns and blue moss, the favourite diet of the unusual child. He loved his morning swim to collect food with his turtle guardian. No sea creature had even been curious about Cornelius as he swam among them. His small wings were stunted and too small to allow him to fly yet, but to his parents he was a bird first and a boy second. They never tired of looking at his beautiful face, sea green eyes and his crown of golden curls. His delicate hands made up for his awkward feet, webbed between the toes. On his head the silver circlet of three fishes was almost buried in the soft hair.

Sargasso and Seraphim had handed over the upbringing of their child to Ptolemy at the request of the Spirit of the Sea, accepting that he was not as other fledglings.

At the small quayside, Cornelius emerged from the water shaking the droplets from his body. Ptolemy followed slowly and clumsily up the steps.

"Mother! Mother! I saw other creatures sitting on the edge just along from here. What were they, Mother?"

Ptolemy listened. He had made Cornelius swim away quickly from the two girls. It was the first time they had encountered humans so close to the water.

"They were girl children, my son, and one of them is our special friend. Soon you shall meet her. They belong to Tellus, they are Earth people. Some of them come and visit the water. They swim a little but they cannot live in the water like us."

"And Caelum, do they ever visit him?"

"No, child, they have no wings. Yours will grow as you get bigger and one day you will soar up in the sky with your father and me. That is why you are so very special, my son."

"Come, eat now," urged Ptolemy.

At that moment Sargasso flew in and landed on the small quay. "Eddie is fishing at the castle," he told his wife joyfully. "I chased a few mackerel his way. Ellie and her friend are at the ferry slip. Well, son, what have you learnt this morning?"

"Father, I saw them too. Two of Tellus's people sitting by the river. One had her feet in the water but they didn't work. Why do they not?" he asked.

"I have no answer to that," replied Sargasso wisely.

Ptolemy spoke to Cornelius.

"The child of the Earth has injured her legs. She can no longer walk on them. There is no energy flowing."

"Poor Earth-girl."

So, unknown to Heather and Ellie, they had been noticed and discussed. Ptolemy made up his mind to be more careful where he took his little charge in future. He knew Sargasso was very keen to show his son to Eddie and Ellie, but he had persuaded him to wait. The wise old turtle was determined to keep their child from discovery for as long as possible. How could he conceal him now the girls had caught a glimpse of him? Not easily, but he would try. But would Sargasso reveal their secret before Ptolemy was ready?

Chapter Thirty-two
New beginnings with a great party

Heather and Ellie returned with their flowers and Patrick and Eddie brought five mackerel proudly home from the castle's rocky edges. Together in the kitchen they fried the fish in seasoned flour and ate them at once.

"We saw Sargasso," Eddie told the girls, and Patrick raised his eyebrows, his mouth full of tasty fish.

"We haven't seen them for a while," sighed Ellie. "Did their egg ever hatch, I wonder?"

"Who are they?" Heather asked. The other three looked at each other, but nobody spoke.

"Is somebody going to tell me?" Heather insisted.

Eventually Ellie and Eddie told her the strange story of their friendship with the seagulls and the robin.

Heather was dumbstruck. "Oh I see," was all she could say, eventually.

"It does seem hard to believe, I know that," said Patrick earnestly, "but the three of us have had the most fantastic adventures together. That's why I wanted to come here so much. Everywhere else is boring and dull compared to Dartmouth."

"We might let you hear some of it, but only if you swear," Eddie challenged her.

"Alright, I swear," answered Heather, bravely.

For the next hour she sat listening to tales of the Seafarers and the Woodlanders, of Captain Avery and the good ship *Fancy*; of Isabella and Ferdinand, the two white mice who had lived at St Petrox church for 300 years; of Umbraluna, the little glimmering shadow from the dark side of the moon; of whales and seals and dolphins, of bats and owls and buzzards. Heather felt dizzy trying to keep up with it all. When at last Ellie, Eddie and Patrick had finished, she sat back, exhausted.

"Well… Nobody would believe that, I can assure you."

"Good," said Ellie. "Now, what about this party?"

Mary and Morag returned with the shopping just then, loaded up with carrier bags. "Good! Here's some helpers!" Mary smiled.

Everyone set to work, and soon the kitchen smelt of sausages, cheese flans, chicken and ham pies, cakes, tarts and meringues, all conjured up in just a few hours. Everyone helped, even the boys.

"There," sighed Mary, "thanks, kids!" She washed her hands and hung up her apron.

"I'll make the tea," offered Ellie.

"I'll never get up again!" groaned Morag, wearily.

After delivering the food to the church hall kitchen in mysterious foil parcels, Morag and Heather went home. The first thing Heather did was to get her binoculars out and scan the river closely, but no mysterious turtles or strange mutant birds broke the surface. She sighed. *When the weather is warmer I shall swim in the river, that's something I can do even with my stupid legs,* she told herself cheerfully.

At five o'clock the following afternoon, Bridget and George arrived at Patrick's house ready to man the tea urn, with a huge boxful of iced fairy cakes covered in tiny coloured roses. Squeezing into Sam's big black car, they set off for Kingswear.

At the church hall they found that Abel, and Will Lane, had transformed it into a party venue. The band had covered every inch of stage with wires, amplifiers and several microphone stands, and some silver mesh had been hung across the back wall. A black and white banner announced THE RIVER RAIDERS in slightly wobbly letters.

Mary, Peter, Eddie and Ellie arrived next, and soon jam jars full of small spring flowers and a candle in a bottle stood on every table. Mr Dodds helped Sam set up the bar, at Irene's insistence as far away from the band as possible. Abel brought the crates of glasses over.

"Here you are, ma'am." Irene was going to be a barmaid for the very first time.

"Thank you," said Irene, eyeing him quizzically. "Is he the one?" as she dug Sam in the ribs, "You know, the diamond robber?" she hissed loudly.

"Shut up, Irene!" Sam replied at once, as Abel blushed, pretending he didn't hear. It was going to take a long time for people to forget.

By seven o'clock it was ready. Jack, Morag and Heather arrived with all the wine and beer, and Will and his friends were tuning up and practising. It was a great atmosphere, the music filling the hall with its bright insistent beat.

Peter and Sam had blown up many red balloons, and tied the long strings in huge bunches. "I'm ready for a beer." announced Peter, finishing tying the last bundle. He sat down heavily and sighed.

"Irene?" Sam called. "Bring us over two beers would you?" He winked at Peter. Irene at once carried two beers over to them obediently. Putting them on the table, she smiled sweetly.

"That will be ten pounds, please," she told them.

"What!" frowned Sam.

"I need some float in my bar money. Some change would be helpful." She continued to smile at them both. Fishing in their pockets they both produced a handful of coins.

"Thank you so much," and she wiggled off across the room in her high heeled shoes, looking back and laughing over her shoulder.

Heather and Philip Dodds kept Abel busy, making sure he was not left to face the public alone. The Rev Watkins had talked for a long time with Abel, helping him to think for himself now that his father was gone.

Heather darted about in her wheelchair, pink faced and with her hair plaited neatly down her back. She was to take the door money and later sell the raffle tickets.

At 7.30pm people started arriving. Heather was ready, and Eddie came to help her, sitting down behind the table.

"Don't you trust me?" Heather said cheekily.

"Yes, of course. Just thought you might like a hand, that's all," shrugged Eddie gruffly.

Sergeant Tim McDonald and Nadia walked in together, holding hands and smiling.

"Good evening," Tim said pleasantly. "It looks lovely in here," said Nadia looking around appreciatively, as they shyly made their way into the hall.

Patrick at once bounded up to Nadia. "It's so nice of you to come!" He was thrilled to see the pretty nurse again.

"You've still got a bit of a bruise left haven't you?"

Patrick stroked his eye gingerly. "Yes, but it's going... He's dead now, you know," he said sadly.

"One less to bother about," remarked Tim dryly.

"Tim!" Nadia was shocked.

"Only joking, Nadia, don't be so serious! Come on, there's eating and drinking to do!" He pulled her away.

The crew of the lifeboat came in and Abel and Rev Watkins looked after them at once, finding them a big table and getting them all a free beer. Will Lane and his friends started the music and the party began. At half time supper was served, and the deserving band sat down together for a rest.

"Great grub!" smiled Will, tucking in. "Where's Abel?" Looking around, he saw him in a corner with Mrs Watkins the vicar's wife, and Mr and Mrs Dodds.

"Oh dear, he's stuck in old fogeys corner! You get him dancing, Miss," he nodded to Heather. "He's allowed a bit of fun too!"

After supper the music began again, the lights were dimmed, and the candles made a calm relaxed atmosphere. Just about everybody got on their feet to dance. Heather showed off her wheelchair dancing skills and Will watched smiling, as he thudded on with his loud drums. He'd seen her dancing in the kitchen before.

The youngsters forgot to be shy. Heather grabbed Abel from the corner and she and Ellie took turns in dancing with him. Abel was actually enjoying himself.

Jack Fraser then got onto the stage and asked everyone to stop for a minute. He took the microphone and cleared his throat.

"This won't take long. Sorry to interrupt, but I've just got a few wee things to say. A big thank you to all who contributed to this evening, and an even bigger thank you to everyone who helped us out in the drama of the last few days. My wife and I are selling the diamond collection at our daughters' insistence, and we are investing the money in the future of Kingswear. Several scholarships will be set up to help further education, and computers will be made available as well. A new course is ready for enrolment now. I want to thank my daughter for pointing us in the right direction – we seem to have been looking the wrong way. This village is a very special place and has become important to me, and so have the people in it. That's all, and thank you."

A cheer and resounding applause followed, and then conversations buzzed around about the exciting plans revealed by Jack Fraser.

"I've already enrolled in a class – "Computers are Kids' Stuff," Will proudly announced to his unbelieving band members.

"So have I," added Abel, going bright red at the thought of it. Everyone agreed it was a fantastic idea.

"Would I be able to join, do you think?" Maureen asked her husband shyly. "I mean, I'm not too old, am I?" Phillip Dodds smiled, looked at his quiet little wife of twenty-three years, and put his arm around her.

"No, my dear, of course not. I think it will be the best thing you've ever done. You'll see." And he gave her a hug.

"Oh good," she replied happily.

The evening ended on an optimistic note, something to move the village on and help everyone forget the strange happenings of recent times. The coxswain of the lifeboat, Robert Brown, approached Jack shyly.

"Mr Fraser, could you point me in the direction of the lad who made the lighthouse work again? I'd like a word with him."

"Certainly, Rob." He pointed to Eddie, where he and his friends were helping to tidy up, mainly consisting of noisily bursting all the available balloons.

"Could I have a word?" Rob approached the rowdy group and singled Eddie out.

Eddie put down his red balloon and joined Rob rather warily. Was he in trouble?

"That light you had, up in the lighthouse, could I have a look at it sometime? Somebody told me you had invented it. It's not solar, is it?"

"No, it's not." Eddie shook his head. "It's – well – it's lunar!" He laughed nervously.

"Lunar?" questioned Rob, "That's unbelievable, I'd love to see it sometime. Would you let me?"

"Yes, of course," said Eddie, "I'll bring it round to you at the lifeboat station if you like."

"Maybe Saturday? 11 o'clock?"

"That'll do," grinned Eddie. "Saturday, 11 o'clock."

"Okay, fine. See you." And off went a very pleased Rob Brown. He'd got ideas for that light.

Reluctantly the party broke up, people drifted home, and the great evening was over, but firm foundations had been laid between people who had only nodded to each other before tonight.

"Mustn't miss the last ferry," warned Mary, looking at her watch and then at her husband who was deep in conversation with George and Jack. Irene and Sam were with Morag, renewing their old college friendship from many years ago.

"Come over and see us, have some supper," said Sam warmly, "we've got the sweetest place at Warfleet Creek."

But Irene looked like thunder.

"Fine. Sounds great. Now you good people should be about your bed, you'll be missing that ferry. Peter, George, time to go," Morag insisted.

Reluctantly the youngsters parted. Patrick had to return to Scotland to Burnside College in the morning. The grown-ups fetched the cars, and waving goodbye, set off for the lower ferry.

"That was such a good evening," sighed Ellie, leaning back against the seat wearily.

"You all did a great job. It was a real success," Peter told them, looking in his mirror. "Do you know how much money you made?"

"No," replied Eddie and Ellie together.

"£520.13p" announced their father, proudly.

"That is fantastic! We're going to give it to the lifeboat, we all agreed that."

"Well, it's a sort of insurance policy for if we ever get stuck out in *Pelican*, isn't it Dad!" joked Eddie.

"I hope we never will," Peter answered. "That would be very embarrassing!"

They arrived home tired. Eddie and Ellie remembered to thank their parents as they slowly climbed the stairs.

"It was a great evening, Mum, wasn't it?" Ellie yawned.

"Yes, dear, now go to bed." And soon the lights went out at Watermill Cottage, one by one.

Chapter Thirty-three
A chance meeting, and the Easter holidays begin

Heather was an extremely resourceful girl, and a very determined one. She could not get the vision of the strange creature she had seen out of her mind. It had been fascinating, streaking under the glassy green water. She knew it hadn't been a bird, but it wasn't a fish either. She made up her mind that before she returned to school she would to go for a swim early one morning to look for it again. She would check the tides, wear her wetsuit and clip a thin line onto herself to ensure her safety. She wouldn't go far, just keep to the rocky edges on the Kingswear side of the river.

Heather laid her plan carefully. Everything fell into place two days later. She got up at six-thirty, packed her bag and quietly left the house. She tracked down the garden until she reached the long flight of shallow steps which led to the small cove. Her wheelchair had to be left behind here.

She pulled on the gloves and her hood, and then some neoprene shoes onto her lifeless feet. Next she put a mask and snorkel on her head, and bumped down to the foot of the steps on her strong arms.

Everything was still, fresh and untouched. The sun began its arrival in the east and the water lapped, clear and inviting. Edging to the gravel beside the river, Heather clipped a cord to a mooring ring in a rock and the other end to her belt. She put on a thin buoyancy aid and she was ready; her heart nervously beat and she felt butterflies churning in her stomach. Was this a good idea? Level with the wide expanse of river stretching hugely both sides of her and far out to the horizon, she felt suddenly afraid.

"Too late now!" Heather told herself sharply, and made an effort to enter the shallows, as bobbing small wavelets covered her feet and one larger wave engulfed her legs. "Here goes!" and with a final push from her arms, she was afloat. The cold water seeped into her suit with an icy trickle and Heather drew a sharp breath in. Gradually the trapped water warmed up and she began to paddle herself along the river in the direction of Lighthouse Beach. All the time, the coil of neatly folded thin blue cord unravelled gently behind her.

Across the river, Sargasso and Seraphim were waking Cornelius and feeding him the last of the seaweed they had been instructed to give him. His mother ran her beak several times through his shiny golden curls and smoothed his small feathered wings.

"He's ready, Ptolemy," called Sargasso, as the turtle lumbered gently across the stones at the foot of the quay steps.

"Come, my little master, ready for your morning swim? We must gather more royal weed today."

Cornelius smiled, his green-blue eyes exactly matching the colour of the creek water that morning. The small bird boy waddled a little clumsily on his webbed feet, his fish-skin shorts and legs smooth and shiny.

"Goodbye Mother, goodbye Father." He turned at the top of the steps and the seagulls both nodded to him, watching proudly. Unlike human children he had grown at the rate of a gull chick and was now walking and learning independence.

The turtle and the bird boy entered the river joyfully, their bodies light and agile in the cold oxygen-filled water. Occasionally they came up for air, gliding on the surface, noting their positions and greeting any Seafarers they encountered. Cornelius was becoming a familiar part of the marine life around the shores of south Devon.

"Look," pointed Cornelius, "one of those Earth-children is in the water, over there." Heather's head was just visible above the surface, a little way across the calm River Dart.

"Yes, you are right," noted Ptolemy, "come, we must be on our way," and he signalled towards the mouth of the River. "Come, Cornelius," he repeated.

"No, I want to see the Earth-child!" and mischievously Cornelius dived under the water and began swimming towards the opposite side. Ptolemy could do nothing but turn and follow the child, who sped off like lightning, streaking across the water. The tide had not yet turned.

Heather, who was enjoying herself immensely, had changed direction and was swimming back up the river towards home. She felt exhilarated and excited by her brave adventure. The buoyancy of the water gave her freedom which she revelled in and her legs floated loosely behind her, no longer a dead weight. Heather's strongly developed arms were easily able to propel her through the chilly water.

She pulled her mask and snorkel down. *Just five more minutes*, she promised herself, *and then I'll go home. I feel really great; I have wanted to do this for so long!* And happily she ducked under the surface.

It was slightly dark with black shapes beneath her, but her eyes soon became accustomed to the gloomy light. Eventually and inevitably Cornelius and Heather glided towards each other. Ptolemy kept a safe distance, just able to glimpse his charge. Heather's eyes widened as something approached her; she kept completely still, her legs floating down as she ceased moving.

Cornelius circled her, recognising her face; he smiled and took her hand, knowing her legs had no power. Heather wasn't quite sure what was happening but she did know that soon she would need air. They swam together along the rocky edges in a kind of synchronised slow duet, until Heather broke away from him and pointed to the surface. She pushed upwards with her arms and immediately broke through the still water with a splash and a spout of water from the snorkel tube. She breathed deeply and fanned her arms on the surface. Cornelius followed, his head, full of glistening curls, appearing next to hers, his lovely child's face dripping with water droplets. His blue-green eyes caught hers and he smiled.

Ptolemy took this chance, and nudging up to the boy, guided him away as quickly as he could between his front flippers. Cornelius had no choice but to leave Heather and was soon past the castle and being propelled out into the open sea, just below the rocky cliffs. When they stopped for a rest, Cornelius frowned and spoke crossly to the old turtle.

"Why did you do that, Ptolemy? I was enjoying myself. I wanted to talk to the Earth-child, why did you not let me?" His face was contorted in a grumpy scowl, his mood petulant.

"I am your guardian, Cornelius, sent by the Spirit of the Sea. It is my responsibility to ensure your safety and education. I am entrusted with this task and therefore I shall choose who you reveal yourself to," he told the boy sternly. "You are but a fledgling yet, not ready to take the world upon you. Just wait a little longer. You do not see the dangers because you are so young," Ptolemy continued rather more kindly. "We must choose your friends carefully."

"Well, I shall tell my mother and my father that you spoilt my swim," Cornelius told him with a toss of his small head, and once again swam swiftly away from the surprised turtle who had to follow the bird boy far out into the ocean.

By the time they reached the Caves of Drach, Cornelius was in a better mood. They gathered the blue moss and the ferny weed together and eventually made up their quarrel. The child was tired now and rode on Ptolemy's back all the way home, even falling asleep for part of the journey, warmed by the overhead sunshine and soothed by the waves which lulled him.

He's only a baby still, the old turtle consoled himself, *he doesn't know anything yet.* But his insistence and surprising independence that morning was duly noted by his guardian who sensed his task may not be as easy as he'd first thought.

Heather meanwhile was in a state of slight shock as she sat on the bottom step getting her breath back. She had coiled up the blue cord, removed her snorkel hood and mask and was trying to relive what had happened. She ran her fingers through her wet hair and closed her eyes, relaxing in the spring sunshine.

It had been real… it was a sort of duck child, beautiful, and an agile swimmer. It had hands too, as she remembered the feel of the small fingers in hers. They had swum together, gliding gently in the half-lit water just below the surface, almost like a dream. She began to doubt her own memory… it had been such a strange experience.

She sighed and opened her eyes, confused and still wondering. The river was waking up and the tide beginning to rush back in. She started her weary climb up the steps backwards, pushing on her arms and at last reached her wheel chair; she elbowed herself onto the seat and turned around with a heavy thump. She had forgotten how much energy was required for swimming. Sitting for a while to regain her strength, she gazed across the river and sea, looking with new eyes, hunting for signs of her extraordinary discovery, but there were none; nothing at all disturbed the peace of the early morning.

***

A few days later, back in Sussex at her boarding school, Heather kept her discovery to herself. She found she didn't want to tell anyone about her chance meeting, not even Ellie or her parents; it was her own special private secret.

Her family continued with their wishes to sell the Scottish jewel collection. Arrangements were made by a reputable firm of auctioneers from Edinburgh to come and view them.

As Easter came around, Patrick returned for the holidays to Waterside Cottage and to work at the café run by his beloved Bridget and George. This year for the first time all the kids were to be employed as waiting staff. Eddie, Ellie and Patrick couldn't wait.

"It's hard work when we're busy," George told them seriously on the very first morning of Easter week as Ellie put small bunches of daffodils into vases on every table. Eddie and Patrick put the metal tables and chairs out and were given a bucket of soapy water to wash them all with. Their eyes met. Maybe this wasn't going to be quite so much fun after all. They set to work with a will and had a bubble fight with the leftover water.

Bridget laughed, holding a towel out through the door. Then the deliveries arrived and Eddie arranged the new postcards in the racks and put bags in all the litter bins. There was more to the café than he had thought. As he walked around the side area with the best view, he gazed across the river to Heather's home. He admired her quiet confident courage. He didn't know if he would be quite so cheerful confined to a wheelchair. She managed so well and hid her feelings about herself whatever they were; he wondered, in a moment of serious silence.

Something caught his eye in the water. As he gripped onto the railings, he thought he saw the shape of a turtle, dark against the light surface. The shadow swam quickly up-river and was gone. Bridget tapped on the window beckoning him in. A party of walkers had turned up all wanting toasted sandwiches and hot cross buns.

He nodded and hurried inside to help. The rest of that day was extremely busy and the team of five worked hard, and most important of all, smiling at each and every customer.

By six o'clock there was the cleaning and tidying up to do, ready to start all over again tomorrow. It had been a long and busy day.

"We're exhausted," announced Eddie, giving Patrick a nudge. "Can we have a day off tomorrow?" with a wink to his friend.

"When you've earned your keep, my boy," Bridget announced crossly, "and until then, you'll work every day, won't they, George?" No one had ever seen Bridget like this.

"Call that work?" she continued. "You youngsters don't know what work is!"

"Only joking – sorry, Bridget," said Patrick at once. Eddie then realised that for two years she and George had worked like this every day, including during a hot summer.

"Sorry, Bridget, bad joke," he told her quietly. "Let's go home shall we? Ready, Ellie?"

"'Bye, George, 'bye, Bridget." And they hurried off.

Patrick and George waited for Bridget. "I think she must be very tired," said George quietly. "I've never known her get cross before." And he smiled weakly at his godson. When they got home Patrick went inside with them.

"Sit down, Bridget, please, I'll make you some tea."

Surprisingly she did as she was told and when Patrick brought the tray she looked up at him rather sadly.

"I don't know what's the matter with me today. I'm sorry I was cross. I'm so fond of you all, and…" She became upset and tearful.

"You need a holiday, Bridget," Patrick said firmly.

In the kitchen where George was preparing supper, Patrick mentioned it to him. Together as they peeled potatoes, carrots and parsnips, they planned a treat for Bridget. Neither of them had noticed she needed a change.

"I'll take her to Madeira, she'll love it there," promised George. "You're right, Patrick, I'll go and book it tomorrow. You'll be back for Whitsun and you can all look after the café together again. This Easter holiday can be your training!" He looked very pleased.

Patrick felt a little horrified. *Left in charge? Just the three of us? We can't do it!*

By the following evening the idea was a reality. True to his word, George had booked a week in Madeira for the May bank holiday and Patrick had booked himself a week of very hard work.

Never mind, he told himself, a week with Eddie and Ellie will be great.

The phone rang and it was Peter.

"Would anyone like to come and join me on Wednesday evening? We're taking *Pelican* out for her first trip."

George and Patrick jumped at the chance.

"Yes, please! What time?"

"Seven o'clock at the Royal Dart pontoon."

"We'll be there. Thanks."

"Goodness me, things are really kicking off," laughed Patrick.

"You must get your little *Sargasso* out soon too," encouraged George.

"There's so much to do," sighed Patrick. "I'd better phone Dad and get him down here to help with the boat."

However, Sam and Irene had other plans for Easter. An invitation from a fellow banker to a ski chalet in St Moritz was a much greater pull.

"But we've just been down to Dartmouth," his mother told him cheerfully. "We'll come next time, my darling. I'm so excited about going to Switzerland. You'll have a wonderful time with Eddie and Ellie. Don't forget to go and see that poor girl, Heather. Such a shame. Well okay, my dear, must dash. Don't be a nuisance, will you?" she added brightly. "Must go, 'bye!" And before Patrick could interrupt her she had hung up.

He was left feeling furious. She hadn't even let him speak to his father, and fancy calling Heather "that poor girl". *How dare she?* he fumed. *I don't know why but I thought they had changed a little since they'd been living in Dartmouth with some real people.* No, he had been wrong. Back in their own world nothing had changed. He went down to his bedroom, suddenly unable to face the sympathetic looks he would get from Bridget and George. He sat on the bed, looking out at the river darkly gliding by.

"I hate my parents," he told himself angrily. "They are so selfish. They have never cared about me. Everything's always about them. Well, from now on I'm going to do everything I want to. I'm going to make a life without them, then they can't hurt me anymore!" and he roughly swept the tears off his face. "No! I'm not going to be upset. I don't need them. I hate them!" and the unwanted tears ran down again. He stood up and looked in the mirror. "They're not worth it." Wiping his face crossly again, he took a deep breath and went to the window. He could see the lights of one or two houses across the river. One of them was Heather's. "Think of Heather, she's got something to cry about!" He composed himself, gritting his teeth angrily.

He went back upstairs. George was putting supper on the table, a large steak and kidney pie with vegetables. It smelt wonderful. He invited him with a friendly gesture. Patrick smiled at these two good people who loved him and gratefully joined them. Bridget was feeling better now and looking forward to her holiday.

"Any news, dear?" she asked gently.

"Mum and Dad are busy this Easter so they won't be coming." Patrick announced it, eating the delicious pie with gusto. "But really, it doesn't matter, Eddie and I can get the boat out and if you don't mind helping too I think we'll manage it."

"Yes, of course, you know I will," replied George, meeting Bridget's knowing gaze. No more was said on the subject of Sam and Irene McNab; they had fallen from grace yet again.

As fate springs its many strange events in life, a surprising twist was awaiting Sam and Irene in St Moritz. On the first evening, their party of affluent bankers were dining out at the best hotel, when across the tables Irene noticed a blonde girl with her back to her. An elegant dark-haired lady and a very handsome gentleman were on either side of her. Facing Irene was a teenage girl with long dark hair, talking and waving her hands about. They were all laughing, and although Irene couldn't hear what they were saying, it was definitely English.

After dinner, everyone was in the lounge for coffee and brandies and Sam and Irene were strolling past the tables when a voice said to her,

"Good evening, Mr and Mrs McNab." Irene turned to see Heather smiling at her.

"Good heavens, Heather! What are you doing here?" Irene said rudely. "I mean, what a surprise!"

"Yes, I'm on holiday with Mr and Mrs Shapiro. Ruth is a very close friend of mine from St Agnes School," and Heather politely introduced them. Sam and Irene had heard about Joel and Evelyn Shapiro. He was a well respected member of the Government. They chatted for a moment, and then Irene and Sam caught up with their group for coffee.

"Well!" said Irene. "Fancy seeing her here. Quite the young lady, isn't she?"

"Yes, she's a very brave girl. Any reason why she shouldn't be here, Irene?" Sam asked sarcastically.

"No, of course not! Only, she can't ski, can she?" Irene sniffed, crossed her elegant legs and sipped her coffee. "Poor thing."

"St Moritz isn't just about skiing, Irene, as I think you know," Sam replied, wishing his wife wasn't quite so unkind sometimes – Irene, who usually only skied for a couple of hours, spent the rest of her day in the shops, beauty salons and little gossipy coffee snugs.

The next day she was the get the shock of her life, as overtaking her on the mountain slopes, Heather and Ruth drove past her on a fast sled led by four husky dogs.

"Hello, Mrs McNab, lovely morning isn't it?" Heather called out, laughing. "Can't stop!" And she urged the dogs on, leaving Irene standing in amazement. Sam stood laughing his head off.

"Well done, Heather, well done! That's not the poor thing you spoke of last night, is it dear?"

Chapter Thirty-four
Sailing in *Pelican* and preparing for a fishing trip

The Easter week ground slowly by and work at the café doubled. Good weather brought crowds of people to Dartmouth. Eddie had discovered that Heather had been whisked off to Switzerland by a school friend and he was more disappointed than he could have believed. The three youngsters worked like Trojans as endless people filled the chairs and tables as soon as one became vacant.

Wednesday evening eventually arrived, and with it the first trip on *Pelican*. The seven of them caught the 6.00pm ferry and walked the short distance to the marina. Ellie was content to relax in the glorious evening and to feel the excitement mounting. At last Peter told Eddie to untie the ropes, and gently they chugged out onto the river and were soon heading out to sea.

Bridget and Mary sat in the comfortable seats with the soft breeze blowing, viewing the passing gardens and riverside houses. George and Peter chatted away as the boat passed the Old Bath House, the church, and the tea shop. How different it all looked from down here.

"Right, let's get the sails up." Peter roused them all and they set to work. It seemed an endless muddle of ropes, winching and shouting, but eventually the wind caught the taut sails and *Pelican* finally took off, slicing through the waves at an alarming rate, spray occasionally blasting over the deck.

Peter brought a bottle of champagne from down below and popping it loudly, the fizzing wine was shared around in plastic glasses.

"Here's to many successful trips in *Pelican*," he toasted them all. "The crew makes or breaks a boat, and I'm very lucky to have such a good one. Cheers! Right, around the buoy and steer her home, Eddie. You can all take turns."

The wind was strong out in the bay and *Pelican* glided firmly through the water.

"Look! Look! There!" called Mary, "Isn't that a turtle?" Everyone rushed to look over the side of the boat, but it had vanished.

"Oh it's gone. I'm sure I saw something."

Eddie looked carefully, remembering how he thought he had seen one a few days before. Suddenly, far above his head he saw Sargasso and Seraphim keeping pace with the boat. He nudged Patrick and Ellie, who watched as well. Once more the turtle resurfaced and this time everyone saw it.

"There it is again!" shouted Ellie, and she noticed that the two seagulls were exactly over the place where the turtle was. Then as before, it disappeared and the gulls flew off.

When the boat returned to the marina and everything was put away neatly, the three had a chance to whisper together.

"Did you see Sargasso and Seraphim?"

"I'm sure they were following the turtle."

"Definitely.

"I've seen it before," Eddie told them.

"So have I," Ellie announced. "Heather and I saw it down at the ferry slip. There was another strange thing with it. I still haven't a clue what it was!"

"What do you mean?" scoffed Eddie, "That's really stupid, you don't know what it was?"

"Well no, I don't actually, it was weird, not like anything I've ever seen," she told him. It was like a duck but Heather and I were sure it had a head like, sort of—" she paused, suddenly feeling very silly." "Like a human being, only very small."

"Don't be ridiculous! You girls! Honestly!" laughed Patrick.

"Well, that's what it was like. If you don't believe me, tough!" an angry Ellie replied.

"I'm going to go and see Sargasso and find out what's going on. He'll know," Eddie told them confidently.

That particular evening was a week before the full moon, known as the Hare Moon. Cornelius had grown at an alarming rate, becoming such an agile swimmer that Ptolemy anticipated it would soon be time for his longest swim yet. This was to be a test; part of the Seafarers' code to establish the independence of marine offspring.

Cornelius was almost ready. He had to swim to Start Point lighthouse and back alone. He had only one week until the Hare Moon. Ptolemy would still accompany him until the chosen time. Sargasso and Seraphim had come to watch his progress on the evening that *Pelican* had gone to sea, when the children spotted the gulls with the turtle.

Of course Cornelius was different; he had three tests to pass, one for each of the three fishes he wore on his silver circlet. Tellus, Caelum and Altum Mare. The boy had to satisfy each one that he could adapt to the three habitats of the Earth and prove to the Spirit of the Sea that his experiment would work.

The boys and Ellie were keen to get out their own small boat which was now in the ownership of Patrick. For two evenings they worked industriously down at the boatshed under the Old Bath House preparing the Cornish shrimper for launching.

"Thank goodness!" said Ellie, breathing a sigh of relief. "My hands are red raw and blistered."

Work at the sea shop took priority and the three beavered willingly, while other sailors enjoyed the freedom of the Easter holidays. After clearing up, the evenings from six o'clock were theirs. Not a minute was wasted. They closed the door, turned the sign round triumphantly and rushed off.

Both the boys wanted to do some fishing and made several rod rests out of old wood and nuts and bolts. The shrimper's launch was planned; the clocks had gone back and the evenings became longer. It was about to happen.

Eddie often looked across the river as he worked away, watching for signs of Heather's return. He was rewarded a week later when he glimpsed someone in a red tee shirt on the terrace. She was back! He felt a wave of excitement and his stomach shivered. He began the longest three hours he had ever spent, until it was closing time.

"What are you looking so pleased about?" asked Ellie, grumbling as she waded through a mountain of washing up.

"Nothing," he replied, still smiling. Ellie rolled her eyes and shook her head. Eddie could be so annoying sometimes.

"I'll go and get some bait. What about putting my lobster pot down?"

"That sounds great," agreed Patrick, "we could sell any lobsters we get at the tea shop, couldn't we?"

"Good, I'll go and check if it's alright. Coming, Ellie?"

"No, I'm too tired tonight."

Ellie went on home letting the boys examine the lobster pot that Eddie had made several years ago. It was dusty and cobwebby, covered in black plastic, right at the back of one of the lime kilns.

"Blast, Sargasso's not here. I wanted to ask him about the turtle." Eddie was disappointed. He examined the lobster pot disdainfully.

"It needs a new funnel and rope, I'll give Joe a ring and he can bring it tomorrow." Joe and his brother Alan ran a larger fishing boat, the *Pride of the Dart* and landed their catch at the small slipway at Warfleet most evenings.

"Did their egg ever hatch out?" asked Patrick, eyeing the scattered sticks and odd feathers where the seagulls had been.

"It's funny you know, they never said anything more about it. We haven't seen a gull chick with them. Maybe it died or didn't even hatch. Ellie didn't want to ask and then we sort of forgot about it," said Eddie, feeling rather guilty and heatless. But surely Sargasso would have told him? Other things had replaced his interest in the gulls; more grown-up things.

"Right, well if you don't need me I'm going up to the cottage," Patrick told him.

"Okay, I might get some bait. See you later," he smiled. Good old Patrick, he was a great friend to have.

Eddie stood for a while thinking about Sargasso and Seraphim. He was annoyed with himself for being thoughtless and spiralled into a bad mood, dark and sad, and kicked a few stones into the water. Seeing an old crabbing line rolled up with a rusty hook sticking out of it, he decided that he didn't want to go home.

Prising some mussels and limpets off the rocks with his Swiss army knife, he sat on the edge of the steps to see what he could catch. It was a fine, dry evening. The wind had dropped and the river was peaceful. He took a deep breath and sighed, twisting the bait onto the rusty hook, relaxing after the busy day and discovering that the time alone and the silence soothed him. He allowed his eyes to drift across the wide river, to the white house tucked into the green hillside.

Come on, admit it, he told himself, *you're only here so you can look for Heather.*

A sharp tug on the line brought him to his senses and he reeled in a small crab struggling on the end of the hook. Shortly after, an unfortunate whiting, two more crabs and a very small mackerel joined each other in his plastic bag. He made no sightings of Heather.

These will do. And with that, Eddie set off for home. When he got back Patrick was in the kitchen with Ellie, Mary and Peter, and supper was ready.

"Hurry up!" complained Ellie. "We've been waiting for you."

"Catch anything?" his dad asked.

"I did, even with that rusty old crabbing line," Eddie laughed, "enough to put in the lobster pot anyway."

"Alan Bailey rang, said he'd leave the funnel and rope in his truck in the morning," Mary told him, dishing out chicken and ham pie with carrots and small roast potatoes, and the delicious meal disappeared very quickly.

"Okay for tomorrow evening? Launch the boat, put the pot down and do a bit of fishing?" asked Eddie eagerly. Patrick grinned.

"I'm the skipper now, just in case you've forgotten! I'll pick my own crew if you don't mind!"

Eddie gasped. "Sorry, Patrick." He went very red. Mary and Peter tried not to laugh.

"You tell him, Patrick," encouraged Ellie. "He'll probably make Heather do everything. I feel a bit sorry for her."

"Heather?" questioned Eddie.

"She's coming to the launch, I invited her," explained Patrick.

"She rang me up to tell me she met my parents in St Moritz. She's had a fantastic time. Apparently she nearly ran my mother over on one of the slopes. She and her friend Ruth were driving a dog sled rather fast!" Everyone roared with laughter.

"She's a great girl," admired Peter, still chuckling. "I'd like to have seen Irene's face!"

Eddie received this news happily, pleased that the next day he would see Heather again.

"But what about the café?" Ellie asked them wildly.

"Don't worry, Ellie, calm down," said Mary quietly. "George and Bridget thought you all might like a day off. It's meant to be a nice surprise for you!"

No one could have believed a week ago how precious one day off could be; a whole day off! That night they went to sleep as excited as if it was Christmas Eve. Mary had prepared them a great picnic and Peter had bought some new lifejackets and flares for them in his usual fussy naval way. It was just going to be like old times again, wasn't it?

Chapter Thirty-five
Heather shares in an amazing day at sea

The following morning started well. The small green Cornish shrimper took to the water, eased in from the boathouse with ropes and pulleys. Sporting their new lifejackets, Ellie, Eddie and Patrick climbed aboard and started the engine. The ropes and fenders were stowed, and waving goodbye to their loyal helpers, they headed straight for the ferry slip where Heather and Jack were waiting. Jack lifted her easily into the boat.

"Bring her back to Woodend, Patrick, and you can all come and have tea with us. Six o'clock alright?" and with that he sped across the river rather fast.

"Hi, everyone!" greeted Heather, her face lightly tanned from her skiing holiday.

"Now, tell me all the latest news," she begged them eagerly. Ellie announced Bridget and George's holiday to Madeira and that they were all going to be left in charge of the tea shop.

"Really?" Heather was almost disbelieving.

"Don't you think we can do it?" Eddie challenged her at once.

"It's just such a big responsibility," she replied cautiously

"You sound like my dad," Patrick told her." I've been working there for over a year now."

"And me," added Ellie, but somehow Heather had cast a slightly unhappy doubting note.

"What else?" Heather asked brightly.

"We've launched *Pelican* and went out one evening for a sail," Eddie replied coolly.

"Yes, and Mother saw the turtle!"

"Really?" It was Heather's turn to be cool.

"I've seen it too, and Ellie tells me you saw something weird one day down by the ferry slip." Eddie's eyes pierced hers.

"Did she? I don't remember."

"You must!" Ellie insisted. "That day you came to get the flowers with me, remember?"

Heather went red and shook her head. "I've been away, don't forget. Heaps of things have happened to me since then." She answered Ellie back in a slightly defensive way. Ellie backed down at once, a little hurt, and an uncomfortable silence fell again between them.

Oh dear, thought Patrick, *I hope this isn't going to be a difficult day. It must be Heather's influence. We don't usually fall out,* and he felt a flicker of unhappiness.

Eddie stared at Heather, who was looking straight in front of her; she wasn't being her normal self, and she was upsetting everyone. He took charge.

"Right. Where shall we go? Any ideas for our picnic?" Nobody answered.

"What about going towards Start Point and sailing into Pennycombe Beach? That's rather small and sheltered. Would that be any good?"

Patrick, Ellie and Heather all nodded in agreement.

"Where are you going to put your pot down?" asked Patrick.

"Just the other side of Spanish Cove. It gets rocky there. I've got to find a spot where the fishermen don't go. Alan told me a place but I haven't had time to put the funnel in yet."

"Let's put the sails up now, and I can steer and the girls man the boom, and you can get on with that," decided Patrick at once.

So the new skipper asserted himself and saw they were all at their allotted tasks, working hard. The sails were slotted into the mast, pulled up, fastened on to their cleats and the tiller was manned. The boom swung as they tacked across the bay, according to the wind.

Patrick concentrated hard and eventually they picked up speed. It was breezy and exhilarating and somehow all the bad feelings from earlier blew away and they started enjoying themselves. Heather and Ellie made a good team, laughing at Patrick and saluting him as he ordered them about.

That's better, thought Eddie as he worked away to fasten the funnel inside the neck of the lobster pot. "Now for the smelly bit!" he grinned as he unwrapped the contents of a small plastic bag.

"Pooh, stink!" complained the girls at once. Eddie tied his blue buoy on to the top and stowed it below the seat until they got to Spanish Cove. Trailing his hands in the water to wash them, he sat back. All hints of dissent had vanished and Eddie heaved a long sigh and relaxed, enjoying the scudding clouds and fresh air.

"Almost there," called Patrick, "shall we get nearer to the shore?"

"Just a bit," replied Eddie, getting the heavy lobster pot up onto the side, and he waited for Patrick's signal.

"Here?"

"Yup, that's fine." Eddie heaved the pot overboard where it splashed and sank at once leaving only the blue marker buoy bobbing on the surface.

"Right, I'm starving," Patrick told them.

Soon the beach came into sight and the boys got ready to jump and take the rope ashore while the girls sat quietly watching and steering gently, waiting for the crunch of the keel on the sandy bottom. Patrick and Eddie pushed the boat towards the shore and tied it to a large rock.

"We must watch the tide, we don't want to be left on dry land," instructed Patrick.

"Aye aye, sir!" Heather and Ellie giggled together. Shouldering Heather between them the boys carried her to the shelter of some rocks for their picnic. Seated comfortably, Eddie asked Heather about her skiing trip.

"It was great," she replied. "I did some tobogganing on a special ski-sled and then Ruth and I had a go at driving a sled with dogs – that was brilliant!"

"Is that where you met my parents?" asked Patrick.

"I first saw them in the hotel having dinner," explained Heather, "then the next day on the slopes I nearly ran your mother over, she did look rather horrified." And they all burst out laughing.

"Poor Irene," said Ellie, glancing at Patrick.

"Oh she's tough, don't worry about her!" Patrick laughed.

"I'm going to look in the pools to see if there is anything for the aquarium," Eddie said eventually. Inactivity was not his strong point.

"I'll come with you," said Patrick and they both jumped up and began their search.

"You can get lunch ready!" Eddie shouted back.

Ellie and Heather ignored him and sat together enjoying the pleasant surroundings as the sun shone on them, watching the boys nimbly climbing over the rocks.

"I wish I could do that," Heather said wistfully, her eyes fixed on the two people darting and weaving further and further away.

"I'm sure you do," Ellie replied quietly, feeling at once an overwhelming sadness for Heather's disability.

"I'm sorry I upset you earlier," Heather said eventually. "I've got something to tell you."

She proceeded to recount the strange incident on her morning swim.

"You see, it was so special that I could hardly believe it had happened. It was almost like dreaming, but I know this: it was truly the most magical experience. I don't want anyone to laugh or make fun of me and spoil it. Can you understand?" Heather put her hand out to Ellie and touched her arm.

Ellie did understand of course and she thought back to her two beloved mice from the church and all the things that had happened since. "Of course I do, I just wish I could see it too."*And I think I know who and what it is*, thought Ellie to herself. It had to be the offspring of Sargasso and Seraphim, whatever form it had taken. It became clear to her at once. *He is* *so precious to them that they have kept him a secret, even from us, s*he decided with very clear insight. Eddie would be rather upset that he didn't know, but they had their own special reasons, she was sure.

"Where do you think the turtle fits in?" asked Ellie curiously.

"I've thought about that," Heather replied, "and I think that he looks after it. He took it away from me rather gently, sort of came between us and guided it off somewhere."

"Possibly some sort of sea nanny or guardian?" cleverly mused Ellie.

"Umm, probably."

"We'd better get the picnic ready, I think they're coming back," pointed out Ellie as in the distance the boys appeared clutching a plastic bag with water in it.

"You're right!" laughed Heather, diving at once into the cold box and fetching out the packets of sandwiches.

"Guess what!" shouted Eddie as he approached. "We found a squat lobster and a tiny plaice!" His excited face revealed that he was exceptionally pleased with their find.

"Wow!" called Heather enthusiastically, "Can we eat them? Will there be enough for four?"

Eddie splashed sea water from the bag at her.

"Ha ha, very funny."

"Food at last! What's been the hold-up?" questioned Eddie cheekily.

The girls refused to even answer him as first an apple and then a banana were hurled at him.

"I only asked!" he grinned, sitting down wet and shingly on the rug beside Heather.

"Get away, you're all wet!" she complained.

Eventually everyone found a place and the food Mary had sent was shared out. There was plenty to eat: sandwiches, potato and onion pasties, fruit cake, yogurts and milkshakes. The four sat in silence munching continuously until it was all gone. Full up and rather exhausted they all lay back against the rocks, sighing.

"I suppose we'd better do some fishing," Patrick said lazily, not budging from his place.

"I suppose we had," agreed Eddie. "Could you thread some bait on a hook, Heather?" he asked, just to see what she would say.

After a pause she relied breezily, "I expect so, if you show me how."

The boys collected Heather and carried her easily into the boat. At one stage Heather's foot dragged on the ground and then jerked up.

"Oh, my foot!"

"What's wrong?"

"I felt a sort of shock in it. It's gone now," she told them.

"Sure you're alright?"

"Yes, it's fine."

With Heather seated comfortably on a cushion and the ropes neatly folded, Eddie pushed the boat out into deeper water and Patrick started the engine. Eddie was thinking about the test he had set for Heather as he surveyed the open sea. He was about to find out.

Chapter Thirty-six
A very unusual rescue

Unflinchingly, Heather cut the bait into pieces and threaded it onto the sharp deadly hooks with their nasty barbs. Eddie also had some sand eels and worms from the garden. Ellie watched Heather and said nothing as she manned the tiller, while Patrick got the sails ready. The wind had changed and was now blowing in a southerly direction.

Ellie cut the engine and perfect peace was restored again. The boat drifted gently in full sail in the direction of Dartmouth; no noise or fumes disturbed them as four rods were hung over the side of the boat on homemade rod rests.

"Those are good, aren't they?" admired Heather.

"It makes it easier to see if you've got a bite," explained Eddie.

Lulled by the rocking of the boat, Ellie trailed her hand in the water, one of her favourite pastimes when out in the boat. Patrick's rod jerked several times.

"A bite!" he whispered, pointing to the fine line bouncing vigorously.

"Wait," instructed Eddie, "it's only playing with it. Hold the rod tightly and get ready to strike."

Heather watched all this, fascinated. A serious jerk on the line made them all jump.

"Strike it now!" yelled Eddie, and Patrick yanked his rod in the opposite direction. At once, feeling the heavy weight on the end of the line, he started to wind the reel slowly.

"Keep the line taut!" Eddie told him as Patrick concentrated on holding the rod the right way. Trying not to tip the boat over, both boys stood up and at last a flash of silver broke the surface and waggled and jiggled on the end of the line.

"Get the landing net," called Patrick to Ellie, and obeying instantly, she grabbed it and reached over the side, holding it under the fish until it dropped still writhing into the green net.

"Well done!" admired Eddie. "It's a bass! A good one. One and a half pounds, I'd say. Nice work!"

Patrick took the fish in his hand very tightly and gently removed the hook from its lip.

"Sorry, old fella," he said rather sadly.

"Let me see it," called Heather, and Patrick showed her his beautiful trophy.

"Isn't it lovely!" she said.

Patrick blocked the way so the girls couldn't see, as Eddie whacked it on the head with a heavy piece of wood.

"Oh dear." Heather seemed upset.

"I know it seems cruel," said Patrick, "that's why we only take the big ones. Usually the little ones are alright and swim away right as rain."

Another rod began to gently bounce.

"Look," pointed Ellie.

"Would you like to do it this time?" Eddie asked Heather.

She hesitated, looking at the dead fish in the bucket.

"I'll help you," offered Eddie encouragingly.

"Okay." She accepted and he brought the rod within her grasp.

"Wait until it really gives a good yank," repeated Eddie.

Ellie and Patrick sat together, watching. They caught each other's eye and smiled, raising an eyebrow slightly as they saw impatient, gutsy Eddie coping with the hesitant attempts of Heather. His patience was rewarded as pulling hard on the rod, rewinding the reel, a glistening zigzagged mackerel danced on the end of the line.

"Hurray!" called Ellie, "Another one!" Eddie caught it, removed the hook swiftly and whacked it on the head. It lay still, all its beautiful colours shimmering like moonlight on a dark blue sea.

"Ahh," said Heather.

"You won't be saying that when you're eating it tonight straight out of the frying pan," said Patrick.

"Maybe not." Heather looked up and grinned.

"I wish I'd brought some feathers," complained Eddie, "you can catch four or five at a time with those."

"Really?" Heather was amazed. "Let's get some for next time," and everyone laughed.

After an hour, three more mackerel lay in the bucket. Patrick and Eddie were pleased with the catch.

"Can we check the lobster pot?" asked Ellie.

"Don't be ridiculous, there won't be anything in it yet!" laughed Eddie.

"Oh go on," begged Heather.

"Alright, but you two can haul it up, it's heavy you know."

It was time to head back. The boys settled down to sail home while the girls sat enjoying the journey, looking out across the sea which seemed very big and wide today.

A black thing passed alongside them. Ellie leaned over and peered into the water as something swam under the boat. She waited, then a turtle appeared a little way off, its head above the water.

"Look! Look! It's the turtle again!" she called out, pointing it out to Heather.

Eddie and Patrick watched too. At once it dived under the surface and headed off again.

"It's going the same way as us!" said Eddie, pointing. The turtle was too fast for them and soon they lost it. Heather and Ellie were thinking the same thing – was the other little creature with him?

"We'll soon be at the lobster pot," Eddie told them. "Look out for the blue buoy."

When they reached it the turtle appeared again, circling the boat purposefully. Eddie took the sails down and Patrick folded them up. They bobbed along towards the lobster pot marker. All the time the turtle was close beside them.

"Shall I do it?" Patrick asked.

"Yes! Go on!" called Eddie. "Quick, grab it!"

Patrick leaned out and heaving hard, pulled on the rough salty rope until gradually the pot came into view. Inside it was the strangest thing any of them had ever seen. That is, all except Heather; because, caught inside the wire cage and unable to get out through the narrow funnel was the extraordinary bird child of Sargasso and Seraphim. His beautiful face was full of fear, his webbed feet caught in one of the wire squares.

"Oh no!" screamed Heather. "We must get him out!"

Eddie and Patrick, realising that whatever it was could not get out, started to cut the strong cord holding the funnel of the lobster pot with Eddie's Swiss army knife. Ellie rushed to watch and help if she could.

Cornelius had nearly drowned; he was on the return lap of his great swim which he had to complete on his own. He had set out from Start Point some time ago and had not yet arrived home. Ptolemy had been hovering and waiting in the sea around the mouth of the river, expecting his precious charge to appear, but there had been no sign of him.

Curiosity had compelled Cornelius to enter the lobster pot, having first spotted the white seagull painted on the marker. Once inside he was well and truly stuck. Without oxygen, he was in a desperate plight. A few more minutes and it would have been too late. Now he lay in the pot on the deck, gasping for air. Ptolemy had heard him calling but couldn't help him. It was the Seafarers' law – the task must be completed by Cornelius alone.

The four teenagers, who had come along just in time, watched the creature in disbelief. Eddie ripped the funnel out and quickly put his hands inside, gently twisting the small body as Ellie threaded his webbed feet out through the bars. Patrick spread the rug onto one of the seats beside Heather, where the little creature was laid and wrapped up very carefully. They had all taken in the details of his body, noting with curiosity his webbed feet, fish-skin legs and shorts, his feathered back and wings and his small perfect human face, arms and hands.

Heather wiped his wet curls and face lovingly with a corner of the rug, and very gradually the wonderful blue-green eyes, fringed with long spiky lashes, slowly opened. The bird boy smiled at Heather in recognition and she smiled back.

"Where am I? Have I finished my task?" he muttered to himself. She smoothed his curls gently and several of the blonde hairs entwined in her fingers.

Ptolemy, hearing his master's voice as he trod water by the side of the boat, banged his body against the wooden hull.

"My little master, I am here!" he called anxiously. All four in the boat looked at one another alarmed. Patrick rushed to the side at once where the turtle was floating, his leathery wrinkled head peering out of the calm sea.

"Put my little master back in the water! He must complete his swim. I thank you most gratefully for your help, but his efforts will all have been wasted if he does not reach home within the hour. I beg you, return him to the water!" spoke the turtle in a deep resonating voice.

"Ptolemy, where are you?" Cornelius tried to sit up but he was enfolded in the wool rug which impeded him. Heather unwrapped him and the delightful little thing slid across the seat and climbed over the side, one leg at a time. He looked up and grinned at them all as they gazed transfixed by his lovely face.

"When I have passed my test I shall come and swim with you again, daughter of Tellus." and he pointed at Heather. "Now I must go." He dropped with a splash into the water, watched by the startled occupants of the boat.

The turtle pointed him in the right direction and the small unknown creature streaked through the water towards the mouth of the river.

"Whew! That was a bit of excitement!" exclaimed Eddie. "He seemed to know you, Heather, you'd better tell us all about it!" and he shot her an inquiring look.

"You've been keeping secrets," Patrick pointed his finger at her, "haven't you?"

Heather blushed deeply and looked very uncomfortable.

"It was only once. I wasn't sure if I had dreamt it! I didn't even tell Ellie, did I?" she looked for back-up from her friend, who didn't let her down.

"No! Not even me! Honestly!"

"It was like a tiny child wasn't it? Half a bird or something. It even talked." Patrick thought aloud.

"Yes, but so did the turtle," added Eddie. "We of all people should be used to that!" He thought about the mice, the seagulls and the robin from their previous adventures.

"Well, I think he's Sargasso and Seraphim's chick, or child," Ellie told them in a superior voice. Eddie fell silent, thinking. They all looked at him, wondering too. How would he react to this idea?

"It's possible. It is, I suppose, thinking about it, *probable.* But if it is, why didn't he tell me?"

Ellie felt sorry for him. "People and animals go to extreme lengths to protect and hide their young. Why shouldn't they? You have to admit he *is* very extraordinary."

"Tell us what happened, go on Heather," urged Patrick, impatient to know more.

"It was after we saw it at the ferry slip that day. I decided I'd like to go swimming in the early mornings because it is something I *can* do. He just appeared swimming beside me. He even held my hand! We came to the surface and he was so lovely, like a tiny child with curly hair, but the turtle must have been close by because he gathered him up and took him away. That's what made me think he was in charge of him. I don't think he liked him talking to me. I didn't see him again until today."

"Did you see the thing around his head?" asked Patrick. "It was silvery, a sort of carved thing like a headband."

"No, I didn't notice that," replied Eddie, annoyed he hadn't seen it. He sighed.

"Well, if it is Sargasso's child, he must live down at the lime kiln. Shall we go and have a look?" He glanced round them all hopefully.

Heather looked at her watch. "Dad's expecting us at six o'clock. It's five o'clock now."

"I'd love to find out," said Ellie at once. "Let's hurry back as fast as we can. Yes?" They were agreed. No one wanted to miss the opportunity of seeing the lovely little bird child again.

By the time they got to Warfleet Creek they were not the only ones visiting the Old Quay to celebrate Cornelius's safe return. The two seals, Solomon and Bathsheba, were waiting in the quiet water until Cornelius was ready to meet them.

"Look, there's the seals!" squealed Ellie in delight. Freddie was also hopping around the lime kilns waiting for a chance to see.

"Why don't you go first, Eddie," suggested Patrick tactfully. "You can tell us if it's okay."

"Alright," agreed Eddie, and nudging the boat in by the old steps, he carefully stepped onto the slippery rocks and up to the grassy quayside. Eddie entered the lime kiln quietly, and saw the turtle, Sargasso and Seraphim huddled around the small figure.

"Hello," Eddie said softly. They all turned round at once and Sargasso was overjoyed to see him.

"Eddie! This is a very special day you have chosen to visit us. Today, our son Cornelius has completed his first task. The Spirit of the Sea will be so proud of him."

"Come," said Seraphim sweetly, "come, Eddie, and meet Cornelius. We need not keep him a secret now."

Sargasso and Seraphim led Eddie to the back of the lime kiln where Ptolemy was feeding the child with his special blue moss. His golden curls had been dried and his feathers preened and smoothed. Eddie could not take his eyes off the beautiful face and was transfixed by his large blue-seagreen eyes. He crouched down and put out his hand.

"Hello, Cornelius, I'm Eddie. I'm very pleased to meet you. Again!" he grinned. Cornelius stood up on his little fish-skin-covered legs and shyly held out his small fingers. They were cold.

"Hello. My mother and father have told me you are our special friend, but Ptolemy said I must wait until I am big and strong to meet you. Today I am big and strong, aren't I, Ptolemy?"

"You are, my little master," acknowledged the large turtle.

"May I bring my other friends to meet you too?" asked Eddie politely.

"Oh yes, I'd love to see them again. Did you tell Mother and Father about my adventure, Ptolemy?" asked Cornelius.

The turtle shook his head silently. Eddie ran quickly back to the boat.

"Come on, it's alright." He beckoned to them all.

"Sorry, Heather, I forgot." At once he climbed down into the boat to help her onto the jetty, one boy on each side of her. Heather's legs gave an electric shock, which sent a spasm through her body. She cried out.

"What's wrong?" Eddie asked anxiously.

"It's only my legs. I just can't control them. They do this weird thing now and again. Sorry."

Up the steps they lifted her, very carefully, and into the first lime kiln.

"I'll sit on the floor over there," instructed Heather, and Ellie followed. Cornelius walked over to them with his plodding little webbed feet.

"You helped me out of the sea box, didn't you? I couldn't have finished my swim if you hadn't set me free. Thank you very much, they saved my life, didn't they Mother?"

And he turned and nodded to her, his golden curls bobbing furiously. Sargasso and Seraphim looked bewildered.

"Tell us, Ptolemy, we know nothing of this. Is it true?" Sargasso asked softly.

"Yes, the child speaks the truth. He entered a lobster pot and was trapped. I heard his calls but could do nothing. Eddie and his friends came just in time to rescue my little master from drowning."

"And you were not going to tell me of this?" The turtle hung his withered, wrinkled neck in shame and was silent.

"You, who would not let me show my child to Eddie and Ellie? You, who told us that the humans would not understand this special gift to us? How many times did we ask to bring Cornelius for Eddie's blessing and to share our joy? Answer me, Ptolemy?"

Sargasso was stern and insistent, while Seraphim shed a silent tear, realising the terrible consequences of what could have been, this very afternoon.

The four visitors, who were now sitting very still, understood at last why they had not seen Cornelius before. It was Ptolemy who had protected his charge from them. They all felt very sad as the turtle struggled to speak. He raised his head, turned to them, and spoke proudly.

"I have been sent by the Spirit of the Sea to be the guardian of this special child who is a gift to Sargasso and Seraphim. It is hoped he will bring unity and stability to our many divisions. Sargasso had loved Eddie and Ellie since they saved his own life, and the human part of this child is a tribute to them; one hair of Eddie's head was included in his genetic make-up. Our Great Father, the Spirit of the Sea, offers this honour to Cornelius.

His fish-skin body, legs and feet are a token to the watery world into which he has been born, and his feathers and wings are a reminder of his true bird parentage. These three elements are combined in his headband of three silver fishes who represent Sky, Earth and deepest Sea, Tellus, Caelum, and Altum Mare. He has been set three tasks to complete to gain his independence and to enter into the three worlds. It is my whole life's work to see him complete these tasks. It is a great honour, and the burden of my duty I carry heavily until completion is achieved."

The turtle's voice began to waver as he bravely tried to continue.

"If in the execution of my duty I have offended any one of you, I am truly sorry. Everything I have done has been for my little master; I only thought of him and his welfare. It was wrong of me to prevent you, of all people, from sharing him," and he turned to Eddie, Ellie, Patrick and Heather sadly.

"I hope you will try to understand, and accept my apologies if I have made you unhappy. You have saved the Seafarers from losing their most precious newcomer."

Then he turned to Sargasso and Seraphim.

"As the moon wanes and turns its face to the darkness I shall leave and you will be free to appoint another guardian, for I have failed." And Ptolemy crept to the back of the cave and began to flip sand backwards over his body to try to bury himself and his shame.

Everyone in the dark cave looked at each other in dismay and said absolutely nothing. This was not for them to decide, uncomfortable though it was to witness. Heather pointed to her watch quietly and Patrick nodded slightly. He nudged Eddie, who touched Ellie's arm.

"We have no part in this," Eddie told Sargasso and Seraphim. "Please excuse us. Thank you for letting us meet Cornelius. It must be wonderful for you to have such an unusual child."

He beckoned to his friends and they crept very carefully out of the lime kiln and lifted Heather back into the boat. As they cast off in silence, the four of them gazed back at the disappearing cave. It grew smaller and darker in the distance as Patrick steered the boat across the river to Kingswear and away from one of the most extraordinary things that had ever happened to them. What would happen next? Would Ptolemy be banished before the new moon? What were the other tasks that had been set for Cornelius?

Half an hour later, in a different world, Ellie, Eddie and Heather were seated by the window in the drawing room at Woodend Manor Farm, telling Heather's parents about their fishing trip. Jack had been pacing anxiously in the garden, waiting with Heather's wheelchair standing by at the top of the steps. He rushed down to greet them and help his daughter out of the boat.

Morag's scones and raspberry jam soon disappeared, along with chocolate cake, sandwiches and many cups of tea. The food comforted Eddie's tortured soul and he looked many times across the dark river towards Warfleet, wondering what was happening. He was not the only one, as each in turn remembered the afternoon's revelations. However, no one could be miserable for long with Jack and Morag, who cheerfully joked and laughed with them.

"By the way, Heather, you've got to go up to London to see Mr Peabody in two weeks' time. We wondered if any of your friends might like to come for the weekend too? Maybe see a show or something?" Jack looked around their faces to see the reaction.

"That sounds great!" replied Eddie. "The only time we can't go is when Bridget and George go on holiday to Madeira."

"But that's not until the May bank holiday," added Ellie, extremely excited.

"I can't come," said Patrick at once. "It's too far from Edinburgh for the weekend," and he looked very glum indeed.

"Don't give up, Patrick," said Jack, wagging his finger. "I shall be up in Scotland myself sometime, working at the distillery, and you might be able to fly down with me. What do you say?"

Patrick's face lit up. "Well, thank you very much, sir, I'll certainly consider it." And soon they were planning exactly what they would do in London and the places they wanted to visit.

"You'll need to go for a fortnight to fit in all those museums," laughed Morag. Heather glowed with pleasure.

Wasn't it a fantastic thing to have such great friends? She didn't realise that she had been lonely before she met them.

Then her mind flashed back to that other special friend, the baby bird child, and she couldn't help wondering how he was. What had happened to poor Ptolemy? She gazed across the river. Her eyes met Eddie's, who was searching the shadows of the river edges too, and they raised their eyebrows at each other in a sort of secret gesture of comfort.

***

At the lime kiln, Cornelius had thrown his arms around the frantic turtle to try and stop him burying himself.

"No! No! It was my own fault! I saw the sea box and I shouldn't have gone inside it. I should have continued my swim. You instructed me not to stop for anything, I remember. I disobeyed you!"

But the turtle, deep in is grief, would not listen to the pleas of the little bird boy, and continued digging.

Cornelius turned in tears to his parents.

"Mother! Father! Stop him! I don't want another guardian. I love Ptolemy! He has taught me everything!" and he raised his tearstained face to beg his parents to help.

Sargasso was heartbroken and said quietly to his wife, "Shall I ask the Spirit of the Sea? He appointed Ptolemy."

Seraphim agreed at once. "Yes, we must ask him. We dare not risk his anger if he does not approve of our decision. Cornelius has still two more tasks to complete."

Sargasso spoke urgently into the small silvered shell he wore around his neck, and his anxious voice reached the ear of the Spirit of the Sea who was lazing by a sparkling turquoise lagoon on a Pacific island. The Lord of the Sea gently roused himself, asking Sargasso if he was in trouble.

"My lord, one of the sea-child's tasks has been interrupted. It was necessary for him to be rescued by our human friends before he completed his long swim alone. Shall the task be counted? Ptolemy is extremely upset as he feels he endangered the boy's life. He wants to be replaced as the guardian, but I cannot decide this by myself. Please help us, Great Master. What shall we do?" Sargasso's voice became weak with sadness.

Frowning, the Spirit of all the Oceans considered this matter. For several minutes there was silence. Then he spoke. "This child was made part human, part bird, and part fish, to reflect your great regard for the friendship of the boy who has now saved his life. Is it not fitting that your son's life should be saved by the very same boy? Ptolemy must continue as his guardian, and learn to accept a little help from the humans in the child's tasks, if necessary. Let him continue this worthy journey towards independence. I judge the task to have been completed. I shall send a messenger to Ptolemy to reassure him of my confidence in him." The words were quickly followed by several sweet notes of music sent through the shell. It was the Seafarers' music and sounded like a French horn.

Sargasso accepted the wise words of his master and the judgement of Ptolemy. He was to stay, and Eddie could help him if he was needed. This was the perfect solution. Happily he gently touched the large back of the half-buried turtle.

"Ptolemy, our great master is not displeased. He has sent his blessing and Cornelius's task is judged to be completed. He can now enter the Seafarers' world. Come, come and join us, we shall celebrate Cornelius's triumph." And Sargasso gently persuaded the turtle to raise his head and look up.

"That's it, old friend. Cornelius is waiting for you." The gull beckoned his child forward. The bird boy started to brush the sandy soil off the turtle.

"We're going to have a party, Ptolemy," his tiny hands stroking the smooth shell of the wrinkled old turtle. "Come and join us," he pleaded.

Solomon and Bathsheba had been waiting patiently in the shallows and shadows of the Creek edges as the drama unfolded.

They began to swim back to home, to the Trip Trap Bridge. As they rounded the castle's rocky shores, a large pelican flew over their heads, up the river, and turned into Warfleet Creek where it landed with a bump on the grassy quayside just in front of the lime kiln.

"I am sent by the Spirit of the Sea. Please accept his good wishes." And with that, the pelican bowed politely and waited.

"Welcome," said Sargasso and Seraphim together. Ptolemy had regained his composure and was thoughtful for a moment.

"What do we call you?" he asked politely.

"Pelorus," was the reply. "May I see the new child I have travelled the oceans to meet?"

Ptolemy pushed the shy Cornelius forward and the pelican bowed his head in reverence and then regarded the newest creature in the universe.

Water was fetched from the tumbling stream, and they dined on the finest ferny royal weed brought from the Caves of Drach and drank the crystal water, which still held its silvery glow. Ptolemy proposed a toast.

"Welcome to the Seafarers, my little master. After two more tasks you will be fully fledged. All of us salute you." Everyone present nodded their approval and whispered, "Welcome, little master."

Cornelius smiled, yawned and snuggled up happily into his mother's feathers. Altum Mare, one of the small silver fish around Cornelius's head, slowly opened his eyes. He had been activated by the music and had received his soul. He would be the first part of the circle of life for the new child.

Sleep gradually came to them all where they had gathered together, only dispersing at dawn when the moon waned into the rose-coloured sky. However, not all Cornelius's friends were enjoying such a perfect rest.

Chapter Thirty-seven
Sargasso and Eddie discuss the next task

Unable to sleep that night, Eddie couldn't wait to find out Ptolemy's fate. He got up early and crept out of the house down to the Creekside.

Peeping into the lime kiln, he saw the bird family asleep together, Ptolemy beside them. The turtle's shell was smooth and polished; no signs of the sandy soil that had covered him remained.

Everything must be alright," Eddie told himself, and was just going to sneak off when Sargasso opened one eye. Rousing himself immediately, he hopped on his one leg and went with Eddie out to the wooden seat on the edge of the quay to talk quietly.

"All is well," Sargasso told him happily. "Ptolemy is to stay as the guardian. His Seafarer's task is complete. Now you and Ellie can share Cornelius with us. You have proved once again to be a true friend and you too have been honoured as you deserve."

"Have I?" asked Eddie modestly. "Have I really?"

"Yes, the Spirit of the Sea has asked for your help with Cornelius and his tasks. You have saved the life of both of us now. Cornelius has mentioned your friend whose legs do not work. He hopes to go swimming with her again."

"Heather, she's called Heather," said Eddie, blushing slightly. "Her legs are paralysed. She fell off her horse and damaged her back."

"We are all damaged in some way," noted Sargasso philosophically. "Some injuries can be seen and some cannot. She swims well and the freedom she enjoys in the water is her comfort."

Eddie nodded, listening carefully to Sargasso. He was right. In the water she was equal to any of them, her disability vanishing.

"We all want to help Cornelius. He is a lovely child. He must have grown up very quickly."

"Yes," admitted Sargasso proudly. "Quicker than we ever thought possible. With it has come the worry of all parents, guarding and guiding their offspring."

"You will let me know when the next task begins, won't you? What is it?" Eddie asked shyly.

"Lord Sunna, Spirit of the Woodland, will tell us. It is to honour the Earth and release the Spirit of Tellus, the second silver fish around Cornelius's head."

"I see," said Eddie quietly, "and the third task?"

"The third task is the most difficult, His conquering of the Sky as he learns to fly. This task is for Caelum, the third fish, to give him his soul and join the others in the circlet. Then, Ptolemy's work will be done. The circlet of the three fishes that Cornelius wears represents the three parts of the world that we live in," Sargasso explained to Eddie. "Our child, it is hoped, may unite all us creatures."

Eddie said nothing, marvelling at the great wisdom and intellect of this incredible seagull. Who would ever have believed it, from a chance meeting that day so long ago on the beach, when he rescued the bird from the hazards of a tangled fishing line?

He spoke at last.

"When Cornelius begins his next task we will be ready if you need us. Thank you, Sargasso. I won't disturb you any longer," and off he went with so much to tell the others.

Heather, who had not slept very well either, was fretting and worrying at home. At last she had a phone call from Eddie, and was delighted with the news.

"I shall go swimming every morning in case I see him again, and all the time I'm getting stronger. Wait till Mr Peabody hears how far I can swim!"

Later that morning Patrick, Eddie and Ellie returned to work as usual. Heavy rain set in, which lasted several days unfortunately. Customers were slow and the time dragged. Even Heather didn't venture out, except to visit Ginny at the stables, and she felt lonely and cut off from her friends.

The Easter holidays drew to a rapid conclusion and poor old Patrick was shipped off to Edinburgh, and Eddie and Ellie took up the challenge of school once more. Heather was driven off to Sussex and the small closely knit group was scattered again. Each time it was harder to say goodbye, and they thought about each other constantly. There was one bright spot on the horizon – Jack Fraser's trip to London. It was a positive focal point in the future to help them through the boring grind of school until they could meet again. The weeks slowly passed and the trip moved ever closer.

Chapter Thirty-eight
The sights of London

When the date for the London visit finally arrived, Mary received a phone call from Morag telling her where and when Harold, Jack's driver, would pick up Eddie and Ellie. Then the three of them would fetch Heather from St Agnes School and head off to London, A booking had been made for them all at Montague's Hotel at Queensgate, in Kensington, close to the museums, shops and galleries. Eddie and Ellie were overjoyed.

"What shall I wear?" was the first thing on Ellie's mind.

"How much money will we need?" was the first thing on Eddie's agenda.

"Have you been saving up your wages?" asked Peter mischievously. Silence was the only reply.

"We'll see what we can do," he said, already knowing that their grandmother had sent twenty-five pounds for each, having heard about the exciting trip. By the time the great day came, miraculously Grandma had sent some money and Mary had taken them to Totnes for new jeans, tops and shoes. They were both thrilled.

"Thank you, Mum," giving her a hug.

"We can't have you looking like a couple of country bumpkins, can we?"

At last they were ready and now they waited in the hallway in their new clothes, happy and excited. Eddie was very keen to see Heather again, and her school. Soon the big car crept into the driveway and Harold, dressed in a grey suit, got out.

"Good morning, ma'am." He touched his hat to Mary. Ellie wanted to giggle as Harold picked up their rucksacks and stowed them in the large boot. Quick farewells were made as Eddie and Ellie sat back in the comfy car, stroking the smooth beige leather and sighing with nervous relief.

"We're off!" whispered Ellie in excitement.

Three hours later they arrived at Bradbury St Agnes. The car entered the school gates, signposted in large letters "St Agnes School for Girls". Ahead lay an old manor house with pointed mullioned windows and a large flat grassy space in front. A flag flew over the rooftops; the grey and red crest fluttered breezily. Harold turned towards a smaller building in the same style.

"This is Miss Fraser's dormitory," he explained. The car drew to a halt and at once the front door opened and Heather came rushing out and down the ramp.

"You've been ages!" she complained. Harold opened the doors as Eddie and Ellie watched Heather transfer from her chair to the car, easily and without any fuss, while her equipment was stowed in the boot. She sat beside Eddie.

"How are you both? Let's go and have lunch. Take us to the Brown Cow, Harold, the one in the village, please."

After soup and crusty bread in the pretty Sussex tea shop they were on the way again, with lots of chatting and laughter. Eventually the grey suburbs of London appeared, the traffic noise increased and Harold pointed out the Natural History Museum and the Victoria and Albert Museum, tall and beautiful. Harold made a right turn and came to a halt in Queensgate.

"We are here, Miss Fraser." Harold fetched the wheelchair, helped Heather out, and sent the three of them to the side entrance where the ramp was. They found themselves in the hotel foyer, where thick carpets and comfortable chairs were occupied by an assortment of tourists.

"I'll order tea," said Heather, while Ellie and Eddie looked around awkwardly.

"There's a table," and Heather was there in a flash. "Sit here, Ellie, and you there, Eddie. Harold will join us in a minute," as she organised them happily. A waitress brought afternoon tea which consisted of sandwiches, cakes and scones. It was obvious Heather had been here before. In no time, Harold joined them for his favourite treat.

"Can't beat the Montague for afternoon tea, eh Miss?" he beamed, as he spread raspberry jam and a mountain of cream on top of a scone. By the time the splendid tea had been demolished, Patrick and Jack came bursting through the revolving door of the main hotel entrance.

"Hi everyone, any left for us? I'll get some more." Jack soon had the waitress buzzing round.

"How was the flight?" asked Eddie, pleased to see Patrick again.

"It was fan-tas-tic! I sat up with Dickie most of the way. I'm definitely going to learn to fly when I'm older."

Jack and Eddie exploded with laughter.

When everyone had finished eating, Jack stood up.

"Well, young lady, better make a few wee plans for tomorrow, okay? Your appointment with Mr Peabody is ten o'clock. Maybe we could meet up at Olga's? Harold can drop them off and then take us to Harley Street. What do you think of that? Of course, there's a pool in the basement at the leisure club, if you'd rather stay here."

"I might swim before breakfast," announced Heather, thinking carefully.

"That's a good idea," agreed Eddie brightly.

"Well, let me know later what you've decided; you're here to enjoy yourselves," grinned Jack. "Now, let's get to our rooms and have a sort out before dinner. Yes?" and he marshalled his troops and sent them to their billets.

Up in their bedroom, Ellie and Heather pulled back the net curtains and gazed out of the window at the hotel opposite and the tree-lined London avenue full of traffic.

"Isn't it gorgeous?" sighed Ellie. "Everyone looks so smart."

The two girls concentrated on their hair and clothes for the next hour. Finally, at 7.30pm, they met the boys and Jack for dinner in the grand dining room.

Eddie found his eyes glued to Heather. She looked stunning. Patrick and Ellie sat side by side, lively and laughing, comfortable together as always. Dinner was as good as expected, and afterwards they followed Jack into the billiards room for some snooker. The girls soon learnt to play, each chalking the cues carefully and keeping the score on the wall-mounted number board. Jack had to force them all to go to bed eventually, as the next day held the shadow of Heather's visit to Mr Peabody.

So far, there had not been so much as a splinter of light to hope for. Jack's jovial exterior hid a heart heavy with sadness for his brave and beautiful daughter. What did the future hold for her?

***

At 7.00am exactly, two small figures broke the perfect surface of the Greek-key-tiled pool in the luxurious spa beneath the Montague Hotel. Heather, arriving in the lift, had come face to face with Eddie, dressed in his track suit, looking a bit lost.

"Only us, then?" he asked Heather.

"Looks like it. See you in a minute." And she wheeled herself through the automatic door to the Ladies' changing rooms.

"Right." Eddie disappeared into the Gents. The pool attendant, Michael, knew Heather and he pushed her wheelchair to the steps and lifted her onto the side.

"Nice to see you again, Miss," he smiled. "Brought a friend with you this time?"

"Yes." She nodded, blushing.

Eddie smiled. "Ready? Go!"

They both plunged into the aquamarine water, swimming furiously towards the other end. Heather touched first and she laughed and laughed while Michael clapped.

"Well done, Miss!"

On the return lap, however, Eddie won easily and their rivalry was friendly and well meant. Half an hour later they emerged to shower and dress. In the changing room Heather dried her hair, smiling to herself.

Today we were equal for the first time, she thought proudly. *He was so surprised when I beat him!* and she laughed.

By 8am the swim was a distant memory as they assembled in the dining room for a traditional English breakfast. While Heather and Jack went to Harley Street to see Mr Peabody, the others agreed to visit the Natural History Museum. They would meet up at 11.30am at Olga's, a smart coffee shop in Old Brompton Road, noted for its fabulous patisserie and Austrian café atmosphere.

"Perhaps you need a swim after all that food!" smiled Jack.

"Oh, we've done that," Heather told them smugly. It was Eddie's turn to blush.

Harold arrived shortly, and Heather went with Jack out to the waiting car.

"See you later, don't get lost!" she called. It was well within walking distance to the Natural History Museum, and Eddie, Ellie and Patrick stood looking up at the awe-inspiring building.

"Huge, isn't it?" Patrick said.

They bought three tickets and entered the most exciting place any of them had ever seen: wandering through the world how it used to be, and how some of it is today. Eddie left Patrick and Ellie looking at fossils and he moved on into an exhibition of extinct small mammals, gazing absently into the cases with neat labels and explanations alongside.

One in particular caught his eye: an extinct species of monkey called the Ghost Monkey, whose remains had been found on the small island of Saba in the Caribbean. This island was rather unique, very small, very steep, with a perfect tropical rain forest at its heart. The monkey was responsible for a legend that had grown up among the natives, that the monkey was a ghost, with its white face that popped up almost anywhere. It could fly, swim and walk, and was reputed to catch fish off the island's steep cliffs. It had been covered in short tufty hair but its forearms were joined to its body with a large flap of skin, enabling it to glide from tree to tree in the forest. It also had the incredible ability to jump off the cliffs into the sea. The lower half of its body was scaled and its feet were webbed, with one toe, like a pair of mittens. This monkey seemed to have been highly intelligent and made a sort of nest with twigs in the lower branches of the trees.

Eddie's interest was immediately aroused. It was only a few genetic steps away from Cornelius; there were definite similarities. Eddie went swiftly back to get the others. "Come and look at this," he beckoned to them. Curious, Patrick and Ellie joined him.

"Isn't this interesting?" He pointed to the skeleton remains of the Ghost Monkey and the artist's impression next to it. They read it in silence and stared at the small white bones for a long time.

"A flying monkey that could fish, with scaly legs and sort of webbed feet. That's a bit weird, isn't it?" Patrick said at last.

"It's the closest thing to Cornelius, isn't it?" added Ellie. "How strange." She stared, puzzled by the creature drawn from imagination. "It's not a bird, but it's very close."

"They must have evolved on this remote island then, they've never been found anywhere else. I suppose the monkeys were forced to fish to get food. See? It hadn't quite got wings but it certainly could glide." Patrick was thoughtful.

Eddie had one thought in his mind, but he wasn't going to tell the others. Why did the monkey become extinct? It worried him slightly; it hadn't been a survivor.

"Cornelius hasn't passed his last two tests yet," he said suddenly. "We still don't know if he can walk and fly, do we? I wish Heather was here. She would have loved to see this. I wonder what she would have made of it?"

Heather was in fact having a thorough examination on Mr Peabody's couch, with Mary Ann, his nurse, taking notes and measurements. He connected her legs up to an electrical machine with electrodes and tested for electrical impulses.

"Try to move your feet, Heather. Good, now your knees. Good. Can you lift your leg up?" as he felt the muscles and tried to assist the movements.

Mary Ann noticed several flickers, and the machine made a pattern. She recorded all the data within a folder of Heather's notes.

"Your legs are in good condition, Heather, there is not much muscle wasting. How have you been managing?"

"I've taken up swimming and I think it's really helping me. My upper body is getting stronger anyway, so that's got to be good."

Mr Peabody unplugged the machine and Mary Ann removed the electrodes. He took his small rubber hammer to test her reflexes, tapping her knees, ankles and scratching under her big toe. The reflex on her toe was not what he expected. He repeated it and found it the same.

"Hmm, unusual Babinski response." He repeated it again and the same result appeared.

"Record reversal of Babinski reflex for today, Mary Ann. Review in three months." He examined her response to touch, heat, cold, and pressure; measured her muscles and recorded her height and weight. He remained slightly puzzled.

"Right, Heather that's all, you're in good shape. Just a blood and urine sample. Mary Ann will do that for you. I'm very pleased with you, let's see you in three months. Your swimming programme is a good idea and you have shown a lot of courage. You're a fine example to others, Heather. You have spirit and determination. Very well done. I know how hard this is, believe me. I have a brother, Andy, who was paralysed in a car crash. He's like you; he won't give in."

"Really? Not Andy Peabody, the Olympic rifle shooting champion?"

"Yes, the very one," he replied proudly.

"I saw him once at a competition," Heather said quietly. "He was brilliant."

"Yes, he is in more ways than one, he has a rich and fulfilled life. Well, off you go and I'll see your father next." He smiled at her kindly, making a mental note to mention her to Andy next time he saw him.

While Heather went off through the next door to the treatment room, Mr Peabody returned to his desk and buzzed.

"Send Mr Fraser in, Laura, will you please?"

Shortly the door opened and in strode the fine figure of Jack Fraser. The men shook hands and both sat down.

"Well, Jack, it's good to see you and that great daughter of yours. She's doing very well, very well indeed. I've got some of the readouts and results of the examination I carried out earlier." In his hand he held a long narrow graph paper with spiky lines all along it. Some he had marked with a red highlighter pen. He held it out to show Jack, and pointed with a sharp pencil to several tall spikes dotted along the paper.

"I haven't mentioned this to Heather as I don't want to give her false hope, it would be cruel, but I have to say, Jack, that there are one or two surprising results here. I think there has been a slight improvement in the electrical impulses sent to the muscles. You see, nerve tissue regenerates so very slowly."

He looked up to Jack Fraser's face over his dark edged glasses. Jack's mouth was open, his hand clutching his chin, and his eyes were closed as he tried to control his emotions.

Shaking his head, he began to speak in a croaky voice.

I've so hoped for this day... this news. I just—" Mr Peabody cut him off.

"No, Jack. You are not to expect miracles. Not yet. I know that this will be the greatest test of all for you and Morag. We must wait to be sure because it might never get any better. The pathways from the spine could be too damaged. I'm sorry but it's just too soon to tell. But, as I say, the signs are there. Under *no* circumstances are you to mention any of this to Heather. I'm sure you understand. False hope is extremely bad for morale. My brother Andy was given all sorts of promises by various quacks and healers. He parted with a lot of money, wanting to believe there was a chance. Finally he accepted it and life has moved on for him. Heather says she met him at a shooting competition. Funny isn't it, this small world of ours?"

Jack composed himself and took a deep breath.

"I see of course how terrible it would be to tell her. I won't tell Morag either, actually. Not just yet. Heather has come on in leaps and bounds since she made some new friends, local teenagers, and they all helped us out over a diamond robbery we had a while back. Bit of excitement! Good detective work! Heather's come out such a lot – sailing and picnicking, swimming and just being normal again."

Mr Peabody smiled and nodded.

"Sounds great."

Jack suddenly had an idea.

"Why don't you and Mrs Peabody come down for a weekend? Bring Andy too, and his family. We could do some sailing and swimming. Heather would love it."

Mr Peabody was rather touched.

"Well, that sounds lovely. Fiona adores the coast."

"Good, get out your diary," Jack insisted. Eventually the date was set for the 21st of June.

"Thank you, Jack, you're very kind. In the meantime keep an eye on Heather's legs. Look for any signs of movement but don't let her see you. Promise?"

"Promise," agreed Jack. The father and daughter left the consulting rooms and found Harold, who drove them back to Olga's for a celebratory coffee and cakes.

"Thank goodness that's over," sighed Heather.

"Yes, but back in three months, eh? Good excuse for tea at the Montague and coffee at Olga's."

Heather laughed and agreed. "I do so love the cakes, Eddie will be in heaven."

Jack smiled. Heather seemed very fond of Eddie, and he obviously felt the same. He was a nice laddie and Jack enjoyed seeing his daughter joking and having a good time with Ellie and Patrick.

Harold dropped them off and they made their way into the café looking for the others.

"They're not here yet." Heather was disappointed.

"Och, they'll be along in a wee minute I expect." Jack summoned the waiter. "Decision time!"

"Oh, it's so difficult. A slice of white chocolate gateau, please," she told the young Italian waiter. "Oh, and a strawberry tart please. I can't resist them. Is that alright, Dad?"

"Yes, have what you like. I'll have the same actually, and two cappuccinos." Jack and Heather laughed feeling very naughty and self-indulgent. Heather put her elbows on the table and looked all around her at the variety of London's visitors sitting in this large popular café.

"I love it here."

She was delighted and happy, enjoying being nosey. A very well-dressed elderly lady came in with a white poodle with two red tartan bows on its curly head, held on a tartan lead. It barked suddenly and pulled away from its lead, disappearing under the table.

"Poppy! Poppy! Come back, you wicked dog!" called its owner frantically. The café was disturbed as the dog raced about barking, and it hid under Heather's wheelchair. One of Heather's legs jumped violently and she called out loud. The little dog stopped barking at once, came up beside Heather and licked her hand. Jack leapt up at once. He had seen her leg jerk. He had seen it with his own eyes.

"Poppy! Poppy! Come here!" called the old lady, very anxious and fraught, her hat askew.

"I'm so sorry," she apologised.

"It's alright, no harm done," Jack told her and they introduced themselves. Mrs Jacqueline Oswald sat down and offered to pay for their coffee as an apology.

"I'm not really supposed to bring Poppy in here," she told them in a half whisper, "but Olga is my closest friend and doesn't really mind. We both live in Bolton Street, but Poppy is naughty sometimes."

"I've got a little white Cairn called Robbie," Heather told her. "I just adore him."

"Good. We both love our dogs so you'll forgive me, I'm sure."

The coffee and cakes arrived, along with Olga, Eddie, Ellie and Patrick. There was total confusion but as soon as Olga appeared, fresh coffee, croissants, gateaux and chocolate cookies turned up like magic and very soon they were all having the greatest fun. Olga spoke with a thick Austrian accent, wore large horn-rimmed spectacles and carried a large handbag. Suddenly a small dog peeped out.

"Suki! Hello, Suki. Say hello to Poppy."

Mrs Oswald shrieked, and the boys burst out laughing. Jack rolled his eyes and Heather nudged his hand.

"Don't say it, Dad," she hissed at him, knowing his opinion of small lap dogs with bows in their hair.

"I insist on paying for you all. Carlos, here to me," she summoned a passing waiter, "Bring a box of cakes at once, assorted cream fancies." The box swiftly arrived. It was large, pink, with white ribbons all over it.

"Thanks very much, Olga, you're very generous," Jack said, backing out of the shop as she blew kisses and made them all promise to come back. Harold was waiting, and drew up alongside the pavement. In the car they laughed about the funny incident.

"What a scream that woman was! Dad, you loved the dog, eh?" Heather joked.

"Aye, she and the dog were a wee bit crazy."

Jack pondered as he looked out of the window on what he had seen, tucking it away to the back of his mind to think about later.

"Right, boat trip up the Thames next, to Greenwich and the Maritime Museum. Dickie is joining us for lunch with his son Antony."

"We've got something to tell you," whispered Ellie to Heather, who nodded with interest.

Firmly ensconced in the glass-sided boat, gliding smoothly up the famous River Thames, Eddie, Ellie and Patrick found a quiet moment to talk to Heather.

"What is it?" she whispered.

"It's about Cornelius—" began Patrick.

"We've found an extinct monkey that is remarkably similar," interrupted Eddie.

"It flies and swims and walks upright, so it has all three elements, like him," finished Ellie, very excited.

"Well that's a surprise, where does this monkey come from?" asked Heather.

"From a remote Caribbean island called Saba. It's quite unique, with a central rainforest, high mountains and steep cliffs."

The conversation was interrupted as Jack appeared with Dickie and a teenage boy with black hair and glasses, wearing all black clothes. He didn't smile, even when introduced to them.

"Hi," was all he said. Jack, Dickie and Harold disappeared off to the saloon bar for a beer leaving the sullen boy to his fate. Although the boys tried to talk to him he obviously didn't want to be there. Eventually Eddie and Patrick gave up and silence fell between them. But Heather wasn't going to give up. She tried again.

"We're going to the Planetarium later," she told him. "Isn't that one of your hobbies, Antony?" He stared at her for a moment.

"Yes it is," he replied. "I wanted to set my telescope up this morning but Dad said I had to come here to meet you. Did you know it is the transverse of Venus today? It's incredibly unusual and I had hoped to see it myself."

He smiled at Heather for the first time.

"We're interested in stargazing too. Eddie and I have invented a light from a lunar source called the Moonmirror," Patrick told him proudly.

"How tremendous! I think that is a very interesting theory and…" he was off, and their interests were sparked. In no time at all Antony became animated, friendly and fun. The girls winked at each other.

"Another astronomy freak!" whispered Ellie behind her hand.

The whole day was full to the brim with interesting places. They all stood on the Greenwich Meridian denoting Greenwich Mean Time and wondered at the clock keeping perfect time, invented so long ago by Mr Harrison.

At the Planetarium, Antony talked nonstop about his favourite subject in the world.

"He's a bit geeky," Ellie told Heather quietly.

"You need to get out in the real world" Eddie told him. "Stuck in Eton and isolated from the rest of society can't be good for you. You must be glad you've met us aliens from Planet Normal today."

"Oh, take no notice of him. Come shopping with us, we'll sort you out with trendy clothes and a new haircut," Ellie teased Antony.

Antony took it all in good humour and at the end of the day they were all firm friends.

"I'd love to see your invention one day," he said rather keenly to Eddie and Patrick. "Maybe I'll come to Devon sometime to visit you."

"I'm sure you will!" Ellie smiled sweetly.

"We'll teach you how to sail," promised Eddie.

By eleven o'clock that evening they were back at the Montague playing their last game of snooker. Ellie was the best, the scoreboard proved it undoubtedly, and Eddie and Patrick were rather sulky, which Heather thought hilariously funny.

"It's only a game!" she teased them.

On the last day, Heather and Ellie begged to be allowed to go shopping and their persistence won the day.

"Och, alright," growled Jack, "anything for a bit of peace. I'll get Harold to drop you off at Harrods while we go to see Churchill's underground bunker."

In the end, Heather and Ellie bought a silk bowtie and a box of toffees between them all for Jack. The grand finale of the trip was tea at the Ritz. Eddie, Ellie and Patrick looked around them at the grand furnishings in wonder. Jack was very touched with his gifts – his bowtie and his toffees with a picture of a London bus on the box.

"Thanks so much," he said quietly.

"Thank *you*!" the three replied, "for a fantastic trip. It's been fabulous." The boys were very grateful that Ellie had remembered a thank you present.

It had been a memorable time for Jack, for many reasons. Young people were so bright and always good company. Heather had been happy and he had a secret parcel of hope, wrapped up tightly and hidden away for another day. He felt great happiness as he sat back in his velvet chair, watching his beautiful daughter enjoying herself.

He thought of Morag, his lovely Scottish lass, and suddenly he was ready to go home; to leave the bright lights and noise of London and find the peace and silence of his home on the gentle River Dart.

"You're quiet, Dad?" Heather remarked, patting his knee. He smiled at her.

"Am I?" and he entered the world again, assuming his parental role to be jolly and entertaining once more. Would the day ever come when he was truly happy? He had been given the smallest hope to cling on to, and cling on he would.

Chapter Thirty-nine
Cornelius attempts his second task

It was very unfortunate that Cornelius's second task coincided with the weekend when Eddie and Ellie were away in London. Sargasso and Seraphim were dismayed when Lord Sunna suddenly appeared outside the lime kiln, holding up his lamp of glow worms above his head.

"Tomorrow will be Cornelius's Earthly task," he announced. "He has from dawn until dusk to complete the journey I have chosen for him. Forest and field, hill and valley, his path will be lit by glow worms, and for these twelve hours only they will shine in the light of the day."

The glow worms all wriggled with excitement – never had the lamp been so full and never had they been chosen for such an important mission. They positively glowed with the thrill of it all.

"What has my young master to do?" asked Ptolemy at once, wishing to be able to prepare Cornelius in some way for what lay before him.

"Remember this. He must find and follow the glow worms wherever they lead. I shall be waiting. Tellus will not receive his Earthly soul until the task is completed at dusk, after the sun sets." And with that he skipped off and disappeared into the woods.

Ptolemy and Sargasso all stared at the sleeping child, his blond curls lying among the feathers and twigs of the nest; they were all thinking the same thing. What of Cornelius's webbed feet? He was flat footed when he walked on the ground. The soft-skinned webs might be torn on rough stones and hard twigs.

"Humans wear shoes," said Seraphim at once.

"Could we not make him some?" said Sargasso. Ptolemy nodded in agreement. A great discussion began about shoes. What should they be made of? How would they be made? Who would make them? Could it be done in time? Would they be comfortable enough to walk in?

Sargasso flew off to consult his dear friend Eddie. After sitting on the garage roof for a while he realised the children were not there; it was a bitter disappointment. Next choice was Freddie or Oliphant. In the second ash tree on the left, he found them both.

"We would be delighted to help, let's get on with it."

Together in the lime kiln they chose the various options for the shoes. Little Cornelius opened his eyes and he looked around at them.

"Hello," he said sleepily.

Seraphim stroked his curls and helped him to get up. "Come child," she said gently, "we need to look at your feet." She led him into the circle, where Freddie drew around his feet with his beak in the soft sand.

"Step back, please," he told the curious bird boy and as he did, two perfect webbed footprints were left behind. Altum Mare, one of the silver fish, spoke.

"It is fitting that one of our brothers gives up his life for this task. The thick skin of a fish will make good leather for shoes. We fish have not had legs or feet for millions of years. We will make the sacrifice."

Everyone nodded in agreement.

"I will choose one. Send a message to our brothers and I will bring the skin back for my master," said Ptolemy.

Altum Mare began humming a strange vibrating note.

"Where am I going, Mother?" asked Cornelius, "And why do I need shoes?" He lifted his lovely face with its sea green eyes to hers. His beauty and innocence was mesmerising and their hearts ached for him.

"Lord Sunna came to visit us earlier this morning and he brought great news for us. Tomorrow is the day of your second task – your Earthly task. He brought with him a hundred glow worms and you are to follow them. You will start as the sun rises and finish as the sun sets. It is going to be an exciting adventure, my son." And she hugged him to hide the tears in her eyes.

"We do not know where you are going," said Oliphant quietly, "but I will alert all the Woodlanders and we will look out for you and support you. No one is allowed to touch you but as you follow the glow worm markers, someone will be there. You must not feel alone on your journey."

"My son, your small webbed feet are not designed for long walks, so we are going to make you some shoes." Sargasso told him.

"Like the humans wear?" asked Cornelius eagerly.

"Yes, just like that." Freddie piped in. "We are all going to help to make them."

"I will wait here with the child and tutor him in the ways of the Woodland," decided Oliphant. "We don't want him falling down a rabbit hole or straying into the fox's den, do we?"

Seraphim's eyes opened wide in horror. She hadn't thought of that.

"Come." Sargasso touched her wingtip and led his wife away. They had work to do at the seashore. Down at the high tide mark they gathered long strips of sea kelp and laid them in a rock pool to keep them wet.

Freddie flew to the farm high up on Little Dartmouth and plucked sheep's wool off the barbed wire fences. When he had collected a large grey-white ball he brought it back to the lime kiln. Then he went off to find Lucinda Spider who was the best stitcher and spinner in the Woodland. Grumbling, she reluctantly climbed onto his back and flew with the robin to the quayside.

"I do not like the fresh air," she complained. "I like dust and dark corners, you know." Freddie promised she could work in the darkest corners of the lime kiln and that seemed to please her. All that was needed now was Altum Mare and Ptolemy to return from the sea with the fish skin. Cornelius watched all this with great interest.

Far out in the bay, a large silver sea bass with shiny scales rippling up and down his body was saying goodbye to his watery world. He was the first to receive the vibrating message.

"I am the chosen one," he told his friends. "I am to go and walk on the Earth. Do not feel sorry for me for I shall have a hundred tales to tell when next we meet. I will not be hung by the mouth on the hook of a hungry fisherman!" Then, with a final leap he somersaulted out of the sea and lay flat on the surface, slowly flapping and gasping as the oxygen failed to reach him from his gills. Finally he was quiet and glimpsed the blue sky above him for the last time.

Altum Mare and Ptolemy waited nearby; the bass closed his eyes as his final gesture. Then quickly and skilfully they slipped his body out of the shiny skin and his flesh sank down, down into the blue-green deeps. Holding the precious skin between them the fish and the turtle swam back to Warfleet Creek where the other materials to make the shoes were assembled; the sea kelp ribbons and the sheep's wool. The footprints in the sand had not been touched and Lucinda cut the skin into two with her sharp snippers while Freddie pecked the neat round holes to thread the sea thongs through. Sargasso and Seraphim stretched the sheep's wool between their beaks until it was smooth and flat.

The shoes appeared slowly as Lucinda stitched and threaded, measured and mused, singing snatches from operas she loved as she worked. Finally she sealed all the edges with freshly spun web to keep the water out, and left them to dry. They were finished at last.

Cornelius had gone with Ptolemy to collect enough royal weed for his journey, and heard the whispers in the great sea bass shoals of the fish who had given his skin for the shoes of the little master. Cornelius felt very sorry indeed but Ptolemy told him the fish had died willingly.

Then Altum Mare, who had returned to the silver circlet around the boy's head, spoke.

"The fish will be with you on your journey. Think of that. He wanted to be the first fish to walk on the Earth."

That night, preparations for the journey continued. The shoes stood in the corner, shiny and smooth, and the package of royal ferny weed had been strapped in strong bindings. Cornelius had been taught some of the Woodlanders' ways and how to recognise some of the animals he might meet. The child was very excited as his father and mother put him to bed.

"We will be waiting for you at the end of your journey," They said, and they sat quietly beside him until he closed his eyes and his lashes touched his cheek in slumber. The seagulls tucked their beaks beneath their wings and slept, haunted by many fears and dreads for the life of their precious child.

Before dawn, Cornelius was up and ready. He slipped on his shoes and tied his package of food around his waist. The seagull parents escorted their child to the edge of Gallants Bower, not wanting the moment to come when he left them.

Lord Sunna had visited the young buzzard prince at midnight with a map drawn on bark parchment. Permission was given to Oliphant to arrange for several Woodlanders to be stationed along the way. They must be volunteers, as it was a brave thing to do to leave the safety of the wood and spread across the long route, but everyone wanted the bird boy to succeed. Only one thing was forbidden - nobody was to physically help him. Oliphant saw to these requests at once.

Cornelius looked around and saw the faint golden lights of the glow worms at the side of the path. Through the misty morning the first shards of sunlight appeared, and waving goodbye he set off up the rough-rooted pathway among the trees. Sargasso and Seraphim watched him go in silence. He followed the track, winding steeply upwards. Many eyes watched him. As he reached the first bend he paused to look down across the river, a little out of breath already.

On he went, the relentless hill still rising up, up, his feet gripping tightly. He sighed and saw the sun glinting through the branches and the dappled leaves.

I'll rest and eat my breakfast when I reach the top, he promised himself.

At the top of the hill the pathway divided into three forks.

Which way? he wondered, searching for a glow worm to guide him. He heard a cough from somewhere above him, and looking up saw a large bird, his beak pointing west. The bird boy smiled and chose the direction of the beak. The bird neither looked nor spoke to him, he just ignored him. Cornelius hurried along until he found a wooden seat overlooking the valley.

This is where I shall eat my breakfast. Carefully he unwound his food.

"If you give me some, I might show you the way," said a cheeky voice. Cornelius stopped eating at once. A small pointed face peeped out from under the seat. It was a smooth brown furry mink.

"Throw some on the ground for me – go on!" encouraged the brown face, sniffing. Cornelius threw one portion of his precious food onto the ground and the mink pounced on it and gobbled it up.

"I might help you. But, I might not. You'll just have to wait and see!" and he ran away laughing.

Cornelius sat for a long time expecting him to come back. The sun moved slowly through the trees as he waited and waited. Then a raucous noise in the branches above made him jump.

"He ain't coming back, mate," said a hoarse voice. Looking up, he saw a black and blue-striped jay nodding his head at him.

Cornelius got off the seat and looked for the next glow worm, feeling rather upset. Why had the mink not kept his promise? He didn't understand. However, as the bird boy walked along the path he had chosen, the brown mink was fleeing for his life: at Oliphant's command he was being hounded out of the Woodland. Two foxes eager for a kill chased him through the five bar gate and out into the world outside. The mink must take his chance now, he could never return.

Cornelius entered the flat gorse-edged field with its long wet grass. Two black rooks stood either side of the path below some large pine trees. Neither spoke but both watched him with their piercing eyes. The sun was now fully up and shone fiercely into his face.

The sea, the sea! He glimpsed the sparkle of the ocean and felt better knowing the water was nearby. Following the glow worms he reached the five bar gate and looked through the bars.

"Must I go out here?" he wondered. "I think I must."

Looking up into the trees again which were now behind him, he saw a buzzard, a robin, and a line of bluetits perched, silently observing him. "Good morning," Cornelius said, but there was no reply. "I suppose I must leave the Woodland now," and he climbed through the bottom bars and into the steep field beyond. Yawning in the sun he stretched his arms out, a little weary.

Freddie, who had followed him for some way, watched him go. He was pleased at the little fellow's progress; he had done well so far, despite giving some of his precious food to the wily mink.

This pathway was covered in stones and rutted with mud and puddles; it was much more difficult across the top of the cliffs. Cornelius made slow progress and became very tired. Reaching a group of farm cottages and buildings, he noticed a grassy bank beside a gateway and could not resist sitting down beneath the honeysuckle hedge. There were no glow worms here but he was too tired to notice.

Almost at once he fell asleep in the warm sunshine. While he slept, grey clouds rolled across the sky and the sun disappeared. A large ginger cat came tiptoeing out of a cottage and noticed something on the bank. It hid behind a bush to watch whatever it was. Slowly, slowly it hunkered down and began to approach Cornelius. It could see feathers. Just as the cat was

297

closing in on him, the first raindrops fell on the boy's face and he opened his eyes.

The cat pounced, catching the small body between its paws, its outstretched claws plucking some of the feathers from his back. Cornelius shouted as he woke up, and swinging out wildly, punched the cat on the nose. Its claws scratched the bird boy's hand, as it withdrew with a loud screech.

"Get away you nasty creature of the Earth!" and the cat ran off extremely perturbed with its bruised nose. Cornelius, thoroughly shaken, watched his red blood drop onto the grass. He noticed there were no glow worms to guide him.

I'd better try harder to stay on the right path. I shouldn't have fallen asleep. I do wish Ptolemy was with me. He was feeling sorry for himself now. The drizzle continued, washing Cornelius's blood away until all traces of him were gone. He scoured the edges of the grass and at last found a pair of glow worms shining brightly in the grey rain. The cloud grew thicker and his feathers were sleek and wet, until he shook himself and fluffed them out to make himself warmer.

Scurrying along, he knew he had some time to catch up on, and the glow worms shone their very brightest to help him. There were plenty of them stationed around a wooden stile which he climbed over, and headed downhill towards the sea. Reaching another stile at the bottom, many glow worms had gathered to prevent him falling over the steep cliff.

"Thank you," he said gratefully, noticing the sheer drop and the jagged rocks below. The worms wriggled in delight at Cornelius's praise.

A roughly hewn flight of steps led through the brambles to the sea's craggy edge, where waves crashed and the breeze blew. The rain stopped suddenly and spaces opened up in the scudding clouds. As the sun pierced the gloom a rainbow appeared, spreading its pretty arc of colours through the sky.

Cornelius stopped to look, delighted at the unknown ribbon of colour. A sea otter watched him from the black rocks.

I want to touch the colours! and he scrambled down the steps, running awkwardly in his silver skin shoes. He reached the Trip Trap Bridge, which extended over a gaping chasm full of rushing, foaming waves.

"Where has it gone?" he cried as the rainbow seemed to disappear and move off somewhere else. He was so disappointed that he ran across the bridge, caught the toe of his shoe, tripped and fell over the side into the roaring wave which engulfed him. He was dragged deep down into the gulley, where he tumbled over and over in a washing machine of revolving water and bubbles, until eventually he was thrown onto the floor of a tiny cave. The tide was not yet full and there was just a tiny patch of wet shingle left.

Disorientated, with a bleeding gash on his forehead, Cornelius retched up the seawater he had swallowed. He shuffled himself as far back as he could to escape the onslaught of the next wave and sat panting and feeling sick. Seawater and blood ran off his curls into his face but he was not afraid of the sea, and he began to talk to himself as he rested.

"I could swim home now, it would be easy. I am tired of these silly shoes and all these walks."

"My little master, do not let the life of the sea bass have been given in vain. Show him the way home," spoke the silver fish on Cornelius's silver headband.

Cornelius knew then that he must climb up the rocks somehow and re-enter the path. The rainbow had disappeared, but the afternoon sun was shining brightly. The shoes felt tight and awkward and he longed to kick them off but he listened to the words of Altum Mare and knew their wisdom. Tellus, waiting for his soul, was depending on him and the sea bass had died for him.

So, sighing and shrugging his shoulders, Cornelius got his breath back, and catching a wave as it left the gulley he rode out on it in his fish-skin shoes and landed on the nearest flat rock. The sea otter watched motionless; his little master had triumphed! The bird boy began the slow climb up to the muddy wet path.

"Eat now, and drink," advised the silver fish very quietly, and after a few steep rocky yards the boy saw a cave with a wooden seat. Down the back of the rocks was a trickle of water which he collected in his hands and drank gratefully. Two tiny mice sat under the seat, excited and very relieved to see him arrive; they had thought him to be lost.

His thirst quenched, he opened his waist pouch to find his food still there. Lucinda's strong web had not let him down despite his fall, but how he wished he had not given the mink a precious portion. He was very hungry now and gobbled up what was left in moments.

I am so tired and my hand is smarting and my head aching but I must go on, he told himself. Wearily sighing, he headed on, following the glow worms through the trees to the last downhill path. The silence of the dark wood he entered soothed his soul and he no longer felt the weight or the tightness of the shoes once he was on flat ground. The sun did not pierce through here and it was dark and still. Squirrels watched him from the branches. Cornelius felt rather tearful; it was getting intolerable now. Weariness engulfed his whole body.

I want to be back home with Mother and be safe in her warm wings. He grizzled for a bit, and picking up a stick he whacked the sides of the path in anger. Pricking up his ears he heard voices, becoming louder as they came towards him.

Oh no, what next?

This time he was not frightened, he was cross. *What are they doing in my wood?*

He hid behind a tree as a young couple strolled by, engrossed in conversation. When they had passed by, Cornelius was just going to step out when from above the path, among the dense ivy, a liver-coloured German springer dog leapt out.

"Get away from me, you nasty creature of the Earth!" Cornelius hissed, and smacked the dog on its rump with his stick.

The dog yelped and bounded away, turning once to look at the strange fierce thing that had attacked him.

"That's it. Look at me! I am Cornelius, child of the Earth, Sea and the Sky! I am not afraid of you!" and with a toss of his head, pulling a stern, frowning face and puffing out his chest, he found new vigour and energy.

Yes, wait until I tell Ptolemy how brave I have been. He will be so proud of me. His little legs marched along and as he strutted he hummed a little tune to himself. He left the wood, and the path joined a narrow tarmac road which was smooth and firm. Searching for the glow worms, he was very aware of the time and did not want to make a mistake now; past a small cottage, then a spiralling path through more woods until he reached Sugary Cove.

"I know where I am now!" Cornelius shouted joyfully. "I am nearly home. Why, I swim past here nearly every day," and he ran enthusiastically down the many steps to the beach, all thoughts of glow worms, paths, the time, the sun and his task, forgotten.

He was not meant to descend these steps: there were no glow worms here. The afternoon was growing late as Cornelius played on the small beach alone, marking the sand with a stick, jumping over rocks, peering into pools and splashing in the edge of the water which lapped invitingly to and fro. He uncovered a crab under a rock but it did not scuttle away, just sat motionless blinking its black eyes. Cornelius was fascinated.

The crab raised a claw and beckoned to the bird boy.

"Come with me. We shall play hide and seek in the deep dark pools and eat the fish in the Earth-man's pots and then run away. I will show you places you have never been, into shipwrecks and lost chasms where the mighty Kraken lived and the Sea Palace which still remains. Come with me, this is where you belong. Cast off your shoes and return to the water."

The boy longed with all his heart to go with the crab, who had tempted his soul. Suddenly Cornelius felt water trickling down his face and a droplet reached his mouth. He licked it away with his tongue: it was salty. He stood still, thinking, as the crab impatiently waved his claw.

"Come. Come with me to the deep!"

At once Cornelius realised he was tasting salty tears; tears shed by the silver fish he wore around his head. Altum Mare was weeping for him. He saw at once that the crab was luring him away from the Earth, away from the path and away from his important task. He looked up and the sun was losing its fire and its heat – it was going down.

"My task! I must find the path and get home, what have I been doing?" and he chastised himself and felt a wave of panic sweep over him.

"And as for you," he pointed his finger accusingly at the crab, "you tried to trick me. Go back into the sea and if I ever see you again I shall crush you. Go!" and he picked up the startled crab and threw it far into the water with a splash. Cornelius scrabbled up the steps, which were very high and pained his legs. By the time he reached the top he was exhausted.

"I must go on." he told himself. "I must go on. Find the glow worms, hurry up. Come on!" He slapped his hand on his fish-skin shorts to encourage himself. "Come on!"

Sure enough, back on the path, the glow worms shone reassuringly.

"There you are." He was so relieved to see them, and grabbing another short beech stick he marched along rather smartly, soon reaching a car park where the glow worms vanished.

"But it's easy from here. Just along by the church path and down into the Creek. Why have they gone?" He despaired and sighed loudly in frustration, looking frantically for the pinpricks of light.

"Oh no," groaned Cornelius as he found them at last, shining across the road and up the steep, root-strewn hill leading into the woods of Gallants Bower. He trudged after them, a last cruel twist in the final stage of his journey. On and on he went, up the steep slopes and back to the top of the Bower, stumbling now with fatigue, the beech stick helping him now to keep his balance. A soft rain began to fall which cooled him first and then made him shiver. A loud roaring noise and a flash of bright light split the sky, terrifying him.

"I must hide, I must find a shelter." Searching wildly around, he found a crevice hollowed in a large tree full of soft dead leaves which he squeezed himself into. He closed his eyes to shut out the fears of the world which had gathered together to test this small creature.

Above him the squirrels gossiped in consternation. The robin and the small white owl were waiting for Cornelius in the second ash tree on the right, farther on in the journey. There was not a lot of time left now. Worry was setting in.

"I'm going to find him," insisted Freddie, "I can't stand this waiting."

"No," said Oliphant, "you will not be able to resist helping him if he is in trouble and you know that's not allowed. Stay here and we will suffer this last hour together."

Freddie knew the wise bird was right and made yet another pot of clover tea.

Lord Sunna, seeing sunset approaching, was curious. He flitted through the tree branches to get a view of Cornelius and knew by the collection of squirrels and birds his exact location. He asked the squirrel leader to bring him a handful of hazelnuts from their store, and he sat on a branch of a silver birch directly overhead, observing the dishevelled sleeping bird boy on whom he had pinned great hopes.

He took one of the hazelnuts, cracked it with his teeth, ate the nut and dropped the shells below him, looking out across the valley and up the river.

"The view is good from this branch, is it not?"

"Yes, Lord Sunna," replied the squirrel, puzzled.

"Will you share some nuts with me?"

"No, Lord Sunna," answered the squirrel, "and neither will any of my people. You alone must eat the nuts."

Lord Sunna laughed. "The right answer, my friend. I shall have to finish them myself," and he cracked nut after nut, discarding the shells below him. The steady stream of falling objects woke the sleeping bird child. He was unsure where he was for a moment. Then, gazing wearily upon a line of golden lights, he knew at once.

"The sun! The sun! I must beat the sun!" and he eased his aching legs and feet out of the hole. Leaving his sturdy beech stick behind, he raced down the hill over roots and ruts and stones and mud, sliding and slipping as brambles reached out to tear him and nettles stood on tiptoes to sting him. He pelted past the second ash tree on the right, where Freddie and Oliphant clasped each other in an emotional embrace, and raced to the very bottom of the hill where his mother, father and Ptolemy were waiting.

"Mother! Mother!" called out the small bird boy, holding out his arms, and he was caught up by them all and squashed in their hugs and chorus of praise.

"Let us look at you, my son," said Sargasso when he could bear to let him go. The sight of him appalled him. Cornelius had blood on his head from a great gash, matted hair and a dirty tearstained face; his feathers had a clump missing and one of his hands was purple, swollen and scratched. His feet he regarded in wonder, because – his feet were perfect: silver, shiny and unsullied. Not a speck of mud had soiled them or thorns torn them and they shimmered in the gathering dusk.

"You have done well," whispered Sargasso. "You have grown today in many ways. I am proud to be your father," and his voice faltered.

"Let us all go home now, shall we?" suggested the voice of Ptolemy, just a little higher than usual, and the joyful reunited family made their way back together.

Another of the silver fish on Cornelius's headband opened his eyes and gazed upon the world, as he too received his soul. Altum Mare winked at him.

"Welcome, Tellus." And then he slept for a very long time.

Lord Sunna laughed as he danced and sang through the woods, recalling all the faithful creatures and insects who had not helped Cornelius in any way. One or two hints given, which he decided to overlook.

"I enjoyed those hazelnuts but they do make such a mess," he said to himself. Now that Cornelius had completed his Earthly task, Lord Sunna was free of his obligation. He could now enjoy watching him win his wings. Would he be able to do this last and most difficult task? It was a good question.

Chapter Forty
Some lessons in life

By the time Eddie and Ellie returned late on Sunday night, the drama of Cornelius's Earthly task was over. It was probable that Cornelius would never again have to walk so far, but he had proved that he could, and the precious fish-skin shoes were packed away in case they were ever needed again.

"I might like to wear shoes sometimes," sulked Cornelius, not wanting to give them up so quickly.

"Of course you might, so they are still here if you need them," Ptolemy told him gently.

"You will often walk on the Earth," Tellus told him proudly from the silver headband.

"As you will often swim in the Sea," added Altum Mare in perfect agreement.

Now Cornelius had three voices to advise him. Was ever such an infant born with this plentiful supply of advisors? Not in all the world had there ever been such a child.

***

A few days later when school was finished, Eddie and Ellie decided to take the boat out. Patrick had told them to use it whenever they liked, and the weather and tides were right for them.

"Shall we go first to see if Sargasso is there?" asked Ellie rather warily, knowing how impatient Eddie could be.

"If you like."

Pleased at this, Ellie and her brother made their way to the lime kiln, where they found Sargasso's entire family and of course heard the exciting story of the Earthly walk. "My goodness, you were brave," Ellie praised the fluffy little bird child with the golden curls, marvelling how two seagulls could have produced him.

"I'm sorry I missed your walk," Eddie said sadly, "I should have liked to have helped you."

"Nobody was allowed to help me," said Cornelius very emphatically. "I had to do it all by myself and I was very brave, you know. I fought with a tiger and a bear and I got a stick and I went like this," and he played imaginary fencing with his hand. "See how good I am? And I fell into the sea and there was loud crashings and flashings in the sky and rain and I was not afraid. I am brave Cornelius now. I have walked over the Earth."

Eddie and Ellie were very amused, and congratulated Cornelius on his success. Ellie looked at the bird boy's feet wondering how he had managed to walk without damaging the fine skin webs of his duck feet.

"So you didn't hurt yourself at all?" she asked.

"Oh, I did. I had blood running on the ground from my head and the tiger ate my feathers, look," and he turned round to show his audience his scars and the small plucked patch on his back.

"Goodness me, you have been in the wars!" clucked Ellie sympathetically.

"And your feet aren't sore?" asked Eddie, thinking exactly the same as Ellie had just moments before.

"I wore my shoes," was the proud explanation. Ptolemy, Sargasso, and Seraphim looked at each other. They had been hoping their son would not mention them.

"Shoes?" came the question in unison.

Sargasso interrupted. "Yes, we made him some shoes from bits and pieces from the sea shore. They worked very well."

"How very clever," said Eddie admiringly.

"Time for your swim, my little master," said Ptolemy, leading Cornelius away.

"We're going out in the boat, we might see you. Let's go down to the beach together shall we?" and she went with the turtle and the little child, leaving Eddie and Sargasso behind for a moment.

"He's done very well," praised Eddie, "I expect it was a long walk."

"Yes, too far for such a small child, but he did it. It was nearly sunset when he reached us, almost too late. He was in a bad state: frightened, tired and several creatures had attacked him, but as you see, he's the better for it!"

"He's certainly braver! He's full of it. A tiger and a bear, pretty good!" The seagull and the boy laughed together.

Ptolemy and Cornelius disappeared into the water as Eddie caught Ellie up. They got the boat out and began sailing down the river towards the sea. Both of them were thinking about Heather as her house came into view.

"We'd better phone her and tell her about Cornelius. Wasn't he funny?" chuckled Ellie. "I think he's going to be a bit of a show-off."

"He's only got to learn to fly now. But it might be difficult because he's not very aerodynamic," mused Eddie thoughtfully. "I've never seen his wings opened out. I wonder what size they are? He won't be able to lift his weight off the ground if they aren't big enough."

Ellie began to see that flying could be a bit of a problem, and it occupied their minds for quite a long time as they sailed along, until their lobster pot marker came into view. Pulling it up, they saw that one medium sized blue speckled lobster and a small crab lay entrapped.

"I feel a bit mean catching them, don't you?" Eddie frowned.

"I know what you mean," agreed Ellie, "But they all eat each other to survive and accept that. Sargasso and Seraphim eat fish and shellfish."

"Yes, but we don't need it to survive, that's the difference."

At that moment Ptolemy and Cornelius surfaced.

"Hello, we've been waiting for you. What have you caught? Can I look?" Ptolemy gave his permission for Cornelius to climb onto the boat. "Let me see inside your sea box," and he rushed eagerly to look. He saw the dark blue lobster and the brown crab, and his eyes narrowed and his lips pursed together.

"You!" he said, aggressively pointing his finger at the crab. "You tried to trick me and make me go back into the ocean, didn't you? Ha, look at you now, you're a prisoner aren't you?" The crab backed into the corner, his round black eyes rolling and his feelers quivering.

"Ptolemy, you'll never guess who is in this sea box," Cornelius shouted over the side. "That horrible crab, the one I told you about."

Ptolemy was swimming close by.

"I hear you, my little master. What are you going to do with him?"

Cornelius looked at the turtle in surprise.

"I don't know. What should I do with him? I want to crush him to death."

"Then do it," answered Ptolemy.

"What would you do with this crab, Eddie?" asked Cornelius suddenly "Eat him?"

That put Eddie on the spot. He had no idea of the incident that had taken place on the task. He spoke thoughtfully. "I think I might throw him back. He is not big enough to eat. He doesn't look as if he is injured, so it's up to you."

Cornelius listened in silence. He watched the crab, sensing its fear, and then he remembered his own frantic attempts to get out of the very same pot. His anger began to subside and he felt pity for the crab and the lobster waiting to hear their fate.

"Throw him back then, it is not what he deserves but I do not want to kill him now. Shall we let him go, Ptolemy?"

"As you wish, my little master," the turtle replied, treading water.

"Let him go, Eddie." And turning his back on the whole affair, Cornelius jumped back into the water and climbed onto the turtle's back for a ride home.

Ellie helped Eddie open the pot and carefully removed the crab and the lobster.

"See you another day," shouted Eddie as he dropped both the creatures into the sea.

"What was all that about?" Ellie asked as they too headed for home.

"We'll ask Ptolemy later, he'll know. Still, he was good to forgive him, wasn't he?"

Arriving back at the Creek, Cornelius begged Ellie and Eddie to come rockpooling with him. There were some lovely seaweed-fringed pools high on the rocks and the little bird boy delved inside them, searching and seeking. He disappeared into a deep one for ages. Ellie got quite worried wondering where he was. She peered anxiously trying to see beneath the water when suddenly he emerged smiling, his face and curls running with water. He held up a small silver locket.

"Look! Look what I found!" Ellie recognised her own lost locket.

"I lost that last year down here. That's mine, Cornelius, it was a birthday present."

"Then I must give it to you, mustn't I?" He was reluctant to give it up, but he handed it over.

"Thank you, and it is very kind of you to give it back." Ellie took his hand. "Come on I'll take you home it's getting dark."

The story of the locket was told to Seraphim and Sargasso. Ptolemy sat on the edge of the quay with Eddie and Ellie and explained the strange happening.

"The crab was sent to lure him away from his task, to try to change his mind to push him into making a decision – the right one or the wrong one. He showed mercy, and even a little forgiveness. It was a good lesson for him. I am glad he did not take the life of the crab."

They all agreed, thinking about the choices little Cornelius had made.

Later, when they reached home, Ellie decided to ring Heather and Patrick to keep them up to date with all the news. Patrick was homesick, of course.

"I'll be back soon in time for Bridget and George's holiday in Madeira. We've got to work for a whole week."

"Thanks for reminding me," grumbled Eddie, wishing they had not been quite so keen to offer their help for the precious time off school. Would Heather also be home? It would make all the difference to him.

Chapter Forty-one
Reunited again in May

May came around. The boat lay untouched, Waterside Cottage was empty, and unseasonal cold weather isolated people indoors. Eddie became restless and unhappy; he hated being inside and he hated schoolwork. In any free moments he studied the physics of flying, marvelling suddenly at each bird he saw. How easy it looked for them, and to think he had never noticed before. Patrick of course was doing exactly the same thing – watching and wondering.

The May bank holiday arrived and so did the two mentally exhausted academic heroes from Scotland and Sussex. Both Patrick and Heather had excelled themselves, each getting the highest marks in their year. Ellie had worked hard to achieve good marks but Eddie's achievements were only fair. They were all exhausted, pale and not in good spirits.

"I hate school," Eddie announced at the breakfast table. "I can't wait to leave."

There was a knock at the back door and in walked Patrick.

"How lovely to see you," Mary hugged him. "Come and have some breakfast."

"Great to be back, I've had a bad time, I can tell you. I feel like throwing all my books into the Creek. I've had enough!"

Edie nodded in agreement with great vigour.

"Huh! Just like me!"

"How did you get here?" asked Ellie, changing the subject.

"Luckily my father drove me down; he's here for a few days too.

"Maybe we could all go for a walk?" Eddie asked, and raised his eyebrows in a knowing way to Patrick.

"Good idea," replied his friend cheerily, as Mary delivered his toast to him and a cup of tea.

"Don't forget, Ellie, we're going shopping today. We've got to find something to wear for the wedding."

"Yes, Mum," Ellie replied reluctantly. She'd forgotten about being a bridesmaid for her Auntie Pamela, and she went upstairs to get ready. Eddie was delighted, he felt better already.

Ellie spent all day at the Wedding Outfitters in Plymouth. She wanted to see Heather and find Cornelius and be with Eddie and Patrick and do so much. She rang Heather as soon as she got back.

"I'm only here for three days and then I'm off to pony camp," Heather told her, "but I do so want to see Cornelius again. Will you tell him I'm back home now? I might just meet him if he knows I'm swimming again in the river."

"Yes, I'll go and look for him today." They said goodbye and rang off.

Eddie and Patrick had gone fishing together off the rocks at the castle so Ellie was alone when she ventured down to the lime kiln.

Sargasso, Seraphim, Ptolemy and Cornelius were sitting together in a circle talking quietly.

Ellie felt a bit of an intruder but Cornelius rushed to meet her.

"Have you come to see me, Ellie? Look how I'm growing," and he twirled around to show her.

"You are," she told him, "you truly are, and soon your wings will grow and you will learn to fly."

He stood still at the thought.

"Mother? Father? Am I going to fly?"

"Sometime I expect you will," Sargasso told him. "Not quite yet. When you are ready. Until then we will swim and enjoy the summer."

Ellie saw her chance.

"Heather is home again, she will be swimming in the mornings. She would love to see you if you happen to be out then."

"We will go, won't we, Ptolemy? The Earth-girl who has no life in her legs, you remember?"

Ptolemy did remember, very well.

"Maybe we can go tomorrow?" Cornelius asked hopefully.

Maybe," replied the wise old turtle, imagining that by the morning the bird child would have forgotten all about it. He was wrong.

At the first light breaking in the sky, Cornelius was rousing Ptolemy to make his breakfast and prepare for a swim. "We will surprise her, won't we?" he laughed to himself. When the sun came up they were ready and at six-thirty exactly the two creatures swam strongly across the river to the foot of the green hills where the tiny cove nestled.

Heather, who was learning the hard lesson of self-discipline through her disability, was determined to swim each morning until she went to pony camp. She struggled into her wetsuit and quietly made her way to the top of the steps where she left the wheelchair. She rested at the bottom, remembering to clip her safety line on to an iron mooring ring. The tide which was coming in met her eagerly and she was floating in minutes off into the dark waters of the River Dart. Paddling her arms slowly, she lay on her back watching the sun rise higher in the sky. Birds began singing and the whole beauty of the morning struck her. It was so good to be home, here by her lovely river in this peaceful place.

Splash! Something made her jump. Heather jolted out of her dreamy float and looked around in panic. What was it? Behind her she saw Cornelius, and not far off, the wizened snake-like head of the turtle, his black eyes watching her.

"You little monkey! You scared me!" and then she started to laugh.

"I just wanted to surprise you."

"Well, you certainly did!" and Cornelius's face broke into a wide smile.

"Are you coming for a swim with us?" he asked.

"I'd love to. Just as far as my safety line allows me, alright?"

Cornelius nodded. Ptolemy followed closely as the strange pair swam off together, hand in hand.

They dived under the cool water, chasing each other and re-surfacing with water streaming from their fair hair, both faces full of joy. When Heather felt the tug on her waistline she signalled to go back, and Cornelius obediently followed her.

She sat on the beach while he searched in the rockpools eagerly looking for a present for her, just as he had found one for Ellie, but Cornelius was disappointed. He hadn't found anything else in the rockpools.

"Maybe tomorrow," the turtle encouraged.

"No! I want to find a birthday present for the Earth-girl now," Cornelius insisted petulantly. The turtle sighed.

"Just one more look, yes?" and he was off before permission was granted. Heather and Ptolemy exchanged the same meaningful smile – he was only a baby after all.

The sun rose higher and shone on the water as a breeze ruffled the surface, dividing the smooth ripples into smaller ones. It looked as if a thousand bright arrows were hitting the water at intervals with a blinding brilliance. Cornelius disappeared under the surface, where he searched among the rocks. His eyes were caught by a sparkling object, and he struggled to loosen it from the rocky crevice in which it was wedged. He pulled hard on the loop he had found, almost running out of breath. It grated free of its jagged prison, and desperately he accelerated to the surface with an urgent kick of his webbed feet.

Ptolemy and Heather were straining their necks to catch sight of him.

"There he is!" She pointed, and they both sat back relieved.

"I did find you a birthday present!" he called in rapture. "I knew I would," and he swam towards the shingly beach holding the string in his hands. When he waddled out of the water he presented his gift to Heather.

"Here you are, it's a birthday present, isn't it? Like Ellie had, only hers was bright and silvery and yours is just a piece of broken glass, but the sharp edges have rubbed off. It does shine, doesn't it?" he said, seeking her approval for his gift.

Ptolemy watched Heather and waited for her reply.

Looking down on her lap, Heather saw a piece of her family's history that had been prized among men; men had sweated and laboured in mines in South Africa for years to produce such items. She turned the stone over in her hand. It was the famous Fraser diamond of enormous value, lost in the robbery, thrown accidently over the side of the boat by Ezekiel King, and firmly lodged in the rocky bed of the river for over six months. As a piece of beautiful sparkling glass shining in the river, it had been chosen for her by Cornelius, and therefore to her this gift was priceless. Tears sprang into her eyes and she swallowed a lump in her throat.

"It does, Cornelius, it sparkles in the sunlight and I love it!" and she stretched out her arms and hugged him.

"Thank you!" He soon wriggled away.

"Shall we go home now, Ptolemy? I want to tell Mother and Father. Goodbye, Earth-girl. I'll try to find you some new legs next time, yes?" and he waved and dived into the sea with the chuckling turtle in pursuit – new legs would not be so easy to find.

***

Heather sat for a long time, thinking of her explanation regarding the chance discovery of one of the only two remaining items still missing from the robbery. She heard her father calling her and gave all her attention to getting back up the steps to her wheelchair.

Jack was waiting for her. "I thought we'd have breakfast together," he smiled at her. "Mum's done some great bacon sandwiches. You've been a long time?"

Heather wagged her finger at him.

"I've told you not to worry about me, Dad. I've got to do things by myself."

Jack held both his hands up. "I know, pet, I know. I'm just a silly old man," and he went to help her into her chair.

"I can do it," she insisted, and as she got her bottom onto the wheelchair seat one of her legs gave a great jolt.

"Ouch!" Heather cried out. "I felt that!" Rubbing her leg, she caught the expression on her father's face. "No, Dad, its only cramp. Right, where are those bacon sandwiches? I'm starving," and went off together to find Morag.

"I've got something to show you," Heather said, as her mother helped her peel the tight wetsuit off. Up her sleeve she had tucked the lozenge-shaped champagne diamond. She held out her hand.

"Look."

Morag and Jack looked, and looked again in stunned silence.

"Where on earth did you find this?"

"In the river, Mother, where do you think?" joked Heather. "It's been there all the time. After all, Ezekiel King did fall in, didn't he?"

"Well, I just can't believe it." Jack picked it up and turned it over in his hand, over and over again, feeling its smooth centre and cut edges.

"Great Grandpa Montague's diamond. It's probably the prize of the whole Fraser collection."

"*Was* the prize," Heather corrected him. "It's gone, remember?"

"Well, shall we keep it?" Jack was undecided.

"Yes," said Heather unexpectedly. "I'd like to have it," meeting her father's steady gaze.

"Whatever you wish." Morag and Jack agreed, taken very much by surprise by their daughter yet again.

***

317

On Sunday the troops all duly turned up at the tea shop to be reminded of the daily routine: Peter was to come each evening to count the takings and bank the money.

Bridget was getting very excited and she was sent home to pack, with hugs and farewell wishes. George checked the stock and deliveries and left umpteen phone numbers. Eventually Peter walked him home, assuring him of a trouble-free week.

"I'll lick them into shape don't you worry, George," grinned Peter. "Off you go and enjoy yourselves."

The next morning the café was in full swing by eleven o'clock, all three focused entirely on making a success of the week. They took turns in the kitchen and waiting on the tables, made endless sandwiches and pots of tea and when the sun came out ice creams began to sell. The fine weather succeeded in making it a very popular spot.

At two o'clock a black car rolled up and parked opposite the tea shop.

"It's Harold!" squealed Ellie and ran to greet him.

"I've brought Miss Heather for lunch, Miss, is that alright?" and he grinned broadly, pleased to see Ellie again, and got the wheelchair out of the boot.

"You've come to check out the cream tea, Harold, haven't you?" accused Elle.

"Well, Miss, it had crossed my mind," he admitted shyly.

Heather wheeled herself across the car park to the café. She was looking for a sighting of Eddie but couldn't quite get into the café with the door obscured by the postcard racks and the drinks chiller, so she sat at a table outside and waited.

Eddie caught sight of somebody sitting down, and rolled his eyes – not another one. What was it going to be this time? He heaved a big sigh and said to Patrick, "I'll go, another cream tea I expect," and off he went with his order pad and pen. He was so tired he couldn't even remember the orders any more. He crossed the threshold of the door wearily and looked up at the table. Heather's smiling face looked back at him.

"Remember me?" she grinned. "The service round here is terrible, isn't it, Harold? How are you, Eddie? Time to sit down for a minute?" and from that minute Eddie's day changed. He fetched the cream tea for two and sat with them in the sun. Patrick and Ellie whispered and giggled in the kitchen and the rest of the afternoon passed happily until Peter came at five o'clock to count the money.

By now Eddie and Patrick had put their guests to work. Heather cleared the tables and Harold served the ice cream, thoroughly enjoying himself, chatting away to the customers and listening to their holiday stories.

"It's quite lonely work you see, being a driver. I like a good yarn," he admitted to Eddie. "Miss Heather's keen as mustard on you, if I know anything. Couldn't get me over here quick enough when she knew I had a few hours off."

Eddie was horrified. "You didn't have to come here on your day off, did you?"

"I don't mind sir, been a pleasure to see you young folk working so hard. Good on you, that's what I say. She's a great lass, bit of go in her, you know what I mean?"

Eddie did know and he realised he was just as keen on her too. He knew then why he had butterflies in his tummy and wanted to keep going to look at the house where she lived, even though she wasn't there. He wanted to spend more time with her during the holidays, time together. He went to the doorway to look for her, and of course she had got Harold to move all the stuff so she could get inside. She was wiping the tables down.

"Are you swimming in the morning?" he asked her directly.

"Yes, want to join me?" Her eyes fixed on his. They were very, very blue.

"I would," he said without smiling. "I'll meet you tomorrow then."

"You guys have done very well. A credit to you," announced Peter, bagging up the takings at one of the tables. "George and Bridget will be pleased."

Harold and Heather got ready to go. She rolled the window down to say goodbye.

"Are you helping tomorrow?" Peter asked her.

"I wasn't going to," she replied, a little embarrassed.

"Why not? We need extra hands in the kitchen, you know. You'll be safe in there, our secret weapon, a buttering and slicing machine," Peter encouraged her in his blunt way.

"Dad!" said two horrified voices.

"Go on, you'll enjoy it! Give it a try," Peter smiled, ignoring his kids. He was used to persuading people to do things. "You won't get the sack, I can promise you that. The staff are a bit difficult but that's nothing new." and everyone laughed.

Heather was silent for a moment. "Alright, I'll see you tomorrow then," and she and Harold swept around the car park and were gone.

"Good work, Dad," said Ellie, watching them go. "Only thing, is Heather told me she was going to pony camp this week."

Eventually they returned to Watermill Cottage to meet Sam, who was coming to supper. Mary had spoilt them, as they sat down to roast beef with all the trimmings and real English trifle.

"I have an announcement to make," said Sam suddenly. He cleared his throat. Everyone stopped eating at once.

Oh no. Patrick's heart sank and his stomach hit his boots somewhere. *He is going to sell the cottage.* They all waited as Sam stood up.

"I've been giving a lot of thought to things; about my job, my life and my family, and I have decided to leave the world of banking."

There was a united gasp around the table.

"I am joining a large finance company in Exeter, to advise and hopefully move them forward. I am also going to work freelance for Fraser Distilleries at Jack's request, therefore I am moving my – our – life to Devon, in one month's time. Irene will continue her own work as usual. I hope it's the right decision. I also hope, Patrick, that this will please you." He turned to look at his son. "After your GCSE exams you can move schools if you wish, son. Your choice." And he sat down, red faced, and heaved a great sigh.

"Well done, Sam, good decision!" and Peter jumped up to shake his hand and clapped him on the back.

Eddie and Ellie couldn't help themselves and cheered loudly, then both looked at Patrick. He was stunned by the news; he just couldn't take it in. It was what he had dreamt of ever since he had met Eddie and Ellie. He looked at his father's face and realised it was true. Patrick managed to speak in a strangled voice.

"I can't believe it, Dad. You of all people, giving up your job." He looked at his special friends, Eddie and Ellie, put his head in his hands and whispered, "Tell me I'm not dreaming, someone."

"I think this calls for a celebration," said Mary, and got up to fetch glasses and a bottle of champagne. She had been keeping it for a special day, and this was it, for sure. She picked up a carton of orange juice as well. *Can't encourage drinking*, she thought.

Soon, toasting each other, glasses were clinked, and huge smiles beamed around the table on all their faces. A lively discussion followed with everyone interrupting and asking questions until each sought the peace and tranquillity of their own beds and their own thoughts. What a day it had been! Things were moving very fast.

Chapter Forty-two
Eddie and Heather swim together, and a magical evening on the river

Anticipating his date with Heather, Eddie was up early the next morning and walked to the ferry slip near George and Bridget's house. He sat on the steps waiting to see if she would turn up. He thought about the previous day and felt great for Patrick who now would be a whole lot happier.

Scanning the river, he noticed something yellow waving from the shore. It was Heather. Eddie had checked that the tide was coming in and it was safe for him to swim across to her. He waved back and entered the water. He had made a good few strokes when something came up underneath him and propelled him across the river at great speed. It was Ptolemy. Eddie was lying on top of the great shell back of the turtle. Then Cornelius popped up.

"We shall swim together, Eddie."

Swiftly the three set off for the small secret cove where Heather was waiting. Eddie was delighted with his escort, and Heather clapped her hands to see them all together coming out of the water on the edge of the shingle.

"Well, good morning!" she called, and she clipped her safety line on and edged towards the water.

"Hi," Eddie smiled. "I had a lift over. I'm not sure I'd have made it without good old Ptolemy. He made a great surfboard."

"You be careful," Heather scolded.

"Anyway, let's go, shall we? I've got to go to work later," he said, rather pointedly.

"Have you put your birthday present on?" asked Cornelius, sitting down next to Heather. Eddie was intrigued. Had they missed her birthday?

"No, I haven't got it on today," replied Heather very sweetly. "I've put it away in a safe place. I don't want to lose it, do I?"

"I suppose not," agreed the child, thinking.

So together they swam, Cornelius, Heather and Eddie, Ptolemy keeping a watchful eye on them all. This time Heather held no one's hand; she needed both her arms to swim beside Eddie, to keep up with him. He marvelled at her strength and agility in the water, and Cornelius darted around them both, begging Eddie to chase him, which Eddie did willingly, listening as the bird boy chuckled in delight.

When Heather felt a tug on her line she signalled to turn back to the shore, and Cornelius raced Eddie, winning easily as Heather was treated to a ride on Ptolemy's back. It was wonderful fun. The turtle guardian steered Cornelius towards home, asking Eddie first if he needed any help getting back, but Eddie wanted a few moments alone with Heather and declined.

They sat on the beach together, holding hands.

"I've cancelled pony camp," she told him, looking into his face, searching his eyes. "I'd rather be here for a week... with you," she added. Looking back into her pretty face and her blue eyes, Eddie kissed her, confident now of her feelings.

Then he laughed. "We're an item now – so Harold says."

"What?" snorted Heather. "He's got a nerve!" and she pretended to be cross.

Eddie kissed her again. "Come on, I've got to get back and you, madam, are going to drudge like us today, aren't you?"

"If you're there I think I might be able to enjoy it," Heather teased him.

"Oh, I'm a bit grumpy when I'm working. There are so many other things I'd rather be doing. We only have one week off, after all. I'd better go while the tide is low. Do you need any help?"

"No I don't, thanks," Heather replied firmly. She rubbed her leg. "But I've got a funny crampy feeling in my leg. It's a spasm, and I'll wait until it's gone. You go, I'll see you later."

Eddie kissed her one more time. It was a wonderful feeling.

She likes me, she really likes me! he kept telling himself, swimming strongly across the river, arriving safely on the other side.

Heather watched every stroke until he emerged at the ferry slip. *He really likes me!* and her leg gave a jolt and she felt a sharp pain.

"Ouch!" she cried out. "What's wrong with you?" and she rubbed her leg furiously. Then it occurred to her that some weeks ago she couldn't actually feel anything, and that gradually these odd twinges and pains, cramps and spasms had come on.

Umm, strange, she thought, and then went back to thinking about Eddie. A delicious warm happiness swept over her.

When Cornelius arrived back he told his mother and father that he had been for a swim with Eddie and Heather.

"Do you know, she is like a fish with her legs behind her. She swims just like me but Eddie is faster. He chased me and I won."

Sargasso and Seraphim were amused as they listened to him, and then his father spoke to him.

"There are stories of mermaidens in the sea my son: of girls with tails just like fish instead of legs, but I have never seen one."

"Then she must be one, mustn't she?" Cornelius insisted.

"No my child, she is not because she has legs but they were injured in a fall," Seraphim said gently.

"Eddie likes her, doesn't he, Mother? And I do. She has hair like mine."

"Yes, my child, the sun has blessed you both with his golden light."

Cornelius was satisfied, and went for his morning nap.

"I am glad that Eddie has found happiness with the mermaiden," smiled Sargasso to his wife.

"Ellie has found a soulmate too, if I'm not mistaken. I can see it in their eyes," she added.

"Then they are both lucky, as lucky as I am," Sargasso told her.

***

The routine at the café soon fell into place and daily the youngsters toiled and served customers, washed up and swept floors. Not until the evening did they have any free time, but love was in the air and they were happy just to be in each other's company, the tight-knit four, joined together by friendship and affection. Heady days of stolen kisses, gentle touches and long gazes. First love is a potent elixir which erases everything else with its power.

Having begrudged the week's work, Eddie now didn't want it to end. Unkindly the world kept on turning and Sunday arrived all too soon. Mary collected Bridget and George from the station at Totnes. The brother and sister looked brown and happy.

"We've had such a lovely holiday!" Bridget announced as she gave Mary a big hug.

"It was a good week," admitted George, also hugging Mary. "Now then, how are those kids getting on? Any of the staff resigned?"

"No indeed," laughed Mary, "but you've gained a few extra ones, Heather and her chauffeur, Harold." Mary enjoyed their surprise. "I've got a feeling they haven't had any wages."

"No wages?" repeated George.

"I think they only needed a free cream tea and they were happy," Mary joked. "Honestly."

"And the takings?" he couldn't help himself asking, always the businessman.

"Very good, I'm pleased to say. The weather has been fine, which helped. Pete's been every evening, counted the money and banked it twice. They have all worked hard and seem very happy. Not a cross word among them. You've trained them to perfection."

"We've booked a small surprise for friends and family this evening. I hope you will all be free to come," Bridget told her.

"Sam's here this week. He's got some great news," Mary told them.

"He's very welcome too. Meet at the ferry pontoon at six pm. I'll ring everyone and tell the kids to close up at four pm today, and we'll see you all later." Bridget and George smiled mysteriously. As Mary continued the drive home she was intrigued as to what the surprise might be.

By six o'clock the word had spread and the party included Mary and Peter, Bridget and George, Eddie and Ellie, Patrick and Sam, Harold, Heather, Jack and Morag.

Harold parked by the pontoon and waited.

A small picnic launch came alongside, its bright striped canopy flapping. Two waiters in black shirts and white bow ties jumped ashore.

"Party for Mr Woodside? Welcome aboard," and the two handsome Italian men stood either side of the small gangplank. As the guests arrived they were greeted by two waitresses in black and white striped shirtdresses with white collars who offered them trays of cocktails.

"Can we?" asked the teenagers tentatively.

"Of course, this is a special occasion. Just one!" their parents gave them permission. George had already made sure they were low alcohol cocktails.

The boat set off up the river with the lively group, everyone talking at once, hearing all about the holiday, the café, Sam's new job, and everything else under the early summer sky. Heather was seated at a table under the canopy, with the other youngsters gathered round her. They were like a group of beautiful brightly coloured birds, chattering and preening together, their happiness infectiously spreading to all the others.

A champagne and lobster dinner was then served; the party seated at elegant tables laid up with black and white linen, an orchid placed beside each napkin. It couldn't have been more perfect.

Small hanging lamps were lit discreetly as the light faded and soft music played at a low pitch. As eyes met and hands touched, the parents began to sense things were different. Something had changed. The boat slid smoothly along in the darkness and the rest of the world disappeared, focused now entirely on the small gathering. Bridget and George, surrounded by the people they loved most, proposed a toast.

"I'd like to thank you all for making it possible to enjoy the rest I didn't know we both needed. You kids have been so responsible and so reliable. I know that you are all going to grow into fine people. So, I propose a toast to you all, thank you." George pointed his glass at each one of them, and Bridget clapped and wiped a few tears away quickly.

Eddie and Heather, Ellie and Patrick looked embarrassed but took the praise. Dear old Harold was pleased just to have been part of the fun. Mary watched her son and daughter curiously; she hadn't realised until now how grown up they were. Their childishness has slipped away through her fingers and she was too late to catch it. They had emerged into the world as changelings, almost fully grown, already winning the hearts and minds of others. She felt suddenly tearful and empty, her eyes pricked and she swallowed. Lifting her glass she drank her champagne, catching a look exchanged between Eddie and Heather – a look she remembered from her own teenage years long ago. Morag caught her eye, and Mary saw the same realisation in her face. She was staring at Heather with a wistful expression.

The picnic boat manager, Don, had been given strict instructions that no tables were to be cleared for dancing. Everyone was to remain seated for the rest of the evening until they returned to Dartmouth. George did not want anything to spoil Heather's evening. A drowsy, satisfied feeling crept over them all as cocktails, champagne, food and excitement created a comfortable mood. The boat had luxurious heaters which kept the cool air at bay. Drifting along watching the river and the magical reflected lights, it seemed like another world, and it was. Even the stars were shining brighter that night, against the blue-black darkness. The four teenagers, struck by their first deep feelings for somebody other than their family and schoolfriends, didn't want the evening to end.

Eventually and inevitably, the boat moored up alongside the quay at eleven o'clock and reality was forced back upon them all. Even the adults had to admit it had been a very special evening. Thanks were heaped upon George and Bridget, who shook hands with everyone and hugged the girls. Reluctantly all the families separated and returned home.

For Morag and Mary it had been an emotional and revealing evening, and neither mentioned anything to their husbands, but disturbing thoughts swirled around inside their heads, reaching into their very hearts – losing one's children was a rather frightening affair.

Chapter Forty-three
Reunited, and some amazing news

It was not until the third week in June that they met up again. But secret letters were exchanged between the four of them, and the postmen were busy in Scotland, Devon and Sussex.

True to his word, Sam took up residence in Waterside Cottage and the well-dressed city banker abandoned his pinstriped suits for a more casual approach to life. Irene came, and went to lectures in universities all around, and Patrick was hugely envious of his father waking up day after day in Devon.

A great reunion had been planned for a weekend of the 20th of June and that longed-for Friday eventually arrived.

Great preparations were taking place at Woodend Manor Farm, as it was Jack who had suggested it weeks ago in London. Morag was expecting Mr and Mrs Gerald Peabody, Andy and Sheila Peabody and their children, Sarah and Toby. Dickie and his son had also been invited and Antony was looking forward to seeing the Moonmirror which he had heard so much about that afternoon in London. Heather was organising an archery competition and a barbecue and Jack had promised a sailing trip, weather permitting.

As Patrick sat in the train carriage which rumbled rhythmically over the track on its way to Devon, he contemplated the weekend ahead of him with growing excitement. Could one go on getting happier and happier? When would it stop? Would there be some terrible disaster waiting to befall him at a certain point because he had had his full share? He spent his time in school longing to return to Devon to Eddie and Ellie. He decided he loved them both equally with a steady ongoing strength, deep and constant – they brought the meaning to his life, he realised in a serious moment.

The train slowed down and Patrick realised he was almost at Totnes station. Relieved, he prepared to get off, and joined the crowd of people thronging towards the exit. Something in red hurtled up to him and grabbed him.

"It's great to see you! Your dad said I could come to meet you!"

Patrick turned around in astonishment to see Ellie's smiling face. She had come to meet him! He took her arm, and then his father appeared, greeted him warmly and took his bag.

"Nice to see you, son. Come on, here's the car," and to Patrick's surprise the black sleek company car had been replaced by a modest, diesel four wheel drive.

"Nice car, Dad!" He was delighted, also noticing the casual cord trousers and polo shirt.

"You'll be keeping chickens next, won't you, Sam?" teased Ellie, whose arm was firmly locked in Patrick's.

"You two lovebirds can sit in the back," Sam told them, and both burst out laughing.

"I don't know about that, but I think she might agree to be my girlfriend," announced Patrick bravely.

Ellie nodded coyly, but was very proud of her new status.

Harold was, at the same time, approaching St Agnes School's leafy driveway.

The car drew up outside the small house which Heather shared with four other girls. She rushed to get her bags as Harold knocked and called her name.

"Miss Heather?" His familiar voice was a pleasure to hear. Freedom beckoned her.

"I'm ready!" she replied, and he began to get everything into the car. As Harold opened the door for her she noticed a shadow inside. She bent forward, and Eddie's face peered out.

"Surprise! Your mother asked me to come up and meet you, she's busy today," he said shyly.

"Brilliant," smiled Heather, "we can go to the Brown Cow together. Harold and I always go for tea."

"Great!" Eddie was pleased.

During that day, the great gathering began. Shady Lane was extremely busy cutting the grass, cleaning all the garden furniture, tidying up the stables and organising the archery equipment. In fact, so much had to be done that he had to ask Abel King to help him, and he too was soon hard at work, sweating in the sunlight up at the stables.

The first to arrive were Mr and Mrs Peabody, who appeared at lunchtime on Friday. Morag wanted to devote some time to this quiet refined couple who had done so much to help their daughter after her horrific accident two years before.

Jack and Morag entertained Gerald and Fiona on the terrace overlooking the river, and organised a walk afterwards to the headland, just the four of them. Tomorrow the guest competitions and barbecue would take place, and Sunday they would go sailing and have a picnic lunch, and by tea time the guests would leave for home.

Eddie and Heather talked quietly in the back of the car. "I've got something to tell you," she suddenly said, mischievously.

"Oh?" said Eddie. "What?"

"Cornelius found one of the missing diamonds! It was wedged between some rocks and he brought it up as a present for me."

"No!" said Eddie in amazement. "He found one of Ellie's silver lockets too, the one I bought her for her birthday ages ago. I bet that diamond was worth a lot of money, eh?"

"It was the pride of the collection – a champagne diamond my great-uncle found. I'm going to keep it actually, but only because that dear little creature gave it to me. He thought it was a piece of glass! Sweet, isn't it?" she smiled, remembering that morning very clearly.

After the Sussex tea shop, Harold sped off to Winchester College where Antony was waiting impatiently. Dressed in black with a large bag by his side, he broke into a huge smile as he opened the car door. All the way to Devon, Antony treated them to his astronomical theories about extra-terrestrial life. Eddie and Heather didn't care, they giggled, holding hands and enjoying being together again. Heather winced and closed her eyes once or twice as twinges of pain shot into her muscles. Eddie noticed her discomfort but said nothing. He turned and smiled warmly at Heather's pretty face. By the time they reached Dartmouth, Eddie and Heather were fast asleep and Antony was still droning on to poor Harold. Eddie, waking up, found himself nearly home.

"I'll see you both tomorrow," and he jumped out of the car. "Thanks Harold, enjoyed the astronomy lecture?" and he slammed the door and went off smiling.

By seven o'clock Sam, Patrick, Mary and Peter, Eddie and Ellie were enjoying fish and chips at the Scallop Shell Inn just along the coast. They sat outside in the cool evening air as the gulls called loudly and the sea hissed on the shingle shore.

"How is the new job going, Dad?" Patrick suddenly remembered to ask.

"I'm really enjoying it. Doesn't seem like work at all. The office staff are all very nice and I think I've made a difference," he added modestly.

"Good," replied Patrick, selecting a prime fat chip for his fork. "So, moving to Devon has been a good thing-yes?"

"Only the best thing I've done for years!" San declared adamantly, unwittingly falling into the careful trap that Patrick was setting for him. "I'm sleeping better than I've done for years. I drink my morning tea down at the slipway, feed the ducks, watch the fishing boats go out, it's just perfect," Sam enthused.

"Pass the vinegar, Ellie, could you?" he asked.

Patrick put his fork down and took a deep breath. *Now!*" he told himself, *Do it now!*

"Then you won't mind if I leave Burnside College at the end of term and move down to Devon like you, will you, Dad?" Patrick's steely eyes locked onto his father's face as Sam digested not only his large portion of haddock but this startling news as well.

Ellie held her breath and caught Patrick's fingers under the table; they were hot and sweaty as she squeezed them tightly. There was an awkward silence and everyone waited for Sam's reaction. They knew Patrick's education meant everything to his parents, especially Irene.

"I'm not going to stop you this time. I know you loved Dartmouth before I did, but I couldn't possibly deny my son the same pleasure. Go for it! Your mother won't stand in your way this time." He looked steadily back at his son's face and nodded, smiling.

It was a very emotional moment but it didn't last long as the truth sank in and the whole table erupted in unbelieving joy. Patrick sat speechless, just smiling and blinking. Things didn't just happen to other people, as he often thought: it had finally happened to him.

"Well," said Mary, "what is it about the McNab men? Is your clan always like this? We'd better watch out, all these determined Scots invading Warfleet!"

Eyebrows were raised by other customers but their happiness was evident and the laughter infectious. It had been a huge milestone for Patrick, who was almost hysterical with relief.

As soon as he reached the cottage, Patrick phoned his mother, who was in Manchester.

She took his news coolly, saying she would be home on Sunday and they would talk about it then. Patrick was triumphant and Irene knew she would never change his mind now; it would be a damage limitation exercise. She had until Sunday to make some plans and to get ahead of him.

***

On Saturday morning the young ones were to assemble at Woodend Farm for the archery competition and the grown-ups were invited to watch. There was also a tennis tournament in the afternoon, and walks and quietness were available for those not inclined to games.

Later, it was 6.00pm for drinks and the barbecue.

In the rose-pink hues of early morning, Eddie and Heather met once more for a swim. This time the tide was not favourable so Eddie had to use his father's dory and he motored over to the sheltered cove below Woodend Farm. The chug of the engine disturbed Cornelius, who watched the blue Dell Quay dory on its journey.

"That's Eddie. I'm going too!" He rushed about getting ready and this time a sleepy Ptolemy let him go alone.

Eddie, Heather and Cornelius played tag, darting and diving until they were exhausted. Sitting resting on the shore afterwards, Cornelius asked Heather a question.

"If your legs don't work we could make you a fish's tail and then you could swim like a real fish, couldn't you?"

Heather thought for a moment, touched by his concern. She was sitting on the shore's edge, Eddie rubbing her long wet hair with a towel.

"I think you mean to make me like a mermaid. Have you seen one?" she asked curiously.

"Yes, the silent one that sits on the rocks down by the ferry, but she doesn't speak to me. I don't think she can swim either," he whispered to her.

Eddie smiled and spoke gently to him. "She's made of a very hard sort of stone and she's not real. She's not alive like us."

"Not real?" repeated Cornelius. "But she's got a fish's tail, and I thought Heather might like one like that."

"It was a good idea, Cornelius, but I think I'd rather have my legs, thank you," Heather chuckled.

"Come on, I'll give you a lift back in the boat if you like," said Eddie, wanting to change the subject. "Heather's in a hurry today, she got lots of visitors coming and tomorrow we are all going on a picnic."

Heather frowned at him but it was too late.

"Can I come on a picnic? I've never seen one before," said Cornelius excitedly. Heather and Eddie exchanged desperate glances. What were they going to say?

"I think your parents would like us to keep you a secret, just to keep you safe until you are fully grown," explained Eddie. "We can't take you, it would be a bit risky."

"Never mind." Heather stroked the soft feathers of his back, loving him for his childish innocence.

"Come on, let's go!" Eddie jumped up holding out his hand, and he and Cornelius scrambled into the boat. "See you soon." They both waved and as the engine roared into life.

Heather waved back, watching as they crossed the river. *Oh dear.* She shook her head, feeling guilty. Had they hurt his feelings? Especially after he had been so thoughtful wanting to turn her into a mermaid. *What a good idea!* smiled Heather. *One I shall consider seriously.* And she burst out laughing.

Ptolemy's searching eyes saw Cornelius in the boat with Eddie and at once he swam back towards the Creek. It was only to be expected, as his little master was part human, that he should be fascinated with the boy and the girl. The turtle followed the wake of the boat and watched his charge jump off the edge of the dory. He automatically lifted both his small webbed feet and flapped his wings several times before he landed on the rocks.

Ah. The turtle knew this was an important new development: Cornelius had felt compelled to use his wings. His development as a bird was beginning. Ptolemy felt a pang of anxiety. Would his work soon be done? Would he lose his little master once he could fly?

Sargasso and Seraphim also watched their little son ruffle his feathers and flap them once or twice. They exchanged glances. So far his wings had remained dormant; maybe the time was drawing near and he would truly be their son? Maybe.

Chapter Forty-four
A summer party at the Frasers', and the lighthouse is lit again

Over at Woodend Manor Farm, there was plenty going on. Heather and Andy Peabody were getting everything ready for the archery competition and there was a lesson at 9.30am for beginners. Antony, Dickie, Patrick, Ellie and Eddie all turned up. Andy was patient and thorough in his explanation. Safety was his first priority; scoring on the coloured boss came later. The time flashed by and soon it was 10.30 am. The other guests slowly turned up to watch.

Heather was serving coffee and tea outside her little cottage and Morag brought a trayful of her buttered scones, still warm, from the kitchen. After coffee, Heather gave out the bows and a glove and armguard to all the competitors. Each quiver held different coloured arrow flights and she stuck a corresponding coloured sticker on each competitor's chest so there were no mistakes. Nobody was allowed to enter the bark arena until all the arrows had been fired, for safety reasons.

Each got ready to shoot and Shady Lane stood by to collect and score. Excitement rose, arrows were loosed at intervals, and at the end the scores were announced by Morag. Andy Peabody was the winner, with Heather a close second. Third place surprisingly went to Patrick, who turned red with pleasure and amazement.

"Well done!" Eddie applauded him and Ellie was delighted. Antony joined them shyly.

"Not as easy as it looks," he told them. "I twanged the string on my arm, look." and he showed them a red angry bruise as he rolled up his shirt sleeve.

"I've done that," grinned Eddie, "hurts, doesn't it?"

The sun came out and Ginny popped her head over the stable door and whinnied.

"Oh yes?" Heather looked up at her beloved pony. "You're on duty too, you know, the little ones are expecting pony rides."

Sheila, Toby and Sarah arrived at the top of the short slope just as Heather was speaking, and the two children, who were seven and nine, rushed to stroke Ginny.

"How did it go?" asked the quiet Sheila, giving a wave to Andy in the distance.

"He won," Heather nodded. "Quite convincingly."

"Good. That's great. Andy's a bit shy in public, it's good for him to have spectators. He's got to get used to it now he's in the limelight. The Olympics no less!"

Andy wheeled himself over to join them. "Pony rides now is it? You did really well Heather _ – you've improved a lot."

"Thank you," said Heather modestly.

After the pony rides, lunch was laid out on the terrace at the main house. A snack of soup, crusty bread, cheese and fruit. Just as they began, Heather excused herself and went into the house with her father. Eddie watched her go, wondering why.

"I'd really like to see your invention," persisted Antony. He had asked Eddie and Patrick several times about the Moonmirror and had received a very weak response. "Any chance?"

"Maybe later. Are you playing in the tennis tournament?" hedged Eddie.

"I don't really want to," admitted Antony, dreading the thought.

"Oh go on," persuaded Ellie, "come in the doubles with me."

"But I'm no good," he said dejectedly.

"That doesn't matter, come on, it'll be a laugh anyway."

Antony surprisingly agreed. Eddie and Patrick decided to partner each other. Eddie told a delighted Antony that they would show him the Moonmirror later that evening. Conveniently, it was still at the lighthouse just along the road.

Heather and Jack then appeared from the house either side of an elderly lady with short white hair, dressed in a kilt and a white blouse with a fine grey shawl over her shoulders. Eddie stared at her. Same blue-grey eyes as Heather's, same shaped face, it must be her grandmother. Morag left her guests at once to greet her warmly.

"Mother, so glad you've come," and she gently kissed her on both cheeks. The lady was escorted by Morag to a comfortable chair, and Jack placed an umbrella over her to keep off the sun, and fetched her a bowl of soup. He then announced to the gathered guests,

"I'd like to introduce you to my mother in law, Annie Fraser. It's her birthday tomorrow. Enjoy your lunch, see you at the tennis tournament later."

Heather sat next to her grandmother, looking after her. Then after a while she beckoned to Eddie, Ellie, and Patrick. "Come on over, and meet my wee granny!"

Rather shyly they were presented to Mrs Fraser senior. She appraised them all with practised scrutiny, and at once picked up Patrick's Scottish burr. "A fellow Scot!" She looked at him and shook his hand firmly, their friendship cemented at once.

After lunch those keen enough assembled down by the tennis court. Jack took charge and as usual his enthusiasm soon changed everyone's mind. The short three-game matches didn't take long and the knock-out began in earnest. All ages mixed up and strange partnerships achieved surprising results. Ellie and Antony emerged the new star duo, getting to the final, where Morag and Sarah just beat them.

Abel arrived armed with lemon squash on trays and handed it out to the sweating players. Later, Mrs Fraser senior awarded two silver eggcups to the winners. Patrick and Eddie received two wooden spoons for being the losers. Heather and Ellie laughed in delight at them. Eddie then told them of his promise to Antony regarding the Moonmirror at the lighthouse.

"Can we come?" both girls asked.

"If you want to. Antony has been pestering us since he arrived to see it."

"But it won't be any good in the daylight will it?" Heather puzzled.

"No, but he only wants to see how it works. Maybe we could turn it on tonight, I'll have to check if it's charged," Eddie decided.

"It's the summer solstice tonight," Heather told him. He looked at her, quiet for a moment, thinking.

"So it is. I'd forgotten that, the longest day."

Heather fetched the key from Jack's office and gave it to Eddie. "We'd better round the others up."

"I suppose so," he said lazily, without moving. It was the first time they had been alone together since their swim earlier that morning. He reached out and moved some strands of hair caught across her smooth face.

"You did really well in that archery tournament."

"Thanks," she replied, blushing.

"Are you swimming tomorrow?"

"No, I don't think so" Heather shook her head. "Not with Granny being here and the picnic and everything. Sorry." She looked up at him and sighed.

"Don't worry, I'll see you at the picnic instead, Okay?"

He took the key from her hand and they left the house to find the others.

Morag looked out of the kitchen window to see them disappearing. She had overheard their conversation quite by accident and had been touched by their concern for each other. She didn't know Heather had been meeting Eddie at the beach. *It's none of your business anyway,*" she scolded herself, and went to find Jack.

Mary, Peter and Sam crossed the river in the blue dory to join in the barbecue. They tied the boat up securely on the beach, and started the climb up the steps leading to the surprisingly lush tropical garden. There were plenty of people dotted about on chairs or leaning over the old stone wall looking at the view.

Morag and Jack spotted them at once and fetched a glass of wine for them.

"Come and meet my mother," and they were swept off to be introduced to Annie Fraser.

"The kids are all up at Heather's cottage, Mary," Morag told her, interpreting their curious glances. "They will all be down at seven for the food. They promised!"

"Eddie won't miss his supper," Mary told her.

Around them the caterers dashed about, and eventually exquisite smells began to filter through the air.

"I'm no good at barbecues," admitted Jack. "Aussie Tucker, the barbecue company, do a much better job – really good steaks, fantastic salads, cold beer, and good wines. Suits me just fine," he grinned. "Can't wait."

Three young men in royal blue aprons began to dish up the food into heated trolleys. "Be ready in five minutes, sir," one of them told him smiling cheerfully, "if you want to tell your guests tucker's up!"

Long tables were laid up with blue cloths printed along the edges with white stars, and white flowers had been put into small red buckets and set all along the centre. Smells of garlic bread and cooked meats enticed all the guests to gather round, and young and old joined in together to eat the wonderful food. Heather and her crowd found a quiet corner by the steps and sat together contentedly eating.

Aussie Tucker did them proud and the tempting puddings were brought on trolleys. Tall meringue confections with cream and summer fruits, castles of chocolate profiteroles with spun sugar cages, and hot jam doughnuts with ice cream delighted everyone.

Eddie groaned as he declared himself completely unable to eat another thing. He lay back onto the grass at the top of the steps. "That was excellent," and shut his eyes. At once Robbie jumped on top of him. "Ouch, get off!" Eddie yelled. "You'll make me sick!" as Patrick pulled the dog away and Heather and Ellie laughed.

"Okay, what's the plan for later?" Patrick calmed them all down.

"It won't get dark until about ten o'clock tonight because of the summer solstice, remember?" Heather said impatiently.

"Oh yes, let's not go down there then until about eight-thirty maybe?" suggested Patrick, "By the time we show Antony how it works and set it up we won't have long to wait for darkness."

"It will be a bit of a squash," worried Ellie, "maybe Heather and I will stay down in the entrance."

"That's a good idea," agreed Heather, "I don't mind. You want to show it to Antony, it will just be fun to come along, really. I'd better go and talk to Granny now. See you later."

Eddie and Ellie found their parents and chatted about the picnic planned for the next day. Antony was also looking forward to it, and to trying his hand at not only sailing but fishing as well.

The food was cleared away and a small group appeared with instruments, one very tall man had a strange-looking object under his arm.

Annie Fraser clapped her hands in delight. "Oh, bagpipes! Jack, you naughty boy!"

An accordion player and a violinist joined the bagpipes; they tuned up and were soon playing a lament. The haunting music spread across the river and the valley beyond. Everyone sat still listening. Next, a lady joined them in a white dress with a tartan sash and sang several Scottish folk songs. Eight young men and women entered the terrace, all dressed in kilts and white dresses with different sashes, and the country dancing began.

The guests swayed to the music, watching the intricate footwork, admiring their skill and energy. When they had finished, the applause was loud and enthusiastic. The whole party had really enjoyed the music and dancing, especially Annie Fraser.

"That was just perfect!" she told Jack. "Thank you."

The folk singer was badgered to perform again, and many joined in the singsong as twilight began to lower its soothing curtain over them all. Candles were lit and coffee was served by the Aussie Tucker staff, and the grown-ups settled down for the evening.

Requesting permission from their parents, the five young people tiptoed away as Heather said goodnight to her granny and wheeled herself along the shrubby path to the main road. She soon caught up with the others.

"It was a fantastic barbecue," they all agreed.

"I loved the dancing." Ellie's eyes sparkled. "It looks such fun!"

"It's very energetic and great exercise," smiled Heather.

Suddenly they all went quiet. Heather must have enjoyed Scottish dancing when she was not confined to a wheelchair. She looked at all their glum faces.

"Oh come on, I know what you're thinking. It doesn't bother me now, I've got used to it. Really. Just don't feel sorry for me, there's no need. Honestly. Eddie? Have you got the key?"

"Yep, got it here," he replied cheerfully as the lighthouse roof with its strange cupola came into view. The wooden arched door set into the stonework looked intriguing to Antony.

"What a funny place to put a lighthouse. Why did they put it here, and not out at sea?"

"It was built to help ships find the harbour as it's completely hidden from the sea," explained Eddie. "And there was a sort of beacon on the turret of the tea shop."

The history lesson over, the door was duly unlocked and the circular entrance vestibule revealed.

"Wow!" Antony gazed around.

"You go on," urged Heather, not wanting to keep them waiting.

The boys needed no further encouragement and were up the steps in no time. Only Patrick stopped to look back. "Sure you'll be alright?"

He shivered looking at the closed door to the beach, remembering being attacked by Ezekiel King.

"Yes, thanks." Ellie smiled fondly at Patrick's serious face.

"How many steps are there down to the beach?" Heather asked Ellie.

"About eight, I think. I can't really remember. Shall I look?" and she crossed the tiny hall to another curved door with a strong latch. She lifted it up, opened the door and disappeared. Heather waited patiently, smelling a damp earth smell from the dark gloom.

"Nine," called Ellie. "There's a handrail, but it's awfully dark. The windows are filthy and there's brambles growing all over them." She returned back up the steps. "What did you want to do? Go down there?"

"I thought I might. It leads to the tunnel, doesn't it?" Heather spoke hopefully.

Ellie was anxious as to how Heather would manage it. "Did you bring a torch?"

"In my bag, at the back of my wheelchair. I've always got one there."

They parked the wheelchair at the top of the steps. "Can you pull out my waterproof leggings?" Heather told Ellie.

Eventually she was kitted up. One of Heather's legs gave a strange kick when a sharp spasm ran up her leg.

"Sorry."

Together they got Heather to the bottom of the granite steps. Quickly turning the torch on, Heather sat looking around.

"Where is the door to the tunnel?"

"Over here." Ellie shone the torch on the old blackened door. Heather stared in silence.

"—and the door to the beach?"

"Down here." In the dark recessed wall, Ellie took the handle off its hanging place and slotted it into the door. She turned it with both hands. The gearing cranked the door open with a creaky groan and the air rushed in, along with welcome daylight.

"The tide's out, I hope."

"Oh yes, I checked that." Ellie replied. As it was only a very short distance across the earthy floor Heather was quickly on the beach, with Ellie beside her.

"This poor old lighthouse could do with some restoration, don't you think?" said Ellie.

"You're right." Heather was very happy sitting on the beach watching the sky darken. She could hear the voices of the three boys above her. They watched the river and the sky blending into one as twilight fell and the first stars switched themselves on.

"I know we keep saying it, but it is so beautiful here." Looking up to her left she noticed the sharp cusp of a new moon in the sky. Darkness crept over the deepening blue and the world stilled. The girls sat together, soaking up the special evening atmosphere.

Then the light on top of the lighthouse suddenly beamed out, pale and white across the sky. The girls gasped.

"They've got it to work. Antony will be loving it!"

On the opposite side of the river, Cornelius, Ptolemy, Sargasso and Seraphim saw the same light.

"What is it?" asked Cornelius, a little afraid.

"It's Eddie's Moonmirror light," his father told him proudly. "It stores the light of the moon. They must be on the top of the old lighthouse at Kingswear."

"I would like to see that." Cornelius was enthusiastic about everything that included Eddie.

"One day you will." Seraphim stroked him gently with her wing. "Now, let's get to sleep shall we?" She let Ptolemy lead his charge towards the large nest and the turtle crooned his strange music of the sea to lull the child. The light had made Cornelius restless, and the summer solstice made darkness come late that evening. The hypnotic crooning was difficult to resist and Cornelius slept at last. The seagulls and the turtle watched the beautiful silver ladder stretch over the sea for a while longer, and then slept themselves.

Cornelius opened one eye; they were all asleep. He eased himself so, so carefully out of his soft bed and padded down the steps, and over the side of the quay into the water. He swam strongly; there were no boats to avoid on this night. A few yards from the shingle beach, crossing in the shadow of the light beam, he saw Heather and Ellie on the beach. Filled with delight and joy, he splashed out of the water to greet them.

"What are you doing here?" they both cried out together.

"I've come to see Eddie's moonlight," he announced proudly. Both girls thought at once about Antony but no sooner had they had the thought than they heard voices from the door of the lighthouse, calling.

"Where are you? Are you two alright? I know we've left you for ages." Ellie and Heather froze in horror as Antony and Patrick emerged stooping from the lighthouse door. Unfortunately the scene was clearly lit by the light from above and Antony's quick eyes noticed Cornelius at once. He ran forward.

"Hello, what's this? What are you?" As Heather tried to stop him he picked up Cornelius in both his hands to get a better look. Cornelius, frightened by the strange boy with his black-rimmed square eyes, because of course he had never seen a pair of glasses before, started to wriggle and flap his wings.

"Hey, keep still, I only want to look at you!" Antony shouted, and laughing hysterically, scaring the tiny bird child even more, he called out to Patrick, "This is the weirdest thing I have ever seen! It can't be real!"

Heather was filled with a consuming anger and screamed out loudly, "Don't hurt him! Give him to me!" She wrenched herself around and clinging onto Ellie, somehow dragged herself to her feet.

Cornelius twisted out of Antony's grip, and flapping his wings furiously, fluttered upwards away from the boy. Heather teetered on her stiff legs and leaving go of Ellie, tried to take a step towards the bird child, holding her arms outstretched. At that moment, as the courageous girl took two more awkward steps, the Moonmirror light went out and the bird child and the girl both fell onto the hard unyielding surface of the beach.

Ellie shrieked. Patrick ran towards her, and Eddie came thundering down the steps of the lighthouse, yelling out Heather's name. Antony stood frozen; everything was chaos in the darkness.

"The torch! Where's the torch?" Ellie sobbed. "It must be here somewhere."

Eddie knelt down by Heather, who was lying unmoving on the beach. "Heather, can you hear me? Heather, what's happened?" He held her hand and stroked her forehead.

Patrick found the torch and with his arm around Ellie shone it beside Heather and all around.

"Where's Cornelius gone?" whispered Ellie, "He's not here." She stopped crying and began to worry about the bird boy. Heather came slowly round, moving her head from side to side and sighing deeply.

"Fetch her chair would you, Patrick?" Eddie asked quietly as he helped Heather to sit up. No one spoke as he cradled her gently. "You'll be alright now. I'll get you back home."

Antony stood awkwardly to one side, biting his nails and feeling terrible. What was the strange little creature he had seen? He was dying to ask but didn't dare.

Heather whispered to Eddie, "Has Cornelius gone? He's not lying hurt, is he?"

Eddie didn't really know but Ellie assured her she had already looked for him and that he wasn't on the beach.

"I hope he hasn't hurt himself," Heather repeated anxiously.

"I'm more worried about you to be honest. Have you hurt yourself? I saw you fall, it was quite a thump," said Eddie. Ellie and Patrick brought the wheelchair close by and the boys lifted her onto the cushions. Together they carried her over the pebbles and up to the dark lighthouse entrance. Holding the torch, Patrick closed the door with the handle, winding the mechanism closed. Just as they were about to pull the wheelchair up the steps, Heather turned to Antony who was silently following them.

"If you breathe one word of what you have seen this evening I'll tell your father that you've been smoking, and I'll personally shoot you, by accident of course, with one of my arrows."

Antony's face took on a horrified expression.

"You wouldn't!"

"I would if I had to – don't tempt me." Eddie knew by the set of her jaw and how her teeth were clenched together that she meant it. Oh boy, she meant it alright!

"Okay," nodded the frightened Antony, "And I'm… I'm very sorry."

"Good!" breathed Heather, relieved.

Eventually they reached the dark road alongside the lighthouse and locking the door hurried back to Woodend Farm. Saying a hasty goodnight to Heather and Antony, Eddie, Ellie and Patrick joined their respective parents who were by now ready to leave. Making their farewells to their hosts Morag and Jack, a smiling Mary asked,

"Did you have a nice time at the lighthouse, dears?"

"Yes, it was great," lied Ellie, "but I'm tired now." She smiled at her mother and took her father's arm.

"Shall we go down to the dory now and catch up with Eddie?"

They made their way down the steps, which were lit up by several bright lights, and got onto the boat. The moon looked sharp and bright and the sky was full of stars.

"Aren't you cold without your jacket on, Eddie?" asked his mother, wrapping her narrow shawl around herself.

"No, I'm really warm, it's such a lovely night, isn't it?"

"You didn't leave it behind did you?" Mary persisted. "It was your new one."

"No, Mum." Eddie sighed. "It's under the seat beside Ellie."

Sam and Patrick soon arrived and off they went. When they reached the other side of the river, Peter helped them all out and Eddie said,

"You take Mum and Ellie back, Dad. I can put the boat away. Go on, I'll only be a minute."

"Okay, son," Peter agreed, as the group walked, tired and happy, up the path and disappeared into the darkness.

The second they were gone, Eddie reached down under the seat and carefully picked up his new jacket, unwrapping it a little. He gazed at the sleeping Cornelius who he had found hidden in the dory asleep. Eddie had quickly covered him with his jacket before his father got into the boat. Holding his precious bundle he ran along the quayside to the lime kiln, and tiptoeing past the sleeping gulls and the turtle, he placed Cornelius into his feathered nest. Eddie whispered goodbye. "You are an impossible little rascal!" and he hurried back to pull the boat into the middle of the river and catch up with his family.

Much later, Eddie sat on Ellie's bed as they discussed the unfortunate events of the evening.

"I hope everyone's going to be alright." Ellie was worried. "Wasn't it awful? That bloody silly Antony!"

"He's an idiot," agreed Eddie, "a stupid idiot."

"Do you think he'll tell?"

"No, I don't," replied Eddie adamantly. "What, and risk being murdered by Heather? Would you? Seriously though, Antony's mother died from lung cancer and his father is really against smoking."

"Oh dear, I see now, that's quite a threat then, that Heather's issued."

"Yes, she's not joking, she'll do anything to save Cornelius."

"What do you think about Heather trying to walk?" Ellie carefully opened the subject.

"Unbelievable," Eddie said proudly. "But her legs have been doing funny things recently. I don't know anything about it but it really doesn't matter to me; I think Heather's fantastic." He blushed and looked at his sister intently, watching her face.

She smiled back kindly and nodded. "She is, she's absolutely fantastic. I'm sure we'll be friends forever now, and with Patrick moving down here soon it's all going to be so different. I can't wait."

"You two have really hit it off, haven't you?"

It was Ellie's turn to blush. "We've always got on, really." Ellie shrugged her shoulders. "You should know how nice he is." She yawned. "Boat trip and picnic tomorrow, got to get to sleep now. Come on, off you go, see you in the morning," and she shooed him off to his own room.

Eddie found it hard to sleep, wondering if Cornelius had recovered from his fright. Pictures of Heather, full of anger and staggering wildly across the beach, stayed in his mind for a long time. Would she even talk to Antony on the sailing trip and would he have the nerve to turn up? He'd have to wait until the morning to find out.

He would have been very annoyed if he had known that across the river at Woodend Farm, Antony was at that moment padding down the corridor to Heather's bedroom, where he knocked on the door. It was quite late but Heather was writing up her diary and stopped the instant she heard the quiet tap on her door.

"Who is it?" she whispered loudly.

"It's me, Antony. Can I come in for a minute? Please, Heather," he called hoarsely.

"Alright," she replied, pulling up the bedclothes around herself. Antony quietly opened the door, and taking a deep breath stepped inside. He stood nervously where he was and cleared his throat.

"I've come to apologise for my behaviour. I'm really sorry about… you know, the strange thing. I've no idea what it was, I just don't want you all to hate me. I know I'm a bit weird. I'm sorry, Heather." He stopped talking and bit his lip, staring at her.

"Well, I suppose you didn't know anything about him. I can't really blame you. Of course I don't hate you, I was just angry because I thought you might hurt him. Anyway, I shouldn't have said those things to you. I'm sorry as well." She smiled her lovely smile at him.

"I think we're quits now. Why don't you go back to bed?"

He smiled weakly and nodded. "Okay. Thanks Heather. See you tomorrow, then."

"Yes."

And he left, quietly closing the door.

Phew! Fancy him coming to apologise! Glad that's over." She locked her diary and turned out the light. She'd have to face him again tomorrow. *I hope he doesn't ask any more questions, because he won't get any answers!*

Chapter Forty-five
A memorable day sailing

After a leisurely breakfast, at which Antony did not appear, Jack took charge of the morning's events. "Meet at the Yacht Club pontoon at 11.00 am. I'll be alongside in *Lochinvar*. See you later everyone," and he disappeared in his car with Andy and Heather, with their wheelchairs in the back. It would be easier to get them installed privately and without fuss. The weather forecast had been checked, tides and times reviewed, and a picnic spot chosen on Hauley Island.

Peter, Mary, Sam and their youngsters were to rendezvous with everyone at the island, having sailed there in *Pelican*, much to Heather's disappointment.

"Why can't I go with the others?" she had grumbled.

"You know why," Morag insisted. "It's not polite to our guests to leave them. You can meet up with your friends for lunch." Morag was slightly waspish as she had offered to stay behind with her mother in law and so had forfeited the whole day.

A large blue van with stars painted on it swished onto the Yacht Club car park to meet Jack. It was Aussie Tucker, with their lunch carefully packed into cold boxes. Three young men soon had it all stowed in the boat.

Gradually the guests turned up. It was a bright June morning with plenty of wind and white scudding clouds. *Lochinvar* was going to look very fine indeed, with her varnished hull and twin masts, when she was under sail.

Dickie, Gerald and Jack were all experienced sailors and Andy a competent navigator, so they were a good crew. Somehow Antony and Heather ended up together and she tried to explain to him what to do with the ropes. Sarah, Toby, Sheila and Fiona were comfortable on a semi-circular seat with plenty of cushions in a sheltered spot away from the wind, and were getting excited as the time drew near to set off.

"Just watch," Heather told Antony, as she and Gerald cast the ropes off and stowed them neatly around the fairleads. Then they were away, heading towards the two castles and out into the open sea.

Today was going to be a great outdoor adventure, and it was impossible not to feel excited as the water hissed by, the breeze blew in their faces, and the blue sea beckoned them towards the far horizon. Heather felt strangely serene. She closed her eyes and let the warm wind blow through her hair and across her face. She was overwhelmed by a feeling of happiness and anticipation, the prospect of something inexplicable overtaking her. Smiling, her face turned to the sun, she entered a drowsy half-sleep.

It was several hours until *Lochinvar* reached Hauley Island, off the coast near to Salcombe. A large shape had been seen on the fishfinder several times, but nobody knew what it was. Jack had telephoned in advance to ask the owner's permission for a family picnic near to the old Pilchard Inn. The island was owned by an ageing rock star who had discovered the joys of painting and developed a taste for fine whiskies. It seemed Jack had worked out a perfect arrangement.

The island was small, with a large Art Deco hotel, fields of sheep and several tiny secluded beaches hidden around its shoreline. A sea tractor connected it to the mainland at low tide but the reclusive owner discouraged visitors to his hilltop house, suffering the summer visitors who flocked to the pub.

As they neared the quayside, *Pelican* could quite clearly be seen, her blue pennant fluttering. Eddie, Ellie, and Patrick stood waving on the deck. *Lochinvar* came alongside. "What kept you? We've been here for hours!" joked Peter, leaping up to catch ropes and help them tie up. Minutes later, Jack opened the Aussie Tucker lunch boxes. They were all starving and the food tasted wonderful as they sat in the sunshine, gently rocking to and fro.

"Can we go and explore?" begged Antony. "I'll help Heather over the rough bits." Heather was rather touched but

Eddie just grinned, knowing how she hated offers of help. Sensing freedom, the youngsters rallied round collecting towels and swimwear, and scuttled off as fast as they could.

Jack stood on the deck and watched them go, then he shouted, pointing to his watch. "We've got to watch the tide. Be back in one hour. I mean it!"

True to his word, Antony did help Heather over the rutted grassy path which led around the top of the island and steeply down to a small cove with high rocky sides. A sandy track halted the wheelchair but they were almost on the beach by then. Heather unbuckled her waist strap. "Shall we go swimming?" She had already got her swimming costume on under a navy tracksuit in anticipation of her swim, and began to transfer herself onto the sandy ground, quickly and with her usual agility, laying her towel on the seat of her chair ready for her return. Antony watched silently, marvelling at her confidence and skill. She was quite something. Patrick and Eddie then took hold of Heather under her arms and gently carried her the short distance to the water without any fuss. Ellie trotted alongside with Antony.

"I found Cornelius asleep in the boat when we went home last night," Eddie whispered. Heather's eyes opened wide.

"Is he alright?"

"Yes, I wrapped him up in my jacket and took him back to the quayside."

"Oh, that's good! I've been worrying about him."

Her feet trailed into the cool refreshing seawater as they reached the edge. When the water reached their waists Heather was gently lowered down, and shouting, "Thanks guys!" she smiled gratefully at them both and took off at great speed with a splash.

"Hey, wait for us, you ungrateful creature!" shouted Eddie, and he and Patrick dived in after her. Ellie and Antony exchanged embarrassed glances, then burst out laughing and high-stepping into the water, shrieking at the cold, both plunged into the frothing waves.

The sun shone out of the clear blue sky and danced on the rippling sea, creating diamond splinters of blinding light. Heads bobbed up and down as the five swam on and out to sea, fronds of kelp sometimes crossing their legs and astonished small fish darting among them. The reality of life on the shore faded into the distance as, floating breathless and tired, they lay in the lapping clear water looking up at the sky in silence.

"Isn't it fabulous?" Ellie remarked dreamily, drifting on her back.

"Yes," agreed everyone.

"Shall we play tag?" suggested Eddie, knowing full well it was Heather's favourite game where she and he were equals.

"Why not?" Patrick at once dived down, and catching Eddie's legs, chased off under the water. Antony was not as fast and he soon became separated from the other four. He wasn't worried and enjoyed listening to them splashing and shouting as they dived in and out.

Suddenly, alongside him a great dark shape loomed, which scared him out of his wits. He froze in the water as the black thing circled him. Panicking, he called out to Patrick who was just coming up for air.

"Hey, there's something funny here in the water! Come and see!" Antony peered warily into the clear water. Without his glasses he could see nothing. Then, bodily, he was lifted up and carried along at great speed, just above the water.

"No! Leave me alone! Help!" he screamed out, and the others, hearing his cries, stopped chasing each other at once. Heather saw something dart alongside her, which surfaced with a splash, frightening her too. It was Cornelius! His wet curls dripped down his smiling little face.

"What are you doing here?" she scolded him.

"Ptolemy and I followed the boat and we've come to meet you. I told him about that boy with the black eyes and he's giving him a ride on his back, I think." Cornelius's eyes twinkled as he listened to Antony's loud screams.

"You little monkey! You're paying him back for frightening you, aren't you?" Heather realised at once. She could hear Antony's petrified voice in the distance.

"That's enough, you've had your fun, let him go, Cornelius, please." Cornelius obediently swam off. Minutes later Ptolemy let Antony fall off his back into the water. By then Eddie, Ellie and Patrick had seen the turtle and what he was doing. Although it was very funny to them, it was rather frightening for Antony. As the turtle swam away towards Heather, the others caught up with Antony and helped him to the shore.

"Was it a shark?" he gasped. "I was so scared. It hasn't bitten me, has it?" and he looked all over himself for blood.

"I don't think so!" Eddie laughed.

Patrick felt sorry for him. "Come and sit down, here's your towel," and the shivering wreck of a boy wrapped himself up and tried to recover from his ordeal.

"Here's some chocolate," offered Ellie kindly, "you'll be okay now."

"I was lucky, wasn't I?" Antony chattered with cold, his teeth clenched. "I could have been savaged."

Eddie, Ellie and Patrick's eyes met and they tried very hard not to laugh.

Cornelius and Ptolemy, meanwhile, turned their attentions to Heather.

"Come with us," Cornelius begged, "come down to the Caves of Drach, we've planned a surprise for you," and he took Heather's hand and dived under the water. Ptolemy gulped a huge lungful of air and then followed the girl and his master down, down to the strange columns of rock with the arches and caves hidden deep below. It was a mysterious, magical place where weird seaweeds waved, tinged with rainbow colours and shiny silver streaks that Heather had never seen before.

On the shore, Eddie wondered where she was. He couldn't see her. Cornelius and Ptolemy had disappeared too. A worried dread seized him. "I'm going to find Heather!" he shouted, running down the beach at full speed and throwing himself into the water.

Heather meantime was feeling as if her lungs were about to burst and pointed to the surface, but the turtle approached her and putting his face close to hers, nudged her mouth open and expelled a quantity of air forcefully into it. She breathed again gratefully.

Cornelius plucked a long strand of the shiny rainbow-coloured weed and wrapped it around Heather's legs. She was anxious and didn't know what he was doing, but the bird boy smiled and nodded, reassuring her. Next a shoal of small squid swam out from the dark caves and Cornelius beckoned them towards Heather. Each squid squirted a strange luminous green and yellow ink out of its body, which encased the girl in a coloured mist. Ptolemy and Cornelius each took one of her hands and floated her upwards to the surface. Heather felt very dizzy now and closed her eyes, almost fainting. As she popped through the surface Eddie swam frantically towards her, calling her name. Ptolemy and Cornelius swam away, leaving Eddie holding her in his arms, still calling her name anxiously.

"What have you done to her?" he shouted angrily, but Cornelius and the turtle had disappeared. Eddie pulled Heather strongly towards the shore, holding her in the lifesaving position and keeping her head above the water. When they reached the shore, Eddie lay Heather in the shallow waves, trying to catch his breath, his chest heaving with anxiety and fatigue. He could see that she was breathing and noticed the seaweed still tangled around her legs. He pulled it off at once and it shrank in the air into a crispy brown strand, losing all its colours and moisture; just a tiny piece was caught between Heather's toes.

Ellie, Patrick, and Antony ran to the water's edge as Heather opened her eyes.

"What's happened?" demanded Ellie, dropping at once to her knees and stroking Heather's wet tangled hair and white face.

"She went under. I found her floating on the surface. This seaweed was tangled round her legs. Maybe she got caught up in a kelp bed, I don't know, but she's alive, I know that." Eddie looked up at his sister with tears in his eyes.

"Oh Eddie, we should all have been looking after her. She nearly drowned." Ellie sobbed bitterly, also realising the danger Heather had been in.

"It was my fault," said Antony in a small voice. "I made such a fuss."

"What time is it?" Patrick suddenly remembered Jack's warning. "Come on, we've got to come back!"

Together they carried Heather to her wheelchair and wrapped her up in a towel. She hadn't spoken but was awake and regaining her composure. A faint greeny-yellow slime had collected around her nostrils and mouth, and Ellie wiped her face with a corner of the towel. She dressed her in her navy tracksuit and covered her completely in the warm, fluffy rug.

"Thank you." Heather spoke at last with a faint smile. Gathering up their belongings, they pushed the wheelchair along the beach and up the grassy rutted track. Antony was very confused and upset by the whole affair. He just didn't understand what was going on.

"Please tell me what happened to us," he ventured.

"Not now, Antony." Patrick told him very firmly. "I'll explain later. We need to get Heather back to her dad or we'll be in serious trouble."

Reaching the brow of the grassy cliff top they looked down over the island to the small harbour where the two yachts were still moored up. Voices and laughter floated up to them.

"We're going to make it!" gasped Eddie, breathless with exertion. "They haven't packed up yet."

"There's a brown Bentley parked on the quayside." Antony was puzzled. "It must be Bradley Ponting's, he owns the island. He likes his whisky, so Dad says. I expect Jack's got a boxful for him."

Heather suddenly reached out for Eddie's hand. She still hadn't said much and he squeezed it, willing her to be alright.

"Can you make it back?"

She nodded, trying to smile, her face a ghastly white tinged with yellow. Ellie thought she looked terrible.

"I'm going to be sick!" Heather said quickly, and spewed up violently on the ground, retching as she doubled up. Yellow-green slime pooled on the track.

"Sorry!" she gasped, as Ellie put her arm around her and wiped her face.

"It's alright, you must have swallowed seawater and seaweed and all sorts," she comforted her, looking in disgust at the strange pool of slime.

"You tell me now!" urged Antony, "before I see my dad." His look was threatening and Eddie realised he might well tell more than they wanted him to.

"Alright, but you know what will happen if any of this gets out, don't you?" he warned him just as threateningly.

"Okay, okay," agreed Antony hastily.

"It was a big turtle that circled you and gave you a ride on its back. It was quite harmless but it is the guardian of the little bird creature you found last night. Heather has been swimming with them in the mornings while he was learning. She adores him. They must have followed us today and took her for a swim, but something happened to her, I don't know what, and she's not in a fit state to tell us. Maybe she doesn't even know, but she's almost alright now and we have to hope that she will be. That's it." Eddie looked up at him fiercely. "We will all keep quiet, won't we?"

"Of course." agreed Antony. "It's just so exciting, isn't it? It's a mutant creature no one has ever seen before – it's a fantastic discovery!"

Eyes met in silence. The Bentley fortunately had left when they finally reached the quayside. Their discussions were halted, and everyone concentrated on getting Heather back on board.

"Had a good time?" beamed Jack, then looking at Heather realised she wasn't herself.

"Alright, hen? Feeling a bit peaky?" He looked in concern at his daughter's pale drained face and wet hair.

"She's been sick. I think she's swallowed some seawater," Ellie told him. "Maybe she should go down to the cabin and lie down."

"Good idea," agreed Jack, and lifting up his precious daughter, he took her down to the main cabin. Eddie folded the wheelchair and stowed the towels. Feeling very upset and worried, he joined the other guests, putting a brave face on it. Heather lay in her parent's comfortable bed, feeling sick and dizzy, with strange sensations running all over her body. She had a headache and her mouth was dry. Closing her eyes, with coloured lights and bright zigzags filling her mind, she fell asleep.

Jack peeped in to check his daughter and smiled to find her asleep. *That's good*, he told himself, leaning her wheelchair against the bedside cabinet for when she woke up. Peter gave permission for the four friends to sail back with Jack, as they were very keen to stay close to Heather.

Eddie, Ellie, Patrick and Antony spent the journey home lounging on the deck in the sunshine, amusing Sarah and Toby. Jack came to tell them Heather was fast asleep and they tried not to worry about her anymore. Later on, leaning over the guardrails, Eddie and Ellie whispered to each other about the strange events but could reach no conclusion about what exactly had taken place, except that Cornelius and Ptolemy were involved, and must know what had happened.

When they moored up at the Yacht Club pontoon, Aussie Tucker's van was waiting to collect their boxes, and the guests prepared to disembark. Suddenly, there was a loud scream from below and the sound of uncontrollable sobbing, which made everyone stop in their tracks. Gerald Peabody went below at once, fearing an accident, but was met by the most unbelievable sight.

Jack was standing in the doorway of his cabin crying loudly, one hand over his eyes and the other pointing at something. Gerald pushed him aside to see Heather standing unaided. She took several steps around the bed, looked up and said quietly,

"I seem to be able to walk again. Funny isn't it?" She then tottered unsteadily towards her father who clasped her in his arms and they both wept. By now everybody had tried to find out what had happened, but Gerald closed the door firmly, assuring them that Heather was alright but that he needed to examine her at once.

Eddie was terrified that Heather had died but it seemed that she was most definitely alive. In fact she was very well indeed. Gerald examined her and questioned her gently as to what had happened out at sea.

"Eddie knows, he found me. I can't really remember. Do go and get him, Dad," Heather begged him anxiously, pulling on his arm. Jack composed himself and did as she asked without question.

"What's this?" Gerald removed a small piece of dried-up sea weed from her toe.

"I'm not sure."

Eddie arrived looking anxious and worried. He sat on the bed beside Heather and Jack, who demanded,

"What happened, laddie? Don't be afraid, we're desperate to know."

Heather's eyes locked onto Eddie's, pleading with him, and he knew at once exactly what he was going to say.

"Antony got cramp while we were swimming and foolishly we all helped him ashore, leaving Heather. When I looked around I couldn't see her so I rushed back into the sea and found her floating on the surface. She had got seaweed tangled all around her legs and a funny greeny yellowy stuff round her nose and mouth. She was breathing so I took her back to the shore. She didn't look well, and she was sick. We thought we'd better get her back here as soon as possible. I'm very sorry, sir, that I left her alone. It was very stupid of me."

"Nonsense, boy, you saved her life," Gerald Peabody told him at once. "This greeny yellowy stuff, have we got any of it to look at?"

"Well, Ellie did wipe her face with a towel so it must be still on there."

"I found this piece of seaweed between her toes, do you recognise it?" and he held up the small piece of crispy curled weed.

"No sir, I don't. It shrivelled up as soon as I unwound it from her legs. It was a multi-coloured strip of stuff I've never seen before."

"Hmm, I'd like to analyse them both. Anyway, I'm quite sure that a miracle has occurred here today. Heather's legs seem to be receiving all the signals from her spinal cord. She can feel everything, for now anyway. I shall have to connect her up to several electrical machines at my clinic and monitor her, but... the signs are good! "

"Thank you, laddie, I'm so grateful to you." Jack took Eddie's hands and pumped them vigorously. Heather beamed her winning smile at Eddie, gazing into his eyes longingly. It was obvious to the two men that she adored him.

"I just don't know how to tell Morag," Jack began again. "She'll be just so amazed, and my mother... It's just a miracle as you say, Gerald," and his eyes filled with tears again.

Gerald continued: "I've been noticing signs of some recovery during these last few months, I think I told you, Jack, but something has accelerated the regeneration process. It's puzzling but of course wonderful. She is one of the lucky ones." Jack and Heather knew he was thinking of his brother Andy, sitting above on the deck, paralysed from the waist down in a car accident.

"Let's get you home to your mother, hen. She'll help you shower and change your clothes," encouraged her father.

"Walking again will make you very tired," warned Gerald Peabody. "I suggest you rest for a while after walking, even use a walking stick for a while to get your balance and confidence back. Just see how you get on." He smiled warmly. "I am truly thrilled for you. You have been a brave and accepting patient." He kissed Heather, shook both Jack and Eddie's hands, and left them together.

"I must go, I'll see you later." Eddie said reluctantly, "I'll phone you, if that's alright Mr Fraser?"

"No! Please come home with me for a while, please. Everyone's leaving soon and we can be together, just us and the families. That's alright isn't it, Dad?" begged Heather.

"I'm happy to have the whole town at my house tonight – we're celebrating!" announced Jack proudly.

"I'll go on then, and maybe see you later. Can I tell everyone?" asked Eddie.

Heather nodded, smiling proudly.

"Sure thing!" Jack replied, and gave his daughter a squeeze.

Eddie ran up the hatchway to find an impatient group eagerly waiting for news.

"It's true! She can walk again! It really is a miracle! Just wonderful isn't it?" He tried to believe it too. A great cheer went up and the babble of voices was deafening.

Down in the spare cabin, Mr Peabody carefully stowed the piece of seaweed in a tissue and cut off the corner of Heather's towel.

Just in the interest of science, he told himself, tucking them into a plastic bag and sealing it tightly.

Heather returned home to an emotional reunion with her mother and grandmother. Gerald had broken the news gently to Morag and Annie before Jack and Heather arrived. Departure time had been six o'clock, but that had been abandoned since the Frasers had decided to have a celebration buffet supper. They had all been invited for eight o'clock. It was an unlikely turn of events, but everyone wanted to share in the celebrations for the young girl's recovery.

***

Across the river on the old quayside, Sargasso and Seraphim heard of Heather's miraculous recovery. Seafarers know that on the summer solstice the influence of the red planet Mars is felt. It is at its very lowest point in the sky, and for one day only these powers exist until the orbit changes. It was this energy that Cornelius and Ptolemy had exploited in their bid to bring Heather's legs back to life. Mars was extremely strong, its influence felt deeply in the ocean and the strength had renewed and revitalised the weak covering of her spinal cord. The seaweeds silver stripes were energising minerals from ancient rocks deep on the seabed. Drinking and breathing the squid slime changed the magnetic constituent of her blood and the newly charged ions had empowered and enriched the blood flow, healing the damaged tissue. The power of the sea was awesome.

***

There had never been such joy and celebrations in the old farmhouse; not since the war ended all those years ago. Scottish music blared out from an ancient record player, champagne and laughter were on the menu in large amounts. The buffet was a sight to behold, with smoked salmon and cold beef, hot soup and oatmeal cakes, raspberries and cream: the Australian boys had tried very hard to cook up a Scottish menu at short notice. This time they had been included in the party, and when the Scottish dancing began they were highly sought-after as partners – young, fit and handsome.

Heather looked beautiful: pale and slightly bewildered in a long blue dress with a cream lace cardigan, and wearing the single champagne diamond around her neck. She walked carefully with a stick, radiant with the immense pleasure of moving around the room unaided; however, her father or Eddie were always at her side. She did not attempt to dance but Ellie and Patrick danced enough for all of them, happy and delighted at their friend's good fortune.

Peter and Mary sat with the Peabodys, enjoying all the fun and marvelling at the miraculous recovery of the deserving girl. Nobody in the whole room felt happier for her than Andy Peabody, who had accepted his fate long ago and held no bitterness.

At last, Heather and Eddie sat together alone, relaxed and smiling. He held her hand and looked at her from time to time. She raised her chin and looked into his eyes.

"I am so happy tonight I feel I could jump up and fly!" she said with a giggle.

"Well, knowing you, you probably will!"

"And now I can go up into the lighthouse and go walking and dancing. We can go out together"

"Fishing and swimming and cross-country running," he interrupted. "You'll try to beat me, and maybe you will!"

She punched him playfully. "Cornelius did this for me, I know he did," and for the first time she told Eddie exactly what happened. He listened, gradually piecing it together.

"What do you think?" she finally said.

"Sounds like it, I agree. He's quite determined, we've seen that, but what's frightening is that he seems to have the power – quite a different thing."

"Will I stay like this? I am a bit afraid I'll wake up paralysed again tomorrow. I couldn't bear it."

"Don't think like that, you won't," insisted Eddie, squeezing her hand. He was determined not to alarm her, but who could really know?

"He's going to learn to fly next, isn't he? I saw him fluttering his wings when Antony got him. That's surely the next stage for him."

Eddie nodded thoughtfully.

"Probably, only natural of course, he is mostly a bird!"

Patrick and Ellie joined them, exhausted after the dancing, red faced and puffing.

"That's too much!" and they flopped down on chairs beside them.

"Everything alright?" asked Ellie, concerned. "Feel okay still?"

"Yes, I can't believe it," laughed Heather. "What a day!"

"It's been a great day, truly wonderful, Heather. I'm so glad for you," Patrick told her quietly, and patted her hand.

Ellie swallowed back sudden tears. He was so very kind.

The music wafted across the river and reached the ears of the seagulls, the turtle and the strange little creature who had been determined to make Heather's legs work again. It was Cornelius who had commanded the squid to transfer the influence of Mars to Heather in the form of the yellow-green slime and the rainbow seaweed. The Spirit of the Sea sighed happily on the faraway shores of Antartica as the child he had helped to create performed his first compassionate task, by healing his human friend.

Heather did not return to school after that special weekend but was taken up to London to have tests at Mr Peabody's clinic. Patrick and Antony returned to their boarding schools, but Irene was already making phone calls and setting up interviews and Patrick didn't really care where he went. He knew his mother too well to interfere at this stage.

Antony had been successfully gagged at last; the four were confident that he wouldn't reveal any information about Cornelius or Ptolemy, despite his hungry interest in the 'mutant species', as he called it.

Eddie and Ellie reluctantly went back to school, still excited and overjoyed at witnessing the life-changing events of the weekend. The news of Heather's recovery was discussed eagerly by all those who knew the family. Would it be permanent? What would be the findings of the doctor in London? Could she say goodbye to her wheelchair for ever? It was nerve-racking waiting for the news.

Chapter Forty-six
Preparations for the third task

Autumn swiftly followed, and Patrick was catapulted from life in Edinburgh to a grammar school outside Plymouth, one hour's bus ride away. He bore the first few weeks of being the new boy stoically, looking forward each day to returning home to his father, his friends, and occasionally his mother.

Mr Peabody was just as surprised as everyone else, and could find no medical reason for the sudden improvement. But it had been maintained, and his private opinion was that he could see no reason why the mystifying recovery should not be permanent.

A botanist friend of his, James Brown-Thomas, had examined both the seaweed and the slime and declared it to be unknown to him. However, it contained many strange elements of metallic and mineral compounds, rich in iron and iodine with a pinkish pigment. James had researched this and matched a substance from a volcanic source millions of years old.

"Can I keep this?" he requested. " I want to store it in my lab as an example. Most unusual, probably came from a vent in the earth's crust millions of years ago. From the sea, you said? Maybe I'll take some samples from that location. Thanks very much."

"Of course!" Gerald gave his permission, thinking all the time of other patients waiting to be healed. Heather came weekly, then fortnightly to his clinic, and all was well. She returned to St Agnes School where her life continued much as before, but without her wheelchair.

***

In the woodland, Lord Sunna had grown into a young man during the late summer, and was now strong and middle-aged, mature in stature and wisdom. He was conscious of the fact that Cornelius still had his last and most difficult task to complete. By the close of the year, the woodland spirit will have aged into an old man, grey and wrinkled, his life over. He still had work to do within this short time remaining.

The new buzzard who had taken over from the acting ruler, Oliphant, was quietly going about his governance after the heroic defeat of the jackdaws. In late autumn, Lord Sunna knocked on the oakleaf door knocker of the Citadel and waited. The door opened just an inch.

"Yes? This is the royal residence. Who is it?" said a croaking voice, and then a black tattered head appeared. It was one of the rooks, guardians of the Citadel, now rather old and doddery.

"It is Lord Sunna, may I come in?" and he quickly slipped through the door before the rook could stop him.

"An audience in the Round Room, I think?" he said with authority, and pushed open the door that he knew led to the Purple State Room with its arched ceiling and book-lined shelves. Almost at once the buzzard appeared.

"You wish to see me, Lord Sunna?" inquired the Lord of the Woodland, claws folded together in his royal robes.

"I have come to discuss the final task of the bird boy, Cornelius. The last element is still to be overcome. Only then will the Earth, Sea and Sky be fully united and our contribution complete."

"What would you have me do? Is this my responsibility?" asked the buzzard carefully, wondering what his commitment would be as he faced this determined man.

"The territory belongs to us both, the woodland, but the boy must have open sky to fly in. You are a bird, so let us co-operate. We must set the date for the task and make an effort to encourage and support Cornelius. All our creatures must be involved and it is clear we shall have to delay hibernation again. I'm sure when you explain how it will contribute towards the success of his flight, your subjects will understand. We cannot countenance failure." He paused meaningfully and fixed his eyes on the buzzard.

The buzzard took all this in at once. Failure would look very bad indeed in his reign. Delay hibernation? That would be extremely unpopular.

"Exactly my thoughts, Lord Sunna. I couldn't have put it better myself. We are of one mind," agreed the royal ruler, smiling. He pulled on a looped rope made of honeysuckle twine, and some Canterbury bells tinkled far off. The door opened at once.

"Yes, Sire?" Another moth-eaten rook wearing a tattered apron was standing there.

"Bring wine and cakes for Lord Sunna at once. We have much to discuss."

"Yes, Sire," and the wretched rook limped out.

"Let us plan the route," suggested the buzzard, drawing a large parchment scroll from one of the shelves. He spread it on the table. This map covered the Seafarers' coastal territory and Gallants Bower. Together they marked the route in deadly nightshade ink with a feather quill. It varied greatly in altitude, from the quayside at sea level to the highest point of the Bower, and was quite a challenge. They agreed on two resting places where Cornelius might set his feet down.

Ptolemy had sent instructions from the Spirit of the Sea who wished to recall to life the two whales waiting in stone at Sugary Cove. They were to be the first resting place. Then when Cornelius had completed the second and most difficult ascent from the sea to the top of the hill, he could have his second rest in the lofty branches of the Citadel. His final journey took him across the Woodland, and sharply down the valley for the descent into his home territory and the finishing line.

"Quite a feat indeed," mused the buzzard. The more he thought about it the more he realised he would be famous, remembered always as the ruler who succeeded in assisting the union of the Earth, Sea and Sky.

"I shall be very willing to supervise this," announced the buzzard as the refreshments arrived and he offered Lord Sunna a heady mix of rosehip and elderberry wine accompanied by sliced truffles in a chestnut tartlet.

"Delicious!" declared Lord Sunna. "You must be the authority to bring this to a successful conclusion. I expect you will want to notify everyone as to their duties. The two Woodland doctors may smooth the way on the subject of late hibernation, my lord, if you get my meaning."

The buzzard picked up the veiled suggestion at once, and nodded furiously.

"Then I shall go and observe Cornelius's training programme, and hope for news posted soon, my Lord." With that, Lord Sunna bowed and retreated from the State Room, knowing all was in hand.

Once he had gone, the buzzard was filled with excitement and set about the preparations at once. The long-tailed tits were summoned and in a twittering flurry were dispatched with bark parchments containing all the news and instructions.

A large notice was pinned to the Citadel door. The curious Woodlanders read out the following orders, crowding around the tree stump.

1. HIBERNATION WILL BE POSTPONED UNTIL 22nd DEC.

2. PLEASE MAKE AN APPOINTMENT AT THE SURGERY FOR A PRESCRIPTION IF YOU HAVE PROBLEMS KEEPING AWAKE.

3. TRAINING PROGRAMME FOR THE FLIGHT PATH ASSISTORS IS 20th DEC.

4. FLAGS AND BADGES WILL BE DISTRIBUTED IN YOUR AREA ON 2lst DEC.

NO EXCUSES ACCEPTED. ABSENTEES CAN EXPECT SERIOUS CONSEQUENCES.

BY ORDER REX BUTEO ANNUS HORNUS 1989.

There were naturally a great many mutterings. Hibernation was a natural instinct, the annual winter weariness invaded their bodies gradually. December was very late for bedding down until springtime.

As suggested, queues of Woodlanders appeared at the treehouse where the Dr Underconstumbles practised. They had been ordered to prepare a special elixir by the buzzard.

"What do you think, dear? This is rather a challenge; sleeping is easy but to keep awake, that is a different matter for us two-oo-oo," said husband to wife. Dr Dew and Dr Yew mixed potions and tinctures tirelessly together, eventually producing a cinnamon-flavoured Elixir of Wakefulness which was diluted in hot mulled wine. This popular combination led to happy congregations of woodland folk drinking wine all around the large tree trunk. The doctors provided enticing green hemp biscuits which Verity, the white dove, passed around in her quiet gentle way. She cooed and soothed away any grumbles, easing the postponement of hibernation along very nicely.

It was therefore all down to Cornelius to complete his training and be ready for his flight attempt. Oliphant and Freddie spent the long dark afternoons together in the ash tree sipping acorn coffee and eating honeyed seed cakes, in deep discussion.

"How's the dear little fellow getting on this week?" Oliphant asked as he cleared the tea tray away.

"He's trying very hard indeed. His mother and father spend hours with him, but—" Freddie paused for a moment.

"But what, old friend?" Oliphant sensed something important was coming.

"But he seems to be having a little difficulty in taking off. You see, it comes so naturally to us that I can't help wondering what the problem is exactly. That's all." He looked up at Oliphant rather sadly.

"What are you saying, Freddie?" Oliphant was shocked. "Don't you think he can do it? But he must, he absolutely must, don't you see? So much depends on it." The owl was so upset and bothered that he ruffled his soft white feathers in a shiver.

"I do see, very clearly," replied the robin slowly. "What I see is that we don't really know what makes us able to fly. What is it that sets us apart from all other creatures? Why can we lift

372

ourselves off the ground and fly about with such ease and very little thought?"

These questions were some of the most profound that have challenged mankind for centuries, but Freddie and Oliphant had only just begun to ask them. The small white owl stared silently at the robin, blinking occasionally.

"I just don't know, my friend." He paused again to reflect. "Little Cornelius is to be the ultimate experiment. So much is hinging on his victory."

"You're right as usual, Oliphant, but is it fair to expect so much of one small creature? Is the design right to blend all three elements seamlessly together? We can only wait and hope, because we shall not know the answer until the day and hour of the task."

Both birds were disconcerted by their deep and serious conversation as doubts about the entire project surfaced in both their minds. Not only about the physical challenge set for Cornelius, but uncomfortable questions about rights and ethics. Was this ever a good plan for the natural world?

The two sat together in deep companionable thought and then the owl got out his pipe which had lain idle for many months. Freddie watched him fill it with an unknown mixture, strike a flint on a tinderbox, and followed the first small curl of smoke to the beamed ceiling. The smell was comforting, woody and sweet. The robin breathed in the scent and it soothed him. After a few puffs Oliphant spoke again.

"It is not our place to disrupt this plan or to sabotage it. All will be as it should be in the end, and we cannot change it. Let us put our own fears and doubts behind us. After all, the Spirit of the Sea is a great power and the Spirit of the Woodland knows all things. Let us keep silent my friend, eh?"

"Yes," nodded the wise robin, "I shall not speak to anyone on this subject."

"Good, we are agreed. Take a puff of my sweetbriar pipe, Freddie, the good doctors make up my tobacco from their pharmacy and it is very pleasing."

Obligingly the robin carefully took several puffs. It was mellow and he felt warm and sleepy. Together they shared the Pipe of Portent and when it was finished a sense of wellbeing seeped over them and both felt ready to accept the inevitable.

Cornelius meanwhile had achieved moderate success at the Creekside with his parents coaching him. He would spring off the edge, flap his wings very hard and fly around in circles. He had fallen into the water many times, much to the amusement of all those watching. His mother taught him how to preen his feathers and keep them in good order. His father weighted his wings with strings of mussel shells to exercise them and give them more strength; they did everything they could possibly think of to help their champion.

The training day at the woodland came around at last. All the creatures were divided into sections to cover the flight path edges. Each was colour coded with corresponding coloured flags, and a flight assister had been appointed in each section. If Cornelius fell or touched the ground they were to mark and record the spot and the task could be deemed a failure by the assister. All eyes were upon Cornelius, and the buzzard had asked for vigilance in their observations.

"History will be hard on us," he told them all. "This is a chance to witness and take part in an event that will be recorded in the Great Book of Time. Let us look forward to this together."

The Woodlanders were so excited they could hardly wait for the day but it was drawing nearer and nearer. Hibernation was out of the question now – nobody wanted to miss this!

Chapter Forty-seven
A dramatic winter's day

Cold and seasonal conditions were expected as the day of the Winter Solstice approached. Many of the inhabitants watched the progress of the bird boy with deepening interest. Cornelius did not waiver in his valiant attempts and was as dedicated to his training as any Olympic athlete. No one could help him; he alone bore the burden of expectation.

Eventually during those last dark dragging days of December he felt himself to be ready. Ptolemy had encouraged him on, exultant in every small success and philosophical in his failures. Sargasso and Seraphim remained silently optimistic.

Patrick, Ellie, Eddie and Heather saw little of their prodigy. They were wrapped up in the great changes of their own lives, school separating them all and interfering with their social life.

Freddie and Oliphant continued to monitor the bird boy's progress for them all, keeping calm and positive.

The long Christmas holidays arrived, sending shivers of anticipation into everyone's hearts. On the morning of the 21st December, Freddie landed on the window sill of Eddie's bedroom tapping, on the glass.

"What's up?" Eddie rushed to the window dragging his sweater on.

"It's today!" Freddie insisted. "He's got to do it today! Sunrise is in thirty minutes and he must have completed the task by sunset at the latest. The highest point is the top of the hill at the Citadel, above the Trip Trap Bridge. The route is up the cliffs. I think that's where you should all be, at the bridge. Can you tell the others?" His anxiety showed in his quavering voice.

"Right. Right," nodded Eddie furiously, as his brain clicked into gear and he actually realised what Freddie was talking about. "I'm on to it, Freddie. What do you think? Is he ready?"

But Freddie had gone, flown off up into the woods to Oliphant's home. Oliphant welcomed him with a hot spicy calming concoction, which he drank gratefully. Nothing more could be done – it was all up to Cornelius now.

Eddie got himself ready in the darkness and roused Ellie, who was full of nervous anticipation. *Oh my, this is the day,* she thought. *Better get on with it, then.*

By the time they were eating breakfast the pale grey light of a winter's morning had crept over the world outside. The dawn of the Winter Solstice arrived, edging the clouds with a coral-pink frill. At eight o'clock they rang Heather, then Patrick was summoned, who appeared almost instantly.

At the quayside, Seraphim woke with a choking feeling and tight bands of tension around her feathered chest, but she made light of it. That morning she was especially kind to her fledgling who was about to fly the nest, feeling as all mothers do the day their children set off on their own – tearful, proud, and a little worried, at their offspring facing an unknown future ahead.

Ptolemy refused to think at all, mechanically following the morning routine, and Sargasso said nothing, a spectator in the final preparations for the most important day in their small lives. The world was still turning, time was still ticking, and tomorrow would creep up inevitably, erasing for eternity whatever happened in the next few hours. The Earth, the Sea and the Sky's perpetual rhythms were unceasing, its inhabitants merely visitors for a fraction of time.

Sargasso's wisdom lifted him apart from whatever events took place this day and he drew comfort from the silvered shell he wore around his neck. His master, the Spirit of the Sea, would be with them to witness this day; he would arrive in his own time from the ocean's rolling winter waves.

The buzzard's instructions were carried out and the route marked with flags. The scroll pinned to the trunk of the Citadel had been read a hundred times and Seafarers and Woodlanders were well aware of their tasks; keen observation of the bird boy was essential. Many eyes, too shy to be seen, peeped and peered, hoping for a view of the exciting spectacle, all the way from the water's edge to the wooded cliff tops.

There were many anxious hearts beating that morning, none more so than Heather's. Her new-found independence had inspired her with confidence and energy, but in her own mind the miracle that had restored her useless legs was all due to Cornelius; she was utterly convinced of it.

Meeting up at the letter-box, Ellie, Eddie and Patrick sat waiting for Heather, and it looked like any ordinary day by the Creek. They shivered in the cold easterly wind, watching the clouds scud across the unfriendly sky. Heather appeared round the corner wearing a yellow knitted beret, brightly cheering up the morning.

"Hi, everyone!" Still unaccustomed to her walking, the others sat fascinated, just watching her approach. "Come on then, what are you waiting for?" she chided them. Jumping up and joining her they made their way to the castle and on up the coastal path towards the chosen vantage point, the Trip Trap Bridge.

At the Citadel the buzzard slipped into his plush velvet robes and his regal hat.

"This is a momentous day, Sire," nodded one of his dressers.

"Indeed."

"We wish you a splendid day, and await your triumphant return, Sire." Both bent low, bowing and retreating from the Round Room backwards. He was alone at last to ponder this day when the poor freak, as the buzzard had secretly called him, was put to the test again.

So ugly, so unnatural, so disruptive, so unnecessary, repeated the Master of the Woodland to himself. Why did everything have to change? It was all just fine the way it was. Everyone had a place and everyone knew their place. It had worked for centuries, his buzzard line stretching back for ages, why interfere with it? These Spirits, so powerful in their own domain, why did they need to join together?

377

He sighed and turned to leave the secure confines of the Citadel, with a trail of followers from the branches of the Great Pine Tree. He was to take up a vantage point and watch for Cornelius from the clifftops. The Citadel was to be his second resting place where the Woodland Lord would welcome him to his territory.

Freddie and Oliphant were determined to follow the whole journey, so stationed themselves at the quayside for the start. Solomon and Bathsheba were gently surfacing at the entrance to the Creek, ready to follow Cornelius around the coast. The first resting place had been decided by the Spirit of the Sea, and at sunrise a wave of energised water, full of light particles which flickered continuously, had been sent across the cold grey ocean. The wave never broke and continued at great speed, travelling across the surface of the sea until it reached Sugary Cove where the mighty whales, Hector and Hercules, lay imprisoned in stone.

As the curving, flickering wave reached them, it dashed against their sides and the particles of light released their energy, transforming the solid rock into flesh once more. The whales rose from the shifting shingle with a loud sucking noise, and floated up on top of the churning sea. Blowing water joyfully out of their spouts, a sonorous echo sounded from their mouths which vibrated through the winter seas and into the far oceans. It was the signal for all the Seafarers. Hector and Hercules took up their positions at the entrance of their cove, proud to be the first resting place for Cornelius.

Sargasso and Seraphim, having wished their son courage and strength for his task, touched wingtips with him and quietly left with Ptolemy. They also had chosen to watch from the rocky edges of the coast between Sugary Cove and the Trip Trap Bridge, in clear view of the whales and the steep cliffs.

Lord Sunna, now in the closing days of his one year cycle of life, was truly an old man with white hair and a long white beard; he stooped slightly and walked slowly with the help of a blackthorn stick. The handle was fashioned into a round mushroom, with pale carved gills on the underside, and would be left behind when he departed this world, ready to be taken over by his successor in his time. The stick was hidden in a secret place known only to the Spirit of the Woodland himself and had particular powers. At the demise of the Woodland Lord, the stick became a mushroom in the ground, spinning itself deeply into place, left untouched until needed. During his last months the aged spirit had lived deep in the woods in a soft mossy hollow, shielded and protected from the eyes of most.

He had considered Cornelius most seriously and had wondered about the future of this new creature, consoling himself with the fact that it was his successor, the next young Spirit of the Woodland, who would guide Cornelius as he took his place among three kingdoms. For today, however, he must soon take up his viewing position high in the woodland for the flight. It was an exciting prospect and he wished the brave little fellow every success.

Within an hour, everyone had taken their place and a nervous energy seized them all. Only two people did not attend the flight path – the dedicated doctors, Dr Dew and Dr Yew Underconstumble. They were only too aware of the two possible outcomes of this day, and had decided to prepare for success or failure. Concocting several remedies which could be administered in various forms to the spectators, they had worked tirelessly and were almost ready. One helper had been lent to them by the Spirit of the Sea: Pelorus the Pelican was their special guest. He and Ptolemy were old friends, both sent to assist Cornelius during his childhood. Now, the two could be proud of his maturity and watch him conquer the skies.

Eddie, Ellie, Patrick and Heather were buffeted by very strong winds as they strode out along the coastal path to a grassy spot the other side of the Freedom Gate, just outside the Woodlanders' territory, and hopefully would see Cornelius clearly as he flew to the Citadel and then over the hilltop and thankfully home. Aware of just how many animals and birds would have ventured out to see this inaugural flight, Eddie wanted to keep his distance and prevent their presence intimidating the Woodlanders. Even he did not know the part he had played in creating Cornelius. One hair from the boy's head had been used for the human DNA: stolen by Freddie, passed to Sargasso, ingested by Seraphim, and the power of the Moon and the Sea had done the rest. Sitting in the cold, waiting for the moment, was very hard for them all and in the silence each boy and girl remembered their personal involvement with Cornelius since discovering him.

On the quiet quayside at Warfleet Creek, Cornelius prepared to leave. He closed his mind to everything, concentrating on a smooth take-off and the route to the first resting place. *I can do this*, he told himself, closing his eyes and breathing deeply.

Ptolemy put his flipper on the boy's shoulder, looked into the blue-green eyes and said kindly, "Whatever happens today is what should be. Accept that, and you will be happy. You have conquered every challenge and in our eyes the tasks are completed. This day is a mere formality. I am proud to have brought you here; my work is done and my spirit is with you. Do not reply, for we will meet again in the oceans, in the breeze, on distant shores. Farewell Cornelius, the Spirit of the Sea is proud. You will have new masters after today." And Ptolemy slid over the side of the little quay and into the water, where the seawater washed his tears away.

Cornelius was quite alone. In the silver band he wore around his head the three fishes whispered encouragement, then the band sprang apart and each fish jumped into the water.

"Goodbye little master, you have given us each a voice and a soul. Now you can fly, our task is over. We can return to the sea," called Tellus, Caelum, and Altum Mare, who splashed their tails and disappeared in a streak of silver.

Inspired by their devotion and amazed by their huge dive into the water, Cornelius took a deep breath and ran along the grass, making a mighty leap into the air. Flapping furiously with his wings and repeating, "I will do this, I will do this!" he glided slowly upwards and tucked his legs beneath him as he executed a perfect take-off. He rose slowly and levelled out, fully extending his grey-white wings over the Creek. Beating them steadily in a good rhythm, he sped along out of the Creek and met the river waters, where he turned sharply right. Below him he heard faint clapping and shouts of encouragement but he heeded neither, keeping all his energies and concentration on one thing – flying. He continued along the rocky edges towards the castle where he wobbled once or twice, until he changed direction again, turning right and meeting a strong wind.

"Oh, this is difficult – steady, – steady now, – readjust, – keep straight," he told himself. The wind unsettled his balance and he struggled to regain his equilibrium, rising slightly and beating his wings harder until he felt secure again.

I must look for the first resting place. Where are they? Black shapes?

He searched for the huge shiny humps of the whales, where he could land and rest. The waves were grey and froth tipped, rising and falling in sharply ordered rows.

"At last! I see them!" Thankfully, he saw the two black whales, stationary in the ripples and troughs of the sea. At that moment a white flake fell upon his beak, cold and wet. Several more landed on his back, melting at once.

All his concentration was focused on slowing down and landing accurately on the back of one of the large creatures. He stopped flapping his wings and glided uncertainly towards the shapes, pulling his legs down ready to land, and slowly, wavering from side to side, he approached the spot. The wind was cruel, gusting fiercely, making Cornelius miss the first whale. He managed to plant his webbed feet on the second whale's back.

"Made it!" he gasped triumphantly. "Rest at last!" He almost slipped off but the barnacles on the whale's tough skin held him fast. He breathed a relieved sigh, and panting hard, tried to catch his breath. Solomon and Bathsheba arrived alongside him. They had followed him faithfully, ready to act as safety guards in the event of an accident.

"Well done, little master!" they praised with their barking voices. "That is the first stage over."

Sargasso and Seraphim watched proudly from the rocky outcrop, unseen by their son. Many had crowded onto the sloping shores to see the miracle of the bird boy, who had been kept a secret for so long. They wondered about him, his face, his hair, his body; he was extraordinary, a marriage of bird, fish and human, so neat and small.

Ptolemy swam in the deep water off the coast, unseen and unheard. He waited for the three fishes that had made up the silver coronet the boy wore around his head. Today Caelum would be officially free, as Cornelius became the first of the new species.

Attention was diverted from Cornelius, however, as the white dots continued to fall, swirled around by the strong, cold wind.

"It's snowing!" the murmur went around the crowd. The four children stood in silence, hardly able to believe it. Almost immediately the small powdery dots turned to large soft flakes and at once they began to shroud the landscape with a white sheet, covering everything.

"Oh no," groaned Heather. "Surely not? It will make everything so difficult for him." "They must stop it!" Ellie burst out in her anxiety. "He can't do it in the snow!"

Eddie and Patrick caught each other's eyes and made a face with closed lips and raised eyebrows. This was not good.

At the end of the resting time, a cormorant on the bridge would raise a flag and Cornelius must fly off, and the whales must descend beneath the water again. Five miles off Land's End a strange water spout was noticed by a fishing vessel, which was ordered to stop fishing and slow the engines. In the snow shower it was possible the skipper had been mistaken, as visibility was very poor. But this was the Spirit of the Sea and the silver tinkling shoals arriving to witness the triumph of his creation – the bird boy flying.

In the swirling white mist the waterspout passed the fishermen and continued on its eerie way, silently advancing towards the coast of south Devon, arriving as the cormorant raised his fluttering green seaweed flag.

Cornelius shook the snow off his wings and whispered, "Help me someone, please!" Then he braced himself, and with a mighty leap launched himself upwards. Even as he began his steep uphill ascent, the snow quickly blanketed him in a chilly, icy softness. He held his breath and beat his fully extended wings madly. For a few seconds he made no progress, and as the crowd gasped, one final effort propelled him upwards and into a diagonal path, across the bridge, then the scrubby gorse bushes, and up, up across the grassy hillside. A sigh of relief was released from all the spectators, who willed the brave little creature upwards.

Eddie spotted him first. "Look! Look! He's coming! There he is!"

Heather, biting her gloves, breathed in, held her breath and could hardly bear to watch. The snow was falling heavily and a gusty wind played cruel tricks, blowing cold and stinging flakes in white swirls.

Cornelius was blinded for a moment and wiped his eyes with his hands. His wings were coated with snow by now and the movement of his arms unbalanced him. The wind seized its chance, lifted him up and whirled him round and round madly. For a moment the boy, disorientated and breathless, was unable to flap his wings which were already heavy with snow.

"Oh, no!" Heather cried out, grabbing Ellie's arm. "No! No!" Her anguish was now real fear. Bravely Patrick, Ellie, and Eddie remained silent, transfixed in dread as Cornelius plummeted downwards in a slow spiral, turning over and over, arms and legs and wings all flailing in desperation.

Lord Sunna waited in fear higher up the hill as he heard Heather's cries and the groans of the crowds lining the route edges.

Cornelius tried vainly to right himself, wavered and stretched his snow-covered wings, dizzy in the gusting wind, but he couldn't maintain his height. Gravity took over and he was dashed onto the black rocks, breaking both his wings on impact.

Ptolemy saw him from the water and accelerated forward towards the shore. Sargasso and Seraphim flew like arrows to his side. The Spirit of the Sea, circling slowly offshore, sent the silver tinkling shoals to help. The little bird boy lay, winded and chilled on the bare snowy rocks, with Seraphim stroking his wet hair.

"Mother, Mother," he murmured, "I couldn't do it. I'm sorry. I'm so sorry. I tried, but—"

"There, there, dear it's alright. You can fly! You *can* fly."

"You did well, my son, the weather has cheated us of your victory," choked Sargasso. Even then they could feel some powerful fate overtaking them. A tiny trickle of blood ran from Cornelius's head onto the white snow and pooled in a growing ruby circle, melting the snow and mixing with its crusty flakes. Seraphim plucked some golden hairs from his curls, and then she Sargasso dipped their beaks in the blood and daubed it on each other's cheeks. Cornelius moved his head from side to side and whispered,

"Mother, Father, I won't forget you. I'm not leaving, I'm going home. Tell Heather I gave her some legs in exchange for my wings. I shall not need them now."

As he closed his eyes, Sargasso and Seraphim laid their beaks one on each other's shoulders and closed their eyes too. They could not bear to look at him anymore, and knew he was lost to the Spirit of the Sea.

Quickly, Ptolemy climbed onto the rock and pushed the boy to the water's edge. Tellus, Caelum and Altum Mare were waiting to receive him. There was now a circling whirlpool beside them of spinning silver fish and smoothly they slipped among them and vanished. Only a few bubbles remained as the silver tinkling shoals carried the boy far away with his beloved guardians.

His parents sat motionless, transfixed in their grief and stared at the empty sea: the whales, the seals, the turtle, the fish and their precious son, all gone. The whole thing was like a dream in the snowy white stillness.

Then the snowflakes took on the rosy glow of sunset, and as they fell onto each face they tasted of a strange sweetness. These were Heavenly Healing Flakes which the two kind doctors had mixed with the snow, and all traces of sadness from witnessing the tragic accident were washed away. The flakes had been sprinkled by Pelorus the pelican whose beak was filled with the prepared elixir.

Within minutes the creatures dispersed like ghosts, creeping back home, and the only two left on the snow-covered shore were Sargasso and Seraphim. Gradually the snow ceased and over the horizon a golden shimmer stretched: the Path of True Endeavour which had been placed there by the Spirit of the Sea for a few moments to mark the passing of Cornelius. It shimmered in the sun's rays, golden and pink, and Pelorus whispered goodbye to Sargasso and Seraphim and flew off, following the gold trail back to his master.

Eddie and Ellie, Heather and Patrick took a few minutes to scramble down the steep slippery hillside. They too had been covered in the sweet flakes, hardly noticing them in their anxiety to find out what had happened to their beloved Cornelius. His crashing onto the rocks had been hidden from them by the steep cliffs. They found everything was quiet and still, just the lapping of the water and two seagulls, necks entwined, sitting on a far rock resting in the pink glow of the sunshine. Strange, because it was well past sunrise by now.

Heather covered her eyes and sobbed, sinking down onto the cold ground. Ellie knelt to comfort her and gazed up at the boys helplessly.

"What happened? Where is everyone?"

Eddie and Ellie began to search frantically around the rocks. A small snowy red puddle caught Patrick's eye. "Here Eddie, what's this? It looks like blood." His friend reached his side at once. Eddie dipped his finger into the redness and rubbed it. It was sticky and slightly clotted. He tasted it.

"It's definitely blood," wiping his fingers on his trousers. Patrick also found a couple of greyish-white small feathers lying caught in a crevice.

"They look like his, don't they?" he said sadly. "I'm going to give them to the girls."

"Where's Freddie?" snapped Eddie suddenly. "He should be here, and where are Sargasso and Seraphim?" He was irritated and upset.

"Is that them over there?" Patrick pointed. "I think it must be, but if anything has happened to Cornelius, and I'm rather afraid that it might have, we don't want to disturb them. Shall we just go home? We can find Freddie later, I'm sure. He'll know. Shall we?" He put his arm out to Eddie who stared out to sea in despair.

"Come on, no point waiting here. Something terrible must have happened. We saw him falling, maybe he crashed onto the rocks and fell into the sea. Who knows?" Patrick beckoned to him. The two boys trudged back across the rocky shore to poor Heather, who was still crying. Eddie put his arms around her and Patrick hugged Ellie.

Eventually, turning to look at the risen sun and staring out to the horizon, they saw the golden pathway across the sea. It glittered and glowed; then it began to dim and fade, mesmerising them, holding their gaze. Their sadness began to slip away like the light, and their memory of the morning became hazy and somehow distant. The elixir had worked.

"Here's the feathers we found," but as Patrick offered them to the girls the wind tried to catch them and blow them out of their hands.

Both girls tightened their grip, shouting, "No! No!" loudly and managed to hang on to them. "We've got to keep them!"

Eddie's fingers tingled where the blood had been, and he felt rather warm.

"He's not dead," he said brightly. "He's alive! Look!" He pointed out to the sea where a turtle, three fishes and a small head surfaced. The sunlight caught the golden curls, but it vanished with the others in seconds, out of sight beneath the rolling waves, leaving the four children blinking, unable to see. "I'm so glad," Heather sighed, and she smiled to herself – Cornelius had not forgotten them.

"And me. He's gone back to the sea where he really belonged. It's the right ending, isn't it?" Ellie added.

"Yes, yes it is," agreed the boys. "Come on, let's find Freddie, he must know something."

Beginning the long climb up the hill, they decided to head for the woods and search for the robin. The sun sank back where it had come from and the day returned to normal. What had really happened to Cornelius? Each one of them was desperate to find out.

Chapter Forty-eight
The conclusion

The little group approached the woodland, entering it through the Freedom Gate as the snow clouds advanced overhead again and the wind began to rise. There seemed to be an eerie glow coming from the heart of the thickest trees. High on a huge pine tree a large buzzard sat, with other birds sheltering on the lower branches. A robin and a white owl flew in and landed on a high branch.

"Get down!" whispered Eddie, and quickly they all hid behind the thick bushes. "I can see Freddie. He's up there." From the way the birds were gathered it was obvious some sort of meeting was going on.

The buzzard and his retinue had not partaken of the Heavenly Healing Flakes, nor had Lord Sunna, and so were not influenced by the Elixir of Fond Memories. The buzzard therefore was shocked and most displeased: his chance of a glorious and memorable reign had been dashed on the bare rocks far below.

Lord Sunna, the elderly woodland spirit, was anguished and remorseful, sorrowing for the beautiful child he had loved. Yet, he was angry: angry at the waste of all the endeavours the boy and his parents and guardians had been through, and that the happiness and joy the child had brought was now lost and wasted.

Over their heads, Pelorus the pelican flew in to join the meeting, landing clumsily on a low branch. The tree shook suddenly with the weight. He spoke at once without waiting for permission: "The Spirit of the Sea has sent me. He wants us all to know how deeply he feels the pain of Cornelius's departure. He fears it was a misjudgement, and that he should never have attempted to interfere with the natural make-up of our being. It was an impossible dream and he is truly sorry." The pelican hung his head, frightened. After all, he was only the messenger.

Eddie and his friends swallowed hard; each one silently agreed. Lovely though Cornelius was, he had an uncertain future in the world.

Lord Sunna leaned on his mushroom-headed stick and spoke angrily. "It was an ill-conceived plan that will bring much unhappiness to those close to the boy. We have all grown to love him, and have followed his progress eagerly. Now we must mourn him. It is not enough to be sorry. I challenge your Spirit, your ruler of the Sea, to come himself instead of sending you!" and he pointed his blackthorn stick at the pelican.

Immediately, the bird turned into a noble stag, snorting and pawing at the ground. Lord Sunna swung the stick above his head, where it twirled upwards and then fell, embedding itself into the woodland floor where it looked like any other mushroom growing. Eyes blazing angrily, the bearded old man was also replaced by a stag, proud and haughty, crowned with a set of magnificent antlers on his regal head.

A murmur of fear spread over the tree and its occupants as the two deer eyed each other from a short distance. The buzzard was forced to speak.

"My kingdom will not witness further bloodshed. My subjects and I have no quarrel with you. It is my task to maintain peace, not to apportion blame. Go and settle your differences in some other place. Come," and beckoning to his remaining subjects, invited them to take shelter inside the Citadel. Everyone obeyed at once, and the four children watched Freddie, Oliphant, the rooks and the others step inside the great door and vanish. It shut with a loud clonk.

"They're going to fight, aren't they?" whispered Ellie, grabbing Patrick's and Heather's arms.

"Yes, but it will all be pointless. Cornelius belongs to the sea. He was never suited to life away from the shore, was he?" Eddie spoke wisely.

Heather said little. All she really cared about was that Cornelius was not dead, and had merely moved his home to the

389

sea. There was still the chance she would see him again, and maybe even renew their friendship. One morning he might seek her out, swimming in the river maybe? This was the shred of hope that kept her heart from breaking.

Both stags scraped at the rough ground and snorted loudly, steam rising from their furred backs. One turned and galloped at speed along the leaf-strewn path to the grassy hillock beside the Great Ash Tree. He turned to face the sea with his great antlers held aloft, raised his head and bellowed fiercely. The lone stag beneath the Citadel stared after him, and whipping himself around, bunched his strong hind legs up and clattered off in hot pursuit, making the four hidden behind the gorse bushes jump.

" Let's follow, come on!" whispered Patrick hoarsely, and holding Ellie's hand they crept as quietly as they could along the grassy edges, with Eddie and Heather following.

"Don't let them get our scent, it'll scare them away," hissed Eddie.

Locked in the Citadel, Freddie was desperate to see what was happening. He knew he ought to be there, something momentous was going to take place. He must get to Eddie and try to help Lord Sunna quickly. He pecked in anxiety at the small slitted window but he could not get out. Then he flew around the royal quarters to try to find another way and came upon a small chimney in an empty chamber. Without hesitation he disappeared up inside it, and emerged sooty and coughing outside at the top of the lofty pine tree.

"Now I'm free!" he gasped, and shot out across the woodland, following the sound of the deer and their antlers clashing. It was frightening to witness these two great creatures engaged in combat as he landed unseen on the top of the Great Ash Tree, quickly scanning around for his beloved youngsters. They were now hidden in a clump of hawthorn nearby.

One of the deer gored the other, and a great roar erupted. Blood spilt onto the ground. Enraged, the injured stag charged at the aggressor, wounding him in the neck. Their antlers locked and as they snorted and steamed with the heat of battle it seemed they had become entangled together, unable to separate themselves. Their hooves kicked and both bellowed loudly.

Eddie could hardly contain himself; he was so afraid that someone else might die on this terrible day. He stood up and showed himself, pointing his fingers, still stained with the blood of the lost child, at the panting animals.

"Stop!" he shouted, "Stop it at once!" and a sizzle of brightness left his finger and lit up both the deer. "Cornelius wouldn't have wanted this! Go home in peace! Go back to your own worlds and be grateful for your lives!" Eddie commanded fiercely.

Miraculously, both their antlers fell off onto the ground with a noisy echo and turned into a pile of sticks. One of the deer nodded and lowered his head towards the four young people, as Ellie, Heather and Patrick emerged and stood beside Eddie, unafraid. The stag turned, ran up the hillock and leapt off into the air with a great bound. Everyone gasped, but as the deer started to fall, it changed into a white pelican, and flapping its wings flew over the cliffs and out to sea, where the Spirit of the Sea was waiting. He had been watching the small hilltop and the struggle that had taken place.

The remaining stag trotted towards Eddie and stopped; the boy held out his hands and the animal sniffed them. Then he licked both his fingers clean, removing the last traces of Cornelius's blood. Ellie, Patrick and Heather stepped forward to stroke the great deer.

A sudden shaft of sunlight emerged from the clouds and surrounded the deer with its brightness. It was such an intense glow that the children were forced to shield their eyes as the deer slowly turned back into an old man who then rose up, disappearing very gradually into the bright light, arms outstretched towards the sky.

"No! No, my lord!" shouted Freddie, who was seized with a compulsive urge to follow him. The bird took off from his branch and flew upwards after Lord Sunna, who was almost out of sight.

"Wait for me!" he begged. Freddie felt lightheaded and bursting with happiness.

"I've got to go, Eddie! It's my time! Goodbye!" he called desperately, trying to follow his master. Up, up he soared, pushing himself higher and higher in the glorious golden light, which was warm and embraced him entirely. They both disappeared into the high clouds and out of sight.

Almost immediately a small shower of raindrops fell to earth. Where the drops fell, a clump of pure white scented bluebells sprang up, with their green foliage swaying in the breeze and their pretty flowered heads nodding. It was to be Freddie's legacy. He was gone forever.

Eddie, Ellie, Patrick and Heather remained silent; a few remaining drops of rain still fell, glistening in their hair. The Elixir of Fond Memories was still working inside them and gradually they turned to one another and sighed, shaking their heads.

"Freddie was very old, wasn't he? Really, far too old for a robin, if you think about it," said Patrick, gazing across the great grey ocean.

"He saved our lives, you and me, remember?" Eddie added.

"He's been a truly loyal friend, and we've had some amazing experiences," Ellie chipped in proudly. "I'm so glad he came to us, all those years ago when we were little kids. We've got to let them both go then, haven't we? Maybe we don't understand their worlds and perhaps we never will, but my life has been changed from knowing Cornelius and I'm grateful to have been just a little part of his life."

Heather too gazed out to sea, watching the rhythm of the waves and looking towards the endless horizon. It was all part of growing up: moving on, leaving childlike things behind, learning the pain and pleasure of adult life.

The two boys and two girls formed a circle on top of the highest point of Gallants Bower, their arms around each other, and shed a few tears to say goodbye to their dearest friends, vowing never to forget them. The smell of white bluebells perfumed the air and they breathed it in happily. Far out at sea, a turtle and a strange bird-like creature swam happily in the cold clear water, followed by three diamond-streaked fish. They were home!

THE END